No matter where she goes, he knows her every move…

Long ago, Rachel Carpenter was a glamorous soap star. She gave it all up to move to Napa Valley with her daughters to open up a bookstore near her family vineyard. Her life is safe and dependable, until she encounters Kane Lafferty at a wilderness camp in the rugged High Sierra. A burned-out police detective struggling with his own demons, Kane is instantly attracted to Rachel. And like Rachel, he isn't sure if he's ready to open up his heart. But everything is about to change…

Someone is watching from the darkness. A fanatic obsessed with Rachel for years has decided to claim what he believes is his. It will be up to Kane to not only protect his new love and her family, but to uncover the identity of the stalker before it's too late for all of them…

Visit us at www.kensingtonbooks.com

Books by Jannine Gallant

Who's Watching Now Series
Every Move She Makes, Book One

Published by Kensington Publishing Corporation

Every Move She Makes

Who's Watching Now, Book One

Jannine Gallant

LYRICAL PRESS
Kensington Publishing Corp.
www.kensingtonbooks.com

In loving memory of my grandma, Lillian Watson. Strong and sweet. Generous and funny. I can only hope to be half the woman you were. You will be missed.

Prologue

Fourteen Years Earlier

He stared at the television screen, his gaze riveted on the girl with the long, auburn hair. The most beautiful girl he'd ever seen. She spoke to a man—a man unworthy of her perfection—her green eyes alight with amusement.

His hand should be the one touching her silk-clad shoulder. *He* should be the one caressing her soft skin. No one else. She should belong to him.

Need surged through him, and he pulled a magazine over his lap to cover the evidence. A commercial flashed on the screen, and the red-haired beauty was gone. He hit the arm of the couch with his fist.

"Honey, you can change the channel if you like." His mother's voice drifted into the room ahead of her. "I don't mind missing my soap just this once."

"I don't care what's on. I'm not watching it anyway."

"You look a bit feverish." She touched his forehead with a cool hand.

"I took some aspirin with my regular meds earlier." *Why won't she leave me alone?* He steadied his breathing while waiting through several more commercials.

An advertisement for tampons ended, and the green-eyed girl was there again. Her beauty tugged at his heart.

"Oh, good, Jordan's on today's show. Her character's new, and I hope they give her a big storyline. Isn't she just the prettiest thing?"

Jannine Gallant

He tuned out his mother's voice the way he would a buzzing mosquito and focused on the television. So...her name was Jordan. None of the other girls on the show were like her. The others didn't feed his desire. They didn't create a burning need inside him. Jordan was special. Perfect.

His gaze followed her every move until the scene ended. A sigh of disappointment escaped as he leaned back against the couch cushions and waited while a different storyline built. More commercials followed. He gritted his teeth.

"You look tired, honey. Maybe you should go back to bed."

"I will in a while."

"How about some soup? Does that sound good?"

He nodded. *Anything to get you to leave me alone.*

Jordan reappeared on the screen. His stomach jumped, and the magazine on his lap twitched. God, how he wanted her.

She wouldn't be interested in someone his age. The time wasn't right, but someday it would be. He'd make her want him as much as he wanted her. Someday the beautiful Jordan would belong to him.

Chapter One

"My baby has pink hair." Rachel Carpenter planted her elbows on the table and held her face in her hands. "No, I take that back. Not pink. Magenta. Her beautiful, blond hair is magenta."

Her sister smiled from across the table, the green eyes they'd both inherited from their mother sparkling with amusement. "Magenta is a lovely color."

"Did I mention she cut it, too? Her hair is short and spiky. She looks like a punk rocker."

Grace Hanover covered her mouth but couldn't hide a smile. "I bet she still looks cute, even with short, magenta hair."

"Of course she does. Lark would be beautiful bald." Rachel let out a deep sigh and poked at a scallop on her plate. "I don't know what to do with her. She's so rebellious and angry all the time. She's only fourteen, for heaven's sake."

Grace reached across the table to squeeze her sister's hand. "Lark is too smart to do anything really stupid."

"Her actions lately haven't shown a lot of forethought. I'm worried about this new friend of hers. Rose is the one who talked Lark into dyeing her hair. Rose's hair is Day-Glo orange." Rachel pleated the napkin in her lap. "Why did Bryce have to go skiing that weekend? He might have been a lousy husband, but he was good with the girls."

"The avalanche was a freak accident—one that wouldn't have happened to him if he'd taken the girls to Hawaii like he promised." Grace's tone hardened. "Oh, no, his current bimbo wanted to hit the slopes instead." She tossed long, brown hair over her shoulder with a sharp flip of her wrist. "Too bad you wasted over ten years of your life on the bastard before you finally divorced him."

"They weren't wasted. He gave me three beautiful daughters. You and I both know Bryce was a cheating idiot, but the girls loved him. They miss him so much. Jade and Ivy are adjusting, but Lark broods. She's been seeing a therapist. The woman assures me she'll come around eventually."

"There you have it. Your daughter just needs more time. Eat your dinner."

If only Rachel could dismiss her worries so easily.

They dined at her favorite restaurant on Fisherman's Wharf. Through the window, the sun cast a golden glow over San Francisco Bay. To their left, the majestic span of the Golden Gate Bridge stretched northward. Farther out in the bay, Alcatraz stood sentinel on its lonely rock.

"How's work? Do you have a full staff for the summer?"

Rachel turned to face her sister. "I think so. Ellen and Chandra are still with me, and I hired a new guy, Tim."

Grace's eyes held a challenge. "How about a quick fling with a young stud?"

"Very funny. I would never hit on an employee. Anyway, I think Tim's gay, and I don't date college boys."

"You don't date anyone."

"Let's not go there. It's your turn for the hot seat. Who's the new guy you're seeing?"

"Nolan Marconi. He's Italian and very intense."

"What does he do?"

"Believe it or not, he's a cop, a detective with the SFPD. Cops usually hate investigative reporters as a rule." She sipped her wine and smiled. "But this one seems to like me—and not just in bed."

Rachel covered her ears. "Too much information. Geez, Gracie, some things should remain private."

"I'm trying to motivate you. Live a little. At thirty-five, you probably still have a few good years left."

She ignored the direct hit. "Am I going to meet him before he goes by the wayside like the legions of men you've dated before him?"

"Yep. He's picking me up when his shift is over." Her eyes brightened. "In fact, here he comes now, and he has someone with him. Talk about hot." She fanned a hand in front of her face.

Rachel glanced over her shoulder. Two men approached, and more than one woman in the crowded restaurant gave the pair a lingering look. They were definitely worth a second glance. One was of medium height with a rangy build. With his black hair tied back in a ponytail, he was movie-star handsome. The other man stood well over six feet and looked like he spent some serious time in the gym. Chestnut hair brushed the collar of his shirt, and sharp blue eyes didn't miss a thing. When his gaze landed on her, Rachel sucked in a breath. Her sister was right about the hot factor.

Grace greeted the black-haired man with a lingering kiss.

"Grace, this is a friend of mine, Kane Lafferty." The detective's gaze never left her sister's face. "Kane, this gorgeous creature is Grace."

"Nice to meet you. Nolan and Kane, say hello to my big sister, Rachel Carpenter."

"It's a pleasure." Nolan reached across the table to shake her hand. "Grace has told me all about you."

"That can't be good." Rachel turned to the man at his side and smiled. When he grasped her hand in his large, warm palm, a tingle jolted through her. The last person she'd felt that kind of chemistry with was her ex.

Kane's brow creased as he released her hand. "Rachel Carpenter... Why does that name sound familiar?"

"Not because you saw it on a rap sheet." Grace scowled. "Her husband was Bryce Carpenter."

The frown cleared. "Of course! I was a huge fan."

Nolan nodded. "Everyone on the force was a fan. With that amazing arm, he led the Niners to some incredible victories. What's not to love?"

"Plenty, but we won't get into it. Have a seat, gentlemen." Grace pointed to the empty chairs. "How about a drink before we leave?"

Despite the temptation to stay, Rachel lodged a quick protest. "I really shouldn't. I have a long drive, and it's getting late. The girls are home alone with Lark babysitting."

"Don't be a spoilsport. You've been nursing the same glass of wine all evening. The girls are fine. Lark is fourteen, and Mom and Dad are practically a stone's throw from your house."

Her sister was right. She was just making excuses, and it wouldn't kill her to be social for a change. "I guess one small drink won't hurt."

"Darn straight. Enjoy yourself while you can. Summer vacation is just around the corner. In a couple of weeks, you'll want to run screaming away from your children."

"Probably." Rachel turned when Kane took the seat beside her. "Do you have a family?"

He shook his head. "Just an ex-wife. No kids. Look, I didn't mean to crash your evening."

"You aren't crashing anything." Nolan tore his attention away from Grace. "Kane and I ran into each other at the station, and I asked him to join us."

"The more the merrier." Grace waved to catch their server's attention. "What does everyone want to drink? I think I'll have a cosmopolitan."

After they ordered, Rachel restarted the conversation. "Do you two work together?" Her gaze wandered from Kane to Nolan and back. Strong was the word that sprang to mind. Kane had a jaw carved out of rock, and those shoulders… She squirmed in her seat. A broad set of shoulders was her secret weakness.

"We're both homicide detectives." Nolan draped his arm over the back of Grace's chair and twirled a lock of her hair around his finger.

"Right now I'm on a…vacation of sorts." Kane's fist clenched on the tablecloth. "I'm headed up to the mountains in the morning for some camping. Hopefully a couple weeks spent under the stars will clear away the cobwebs."

Before Rachel could ask what he meant, Nolan spoke up.

"Which is why I insisted he join us. Anyone who plans to commune with nature for more than a night deserves a civilized send off."

Their server delivered the drinks.

Rachel took a sip of her Irish coffee. "Where're you camping?"

"My brother runs a wilderness camp on Donner Summit called Granite Lake Retreat. There're cabins to sleep in, and all the food is provided for the guests. He offers nature hikes and canoeing, that sort of thing. I volunteered to give him a hand until the rest of his summer staff arrives."

Rachel smiled. "Sounds like fun. I haven't been camping in ages."

"My sister actually enjoys sleeping in a tent." Grace shuddered. "She hikes for fun. If I'm on vacation, I want a luxury hotel with a gym."

"I'm with you there, babe."

"You two are soft." Rachel shook her head. "You're missing out. Nature is good for the soul."

"You didn't tell me you had a crazy sister." Nolan gazed into Grace's eyes.

"I try to keep it a secret. A whacko in the family might reflect badly on the rest of us."

Kane raised a brow. "How many of you are there?"

"Five." Grace rolled her eyes. "We have another sister and two brothers. It was always a battle for the bathrooms when we all lived at home."

"That's nothing." Nolan tapped his chest. "My mama raised seven boys and two girls."

"I thought having one brother was more than enough." Kane swallowed the last of his cocktail. "I'm sorry to break up the party, but I really should go. I still have to pack, and I want to hit the road early to beat the morning traffic."

"Me, too." Rachel pushed back her chair. "It was nice meeting you, Nolan." She turned to face the man beside her. "I hope you enjoy your vacation."

"I'll walk you to your car."

"Thanks, but it's a bit of a hike. I couldn't find any parking close by."

"All the more reason to have an escort. Are you ready to go?"

"As soon as I pay the bill." She stood and swooped to retrieve the folder from the approaching server.

"I'll get the drinks." He pulled his wallet out of his pocket.

"Don't be silly. You're our guests, right, Grace?"

"Right. Let her pay. She always gets her way in the end, so you may as well save the argument."

After Rachel handed the young man her credit card, he retreated, nearly bumping into an older woman hovering nearby. The woman stepped around him with a broad smile.

"It is you! I told my husband I couldn't be mistaken. I said, 'Ted, that's Jordan Hale.' Sure enough, I was right. Honey, would you mind signing an autograph. I adored you before you fell off that cliff and drowned." The woman paused for breath and pulled a notepad from her purse.

Rachel pasted on a smile. "I'd be happy to."

"Make it out to Mary Cooke, with an *e*, please. And can you sign it from Jordan Hale and then your real name? I can't tell you how thrilled I am to meet you in person. I don't know why those horrible writers had to go and kill you."

"Here you go, Mrs. Cooke. It's always a pleasure to meet a fan who still remembers me."

"Thank you, dear. Why you're just as nice as you were on the show." The woman backed toward her own table. "Wait until I tell Mildred. She's going to be green with envy."

Rachel laughed. "Tell Mildred I said hello." When the server returned with the credit card slip, she signed it.

Nolan looked from Rachel to Grace. "What was that all about?"

Kane's brow creased. "Yeah, why did that woman call you Jordan Hale?"

"Because that's who she was back in the day. My sister was Jordan Hale, seductress extraordinaire on *Days of Desire*." Grace grinned. "Pretty cool, huh?"

Rachel shook her head. "Neither of them looks like a soap fan, so I doubt they know what you're talking about."

"Don't be such a sexist. Plenty of men watch soap operas. After all, the women are hot. Why shouldn't men watch them?"

Nolan scowled. "Grace, what the hell are you rambling on about?"

Rachel took pity on him and explained. "I was on a soap opera while Bryce and I lived in New York. You might remember he played for the Giants before he was traded to San Francisco. Anyway, my character's name was Jordan Hale."

Kane pushed his chair in and stepped closer. "That was, what, a dozen years ago?"

"Soap fans have long memories, and mine was a popular character. I had quite a following back then."

"You still get recognized, though not as often since you cut your hair shorter." Her sister studied her and tapped one manicured nail on the table. "Jordan Hale looked a lot younger than you do."

Rachel rolled her eyes. "Thanks, Gracie. Remind me to break out the support hose."

"I don't think you're ready for a nursing home yet." A smile tugged at the edges of Kane's firm mouth. "Shall we go?"

She nodded. "Good night, Nolan. Grace, I'll talk to you soon."

"You certainly will." A speculative gleam lit her eyes. "I'll expect a full report."

Kane guided Rachel through the restaurant with a warm hand against the small of her back. "What did your sister mean by that?"

"Nothing. Grace is just being Grace. She's a nut." Rachel's cheeks heated. She knew full well what her sister had meant. Unfortunately,

Grace had seen her attraction to Kane and was undoubtedly hoping for a juicy end to the evening. As Rachel wasn't in the habit of jumping into bed with relative strangers, her sister was doomed to disappointment.

"Where'd you park?" Kane waited for her response as they stepped out into the brisk spring air.

"Down the Embarcadero." She shrugged on the sweater her mother had knit her the previous Christmas. "I suppose you're in the opposite direction."

"No, I'm that way, too." Taking her arm, he led her around a crowd of people who'd stopped to listen to a street musician.

The clear, clean notes of his saxophone followed them as they strolled down the brick-paved sidewalk. The moon was out, a silver orb shining over the bay.

She tilted her chin. "Look at that sky."

"Beautiful, isn't it?"

Rachel nodded. "I'm glad I don't live in the city anymore, but I do miss nights like these."

"Where do you live?"

"Up in Vine Haven, north of Napa."

"I know the area, lots of rolling hills and grape vines. What do you do there?"

"I own a combination bookstore coffee bar. The town has enough of a tourist trade to survive, but not enough to ruin the small town atmosphere."

"I think I've been there. Years ago, my ex-wife dragged me through Napa County on a wine-tasting tour. Is there a small winery in Vine Haven?"

Rachel smiled. "Only the best one in Northern California, but I may be a teensy bit prejudiced. Hanover Vineyards belongs to my family. I grew up there, and my father and brother still run the vineyard and winery. We offer tours on the weekends."

"Oh, yeah? So you moved back to the family homestead after your husband died?"

"Actually, the year before. Bryce and I were divorced when he died in the skiing accident."

"I remember hearing about that. I don't imagine living with a professional athlete was easy."

"There were some negatives." Bitterness edged her voice, and she forced herself to relax.

"Cops make lousy husbands, too. Just ask my ex-wife."

"You seem like a good guy. What happened?"

"The usual. I spent more time at work than I did with her. Diana is a very nice person, and she's a fighter. She stuck it out for five long years before she finally gave up. I guess she came to the conclusion I wasn't going to change."

Rachel stopped walking and looked up at him. The breeze blew her hair across her face. One strand caught at the corner of her mouth, and Kane reached out a finger to free it. Her breath stuck in her throat as she struggled to remember what they were talking about.

"Did you want to change?"

"Not really. I was younger and had a lot to prove."

"And now?"

He ran a hand through his hair. "I'm not sure anymore, but I do need a break."

"Did something happen?"

His expression closed. "Yeah, something happened." After a moment's hesitation he took her arm to lead her forward. "I don't know why I'm boring you with my problems. How did we end up talking about me?"

"I have that effect on people. Something about me makes everyone I talk to want to spill their guts."

He grimaced. "I'm not the only one? There's a crowd of needy jerks bending your ear? Terrific."

"Mostly just family." She gave him a teasing poke to lighten the mood. "I'm no psych guru, and even if there was a crowd, I'd say you're unique."

"Hardly. I'm just one of a million divorced cops. You may want to warn your sister we're bad relationship risks before she gets too involved with Nolan. Not that he isn't a great guy."

"I'm sure he is. Anyway, I'd be more inclined to worry about him. Grace discards men faster than empty pizza boxes."

Kane grinned. "Your sister seems like quite a dynamo."

"She is. When God passed out inhibitions, he skipped Grace and gave me a double dose."

"I doubt that. Anyone who was a soap star can't have too many restraints."

"Ask my oldest daughter. She'll tell you all about them. Here's my car." Rachel stopped beside her red SUV.

"I rest my case. Inhibited people don't buy red cars."

"I chose the model, but I let my girls pick the color. They take after their aunt."

He smiled, his rugged face lit by an overhead streetlight. Kindness—and pain—was reflected in his eyes. Lines radiated from the corners of his lips, and creases marred his broad forehead. He looked like a man who'd seen the darker side of humanity and was worn down by the experience. It took all her willpower not to reach up to stroke his cheek.

"It was nice meeting you, Rachel Carpenter. More than nice."

"I hope you have a wonderful time camping. I must admit I'm a little jealous."

"You should come up. My brother's retreat is a great place for families. I bet your girls would love it."

"Jade and Ivy probably would, but Lark's another story. Anyway, I imagine the camp is fully booked for the summer."

"It is for July and August, but I think there's space left in June. People tend to wait until it's warmer to go camping in the Sierras. It can be pretty cold at night this time of year. I wouldn't be surprised if there's still some snow left around the lake."

"In other words, pack a warm sleeping bag."

"You've got it. If you decide you're interested, Jed has a web site. Look up Granite Lake Retreat on the Internet, and you can get the phone number to make a reservation."

"I'll think about it." She let out another sigh before she could stop herself. "I'd better go. The drive isn't getting any shorter standing here." She touched his arm. "Thanks for walking me to my car. I know you're anxious to get home."

"My pleasure, and it wasn't out of my way. I own the Jeep parked three spaces over. Anyway, it's not safe for a woman to be alone on the street this time of night."

"True, more's the pity. Good night, Kane. Maybe I'll see you again sometime."

He enclosed her hand in both of his, and a tingle shot through her.

"I certainly hope so." He hesitated then released her. "Drive carefully."

She unlocked her car door. "Careful is my middle name."

Chapter Two

Rachel eyed Kane through the rearview mirror as she drove away and wished she could be more like Grace. Toss caution to the wind, forget her responsibilities and hook up with an attractive man for the night. Too bad having a one-night stand wasn't in her nature. Chances of a more meaningful relationship with Kane Lafferty didn't seem likely.

She took the onramp to the Bay Bridge, thankful the traffic at this hour was light. Though it was a complete waste of time, her conversation with Kane played over and over in her mind. The man was thoughtful, attentive and just plain nice. The fact that he was gorgeous and sexy didn't hurt. Perhaps he had a few hang-ups, but who didn't?

God, maybe Grace is right. Maybe I do need to get laid.

It had been too long since she'd felt a man's arms around her. Her first and only love had been Bryce. After the divorce, she'd dated occasionally, feeling she owed it to herself to meet someone new. At the same time, she'd known going into those relationships they wouldn't work. Her girls were her number one priority, and not many men wanted a ready-made family.

Rachel counted back the months since her last attempt at a relationship, and her jaw sagged. Could it really have been nearly a year?

"No wonder Kane sent my hormones up in flames. I guess I should make an effort to throw myself into the dating pool again."

Exiting the freeway, she drove faster than she should along the two-lane country road that wound through the rolling hills of Napa Valley. It was pushing eleven-thirty, and she was anxious to get home. Her mouth opened wide in a bone-cracking yawn.

"What the..."

A fallen limb from a giant oak lay across the middle of the road. She swerved hard left to avoid it. *Whump.* Her SUV jolted as the rear tire hit the end of the branch. A moment later, an ominous thumping sounded from the back of the car. Swearing under her breath, she pulled to the side of the road, stopped and got out. In the faint moonlight, one look at the rear tire confirmed she had a flat.

"Five more measly miles and I would have been home."

She got back in the car and pulled out her cell phone. Turning on the dome light, she punched in the number for roadside service and waited for the operator to come on the line. Three minutes later, she threw the phone across the seat. An accident had both their area tow trucks tied up. It would be at least an hour before someone could get there.

"Forget that."

Rachel pulled the owner's manual from the glove box. After reading the section on changing a tire, confidence surged. Not hard at all.

Until she got started. After she released the spare tire from beneath the car, she took out the jack. Grunting with effort, she managed to pump the jack enough times to raise the flat clear of the ground.

"All right!" Her fist pumped the air.

A bird in the granddaddy oak emitted a small chirp.

"Next, off with the old tire and on with the new. Piece of cake."

Except it wasn't. The lug nuts must have been soldered on. As hard as she tried, she couldn't budge them. Tired and frustrated, she admitted defeat and went searching for her cell phone. Finding it on the floor of the passenger side, she entered her brother's number.

Four rings later, a groggy voice answered.

"Hi, Will. It's me."

"Rachel? What's wrong? It's almost midnight."

"I know, and I'm sorry to wake you, but I got a flat coming home from San Francisco."

"Did you call the auto service?"

"Yes, but they can't get to me for an hour or more. I took the spare out and jacked up the car, but I can't budge the lug nuts. I've tried. They're on too tight."

"They usually are. I'll come get you." He sounded slightly more awake. "Where are you?"

"About five miles south of town. I'm really sorry."

"Yeah, well you'll owe me. I'll see you in a few minutes."

"Thanks."

She leaned against the side of the car and closed her eyes. The world around her was dark and silent, the moon having sunk behind the hills. Minutes later an engine rumbled in the distance. She shielded her eyes as twin beams of light speared through the darkness.

The car approaching wasn't her brother's Volvo.

An older pickup pulled to a stop, and a man's voice called from the open window. "Need some help?"

In the glare of his headlights, she could only make out a shadowy figure wearing a baseball cap and dark glasses.

"No, thank you. I have a flat, but my brother is on his way. I appreciate the offer."

"A pretty lady like you shouldn't be out alone this time of night. I don't mind getting started on the tire while you wait for your brother. Better yet, give him a call and tell him you've got it covered. I'll be happy to change it for you."

Rachel shifted from one foot to the other and glanced up the deserted road. The guy made her nervous. Who wore sunglasses in the middle of the night? "Really, I'm fine. Don't let me keep you."

"I insist." His door creaked as it opened.

She took a step back, heart racing. Before real fear could take hold, a second set of lights appeared on the road. Her breath whooshed out. "Here's my brother now."

"I'll be on my way then." The door shut. Truck gears grinding, he accelerated around the branch and headed down the road.

"Who was that?" Will stepped from his car into the glow of its headlights. Ten years her senior, her brother was tall and thin with a shock of red hair beginning to recede. He stared after the retreating pickup.

"Some guy who stopped to help after I called you. I know this isn't exactly a high crime area, but I was a little nervous out here alone with a stranger."

"I'm glad you called when you did. It looks like you made good progress with the tire." He hunkered down beside it.

"I thought I could change it by myself. I was feeling pretty cocky until I tried to loosen those damned lug nuts."

"They are on tight." He grunted even more than she had as he threw his weight into the task. Ten minutes later the spare tire was on. Will stowed the flat in the back of her SUV. "Don't forget to drop it off to be repaired tomorrow. You wouldn't want to get stuck again without a working spare."

"God forbid I should have another flat. Fate couldn't be so cruel twice."

"You never know. Help me drag this limb off the road so the next driver doesn't hit it."

They moved the heavy limb then Rachel gave her brother a hug and slid into her car.

"Thanks for bailing me out. I hated having to wake you at this hour when I know you'll be up at dawn."

"No problem. What were you doing out so late, anyway?"

"I had dinner with Grace, and it lasted longer than usual. Her latest boyfriend showed up with a friend, and we talked to them for a while. I should have left sooner."

"Grace has someone new?"

"When doesn't our sister have a new guy? You know Grace, but she really seems to like this one. He's a cop."

"She hasn't dated a cop before, has she?"

"No, but I can see why she decided to broaden her horizons. Nolan is very handsome. So is his friend."

"Interesting. Should I assume you dragged this friend off for a round of mad, passionate sex? Is that the real reason you're late getting home?"

Rachel laughed. "Not a chance."

"Too bad." He gave her door a thump. "Let's go. Sharon's probably wondering what's taking me so long."

"Thanks again, Will."

Minutes later, Rachel rolled into her driveway and turned off the engine. The porch light illuminated the pale blue paint on her old Victorian home. She entered the house quietly, flipped off the outdoor light and left her shoes in the entry. Crossing the hardwood floor to the stairs, she stumbled when she tripped over a big, furry shape.

"Geez, Daisy. You picked a fine spot to sleep."

The golden retriever stood and wagged her tail, wiggling with excitement at this unexpected activity in the middle of the night. She followed, toenails clicking, as her mistress went up the stairs.

Before going to her room, Rachel looked in on each of her girls. Ivy was a small lump beneath her quilt, the top of her blond head shining in the glow of a nightlight. Across the hall, Jade lay sprawled on her bed, blankets in a tangle at her feet. Lark's door was locked. Sighing, Rachel entered her bedroom as quietly as she could and shut the door behind her then turned on the lamp.

Daisy thumped down on the rag rug next to the bed and let out a groan.

Rachel smiled at the dog. "That's exactly how I feel." She stripped off her clothes and dropped them into the hamper. Shrugging on an oversized T-shirt, she walked into the adjoining bath and quickly brushed her teeth. After splashing a little water on her face, she headed back toward the bed to stretch out on cool sheets.

She flipped from lying flat on her back to her side, but couldn't sleep. Her mind conjured up disquieting memories of Kane Lafferty. Firm lips quirked in a smile, blue eyes piercing and direct as his gaze rested on her. Broad shoulders, strong arms...

"I need to get a life." Rachel punched her pillow, flopped to her back and closed her eyes.

Still, it was a long time before those images faded...

* * * *

Kane lay in bed, bone-tired but unable to sleep. Sitting up, he punched his pillow then lay back down. Insomnia was just one of the lingering after-effects from *the night*. The night he'd lost his partner and good friend. The night he'd killed another human being.

The night he'd started to ask himself some tough questions.

Was he so caught up in saving the world he'd lost sight of the bigger picture? His kind of work was necessary. Vital. But it had cost him his marriage. Sometimes he wondered if it was costing him his soul.

Gazing at the ceiling, he groaned. A cop who second-guessed himself was a liability, which was why his lieutenant insisted he take all his accumulated vacation time. Maybe after spending a few weeks in the mountains, he'd figure out what was important. If he was lucky, hanging out with Jed again would take him back to his roots and help him remember why he'd wanted to become a cop in the first place.

To serve and protect.

To watch his partner's head explode.

To kill a child.

"Son of a bitch!"

He stumbled out of bed and into the bathroom where he turned on the light. It wasn't the wound in his chest that hurt. Surgery had removed the bullet, but not the memories. Staring into the mirror, a man with haunted eyes looked back. Somehow he had to get beyond what had happened and think about the future.

When he lowered his head, an image of Rachel Carpenter drifted through his tortured mind. Unquestionably, she was beautiful. Just the memory of her smile and the touch of her hand on his arm sent an arrow of feeling straight to his groin. He'd sensed a sweetness in her that attracted him. When he got back from the mountains, maybe he'd give her a call. His jumping nerves calmed at the thought.

The love of a good woman certainly hadn't been his savior the first time around, but it might not hurt to try again. The type of women he'd been dating—women who knew the score and didn't expect a commitment— satisfied a primal urge, but not much else. Could be it was time for a change.

Kane splashed water on his face then squared up to the mirror again. His eyes looked clearer, more focused.

This time when he went back to bed, sleep took over at last.

* * * *

Lying in bed, he could think of nothing but Jordan. Eyes cautious, her figure hidden by an ugly sweater. Her beautiful hair had been longer before, and those ripe curves were showcased in silk and satin. His breath came quicker as he reached down to stroke himself. He'd almost taken her tonight. He'd been so close to the culmination of all his dreams. Earlier, as the hours ticked by but she hadn't come home, he'd grown worried and gone looking for her. His timing had been off, and he'd missed his chance on the deserted roadway.

No matter. He'd have to be patient a little longer. He was good at being patient. After all, he'd waited fourteen long years. He'd wait an eternity if need be. But he didn't think it'd be much longer. His reward was near. He could feel it. In his heart, Jordan already belonged to him.

Someday soon, she'd know it, too.

Chapter Three

"Wake up, girls. Last day of school." Rachel gave a perfunctory knock on Lark's door before pushing it open to poke her head inside. "Rise and shine."

Standing with her back to the doorway, hair damp from a recent shower, her daughter wore nothing but a pair of panties and a bra. Soft light from the bedside lamp highlighted the small blue tattoo on the white skin of her left shoulder.

Rachel gasped and closed her eyes. Surely she was seeing things. When she opened them, the tattoo was still there, a delicate bird perched on a leafy branch.

"Oh, my God." She started to speak again then stopped, struggling for words. "What have you done?"

Lark spun, eyes defiant as she stared at her mother. "It's just a tattoo. It's no big deal."

Stomach churning, Rachel shook her head. "You're wrong. It's a very big deal."

Don't yell. Stay calm.

She took a breath. "Cutting and dyeing your hair was bad enough. Hair will grow out. That tattoo is permanent."

"Lark got a tattoo?" Jade peeked around the doorframe wearing a pair of pajamas with *Girls Rule* emblazoned across the front. Her red hair hung down her back in tangles. "Wow, do you have a death wish or something?"

Jannine Gallant

Ivy floated up in a long white nightgown. "I want to see. Can I see it?"

"Get lost, both of you." Lark's voice quavered.

Neither of her sisters moved an inch.

"Turn around, Lark. Let me see what you've done to yourself."

Slowly her daughter turned, presenting her back for inspection. Rachel examined the tattoo. Thankfully the skin around it appeared to be healthy.

"At least it's not infected. Why did you do it?"

"Don't be so dramatic, Mom. It's just a little bird. Rose got a rose, and I got a lark. Get it?"

"Cool." Jade's voice held awe.

"Can I get a tattoo of some ivy when I'm older?" Her youngest flipped her long, blond hair over her shoulder with a mischievous smile.

Rachel turned to glare at them. "Shouldn't you two be getting dressed for school?"

"We have to miss all the good stuff." Jade pushed her sister in front of her as they headed back to their rooms.

Rachel forced her hands to unclench. "When did you have this done?"

"Last weekend in San Francisco. Rose's brother drove us." Lark dropped her gaze and ran a toe through the carpet.

"You didn't ask me first?" The final word ended on a screech. "You said you were spending the night at Rose's house. You didn't think I needed to know where you were?"

"If I'd asked, you would have said no." A spark of her usual defiance surfaced. "Anyway, Rose's mom knew where we were going."

"She knew about the tattoos?"

"Maybe not, but she knew about the haircuts. She likes them. She said they rock. She's not stuck in the Stone Age like you."

Mentally, Rachel counted to ten before she spoke again, trying to regain some control. "I don't understand how this happened. No reputable shop would tattoo a couple of fourteen-year-olds. There are laws against it. You could get in trouble. *I* could get in trouble." Her voice grew louder.

"Did you let some deviant on the street poke you with a dirty needle? For God's sake, Lark, people contract HIV that way."

Her daughter's eyes widened. "It wasn't like that, honest. Rose's cousin did it at his house. Everything was very clean, I swear."

"Why would her cousin do such a thing? He'd lose his license—"

"I don't think he has one. It's just a hobby." Lark stared down at her feet.

"I should press charges."

Her daughter's head snapped up. "Mom, you wouldn't! It isn't Rusty's fault. He's only a little older than Gavin, but he's an artist." She touched the tattoo. "His work is amazing, and we told him we had our parents' permission. I'll die if you call the cops. Rose would never forgive me."

"I don't care what Rose thinks. You let some little punk stick you with a needle. It doesn't look infected, but—"

"I swear I'm not going to get a disease. He's Rose's cousin not some stranger. Rusty made sure we knew it was safe."

"Illegal, Lark. Getting a tattoo is illegal."

"So's underage drinking. Kids do it all the time."

Rachel massaged the back of her neck. "Unfortunately, we don't have time now to discuss this further. Get ready for school."

"What're you going to do to me?"

"I don't know yet. You're a little too old for a time-out or a spanking. This is serious."

"It's just a little tattoo. You have to admit it's adorable."

Rachel didn't smile. "You drove into San Francisco with a sixteen-year-old boy and got a tattoo without my knowledge. Don't kid yourself. There'll be consequences."

"Are you going to tell Grandma and Grandpa?"

"Probably not today, but they'll find out soon enough. It's the beginning of summer. You can't keep your shoulder hidden forever."

"Grandma's going to freak." Lark's head drooped. "I guess I shouldn't have done it."

"You shouldn't have done a lot of things. Get dressed. We have a long day ahead of us."

* * * *

Somehow, Rachel got the kids to school on time. Balancing a tray full of banana bread and a bag of muffins in one hand, she unlocked the rear door of her shop, went inside then pushed the door closed with her foot. After setting her load on the front counter, she glanced around the store she'd worked so hard to create. The Book Nook was her pride and joy. Opening the shop had restored her self-esteem after her divorce and given her life purpose beyond mothering her girls. A coffee bar and sitting area occupied the front with the remainder of the large space filled with books. In back were a supply room and her cubbyhole of an office. Up a set of spiral stairs, she displayed gift items and office supplies.

A short time later, the coffee was brewed and the espresso machine steaming when she opened the front door to let in her first employee.

Chandra entered on a wave of perfume and trailing skirts. "Wow, you look great." She eyed Rachel's hunter green dress and matching jacket. "What's the occasion?"

"Jade's fifth grade promotion ceremony is this afternoon."

With gorgeous brown eyes, toffee-colored skin and high cheekbones, Chandra Jabeaux was nothing short of stunning. Today her black hair was braided into dozens of tiny cornrows.

"That's right. This is the last day of school, isn't it?"

Rachel nodded. "Lark's eighth grade graduation is this evening." She took a deep breath. Just thinking about her eldest daughter sent her blood pressure soaring.

"What's wrong? Are you sad your little girls are growing up?"

"I wish motherly sentimentality was all I had to contend with."

One brow lifted. "What's Lark done now?"

Rachel grimaced. "She and her friend got tattoos."

Chandra covered her mouth with both hands, eyes wide. "You must have flipped when she told you."

"You could say that. I might feel better if she'd had the sense to confess. I discovered what she'd done when I walked into her room this morning."

"It's not the end of the world. I have a tattoo." She stuck out her foot to display a blue flowering vine circling her delicate ankle.

"You're twenty, and Lark is fourteen. You've earned the right to make your own decisions. Anyway, it's illegal."

"Good point. If I'd gotten a tattoo when I was your daughter's age, my mom would have skinned me."

"Exactly." She turned to walk behind the small counter. "I'm working on a suitable punishment. I don't think Lark will be seeing Rose for the rest of the summer."

"She isn't going to like that one bit."

Rachel glanced up from counting the change in the cash register. "It's a punishment. She's not supposed to like it."

"If it's any consolation, I think you're making a wise decision. That Rose girl is trouble. I don't know what Lark sees in her."

"Her sixteen-year-old brother is cute, and he has a car."

"That would explain it."

She slid the register drawer shut. "You're all set. I have some paperwork to do in back. Call me if things get too busy."

"Will do."

Stopping to pour coffee into a mug with her name on it, Rachel headed to her office. Sitting at her desk, she reached for the file holding time cards, ready to tackle payroll.

Her hand shook as she pictured her daughter wandering through one of San Francisco's less savory neighborhoods. Anything could have happened. The police—

A vivid memory of Kane's steady blue gaze intruded on her thoughts.

The attraction between them had been instant, and the idea of seeing him again was enticing. A vacation might well be the answer to her current problem. At the moment, her goal was to keep Lark away from Rose. A camping trip to the Sierras would certainly accomplish that. She turned on her computer, waited until it hummed to life then pulled up the website for Granite Lake Retreat.

Photos portrayed a crystal clear lake surrounded by mountains. Tiny cabins dotted a shoreline where several canoes were tied to a dock. The number to call for reservations was prominently displayed in the top right corner. Rachel was tempted enough to reach for paper and pen to jot it down. Jade and Ivy would have a blast. They deserved a vacation. So did she.

She flipped open her day planner. Nothing important was scheduled before the end of the month except an orthodontist appointment for Jade that could be changed. The week following, Jade had soccer camp, Ivy had swim lessons and Lark was enrolled in a jazz dance clinic at the community college. She and the girls would be in Tahoe the last few days in June for her ex-mother-in-law's sixtieth birthday party. The camping trip would have to come before the party. Taking a breath, she dialed the number.

"Granite Lake Retreat." A pleasant female voice chirped the greeting. "How may I help you?"

"Hi. I was wondering if you have any openings starting next Thursday."

"How many people in your party, ma'am?"

"Four."

"Actually, we do. We just had a cancellation that opened up two cabins. How many days will you be staying?"

"Seven nights." *May as well jump in with both feet.*

"Terrific. Let's go over a few details."

Rachel grabbed a note pad to write down the list of items she'd need, along with directions to the pick-up point. Apparently customers hiked to the actual campsite.

When the woman asked, Rachel provided her pertinent information and credit card number. She was about to hang up when she remembered Daisy.

"Are dogs allowed?"

"Only if they're obedient and kept on a leash. Would you like to bring your pet?"

"Yes, she's a golden retriever and very well behaved."

"I'll make a note of it on your reservation. Is there anything else I can help you with?"

"No, I think I have all the information I need."

"Great, we'll see you next week. Have a nice day."

"I'll try. You, too."

Rachel hung up the phone. Behind her, a board creaked. She spun around in her chair expecting to see Chandra, but the doorway was empty. The back door to the shop closed with a thud. Frowning, she left her office to open it and check behind the building. Her SUV was parked alongside Chandra's compact car. Otherwise, the small lot was deserted. Shrugging, she went back inside.

The next couple hours were spent finishing payroll and helping with a rush of customers.

It was noon when the bell over the door jingled and Ellen Patterson sailed through. "I came in a little before I was supposed to. I thought maybe you could use the extra time, Rachel."

"That was sweet of you. School is dismissed early today, and I have to take Jade home to change before the promotion ceremony."

"I guessed as much." Efficient and eager to please, Ellen had been with Rachel since she opened the shop soon after her divorce.

"Now that you're here, I have a question. How would you feel about putting in some overtime at the end of the month?"

Ellen set her purse on a shelf and glanced over. "I'd love to. I could use the extra money."

Chandra looked up from itemizing a stack of books. "I don't have a problem with it either. Are you expecting the shop to be extra busy?"

"No, I was thinking about taking a vacation, a camping trip to the mountains with the girls."

Ellen's smile lit her plain face. "That's great. You never take any time off."

Chandra nodded. "Between the three of us, we can handle the shop. I'm sure Tim won't mind working a few extra hours."

"Thanks, both of you. I appreciate it."

Rachel finished in the office and left to pick up her kids. All three girls were full of talk about the last day of school. Even Lark made an effort to be pleasant. The cynical side of Rachel assumed it was an attempt to butter her mother up before a punishment was handed down.

Jade's promotion ceremony went smoothly. With her hair flowing in curls down her back and wearing a short, lavender dress, she looked so beautiful Rachel's heart ached.

Her mother leaned forward and squeezed her hand. "It's like seeing you again at that age."

"And you, Mom. We're definitely three peas in a pod."

After the brief reception following the ceremony, Rachel drove the girls home for a short rest before they had to take off again.

She was sitting on the couch, sorting through the mail when a piece of paper floated into her lap.

She glanced up at Lark standing above her. "What's this?"

"My report card."

Unfolding the paper, a smile spread. "You got all A's. Honey, I'm proud of you."

Lark frowned. "Ivy isn't the only one who can get straight A's around here."

"I never thought she was. This is terrific. Your teachers have given you nothing but good comments."

"I hope you'll take my grades into account when you decide on my punishment." She stuffed her hands into her pockets. "I don't know why I got the tattoo. It seemed like the thing to do at the time."

Her daughter's eyes were filled with misery. It would be so easy to let her off the hook, but that wasn't an option. If Lark thought she could get away with breaking the rules once, God only knew what she'd do next. The tattoo was beyond serious. Just thinking about it raised her blood pressure.

"I've given your behavior a lot of consideration, and I'm pleased you recognize you made a mistake. I don't want it to happen again."

"It won't, cross my heart. I won't get any more tattoos, and I'll let my hair go back to its natural color."

"The hair and the tattoo aren't the only problem."

"I don't know what you're talking about." She scowled at the floor. "I thought you were mad about the tattoo."

"Oh, I am, but I'm equally upset you left town without telling me. I'm your mother. I need to know where you are all the time."

"I promise I'll tell you from now on."

"I certainly hope so, but for a while you won't be going anywhere with Rose. You're not allowed to spend time with her until I say differently."

"That's not fair! Rose is my best friend."

"She hasn't always been. Why don't you hang around with Amy or Natalie anymore?"

"Because they still act like kids. Rose doesn't. Anyway, it's not her fault I got a tattoo. I made my own choice."

"You certainly did, and it was an extremely poor one. You used to have better judgment. Rose—"

"You can't pick my friends for me, Mom."

Rachel sighed, hating the defiance in her daughter's eyes. "You're right, I can't. But I can choose who you spend your time with, and this summer it won't be Rose."

"All summer? You can't do that!"

"If your choices improve over the next couple of months, we'll re-evaluate when school starts."

Lark's eyes narrowed. "Dad would never have been this mean. I wish he hadn't died. I wish..." She clamped her lips together.

"I wish he hadn't either. I don't like making these decisions on my own."

"Is that all?" Lark's chest heaved as she drew in a ragged breath.

Thinking about the camping trip, Rachel held her tongue. "It is for now. Why don't you go get dressed? We need to leave in about an hour."

"Am I allowed to talk to Rose at our graduation, or is that asking too much?" Sarcasm accompanied the defiance in her voice.

Rachel's temper flared. Silently she counted to ten. "Of course you can talk to her. You just can't go anywhere with her or with her brother."

"Fine!" With one last icy glare, Lark stomped off.

Rachel collapsed against the back of the couch.

"Is the coast clear?" Grace stepped into the doorway.

"Gracie! I thought you weren't going to be able to make it today."

"I changed my work schedule. Rough day?"

"The worst."

"Do you want to talk about it?"

"Maybe later. I can't face a rehash right now."

"You can tell me all the gruesome details after dinner. I was planning to spend the night at Mom and Dad's, but I'll stay here instead."

"You know you're welcome. If we're lucky, seeing her favorite aunt will improve Lark's mood and make the evening bearable."

"We can hope." Grace smiled. "Come on, let's go rally the troops."

After the earlier theatrics, the eighth-grade graduation ceremony was anticlimactic—the only bit of drama created when Lark walked across the stage wearing a summer dress that bared her tattoo for the world to see. Rachel's mother sagged in her seat, her gasp audible through the applause.

A short time later, Audrey Hanover entered the kitchen of her big, rambling farmhouse, still in a huff. "Neither of you would have gotten away with a stunt like that when you were teenagers."

Though she'd grown plump over the years, and her red hair was mostly gray, she was still a beautiful woman—and a force to be reckoned with. She cast another dark look in her granddaughter's direction.

"Believe me, Lark isn't getting away with it either." Rachel washed her hands and dried them on a dish towel. "Now, what can I do to help with dinner?"

Audrey ignored her daughter's attempt to change the subject. "Then why wouldn't you let me speak my mind when we were at the school?"

"Because I didn't want a public scene. I'm handling the situation, and Lark is well aware of my displeasure. Please, can we just drop it for now?"

Grace took her mother's sweater from her and hung it on the hook by the door. "Don't worry, Mom. Lark is in serious trouble. Rachel let her have it earlier. Now, let's get the ham out of the oven and eat. I'm starving."

Her sister led their mother away, and Rachel reached up to massage her temples.

"Here." Will handed her two aspirin and a glass of water. "You look like you could use these."

"My savior." She gulped down the tablets.

"Is Mom giving you grief?"

"She doesn't bother me. It's the situation in general. Lately I feel like my life is one disaster after another."

"Keep your chin up, kid. You'll survive."

"If you say so."

Dinner was eaten with the usual noise and confusion that accompanied a Hanover family gathering. Afterward, Grace followed Rachel home. When she came downstairs after changing into a pair of old sweats, her sister handed her a glass of wine.

"Are the kids asleep?" Grace leaned against the kitchen counter and tapped one polished nail on the granite surface.

"Jade and Ivy are. They were both exhausted. Lark is listening to her iPod and ignoring me."

"She'll get over it."

"Maybe not after I throw her the next curve ball." Rachel took a sip of wine then set down her glass to pull flour and sugar out of the pantry.

"What curve ball are you talking about?"

She set to work mixing up a batch of apple bran muffins. "The camping trip I'm planning. It'll be easier to enforce the no Rose rule if they aren't in the same town."

Grace eyed her sister with raised brows. "This camping trip wouldn't have anything to do with the retreat Kane Lafferty was talking about, would it?"

"It might. I booked a reservation for seven days starting next week." Rachel cracked the last egg into the bowl then stirred vigorously.

"I knew it! I told Nolan you had a thing for his buddy. You could barely keep your eyes off him while we were having drinks."

Rachel squirmed as she poured the batter into prepared tins. "I don't have a thing for Kane. Sure, I think—thought he was attractive. Who wouldn't? But it's not like I ran off and jumped into bed with the man."

"Are you sure?"

"Grace!" Rachel shut the oven door and turned to glare at her sister. "Of course I'm sure."

"Just checking. Did he kiss you?"

"No, he walked me to my car and left. End of story."

"Obviously not or you wouldn't have planned this camping trip."

"The trip isn't about Kane. It's about giving Jade and Ivy a great vacation and getting Lark away from her friend. I looked up Granite Lake Retreat online and it seems like a really fun place. That's all there is to it. Honestly."

"I hope so."

Rachel set the timer and turned. "Why? I thought you'd be thrilled I'm actually interested in someone for a change."

"Normally I would be, and I'll admit Kane is very sexy in that macho way you seem to go for. Not my type, but seriously hot."

"Do you have a point?"

"I was getting to it. Nolan told me all about Kane, and he doesn't sound like someone you want to be involved with at the moment."

She sat down at the table across from her sister. "Why not? He seems nice."

"He is, and Nolan has a lot of respect for him. But Kane has some problems. He was involved in a shooting that left his partner and a sixteen-year-old kid dead. Kane was wounded. Their lieutenant ordered him to take some time off to get his head together. Which means he isn't the ideal candidate for a relationship."

"That's awful. I thought I had problems."

"You do. So find a nice, uncomplicated man who's good in bed and isn't an emotional mess. Kane is probably more trouble than you want to tackle right now." Grace reached over and took Rachel's hands. "I don't want you to get hurt again. You aren't tough like me, and taking on a project the size of Kane Lafferty seems like more pain than it's worth."

"You're probably right. It's too bad, though, because I really did like him."

"Hey, if you could have a fling with the guy and walk away, I'd say go for it."

"What makes you think I can't?"

"Come on. I know you. You'd do something stupid like falling in love."

"I slept with Alan, and I didn't fall in love with him."

Grace wrinkled her nose. "Let's face it, Alan was a little on the boring side. He was certainly no Kane Lafferty."

"True."

Outside a vehicle slowed and idled, its headlights illuminating the empty street.

Rachel stepped to the window to peek out. "I wonder who that is."

Grace joined her as the pickup drove away. "Someone must be lost."

"I suppose." The timer dinged, and Rachel pulled the muffins from the oven. "Let's go to bed. I'm really tired. Plus, tomorrow I have to break the news about the camping trip to Lark."

"Do me a favor and wait until after I've left to talk to her. I don't want to get hit by the fallout."

Grace ducked when Rachel threw a potholder at her.

"Aren't you sweet and supportive. Good night, Gracie."

Chapter Four

The early morning sun was just peeking over the hills as Rachel and the girls left Vine Haven. Traffic heading east was light, putting Rachel in a good mood. She sang softly with the radio as the miles passed. In the back seat, Jade and Ivy told jokes, played games and consoled Daisy, who moaned pitifully.

Lark turned around in the front passenger seat and frowned at her sisters who were giggling helplessly at one of Jade's jokes. "They won't think it's so funny when Daisy throws up on them."

"That's a cheerful thought."

"You can't expect me to be happy. I didn't want to come on this stupid camping trip."

"Lark." Rachel's tone held a warning.

Her daughter retreated into sullen silence. She'd been sulking all week. After her initial explosion, she was punishing the rest of the family with her long face and dramatic sighs.

Jade leaned forward between the seats. "What's so bad about going camping, anyway?"

"Everything. When are we going to get there? I'm sick of sitting in the car. We've been driving for hours."

"It's not too much farther."

"I still don't see why *I* had to come."

Rachel sighed. "We've been through this already. This is a family camping trip, and like it or not, you're part of the family."

"Not. Definitely not."

Jade bounced and squealed. "Mom, this is our exit."

Rachel drove down a two-lane road lined with pine trees. Here and there piles of dirty snow lay in shady patches. The girls sat quietly, watching for the signpost that marked their destination.

"There it is." Jade pointed at a weathered sign with the camp's logo.

The car bumped along a rutted track as Rachel pulled to a stop in a makeshift parking lot.

A battered wooden fence lined the parking area, separating it from a stable and corral. A couple of horses and several mules dozed in the sun. Every now and then one switched its tail to shoo away a fly.

"This rocks. They have horses." Jade climbed out of the car.

"Do we get to ride them?" Ivy ducked as the dog leaped over the back of the seat in a scramble toward freedom. She ran to the fence. "Look at the donkeys. Aren't they cute?"

"Actually, they're mules." A young man with dark blond hair, glasses and an engaging smile approached, his hand outstretched to shake Rachel's. "I'm Jason, and you must be the Carpenters. Welcome to Granite Lake Retreat. I'll be your guide for the hike up to the actual camp."

Rachel introduced the girls as he made short work of unloading their gear.

"Is that it?" He pointed at the pile of suitcases, sleeping bags and guitar case at his feet.

"Maybe we over-packed." Rachel frowned. "It looks like an awful lot to carry."

"This is nothing. You should see the stuff some people bring."

She glanced down at her dog, who sat nearby keeping an eye on the horses. "Oh, where's Daisy's food?"

"It's right here." Ivy pushed a heavy burlap sack off the backseat floor. "Jade moved it up here so Daisy wouldn't eat it while we were driving."

Rachel smiled at her daughters. "That was smart thinking."

"I didn't want her to throw up on me."

Jason laughed. "That would motivate me. If we have everything, I'll load your gear onto a couple of the mules."

Ivy climbed out of the backseat, clutching a dark-haired doll to her chest. "I can't believe I almost forgot Samantha."

"Mom, she's not taking a doll with her, is she?" Lark rolled her eyes. "How embarrassing is that?"

Rachel rested a hand on her youngest daughter's head. "I don't mind as long as she carries her."

"Geez, Lark, she's nowhere near as big as your guitar."

"I can't leave it. I have to practice."

Their guide smiled at her. "Sometimes at night we sing around the campfire. Maybe you could play for us one evening."

Lark responded with a shy smile of her own. "I'd like to, but I'm not a professional or anything."

"Don't worry. We aren't picky. Jed plays the fiddle, and you can accompany him. Jed's the owner of Granite Lake Retreat. He's a great guy, but be careful." His grin was teasing. "Most of the single girls fall crazy in love with him before they leave."

"He must look like his brother." Rachel grabbed two suitcases and followed Jason toward the corral.

"Do you know Kane?" He turned to look at her.

Her face heated. She hadn't meant for him to hear her comment. "I met him once."

"Kane's great, too. He's been terrific about helping out. Right now it's just me, Jed, Hillary and Ozzie, but we have more staff coming before the holiday."

They made a return trip for the last of the bags, and Rachel locked the car. "Does everyone have their day pack and water bottle?"

The girls nodded.

Jason secured their gear to the mules. "Who wants to lead the second one?"

Jade volunteered. "What's his name?"

"Dozer. This one's Mandy."

"Cool. Are the horses coming with us?"

"No, a man down the road owns them. He boards them in our stable and feeds the mules for us in exchange."

"Too bad." Ivy sighed. "I'd love to ride one."

"I'm afraid we don't offer trail rides, but don't worry. There're plenty of other activities to keep you occupied."

They followed a beaten dirt path through a thicket of trees out onto an open hillside and walked for a half hour before Jason stopped his mule.

"Check out the view."

An open vista stretched before them with towering granite peeks and dense conifer forests reaching to the horizon. A crystal clear lake rested at the bottom of the bowl.

"Wow, it's really pretty," Ivy called. "Come look at the lake, Jade."

She handed the lead rope to Rachel and ran over to stand next to her sister. "This is so awesome. Are we on top of a mountain?"

Their guide shook his head. "Not really. We're on a ridge above the camp. The trail leads down from here."

"The cabins sure look tiny." Lark started down the slope behind the others.

"They aren't very big, just a room lined with bunks and storage space for your gear underneath."

Lark stopped. "And a bathroom."

Jason grinned at her. "I'm afraid we don't have indoor plumbing at Granite Lake. That path at the far end of the cabins leads to the outhouses. We use a lot of lime, so they don't smell too bad, as outhouses go."

She gave her mother a horrified look. "You didn't mention anything about outhouses. What about showers? Please tell me there're showers."

"We jump in the lake, right, Mom?" Jade pushed on the mule to get him moving again.

Their guide took pity on Lark. "We have solar showers. The water is pretty warm after hanging in the sun all day."

"Super. It's practically five star accommodations." Lark wrinkled her nose as one of the mules stopped to lift its tail. "Gross. That's so disgusting."

"Pee-yew." Ivy waved her hand in front of her nose. "What do you feed him?"

"Hay and the occasional bologna sandwich. Dozer loves bologna."

"You might want to think about changing his diet."

Lark frowned at her sister. "Your doll is going to lose its shoe."

Ivy screamed and grabbed the dangling shoe. "Thanks. I wouldn't have liked fishing it out of that steaming pile."

Jade shrieked with laughter, her braces flashing in the sunlight, and even Lark was smiling as they entered the camp.

A tall man with brown hair, blue eyes and a strong resemblance to Kane jogged up the slope from the lake to greet them. "It sounds like you enjoyed your hike." He extended a hand. "I'm Jed Lafferty, your host."

Jason introduced Rachel and the girls to Jed and Ozzie Thompson, a short man with sparse white hair. The cook was probably in his mid-seventies. He shook Rachel's hand and then went back to the campfire he was tending.

"Kane took some guests on a hike, and Hillary drove into Truckee for supplies. You'll meet them both later. Kane's my brother."

Rachel opened her mouth to say she was already acquainted with his brother but closed it when Ivy interrupted.

"Is this our cabin?"

Jed nodded. "Go ahead and settle in. Ozzie should have lunch ready shortly. I imagine you're hungry after your hike."

Jade peeked inside. "Starving."

"Come out to the central picnic area when you're ready. That's where we eat all our meals. Toilet facilities are at the end of this path, and there are a couple of shower stalls over near that grove of trees." He pointed to a bucket of water by the door. "This is just for washing. We keep a supply of bottled water to drink."

Jason had unloaded the mules while Jed talked, and both men left them to get organized. Her youngest daughters claimed the upper bunks.

"This is so cool." Jade climbed up to her bed and bounced on the bare mattress. "It's comfortable, too."

"That's good." Rachel sat on a lower bunk to test its firmness. "This beats sleeping on the ground."

Other than the four bunks, the furnishings consisted of a small table with two chairs, an old fashioned basin and water pitcher, a mirror in a copper frame and a lantern, which hung from an overhead hook.

"It's nice." Ivy reached up to touch the lantern. "I like this place."

"The cabin seems functional."

Rachel smiled at the girls. Their eyes were bright with anticipation. Even Lark had stopped moping.

"Let's spread out our sleeping bags and then go eat. I'm pretty hungry."

They stowed their suitcases under the bunks and washed their hands and faces in the basin. After tying Daisy in the shade with a bowl of water and a dog treat, they left the cabin to follow the trail to the area set up with picnic tables Jed had mentioned. A buffet of sandwiches, salads and chips was spread out on vinyl tablecloths. A big tub of iced drinks rested next to the food table.

"It certainly doesn't look like we're going to starve while we're here." Rachel sat down with her loaded plate.

Jade swallowed a mouthful of macaroni salad. "It's really yummy, almost as good as Grandma's."

"Don't let your grandmother hear you say that. You're right, though. It's very tasty."

"Ozzie is one heck of a cook. We've been eating like kings since we got here."

Rachel turned around and smiled at the speaker, a young man in his late twenties with long hair pulled back in a ponytail and a scraggly beard. His friend had short, dark hair under a Chicago Cubs baseball cap and brown eyes. They introduced themselves as Chip and Bob.

"Did you just arrive?" Chip asked.

Rachel nodded, wondering how he could possibly eat the Dagwood sandwich without half of it ending up in his beard. "We're staying for a week. Have you been here long?"

"This is our second day. The place is great. We hiked fifteen miles yesterday, so today we're taking it easy with a little fishing and lazing around at the lake."

"We'll probably go down to the beach after lunch."

"Mom, that lady over there is staring at you." Ivy tugged on her arm. "I think she's trying to get your attention."

Rachel's gaze followed Ivy's pointing finger. A woman who looked to be in her mid-forties with shoulder-length brown hair and an eager expression sat at a table with a man and two teenaged kids. She spoke to them in a low voice before coming over.

"I'm sorry to bother you." Her smile was uncertain. "I've been going mad with curiosity. Were you by any chance on a soap opera a dozen years ago?"

"I was, but I'm surprised you recognized me. I was a lot younger and better dressed at the time."

The woman shook her head. "Maybe better dressed, but you're still just as beautiful as you were then." She stuck out her hand. "I'm Mimi Andrews, and that's my husband, Greg, with our kids, Kevin and Lauren. It's a pleasure to meet you. I'll admit I watched you religiously back when the children were still in diapers."

"It's nice to meet you, too." Rachel took the offered hand. "These are my girls, Lark, Jade and Ivy."

"You're all as pretty as your mother. I'll leave you to finish your lunch. Maybe we'll see each other down at the lake later."

Rachel picked up her sandwich after Mimi left. "She seems like a nice woman."

Lark rolled her eyes. "Another fan?"

Ivy frowned at her sister. "Mom was famous. You're just jealous because no one knows you were on the show."

"She was only in a couple of episodes." Rachel reached for a chip.

"And I was a tiny baby. You're such a dork, Ivy."

Jade poked her younger sister. "Hurry up and eat your sandwich. I want to go swimming."

Rachel frowned. "The lake is probably pretty cold."

"Who cares? Can I go change into my bathing suit?"

"If you're finished eating, you may."

Jade dumped her paper plate in the trashcan and hurried off with Ivy right behind her.

"Don't you want to go swimming?" Rachel glanced over at Lark.

"Maybe later. Can I go talk to that girl over there? She looks like she's my age, and if I'm going to be stuck here for a week, I may as well make friends."

"Do you mean Mimi Andrews's daughter?"

Lark nodded. "Her mom said her name's Lauren."

"That's right, Lauren and Kevin. Sure, go introduce yourself. I want you to have fun this week."

"Don't push it, Mom."

Rachel grinned. "A mother can dream, can't she?" She dropped her plate in the trash. "I'll be down at the lake with your sisters if you need me. And please don't wander off without checking with me first. I don't want you to get lost."

"Or eaten by a bear or kidnapped by an escaped lunatic. I know the drill. See you later." She hurried off to catch up with the other two kids before they left the picnic area.

The boy was tall and good-looking like his father. Rachel had a feeling he was the attraction, not his sister. Which wasn't necessarily a bad thing. Anyone who could distract Lark from her crush on Rose's brother earned a gold star in Rachel's book. Leaving her eldest to her own devices, Rachel headed back to the cabin where she changed into a bathing suit and wrap.

She grabbed a towel and a book, put Daisy on a leash and headed out at a fast clip. As they approached the lake, the dog lifted her nose to sniff the air then tugged even harder.

It was warm for mid-June. With the sun riding high in the sky, a quick dip in the lake would be refreshing after their earlier hike. As Rachel neared the dock, Jade jumped in with a splash and came up gasping.

"It's freezing." Her teeth chattered. "Don't be a chicken, Ivy. Just close your eyes and jump."

Ivy did, then screamed and flailed. Rachel smiled. Maybe she'd skip the swim and settle for a bit of sunbathing. She spread her towel in a patch of sand between two boulders. A perfect spot with a towering pine creating just enough shade to keep her cool, and a spectacular view of the lake shimmering beneath the afternoon sun. The girls jumped in again, their laughter ringing across the water. Rachel sighed. It had been far too long since her last vacation. She could only think of one thing that would make it better.

"Would you like a cold drink?"

Shading her eyes, she glanced up as a shadow loomed over her. Anticipation. Excitement. Delight. A conflux of emotions swirled inside her. *Settle down, Rachel.* With an effort, she composed her voice, afraid she'd sound like a school girl with a mad crush.

"I'd love one."

Kane sat on the boulder next to her and opened a small ice chest. "Cola or beer?"

"Cola, please." She took the cold can then offered a smile.

He opened a beer with a hiss and took a swig. "I recognized you from the trail above. Nobody else has hair quite that color of red. I was afraid I was imagining things."

"Should I take that as a compliment?"

"Definitely. When did you decide to come up here?"

"Last week. I wanted to get away for a while, so I looked the place up online like you suggested. It appears I made a good choice. My girls are having a great time."

"Are those two yours?" He pointed toward the dock.

Both her daughters bent at the waist. Simultaneously they dived into the water and came up screaming.

"The taller one is Jade, and the blonde is Ivy. I have a feeling they're going to disturb the peace around here."

"That's okay. Kids should be able to make noise when they're outside."

Rachel smiled. "Let's hope the rest of the guests feel that way."

"And who is this?" He scratched Daisy behind one ear.

The dog moaned in delight then leaned against him.

"Apparently, your new best friend. Her name's Daisy."

"Why isn't she swimming with the girls?"

"She's not a big fan of the water." Rachel stroked the dog's silky coat. "She has a few hang-ups, but she's very sweet."

"I thought you had three daughters."

His eyes were a clear, beautiful blue as he held her gaze. Her stomach fluttered.

"I do. Lark's up at camp with a couple of other kids."

"Blond hair with pink streaks, but still pretty?"

Rachel laughed. "That's a very good description."

"I saw her before I came down. She and the Andrews kids were talking to Jed about taking out a canoe."

"I'm glad she's found someone her own age to hang out with. My oldest wasn't exactly looking forward to this trip."

"You didn't want to leave her home alone?"

"Not a chance. She got a tattoo a couple of weeks ago along with that awful haircut."

Kane choked on his beer. "Now I remember why I wasn't in a rush to have kids when I was married."

"They've given me more than my fair share of headaches, but the rewards are worth it. How can you resist those happy faces?"

Jade and Ivy ran up, their curious gazes on Kane. Water dripped from their hair and bathing suits to form a couple of growing puddles.

"Can we swim out to that big rock and back?" Jade asked.

The rock in question was probably more than a hundred yards from shore.

Rachel frowned. "You can go, but I'm not so sure about Ivy. That's an awfully long way for you to swim, honey."

"I can do it. I'm much better than I used to be. Please."

"I don't know. If you got into trouble, it would take me too long to reach you. I don't think it's a good idea."

"That's not fair!"

Kane touched her knee. "Would you let her go if I swam with them? I came down here to cool off, anyway."

She glanced over at him and smiled. "Girls, this is Kane Lafferty. You met his brother, Jed, earlier. Are you sure you don't mind? I imagine the water's pretty cold."

"It is, but cold doesn't bother me. Is that a yes?"

She waved her hand. "Have fun. I'll watch you from my nice warm spot on shore."

"Last one in's a rotten egg!" Ivy took off laughing with Jade close behind.

"Guess I'd better get a move on." Setting down his beer, Kane followed close behind the girls as they all hit the water.

His head bobbed next to Ivy's small one while Jade swam ahead in a strong crawl.

Lark made brief eye contact as she came down to the shore with her two new friends. They strapped on life vests and climbed into a canoe, which rocked precariously as they shoved off. Greg and Mimi Andrews settled under a beach umbrella a short distance away, and Rachel gave them a smile and nod. The two young men she'd met at lunch walked by carrying fishing gear. They called out a greeting as they passed. She waved in return then covered a yawn. It was that sort of afternoon. Apparently, Daisy agreed. She flopped down in a patch of shade and let out a groan.

Relaxing under a warm sun, Rachel closed her eyes as she drifted in a languid state between sleep and wakefulness. When a quiver of unease shot through her, she sat up to look around, wondering what had disturbed her. Kane and the girls were swimming back, and Lark was still out in the canoe. Mimi stood knee-deep at the edge of the lake while her husband read a magazine. The two fishermen had disappeared from sight. A scuffling noise sounded behind her. She turned her head as a young boy tore down the path toward the lake. He was followed by a man wearing walking shorts and a tan camp shirt. Rachel frowned. He looked familiar.

Jade and Ivy swam ashore. Shivering, they ran to her, looking for towels.

"Didn't you bring them down with you?" She twisted and inched sideways to see behind them.

As Kane swam back toward the rock, his strong arms cleaved the water in graceful strokes.

"We forgot." Jade's teeth chattered as Ivy huddled close to her.

Rachel returned her attention to the girls and levered to her feet. "The two of you can share mine while I go get a couple from the cabin."

She hurried up the path. A squirrel chirped at her from the protection of a bush, and a blue jay squawked on an overhead tree branch. Reaching the cabin, she paused to look around. The breeze blew lightly. Nearby, a rock clattered. Rachel peered around the side of the structure. Something moved in the trees up the hillside.

Another camper or an animal—squirrel or bear?

A shiver worked down her spine. Grabbing the towels from the cabin, she headed back to the lake. "Here you go."

Jade took the towels. "Thanks. We're going to go lie on the dock and warm up."

Kane walked up from the water and stopped beside them.

Ivy peeked at him from behind dripping bangs. "Thanks for swimming with me. Maybe we could do it again tomorrow."

He smiled back. "Any time you like."

"That was nice of you." Rachel sat down on her damp towel. "I appreciate it."

"Swimming with your daughter wasn't exactly a chore." He stretched out beside her. "I even swam a couple of extra laps."

Rachel tried hard not to stare and failed. Kane's broad, tanned shoulders glistened with moisture. Droplets of water clung to the dusting of hair covering his chest, which narrowed to a damp trail that disappeared inside his shorts. She licked dry lips and took a sip of her lukewarm cola. "I appreciate it anyway."

"Did you take a nap while we were gone?"

"I was almost asleep when something disturbed me."

"What woke you?"

"Um, probably a squirrel."

"You seem a little distracted." His eyes were bright with amusement as he studied her.

"I noticed your scar." It was a lame attempt to excuse her fascination with his chest. "Grace told me you'd been shot."

He ran a finger over the ridge of puckered flesh below his collar bone. "Does it bother you?"

She shook her head. "It's not exactly disfiguring. Is it painful?"

"Not anymore."

Kane stretched, and Rachel's choked on her drink.

He glanced her way. "I should probably head back up to see if Jed needs any help."

"Will I see you around later?"

"Count on it. We're planning a bonfire for this evening. I'll be sure to look for you there. Dress warm. It gets cold as soon as the sun goes down."

Rachel nodded. "Thanks again for swimming with the girls."

"I enjoyed it." A smile tilted his lips. "Maybe next time you'll shed that cover-up and join us."

He left before she could answer, and Rachel let out a deep breath. The man was lethal. She fanned herself with her book. His sex appeal quotient was off the charts, and she felt like a walking hormone, which was ridiculous. She was thirty-five and the mother of three, not a sex-starved teenager. She had more than enough on her plate dealing with the girls. Getting worked up over a man was just plain foolish.

Maybe she would take a swim. After her conversation with Kane, a dip in icy water was just what she needed to cool off. Scrambling to her feet, she ran down to the lake and jumped in.

Chapter Five

"Make sure you put on a warm jacket." Rachel zipped her coat. "Don't forget a flashlight. It's going to be dark when we come back."

Jade sorted through her suitcase. "I can't find one. Where did you put them?"

"They're in the bag with the extra towels. Lark, are you ready to go?"

Lark nodded, an actual smile curving her lips as she tugged a knit hat over her hair. "Can I bring my guitar? Lauren has a flute, and she wants us to play something together."

"Of course you can, honey. Where the heck is Daisy's leash? I thought I left it on the table when I tied her up before dinner."

"Here it is." Ivy came out from under the table. "The leash must have fallen off when I set the water bottles down earlier."

"You do tend to meet yourself coming and going in this place." Rachel looked around their cramped quarters. "It seemed bigger when we first got here."

"That's because Jade hadn't spread her stuff all over the place yet." Lark edged toward the door.

"Your sister has a point." Rachel eyed Jade's scattered clothes. "You're going to have to keep your stuff cleaned up. There isn't room to swing a cat in here."

"I will when we get back. Let's go."

Pleased that her daughters—all her daughters—seemed eager to get down to the campfire, Rachel shut the door, clipped Daisy's leash to her collar then followed them down the trail toward the southern end of the lake where a huge bonfire burned brightly against the darkening sky. The last few rays of light glimmered on the mountain peaks as the sun sank below the horizon. Other campers were leaving their cabins. A little boy broke loose from his father and ran full tilt into Lark, knocking them both to the ground. Rachel hurried forward as Lark scrambled to her feet.

"I'm so sorry." The father lifted his son off the ground. "Rex, you need to apologize to this girl. You could have hurt her."

"I'm fine." Lark brushed off her jeans. She retrieved her guitar case and looked up at the man. Her eyes widened. "Mr. Olmstead, is that you?"

"My goodness, Lark, I didn't recognize you in the dark. Fancy meeting you up here. Hello, Mrs. Carpenter. Hi, girls."

"Please call me Rachel. Now I know why you looked so familiar when I saw you down by the lake earlier. I wasn't expecting to see a face from home."

"Is this your little boy?" Lark glanced down at the pint-sized dynamo covered in dirt.

"Yes, this is Rex, and I'm Dennis. No 'Mr. Olmstead' while we're here. It makes me feel like I'm back in school."

"Are you vacationing with your family?" Rachel tugged Daisy away from the boy.

"Just with Rex. I'm divorced. Oops, there he goes again. I'd better catch him before he gets into more trouble." He smiled, making his ordinary features more attractive. "Maybe we can talk again later." He sprinted after his son.

Lark rolled her eyes. "I think Mr. Olmstead likes you, Mom. Believe me, he was never that animated when I had him for seventh grade math."

"He's probably lonely. He sounded sad when he said he was divorced, and he obviously has his hands full with Rex."

"I bet he bored his wife into a stupor. He used to go on and on about the dumbest stuff."

"That's not very nice, Lark. Just because math isn't your favorite subject doesn't mean it's dumb."

"I know, I know—*if you can't say something nice...*" She turned away. "Hey, there's Kevin and Lauren. Can I go sit with them?"

"I guess so, but find us when you're ready to leave. I don't want you walking back to the cabin alone in the dark."

"Fine. Whatever. I'll see you later."

Rachel sat down on a log with Jade and Ivy. A minute later Kane appeared.

"I think Ozzie's handing out marshmallows. You'd better go get some before his supply runs out."

"Can we?" Ivy bounced up and down.

"Sure."

Both girls shot off to join the group of kids surrounding the elderly man.

"We have quite a crowd tonight." Rachel scooted over to make room for Kane on the log.

He sat next to her and stretched his legs toward the fire. "The big group over there is some sort of family reunion. The parents are George and Rita Dawson from Nebraska." He pointed to a dark-haired, older woman and a heavyset man. "They have two married daughters who came with their husbands and children and one unmarried son who brought along his girlfriend. The son lives somewhere in the Bay Area, and I don't think Mrs. Dawson is a big fan of the woman with him."

"Why not?"

"The rest of the family looks like an advertisement for middle America, but check out Tiffany the Temptress."

Kane put his hand on her chin and turned her head toward the right. For a moment the touch of his warm fingers against her face made her forget why he'd placed them there. When she finally focused on the woman in question, she gaped.

"Do you think they're real?" His whisper tickled her ear.

"They can't possibly be. Oh, my."

"Fake or not, I'm looking forward to seeing her in a bathing suit tomorrow." He wiggled his eyebrows.

Rachel punched his arm lightly. "So is every guy here. Wow, I can see why his mom is upset. Having a Playboy centerfold as a prospective daughter-in-law would be tough."

"It should make for a few interesting conversations this week. All the cabins are full now, so you may as well get to know your fellow campers if you're feeling sociable."

"Let's see if I can remember them all. There's Greg and Mimi Andrews and their kids, Dennis Olmstead and Rex the human torpedo, Chip and Bob who might or might not be a couple, the Dawson group and us."

"I don't think Chip and Bob are gay. Chip's eyes popped out of their sockets when Tiffany walked by in a tank top earlier."

"Not surprising. Did I remember everyone?"

"You did. Then there's me and Jed and Ozzie and Jason. Hillary was away today, picking up supplies. She'll be back in the morning. You'll like her. She's a tiny little thing but full of energy."

Jade and Ivy raced back, carrying sticks and marshmallows. Jade dropped to her knees and poked her treat toward the flames. The marshmallow crackled and burned. Ivy sat back and toasted hers to a golden brown.

When she finished cooking her third treat, she offered it to Kane. "Would you like one? I'm full."

"Thanks, but maybe your mom wants first dibs."

Rachel waved her hand. "It's all yours."

Kane dropped the oozing glob of sugar into his mouth then licked his lips. "That was delicious. Thanks, Ivy."

Her daughter giggled.

"I'm going to go get another marshmallow." Jade stood. "My last one fell into the fire, and Daisy ate the first one. She seems to like them burnt." She rubbed the dog's ears.

"You can have another one, but Daisy can't." Rachel grimaced. "The last thing I want is a sick dog."

Kane nodded. "Especially since you really should keep her inside the cabin at night. We have bears around here, and she'd probably bark her head off if one wandered through the camp."

Ivy's eyes grew wide. "There're bears?"

"Don't worry. They won't try to get into the cabins if you don't keep any food in there. We lock all the supplies in bear-proof bins."

"Do you think I'll get to see one while we're here?"

"You might. They're pretty common in this area. Keep your eyes open while you're hiking."

Jade returned in time to hear the end of the conversation and sat on the other side of Kane, holding her marshmallow above the flames. "Cool. Maybe we can go looking for bears in the morning. I want to take a picture of one. Can we, Mom?"

"We'll see. I have zero interest in meeting a bear up close and personal. Anyway, there might be other activities you'd prefer."

"Yeah, like what?"

"I think Hillary is planning an art walk." Kane stroked Daisy's head when she rested her chin on his knee. "She mentioned taking anyone who's interested up to a meadow full of wildflowers to paint. Jed is planning some kind of game day with races for the kids."

Ivy dropped her marshmallow stick. "I want to go on the art walk. Please, Mom."

Jade snorted. "The races will be way more exciting. I want to do that."

"As far as I'm concerned, you can each choose the activity you prefer. We might have a problem, though, if I need to supervise you both."

"Nope. The staff will handle it." Kane turned, his knee bumping hers. "You and I can go for a hike while they're busy."

Rachel's gaze met his. "That sounds like fun."

"Then it's a date."

"What about Lark?" Ivy pointed at her sister sitting on the other side of the fire. "She's not going to want to paint or be in a race."

"She never wants to do anything fun." Jade wiped her hands on her jeans.

"Lark can hike with us if she wants, or she can hang out with Lauren and Kevin. Looks like they're ready to start the music. Your sister is warming up on her guitar."

Jed clapped his hands for attention. "We thought we'd have a sing-along this evening. Feel free to join in. I'll play the fiddle, and tonight we have a special treat. These two beautiful young ladies have agreed to accompany me. Lark is playing her guitar, and Lauren the flute. Give them a round of applause, folks."

Everyone clapped, and Jed raised his bow. He played folk songs and camp songs, one after the other, and most of the guests sang along. Kane had a pure, deep voice that was a pleasure to listen to. Rachel wasn't a terrific singer, but she didn't let that stop her.

"Your daughter's very talented." Kane touched her arm when the musicians took a break. "Has she been playing the guitar long?"

"For a couple of years now. Lark has a terrific singing voice, too. She used to sing in the church choir, but now she wants to play in a band."

"You don't sound very enthusiastic about it."

"She's still so young. I don't want her to quit the other things she's good at."

Ivy giggled. "Lark's great at getting into trouble."

Rachel frowned at her youngest. "Let's just say she doesn't always follow the rules. She's a free spirit."

"Is that why she has pink hair?"

Jade poked her sister. "And a tattoo. Don't forget the tattoo."

Rachel grimaced. "Enough. I think they're ready to begin again. Are you two comfortable down there?"

"The ground is kind of sandy, and we can lean against the log." Ivy looked up. "You should try it, Mom."

"I'm all right where I am."

"You can lean against me." Kane scooted closer and put his arm around her. "How's that?"

"Nice." Rachel rested against his shoulder, letting his strength surround her. It had been a long time since she'd leaned on anyone, and it felt good. She tried not to think about the fact that any relationship she forged with Kane would only be temporary. Her sister's words echoed in her head. *Kane has problems. Don't let yourself get hurt.*

She let out a sigh. His problems, not to mention her own, were a non-issue. In a week, she'd go back to her normal life, and he'd go back to his. The burst of happiness fizzled.

Jed and the girls played for another half hour before quitting for the evening. Reluctantly, Rachel left Kane's side to make her way around the circle of campers. Darkness encroached as the campfire settled into glowing embers. When she stumbled on a loose rock, a hand reached out to steady her.

"Careful, you could twist an ankle."

Rachel smiled at Bob. "I guess I should have used a flashlight."

"Would you like to borrow mine?" Chip held out a red plastic light. "We only need one to get back to our cabin." He rose to his feet. The light from the fire gave his cheeks a warm glow above his beard. "Or, I could walk with you."

"Thanks, but I'll be fine."

"Have a good night then."

Rachel slipped past part of the Dawson group and reached Lark. "You were terrific, honey. So were you, Lauren."

"Thanks, Mrs. Carpenter. It was fun."

Jed turned away from a conversation with George Dawson. "Too bad I can't hire you both for the summer. This was our best campfire night yet. Maybe you'd like to play for us again before you leave?"

The girls nodded and smiled.

Jed gave Rachel a curious look. "I get the feeling you and Kane knew each other before tonight."

"My sister is dating one of his friends on the force. We met just before he came up here."

"Ah, you're the one."

She shifted and frowned. "The one, what?"

"The one he mentioned. Excuse me. It looks like the Dawsons could use some help with those chairs they brought down."

Jed hurried off, leaving Rachel to wonder what he'd meant.

"Can I go for a hike with Lauren tomorrow?"

"Please, Mrs. Carpenter. My mom said it's okay."

Rachel smiled at the girls. "It was kind of you to include Lark. Of course she can go."

"That's great. I'll tell my mom. See you in the morning." The girl hurried toward her waiting parents.

Lark picked up her guitar case and followed Rachel back around the fire. "Where're Jade and Ivy?"

"They're over there with Kane. I told them to wait."

"So, who's this Kane guy?"

"He knows your Aunt Grace, and he seems like a nice man. He swam out to the big rock with Ivy while you were canoeing."

"You looked awfully cozy with him earlier." Lark's voice held an edge. "Do you like him or something?"

"Sure I like him." Rachel spoke with deliberate cheer.

"You know what I mean."

She turned to face her daughter. "I just met the man. Don't make a big deal out of nothing."

"If it really is nothing."

"Can we please drop it?"

"Hey, Lark, you actually sounded pretty good." Jade strolled up with Ivy and Kane following.

"I would hope so with all the time I spend practicing."

Kane handed Rachel her flashlight and the end of Daisy's leash.

"Thanks." A familiar tingle sizzled along her nerve endings when their fingers brushed. "Kane, this is my daughter, Lark."

"It's nice to meet you."

Lark mumbled an acknowledgement. "Can we go? I'm cold."

"Sure. I guess I'll see you tomorrow."

He touched her shoulder. "Ask Ozzie for a sack lunch in the morning. We probably won't be back until mid-afternoon."

She nodded. "Good night."

"Night, Rachel. Sleep well, girls."

"What was that all about?" Lark kicked a rock in the path as they left the campfire area. "Where's he taking you tomorrow?"

"For a hike."

"I'm going on an art walk to paint flowers." Ivy skipped ahead.

"So you're just taking Jade with you?"

"Nope. I'm going to be in a race."

Lark snorted. "That's convenient."

Rachel gritted her teeth. "All of you head down to the outhouse before getting ready for bed. You don't want to have to get up in the middle of the night."

"And run into a bear." Ivy shivered.

Lark stopped as Rachel stepped off the path. "Where are you going?"

"Up the hill so Daisy can do her business. I don't want to take her out again later."

The stars shone brightly overhead as the dog stopped to sniff a bush. Behind her, a branch snapped. Rachel glanced over her shoulder.

"Come on, Daisy. Go pee and make it snappy. Ivy has me imagining bears behind every tree."

Finally, Daisy squatted.

"Good girl."

When the dog finished, Rachel took a quick trip to the outhouse then hurried back to the cabin. The girls were already in bed. Someone had lit the lantern, and a soft glow illuminated the room. She brushed her teeth at the basin, undressed and pulled on a pair of sweats then turned off the lantern before climbing into her bunk.

"G'night, Mom."

At Ivy's whisper, Rachel smiled. "Good night, girls. Sweet dreams."

Jade turned in her bunk. "I'm glad we came."

Ivy's head poked over the edge. "Me, too."

Across the cabin, Lark turned to face the wall, presenting her back.

Rachel sighed. "I'm glad we came, too. Now, go to sleep."

* * * *

His heart pounded with a surge of adrenaline. He'd almost approached Jordan walking her dog, but the desire to talk to her—maybe touch her— battled with his cautious nature. In the end, he'd forced himself to wait. It was too soon. She needed time to get to know him before he made a move.

He lay still in his bunk, too excited to sleep. Today had been the best day of his life. He'd watched Jordan at the lake, wearing a bathing suit that revealed her beautiful body. The water had glistened on her flawless skin when she emerged from the lake, and her nipples were hard little points. Someday they would respond to his touch the way they had to the chilly water. Someday she would look at him with love in her eyes. Maybe not yet, but soon.

A frown drew his brows together, and his burgeoning erection wilted. The day would have been a perfect if Jordan hadn't ruined it by sitting with Kane Lafferty at the bonfire. Jealousy roiled in his gut. She shouldn't have sat so close to another man. She shouldn't have let him put his filthy hands on her. She should save herself for the only one who truly loved her.

He was a patient man, a forgiving man, but there were limits to what he could endure. Watching Jordan with someone else wasn't something he would tolerate.

He'd waited fourteen years for this moment, fourteen long years to make her his own. Failure wasn't an option.

Chapter Six

"Daughter number one off to paint flowers. Check. Daughter number two staring down her competition with a gleam in her eye. Check."

Kane smiled at the humor in Rachel's voice then raised a brow. "Daughter number three doing her own thing as usual, I suspect."

"At least she's not moping."

His spirits lifted as he and Rachel hiked toward the north, following the Pacific Crest Trail on a steep uphill climb. Sweat stuck his shirt to his back and glistened on Rachel's brow before he finally stopped near a stream. The temperature was climbing, and looking at this woman with her toned arms and slim hips made him even hotter. Definitely time to cool off.

She tipped back her water bottle and gulped then wiped her mouth with the back of her hand. Daisy teetered on the edge of the creek. When the dog's front feet slipped, and she landed nose first in the water, Rachel laughed.

Kane grinned. "You have a weird dog. Doesn't she know retrievers are supposed to like water?"

"I don't think she even knows she's a dog."

"That's because you treat her like one of your kids. Are you ready to go, or would you like to rest a while longer?"

If they didn't keep walking, he wouldn't be able to keep from touching her, and the last thing he wanted was to scare her off.

"I'm ready." She shoved the water bottle back into her daypack. "Where're we headed?"

"There's a pretty little lake about an hour from here. I thought we'd stop there for lunch."

"Sounds like a plan."

A short distance later, the trail leveled out and they were able to walk side by side with Daisy leading the way. A light breeze set the pine trees swaying as Rachel tucked a stray curl behind her ear and lifted her face to the sun.

Kane gave her ponytail a gentle tug. "Did you put on sunscreen? At this altitude, people burn easily."

She nodded. "I slathered it on all of us this morning before breakfast, and the girls have strict instructions to reapply. What about you? You look awfully tan."

He glanced down at his nut-brown arms. "I wear it, but I still tan. Jed does, too, so it must be in our genes."

"I've been wondering how your brother owns a camp in the middle of all this." She spread her arms wide. "Isn't this area part of the Tahoe National Forest?"

"Yes, but Jed has some sort of ninety-nine year lease from the Forest Service. I'm not sure exactly how it works."

"What does he do in the winter?"

"He lives up here year round."

"Surely not at the camp! It must be buried under twenty feet of snow by February."

"Sometimes more." Kane laughed. "Don't look so horror-stricken. He has a cabin near Norden, the little town just off the freeway. He works out of a ski rental shop, offering guided cross-country tours."

"Your brother's obviously the outdoorsy type. What about you?"

"I am, too. I hike and mountain bike in the summer and ski in the winter whenever I have time. With my job, it isn't as often as I'd like. Sometimes I envy Jed his lifestyle."

She was quiet for a moment then blurted, "I know about your partner getting shot and the boy you killed. Grace told me."

Kane sucked in a breath. Pressure weighed on his chest like a ten-ton boulder. The day had been going so well, too. They'd been getting to know each other, taking it slow. Now this.

"Nolan has a big mouth."

She touched his arm. "Grace was concerned about me. She noticed the chemistry between us right away. I'm sorry. I don't want to spoil the day, but I wasn't comfortable keeping it a secret."

The trail meandered out of the trees onto a ridgeline, which dropped off in a sheer descent to a valley below. Kane stopped and turned to face her, holding her gaze.

"Are you attracted to me?"

A blush colored her cheeks, but she didn't hesitate to speak. "Yes, my sister knows me well."

A bit of the weight eased. "The feeling's mutual." He bent to pick up a rock then sent it soaring into space. "So, Nolan and Grace wanted to warn you I'm a head case."

"It wasn't like that."

"Then what was it like?"

Rachel sighed. "My marriage ended in disaster, and I haven't dated much since. When it comes to men, Grace is overly protective. She doesn't want me to get hurt again."

"And based on a half-hour conversation, she thought I would hurt you? Or was that Nolan's idea?"

"Grace wanted me to know you have some personal issues to deal with. She thought you might not be a great relationship risk at the moment."

"All I did was walk you to your car."

Rachel crossed her arms and gazed out at the view. "She didn't say a word until I told her I was coming up here. Then she got it into her head I was planning this vacation as a way to see you again."

His heart jumped. He reached out a finger to stroke her cheek. "Was she right?"

"I had several reasons for wanting to make this trip."

"Was I one of them?"

She nodded and licked her lips. The flick of her tongue destroyed his self-control. Stepping forward, he gripped her arms as his mouth covered hers in a quick hard kiss. When it ended, he didn't release her.

"I like being a reason." His breath stirred the hair at her temple as he inhaled an intoxicating scent of floral shampoo, sunscreen and woman. "Are you sorry you came?"

"No." She rested her forehead against his chest for a moment. "Should I be?"

He pulled back far enough to look her in the eye. "I hope not. Seeing you again has made me happier than I've been in months, but Nolan was right." The tightness in his chest returned. "Shooting that kid screwed me up. I'm not sure what I'll do when I get home. When I think about going back out onto the streets, I want to chuck my whole career."

"What would you do instead?"

He ran a hand through his hair. "I don't know. I've never been anything but a cop. My dad was a cop, too, and I always wanted to be just like him."

"I'm sorry, Kane."

"Yeah, so am I. Your sister was right to warn you about me. I probably am a bad relationship risk."

"Well, I have plenty of baggage of my own. I have a business to run and three girls who will always be my top priority. Right now Lark isn't exactly a pleasure to be around, and I have a feeling her reaction wouldn't be positive if I started dating someone seriously."

"She doesn't want you to have a life of your own?"

"Fourteen year olds tend to be a tad self-centered. She's still struggling with her father's death. It's been rough on her, and she's acting out.

Hopefully with therapy and support, she'll work through it sooner rather than later."

"What about Jade and Ivy? They seem to like me."

"They do. I don't think they'd mind if we saw each other after our vacation ends, but it's hard to know for sure."

"So is this going to be our first and only date?" He tilted her chin, caressing the soft skin.

Concern clouded her eyes. "I hope not, but I have to consider my daughters and their feelings. My choices affect them."

With an effort, he forced a lighter mood. "So, no making out while the kids are watching?"

Rachel smiled, and some of the worry in her eyes faded. "I'm afraid dating a woman with three children has its drawbacks."

"It also has rewards." He ran a finger across her lips. "I'd rather have you, your girls and your dog than Tiffany the Temptress any day."

"That's because mine are real." She stepped back, and his hand fell away. "Where's that lake? I'm hungry."

Time to recapture the easy companionship they'd enjoyed before the conversation turned serious. No matter how attracted to her he was, she was right. He probably wasn't ready for anything else. Not yet. Not until he figured out where the hell his life was headed.

He released a long breath. "Our destination is just ahead."

They reached it a few minutes later. The lake was small but beautiful, surrounded by trees on one side and a granite apron on the other. Located a short distance from the trail, the spot he chose was sheltered from the breeze.

They stretched out on the warm granite to eat their lunch. Daisy wandered around the shore, sniffing here and there before coming back to settle near Rachel.

"This place is gorgeous. Thank you for bringing me."

"My pleasure." Kane finished the last bite of his sandwich and polished an apple on his shirt. He bit into it with a crunch. "We can take a swim after lunch if you'd like."

"I'm tempted, but I didn't bring my bathing suit."

His pulse jumped then raced ahead. "We could always skinny dip."

Rachel peeled a banana. "I'm a little too old to get caught swimming naked. I'm not seventeen anymore."

"No, you're a whole lot better." His gaze moved over her curves, and his fists clenched at his sides. "Anyway, no one will see us. The lake is hidden from the trail."

"It is hot." She scratched a mosquito bite on her elbow. "Maybe I could wear my underwear."

"And I'll leave on my shorts if it'll make you feel better."

Rachel took a bite of the banana. "I'm pretty sure that's not what would make me feel better."

Two seconds later, he had her flat on her back with the banana lying on a nearby rock. He cradled her head in his hands and kissed her. When she kissed him back, desire surged even stronger.

So much for the slow approach.

"Do you know how much I want you right now?"

She bit her lip. "I'm sorry. I wish I could say yes, but I can't."

"I know. Can we do this?"

He trailed kisses down the side of her neck, burying his nose against her skin. She smelled like fresh air and woman. His breath came fast as he moved back to cover her mouth with his, his tongue stroking until he wasn't certain he could stop.

A cold nose thrust between them. At a blast of stinky dog breath, they separated in a hurry.

"My savior." Rachel's smile shook as she gave Daisy a shove.

Kane stretched out on the rock with an arm over his eyes. His chest rose and fell. Frustration filled him, edged with disappointment and a touch of guilt. "I wouldn't have pushed."

"I know. It wasn't you I didn't trust."

He sat up slowly. "I'm ready for that swim." With swift, jerky movements, he untied his hiking boots, shucked his T-shirt and took a running dive into the lake.

* * * *

Kane's powerful body cut through the water as he swam to the far side of the lake. The woods were still except for the buzz of a mosquito. Rachel swatted at it and untied her boot laces, then waited for her pounding heart to still. She'd been so tempted...

Daisy sniffed the banana.

"I'm not sure if I should thank you or tell you to get lost." Rachel scratched the dog's ears. "I know what I'd like to do."

She pulled off her boots, socks, shorts and tank top, leaving them in a neat pile. Wearing only a pair of cotton bikini panties and an electric blue jog bra, she walked down to the lake to wade slowly away from the shore. The water was freezing, and the pebbles on the lake bottom dug into her feet.

"It's easier if you just dive in." He swam closer.

"I don't think I can." Rachel inched forward. "I'm not usually one to jump in with both feet."

Kane reached out and caught her hand. "Then I'll help." With a quick tug, he pulled her into the water next to him.

"Oh, my God, it's so cold." Her teeth chattered.

"Right now, that's working in your favor. I'm not the man I was before my swim."

She grinned. "Maybe we should stay in here all day."

"Not a chance. I think I'm turning blue."

"A little exercise will warm you up. Let's race."

Rachel was a decent swimmer, but she was no match for Kane. He passed her and was waiting when she reached the far shore.

"It looks like I won." He pushed a strand of wet hair out of her eyes. "What's my prize?"

"Your choice."

Slowly he pulled her against him. The wet cotton bra wasn't much of a barrier as she hooked her arms around his neck. Skin slid against skin before a searing kiss stole her breath.

"Want a rematch?" His breath came in a gasp.

"You're on."

Rachel flipped backward into the water and swam hard enough to reach the shore seconds before he did, then climbed out onto the warm granite.

He flopped down beside her, water running off him in streams. "You beat me. What's your prize?"

Lying on her stomach, she glanced up and blinked fat droplets off her lashes. "I get to dry off on your shirt."

He grabbed his shirt, but instead of handing it to her, ran the soft cotton over her back and down her legs. "How's that?"

"Nice." She closed her eyes, afraid to see the expression in his. Afraid the temptation to let him do more would destroy her control.

"Turn over." The words were a whisper in her ear. When she rolled onto her back, he dried her arms and bare stomach. "Look at me, Rachel."

Slowly, she lifted her lids.

"We can leave now, or we can stay. Your call."

She met his direct gaze. "I don't want to be a tease. If we stay, I don't intend to make love to you on this rock. I'm not good at casual sex, and we haven't known each other very long."

His finger ran along her rib cage. "I won't push you."

"It isn't fair to let you kiss me then ask you to stop."

"Why don't I decide what's fair?"

Rachel glanced over his shoulder. "Daisy might object. She looks ready to pounce."

"You don't need a furry protector. Tell her to stay."

"Daisy, sit." She cleared her throat. "Stay."

"Will she behave?"

"She'll only disobey if she thinks I'm in danger."

"I won't give her a reason to think anything close. Just a few kisses, and then we'll go."

He took her in his arms and rolled with her until she was laying full length on top of him. Their bodies fused, leaving little to Rachel's imagination. The hard length of his need pressed against her. She caught her breath.

"The effect of the cold water appears to have worn off." She stared down into the depths of compelling blue eyes.

"Holding you would make a monk horny. You're beautiful, Rachel Carpenter."

She leaned down and touched her lips to his. "So are you, but it's more than attraction. I genuinely like you. That's what's making this so difficult."

He cupped her head and brought her mouth down to meet his. Their tongues mated and explored as the kiss went on and on. Rachel squirmed against him, and he groaned.

"Move like that again, and I'm going to disgrace myself."

With a nervous giggle, she dropped her face onto his chest, loving the way the hair tickled her nose. She wanted to take off her bra and feel its softness against the sensitive tips of her breasts. She wanted to reach between them and touch the part of him that poked so insistently against her belly.

"We should go before I forget I promised not to rush you." One hand stroked her hair.

"I want to. I really do, but then what? When this week is over, I'll go back to my bookstore and my girls, and you'll return to a job that's killing you. We might see each other once in a while and have great sex, but we won't really be a part of each other's lives."

He winced. "A real relationship can't survive on sex alone, great or otherwise. Maybe we should take a step back and see how we work as friends first. We've gotten a little ahead of ourselves."

"Smart idea. I'm not like my sister. I can't indulge in a quick fling without winding up with a broken heart."

Kane ran a finger along her cheekbone. "I don't know if I'd be able to either. Rule number one: No more getting almost naked when we're alone."

"Rule number two: Kissing is okay, but not the soul-sucking kind that makes me forget rule number one."

He sat up and handed over her clothes. "You'd better get dressed before I forget rule number three."

"Which is?"

"I can hold your hand, but I can't feel you up."

She threw back her head and laughed.

He bent and kissed her throat, his hand sliding across her breast in the process.

A quiver shook her, and her laughter quieted. "What happened to our rules?"

"They don't go into effect until we're back on the trail."

"Too bad we have to leave, but it's getting late." She glanced at her watch. "After two now, and it'll take a couple of hours to hike to camp."

"Don't worry. Jed will keep an eye on your girls. I told him we'd probably make a day of it."

Rachel pulled her tank top over her head. "Did you tell him why?"

"He's a smart man. I'm sure he'll figure it out for himself." Kane tied his boots. "Ready?"

She nodded.

The hike back was uneventful. The only time Kane touched her was to help her over a fallen tree in the path. By the time they ran into Chip a half-mile from camp, she was starting to regret all their new rules.

Chip's brown eyes shone as he offered a friendly smile. "Fancy meeting you out here."

Kane raised a hand in greeting. "This is a popular trail. I'm surprised we didn't meet anyone else from camp."

"Bob and I saw Olmstead earlier. Then, not long ago, I ran across the guy who brought the blond bombshell."

"Curt Dawson. The blonde is Tiffany." Kane pulled out his water bottle.

"Well Tiffany wasn't with him. She doesn't strike me as much of a hiker. Did you have a nice day?"

Rachel nodded. "We ate lunch up at a little lake. Where's your friend?"

Chip shrugged. His gaze rested on her for a long moment before he glanced away. "I'm not sure. We got separated a couple of hours ago. Bob's probably back at camp by now."

When they reached the cabins, Chip went into his, and she walked down to the lake beside Kane to look for her girls. Ivy and Jade were with Hillary, a petite Asian woman, building a castle out of sand and rocks. Lark sunbathed on the dock with Lauren.

"Hi, Mom." Ivy glanced up and smiled. "I painted the most beautiful picture. You're going to love it."

"I'm sure I will. Did you have fun?"

She nodded, her ponytail bobbing. "Hillary showed me how to paint shadows. It was so cool."

Rachel smiled at the young woman. "Thanks for taking Ivy with your group."

Hillary's dark eyes sparkled with good humor. "We had a great time. Kane, I think Jed was looking for you earlier."

"I'll go find him in a minute. How were the games, Jade?"

"I won the running and swimming races, but this boy name Leo beat me at rowing. Of course it wasn't exactly fair since little Rex was my partner."

Rachel squeezed her shoulder. "Sounds like you had a good time despite the loss."

"Yeah, it was pretty fun."

"I'm going to go talk to Lark, and then maybe we should all take showers before dinner."

Jade rolled her eyes and pushed Daisy away from the castle. "Geez, Mom, I was in the water half the day."

"Yes, but it wouldn't kill you to use soap."

"I'd better go see what Jed wants. I'll see you later." Kane touched her cheek in a gentle stroke before hurrying up the path.

Rachel let out a breath then walked over to the dock and sat down next to the two older girls. "How was your hike?"

"It was really great." Lauren flipped long hair over her shoulder. "Lark and I got tired after lunch, so Kevin brought us back to camp. Dad kept going. I think he's still out there."

Lark wore a hot pink bikini with her tattoo prominently displayed. "We've been here for hours. You were certainly gone long enough."

"We hiked quite a distance before stopping to eat."

Her daughter's eyes narrowed. "Your cheeks and chin are pink."

"I guess I should have used more sunscreen."

"Or Kane should have shaved closer this morning."

Rachel grasped the edge of the dock and counted slowly. "I'm taking your sisters up to the shower. Would you like to join us?"

"Maybe later."

"That's fine, but don't stay out here too long. Both of you look like you've had enough sun for one day."

"We won't." Lauren gave her a friendly smile. As Rachel walked away, the girl spoke in a low voice. "It must be so cool having a mom who used to be an actress."

"She was just on a soap opera. It was no big deal." Lark sighed. "My dad was really famous. I wish he hadn't died."

Silently Rachel cursed Bryce for the millionth time, damning him for leaving his girls without a father. If he hadn't been skiing out of bounds, the tragedy never would have happened.

She called to Jade and Ivy then headed back toward the cabin. As they reached it, Kane approached.

"Get your shower stuff and a change of clothes, girls. I'll be with you in a minute." They went inside as Rachel waited by the door.

"What's up?"

"I have to go." He swept a hand through his hair. "My dad threw his back out playing golf, and he's confined to his bed for a few days."

"Is he going to be all right?"

"I think so. It happened once before, and he recovered fairly quickly. That time my mom was still alive to take care of him. Now it's up to me and Jed, and obviously I'm the logical choice for the job."

"Of course you should go. Where does your dad live?"

"Down in Reno. I'm really sorry about this. I was hoping to spend a lot more time with you this week." Lines radiated at the corners of his eyes as he squinted against the sun.

"Maybe you'll get back before we leave."

"Let's hope. Damn." He pulled her roughly into his arms and kissed her.

She was breathless when he let go.

Reaching into his pocket, he pulled out a business card. "I wrote my cell number on the back. If I don't see you again before you leave, I hope you'll call me when you get home."

"I will."

"I'm sorry, Rachel." He cupped her face in his hands and kissed her one last time. "I'll see you."

A giggle distracted her as Kane strode away. She turned slowly. Ivy's face was pressed against a crack in the door.

"Kane kissed you."

"It was a good-bye kiss. He has to leave. Are you ready for a shower?" Her youngest nodded. "Is Daisy coming with us?"

"No, you can fill her water bowl while I get my things together."

Rachel showered then went to dinner. She chatted with the other campers and toasted marshmallows with her girls, but her heart wasn't in it. The spark that had made the previous evening so much fun was missing. Sternly, she told herself to get over it. They had five more days in camp, and she was determined to enjoy them. Kane was only a temporary fixture in her life. She'd do well to remember that.

Chapter Seven

Rachel lay between Mimi and Tiffany, soaking up the late afternoon sun by the lake.

"I think Curt brought me along just to stick it to his mother. He's tired of her trying to run his life."

Rachel turned her head and smiled. Despite her centerfold figure, the younger woman was charming and witty, and Rachel suspected even Mrs. Dawson was warming up to her.

"That's what mothers do best. Just ask my three girls."

"My mom is still very free with her advice. I don't think it ever stops." Mimi propped herself up on one elbow. "So, Tiff, are you and Curt serious about each other?"

The blonde shook her head. "We see each other now and then, but we aren't exclusive. I was surprised when he asked me on this trip."

"Is that why you think he had ulterior motives?" Rachel reached for the sunscreen and added another layer to her nose and cheeks. "Men."

"Most of them are a pain in the ass." Tiffany shrugged one shoulder. "But I'd hate to live without them."

Mimi laughed. "I doubt you'll ever have to. When you walk by in a bikini, they drop like flies. There've been times when I thought Chip might need mouth to mouth resuscitation."

Sitting up, Tiffany wrapped her arms around her knees. "I wouldn't mind volunteering. He's cute in a rebel hippy sort of way, but the scraggly beard would have to go."

Rachel squinted into the sun. "Is there any man here you haven't thought about in the biblical sense?"

"Let's see. Bob has a reflective quality that probably hides a volcano waiting to erupt. Guys like that are either amazing in bed or go off too soon, if you get my meaning. Then there's Dennis Olmstead. I'm afraid he's just pathetic. Anyway, he has a huge crush on you, Rachel. The poor guy practically drools at your feet. And don't get me started on Jed. I nearly cream my panties just looking at him. Oops, here comes Curt. I guess our little gossip session is over."

Curt joined them, bragging about the fish he'd caught earlier. The man was easygoing and had a certain charm, but Rachel didn't see the attraction. When he finally got up to leave, Tiffany went with him.

Mimi looked over at Rachel and raised a brow. "Have you ever wondered what she sees in him?"

"Actually, I was just thinking about that. She's so vivacious, and he's kind of a dud. He does seem like a nice guy, though."

"He's a dud with a secret weapon. I was up early this morning and caught him outside his cabin taking a leak. Let's just say his generous proportions might have something to do with the spring in Tiffany's step."

Rachel's smile broadened. "This place is better than a college dorm for gossip."

"Girlfriends are fun, but they don't keep you warm at night." Mimi turned over onto her stomach.

"That's why I own a down sleeping bag."

"You wouldn't need a heavy-duty bag with Kane around."

Rachel sighed. "No, but I'd probably need a mile of surgical tape to put my heart back together when the relationship was over. Best not to even start one."

"Who says it would have to end? The looks he gave you your first day here were hot enough to start a forest fire."

"Maybe, but it takes more than attraction to build a solid relationship, and I have my girls to consider."

"Speaking of attraction, Kevin has a bit of a thing for Lark. I hope you don't mind."

"Not at all. Lark and I are going through a rough patch, and she could use some new friends."

Mimi patted her arm. "It's tough to have perspective with your own child. I realize Lark tests you, but honestly, when she's with us, she's polite and funny and caring. We'd be happy to see more of her."

"Thanks. I appreciate that."

"Hey, girlfriends are good for more than just gossip." She rose to her feet. "I'm heading back to my cabin."

"That's probably a good idea. It must be close to dinnertime, and Jade and Ivy have got to be waterlogged by now." Rachel stood and gathered up her towel.

"Do you have plans for tomorrow?"

"The girls and I are going on an all day hike. Lark even consented to join us. What about you?"

"We're hiking, too. I could use the exercise to work off the meals Ozzie feeds us. At this rate I'll be afraid to step on a scale when I get home."

"I know what you mean. My jeans are snugger than usual."

"Boohoo. If you don't watch out, you'll be a size six."

Laughing, Rachel went to collect her kids.

* * * *

"I can't believe tomorrow is our last day here." Jade kicked a rock. "I wish we could stay longer."

"It has been a lot of fun." Rachel gave her daughter a commiserating smile. "We aren't going home yet. We still have your grandmother's birthday party to look forward to."

Lark rolled her eyes. "Not to mention hot showers and toilets that flush. How far do we have to hike? We must be miles from camp, and I think I'm getting a blister on my heel."

"Do you want to stop and put a bandage on it?"

She nodded then sat down on a rotted log to unlace her hiking boot. While Rachel dug out the first aid kit, Ivy threw pine cones for Daisy. The dog ran around in circles, barking like a lunatic.

Jade squatted down by the creek they'd been following and splashed water on her face. A moment later, her head popped up, and her back stiffened. "Make Daisy be quiet. I thought I heard something."

Rachel frowned. "What sort of something?"

"Like someone stepped on a branch."

"It was probably just a squirrel." Lark held out her hand. "I need a bandage, Mom. I do have a blister."

Jade scowled. "It sounded a lot bigger than a squirrel."

"I wouldn't worry about it. If you're ready, Lark, let's get moving. The waterfall shouldn't be much farther, and I'd like to reach it before we stop for lunch."

Ivy groaned. "I'm starving now. We ate the trail mix hours ago."

Rachel pulled an apple out of her pack and handed it to her. "You can eat that while we're walking."

"I think someone's following us." Jade moved closer and glanced over her shoulder.

"Other hikers could be on the trail. They'll probably catch up to us by the time we reach the waterfall."

No one passed them, but the falls were beautiful, twin cascades dropping twenty feet into a pool below. They sat on rocks near the creek bank and ate their sandwiches while sunlight sparkled on the water in a rainbow of colors. The girls waded in the creek and splashed each other, their joy in the moment infectious. Rachel pulled out her camera and snapped several pictures, trying to capture their happiness.

Her thoughts drifted to Kane, and she wondered if he was thinking about her, too, maybe missing her. Having him along on the hike would have made the day perfect. And more complicated. Probably it was for the best she didn't have to decide whether or not to pursue a relationship. The choice had been made for her.

As the afternoon lengthened, she stood. "Girls, come put on your shoes. If we don't start back now, it'll be dinnertime before we reach camp."

They left a few minutes later with Jade leading the way. They hadn't gone far when she stopped. "Mom, look!"

Rachel stepped up behind her, keeping a firm grip on Daisy's collar. At the edge of the trail, two adolescent bear cubs peeked out from behind a huge cedar tree. She handed the leash to Lark, reached in her backpack for the camera and took three shots before Daisy lost her battle with self-control. Her barking sent the bears bolting into the forest.

"Weren't they the cutest things you ever saw?" Ivy cried. "Why did Daisy have to scare them away?"

"Don't let go of her, Lark." Rachel grabbed the dog by the collar. "We'd be out here all night searching for her."

"Geez, she almost pulled my arm out of its socket."

Daisy trembled as she stared into the forest and growled.

"No, girl." At Rachel's firm command, the dog sat.

Jade adjusted her pack. "Do you think they'll come back?"

"Probably not, but I'd rather not be around if their mother shows up. Let's get moving. It's late."

Two hours later, Ivy was beginning to lag behind when Rachel called a halt.

"It's not much farther to camp, but maybe we could all use a break. I brought power bars if you want one."

The girls grabbed them eagerly.

Jade shoved the empty wrapper in her pocket then lifted her head. "I heard a noise again."

Ivy stared into the woods. "Maybe it's the bears."

"Or Jade's overactive imagination." Lark drank from her water bottle before returning it to her pack.

"No, I heard something, too." Silence echoed in Rachel's ears, sending a chill through her. "Is anyone there?"

Shadows stretched across the trail. Wind blew softly through the tree branches, and a bird chirped somewhere overhead. The forest was beautiful and peaceful, but the hair stood up on the back of her neck.

"No one's there. Can we go?" Lark let out an exasperated sigh.

"Fine. I'm sure it's nothing." But she couldn't resist one last look behind them.

Rachel set a swift pace. Ivy's feet were dragging when they finally reached the camp.

"Geez, Mom, we didn't have to rush so fast. Ozzie doesn't even have dinner ready yet."

"I'm sorry, honey. I felt like hurrying. Why don't you take Daisy back to the cabin and go wash up. I need to talk to Jed for a minute."

The camp host was stashing food in the bear-proof boxes near the barbecue pit. He looked up and smiled at her approach.

"That's a lot of supplies."

"Jason just got back from town with enough to hold us over until the weekend." He shut the door on the last box then turned to face her. "How was your hike?"

"The waterfall was beautiful, and we saw a couple of bear cubs. All in all, the day was pretty spectacular."

"Then why do you look worried?"

Rachel rubbed the toe of her hiking boot through the dirt. "This is going to sound stupid, but I think someone was following us."

He frowned. "Are you sure?"

"No, but Jade heard someone several times today. She has excellent hearing, and she wouldn't joke about something like that. I called out, but I didn't get a response. Is everyone back in camp?"

"You're actually one of the first groups to return. The senior Dawsons are in their cabin, and I saw Tiffany down by the lake. Oh, the Andrews got back a few minutes before you did. Everyone else is still out hiking. Hillary took a group with her, but most of our campers spent the day on their own."

"So, it could have been anyone on the trail with us."

"I'm afraid so." Jed gave her shoulders a squeeze. "I wouldn't worry about it. Maybe one of the guys was following you, enjoying the view, and was embarrassed to admit it when you busted him. You've got great legs."

Rachel laughed. "Thanks, Jed. For some reason, that makes me feel better."

"Glad I could help."

"Looks like the two of you grew pretty cozy while I was gone."

Rachel spun.

Jed stepped away. "You're back."

"Not expecting to see me?" Kane's brow rose.

"Not this soon. How's Dad doing?"

"A lot better. He was out of bed this morning, fixing his own meal and insisting he could drive. I stuck around until I was sure he could manage and then left. Maybe I shouldn't have rushed back. You seem to be doing fine without me."

A grin stretched Jed's lips. He reached over to give Rachel another hug. "Jealous?"

Kane scowled.

His brother laughed, released her then gave Kane a slap on the back. "I'll leave you two alone to talk. See you at dinner."

"Jed was just being friendly." Rachel smiled. "I'm glad you're back."

"I know he was, but the guy's a magnet for women." Kane stepped forward and reached for her hand. "How've you been?"

"Good." She sucked in a breath when his thumb stroked her palm. "We went on a long hike today."

"Yeah? Where'd you go?"

"Up to a waterfall west of here."

His eyes glowed with an interest she suspected had nothing to do with their conversation.

"Where're your girls?"

"Washing up for dinner. They'll be back any minute."

"Then I guess I should let you go. Would you be interested in taking a canoe out on the lake with me later this evening?"

She nodded. Heat crept up her neck and bloomed in her cheeks. "I'd like that a lot."

"It's a date. I'll see you at dinner."

As he walked away, her whole body tingled. When Ivy skidded to a stop next to her, she tore her gaze away.

"Was that Kane?"

"Yes, did you wash your hands and face?"

Her daughter nodded. "Jade is helping Rex find his football, and Lark went to take a shower."

"Maybe I'll take a shower, too. Do you want to come?"

"I'd rather help Hillary set up for dinner. Can I?"

"If you don't get in her way."

"I won't."

In the cabin, Rachel grabbed clean clothes, soap, shampoo, and a towel then set off for the showers. She passed Bob and called out a greeting.

"Hi, Rachel. Did you have a nice day?" He adjusted his ball cap and rocked back on his heels.

"I did. How about you?"

He nodded. His sober gaze lingered on hers before he smiled. "I caught a couple of trout. Ozzie is cooking them for me."

"Sounds delicious."

"Would you like to try some? I'd be happy to share."

"Twist my arm. Well, I'm off to wash off a layer of dirt. The trails are sure dusty."

"That's because it hasn't rained in a while. Good thing getting dirty never killed anyone."

With a laugh and a wave, she walked away.

Lark was bent over wrapping a towel around her wet hair when Rachel reached the shower stalls.

"Does it feel good to be clean again?"

Lark ignored her question. "I saw you talking to Kane."

"He just got back. His dad's a lot better."

"I bet you're happy to see him."

Her daughter's tone set Rachel's teeth on edge. She put down her clothes and shampoo before turning to face her. "As a matter of fact, I am. What have you got against Kane? He's really a very nice man."

"Nothing, I guess."

"Then what's with the attitude? I've dated men before, and you didn't seem to mind."

She shrugged. "I could tell you didn't like those guys very much. But you smile at Kane the way you used to smile at Dad when I was a little kid. It bugs me."

"Don't you want me to be happy?"

Lark sighed. "Sure. Whatever." When she raised her gaze to meet Rachel's, her blue eyes clouded. "What I don't want is some guy thinking he can replace my dad. Jade and Ivy might be dumb enough to fall for it, but I'm not."

"No one can replace your father, honey, and I wouldn't want anyone to try. Besides, I think this conversation is a bit premature. I barely know Kane. I don't think you have to worry about picking out bridesmaid dresses just yet."

"Funny, but you don't fool me. You really like him."

"Yes, I do, and I'm going canoeing with him tonight. I'd appreciate it if you'd be civil."

Her daughter's expression reflected pure disgust. "That's so gross. How am I supposed to sleep knowing you're making out with Kane in a boat?"

"Try hard. If you're done here, I'd like you to keep an eye on your sisters. I'll be up in a few minutes."

Lark whipped the towel off her head and trudged up the path as the last rays of dying sunlight highlighted the magenta streaks in her hair.

* * * *

A full moon rose above the mountaintops, casting a faint trail of light across the lake. Stars shone brilliantly in the night sky as Kane paddled the canoe away from the shore. Rachel was more beautiful than he remembered as she leaned back against a heap of inflatable cushions and blankets and gazed upward. His arms flexed as he pulled the paddle smoothly through the water. He'd rather wrap them around her.

"Are we going someplace in particular?"

"Just following the moon path."

Her teeth flashed in the darkness. "Kane Lafferty, I believe you're a romantic."

"Promise not to tell. It'd ruin my tough-guy image."

"You're about as tough as a marshmallow."

He dropped the paddle and held out a hand. "Come over here and say that."

"I would, but I have all the blankets."

"Good point." Stepping carefully, he left his seat to settle with her in the bottom of the canoe. His arms came around her as he pulled her against his chest.

Rachel unfurled a blanket to cover them. "This is cozy. I could stay out here all night."

"Suits me."

"Unfortunately, Jade and Ivy would worry."

His chin rested on her head. "Lark doesn't worry about you?"

"Not when she thinks she knows what I'm doing. She said this canoe ride was just an excuse to make out."

His laughter echoed across the lake. "That's one smart girl you have."

"I know. It's part of our problem."

"Right now I can't remember any of mine."

He tilted her head to cover her lips with his. She responded with an eagerness that left him shaken.

Drawing a ragged breath, she leaned against him. "How do you do that?"

"Do what?"

"Make me feel like I can fly to the moon on a single kiss."

"Honey, I'm right there with you." He kissed her again, his lips trailing down the side of her neck.

Her eyes closed on a soft moan. "I'm ready to chuck those rules we made."

"You couldn't have told me that while we were on dry land?" His palm stroked up the length of her arm. "If we chuck them right now, we'll capsize the canoe."

"What if we bend them a little?"

"We can bend them all you like, but first you're going to have to turn around. I'm getting a kink in my neck."

The boat rocked dangerously as Rachel squirmed until she was lying half on top of him. "Better?"

"So good it hurts." His arms shook as he held her and poured all the frustration built over their days apart into another kiss. Taking a deep breath, he broke away. "Unless you're willing to peel those pants off right now, I think we'd better stop."

One finger traced his mouth. When he drew it between his lips, she gasped.

"I'm willing."

His heart stuttered then pounded in an erratic beat. "I'm not joking, Rachel."

"Neither am I. If I could just get my shoes off…"

"Oh, Christ, I don't have any protection."

"That's okay. I'm on the pill."

"I promise I don't have anything contagious. Are you sure about this? I don't want you to have any regrets."

"I thought about you a lot while you were gone." She touched his cheek. "I missed you. I thought I was making the smart choice by not getting involved, but life doesn't come with guarantees. Putting your heart on the line is always a risk. You're worth it."

He cradled her face in his hands. "I missed you, too. More than I thought I would. More than I felt comfortable missing any woman. It isn't just about the sex. I hope you know that."

"I do. We may find a relationship between us is just too complicated in the long run, but at least we'll have tonight."

His mouth covered hers, kissing her until she whimpered. With quick movements, she jerked off her shoes and pulled her legs free of her pants. His hand explored her wet readiness. Knowing she wanted him made him ache even more. With trembling fingers, he pushed down the waistband of his sweatpants. When her hand closed around him, he gently pulled it away.

"I'm not going to last long as it is."

"That's okay because neither am I. I can't remember the last time I felt like this."

Lifting her hips, he settled her on top of him. The breath left him in a whoosh, and it took a moment to find some control. When he urged her into motion, she slid up and down, up and down, tearing away his defenses. Gritting his teeth, he held on until her body quaked around him then let himself go. Rachel collapsed against his chest, her heart pounded in rhythm with his.

He stroked her back as all his tension drained away.

"If I wasn't afraid of capsizing us, I'd prove I can last longer than a half a minute."

"You didn't hear me complaining." Her hair hung in tangles around her face as she gazed down at him. "I don't know if I can move."

"You don't have to." Very carefully, he rolled them over.

When they made love again, it was slow and sweet and lasted a lot longer than thirty seconds.

An hour later, Kane docked the canoe and helped her ashore.

She glanced back. "What about the blankets?"

"I'll get them in the morning."

Hand in hand, they walked to her cabin. Taking her face between his palms, he kissed her slowly and thoroughly before finally letting her go. She went inside, closing the door behind her, leaving him alone in the night.

* * * *

He rose from the shadows and walked down to the canoe. Pulling out a blanket, he buried his face in the soft folds. It smelled of sex. Jordan had betrayed him. After all these years of waiting, she'd betrayed him. His face crumpled.

No more Mr. Nice Guy. No more waiting for her to realize they were meant to be together. Obviously, she wasn't as sensitive as he'd thought if she believed Lafferty was the right man for her. Or maybe she didn't care. Maybe she just wanted sex. If that were the case, he'd be the one to give it to her.

He was through being patient. Jordan didn't deserve such thoughtfulness. Obviously, his concern for her feelings had been misplaced. If she was going to act like a slut, he'd treat her like one.

Chapter Eight

Their last morning at the lake, the girls swam while Rachel sunbathed with Mimi and Tiffany. The three women had formed a strong bond during their week together. Exchanging phone numbers, they promised to get together again before the summer was over.

Ozzie outdid himself for lunch, serving delicious barbecue beef sandwiches. Rachel had just finished her meal when Dennis Olmstead cornered her.

"Since you and I are both nature fans, I was wondering if you'd like to go hiking with me once we're back home again. I know some great trails."

Rachel hesitated. She didn't want to encourage the man, but she didn't have the heart to issue a flat out rejection. His expression as he gazed into her eyes reminded her of Daisy begging for a treat.

"Actually, Dennis, the girls and I aren't going home yet. We'll be spending some time in Tahoe with their grandparents. Afterward, I'll be awfully busy catching up at work."

"I understand. Maybe sometime later in July?"

"If not, I'm sure we'll bump into each other once school starts. Jade will be in middle school this year."

"I'll give you a call in a few weeks to see if you're free. I don't have a lot of commitments in the summer, so I can work around your schedule."

He hadn't taken her hint. Rachel forced a half-hearted smile and backed away. Turning, she nearly ran into Tiffany and Curt.

Tiffany pressed a hand to her mouth but couldn't cover a broad smile. "Aren't you Little Miss Popular? First a private canoe ride with Kane, and now Dennis is begging you for a date."

Rachel grimaced. "I tried to let him down easy."

"I bet you didn't say no to Kane last night."

Her cheeks heated. "Uh, are you going down to the lake this afternoon?"

"Maybe later." She tucked her hand through Curt's arm. "All this talk about dating has put me in the mood for a...nap. We'll catch you later, Rachel."

"Sure. Have fun." Grinning, she turned and bumped into Kane. His hands came out to steady her then remained at her waist.

"I guess I should look where I'm going. I keep running into people."

"You can run into me anytime." His eyes twinkled. "Want to go for a walk?"

She nodded. "Let me get Daisy and check on the girls first."

"They can come with us if they want. I'd like to get to know them better."

Warmth seeped through her. If Kane was interested in spending time with her girls, then maybe their evening together had been about more than sex. She'd lain awake half the night, shaken by her own audacity. Rachel Carpenter didn't have one-night stands. The fact that she'd been willing to throw all her standards aside for this man she barely knew frightened her more than a little. She wanted—needed—normal, and a stroll by the lake was a good place to start.

"Where were you this morning?" She let her arm rub against his as they walked toward the cabin.

"I had a few phone calls to make, and the reception is better up above the camp. I talked to my lieutenant and told him I'd gone for a couple more weeks. I'm not ready to go back to work yet." He brushed a hand over his chest. "I'm not sure I ever will be. Truthfully, I've considered resigning."

After she untied Daisy and snapped on her leash, they turned down the path toward the water. "Have you thought about what you'd do instead?"

"My options are limited. I'm not trained for anything but police work."

"There must be plenty of opportunities for someone with your experience. After all, you have some unique skills."

He grimaced. "I'd make a hell of a bodyguard. Seriously, though, I might look into security, or maybe I'll get my PI's license. I'm not ready to make any big decisions yet." His smile didn't reach his eyes. "Right now I want to be like Jed and spend all my time outside playing. I think I'll stick around here for a while longer."

"Then that's exactly what you should do. Give yourself a break." When they stopped at the lake's edge, Rachel shaded her eyes against the glare off the water. "Do you see the girls?"

He pointed. "They're over on those rocks."

They walked down the shore to an outcropping of rocks that jutted into the lake. Jade and Ivy were hunched over a fishing line dangling in the water.

Kane squatted. "What have you got there?"

"Crawdads." Jade held up a bucket. "The biggest one snapped the leg off a littler one. It was so cool."

Rachel made a face. "Are you planning on eating them?"

"Eew! That's gross." Ivy poked one of the crawdads. "We're just seeing how many we can catch. Ozzie gave us some leftover chicken to use as bait. When we're done, we'll dump them back in the lake."

"Kane and I are going for a walk. Would either of you like to join us?"

Ivy shook her head. "We hiked too far yesterday. My legs are still tired."

"What about you, Jade?"

"I'd rather catch crawdads."

"Then I guess we'll go without you. Have you seen Lark?"

"She went out in a canoe with Kevin." Jade pointed toward the far side of the lake.

"Lauren didn't go with them?"

"I think Lark and Kevin wanted to be alone. I saw him kiss her earlier."
Ivy giggled.

Jade frowned. "You're such a tattle-tale."

"I'm not tattling. I'm sharing an observation."

Rachel crossed her arms over her chest. "What your sister does with
Kevin or any other boy isn't your business, Ivy."

"Fine, but you might want to check her for hickeys when they get
back."

Jade gave her a push. "I bet you don't even know what a hickey is."

"I do, too. Grab the line. We've got another crawdad."

Rachel and Kane left the girls and continued their stroll along the lake.
In the heat of the afternoon, sweat dampened her back. Kane took off his
T-shirt and slung it over his shoulder.

"Are they always like that?"

Rachel rolled her eyes. "Frequently they're worse."

"They seem like good kids. Are you worried about Lark being alone
on the lake with a boy?"

"After what we managed to do in a canoe, I can't help being a little
concerned. Still, I'm not going to overreact. Kevin's a nice boy, and
they're in view of half the camp."

He draped an arm over her shoulders. "About that? When do we get
to do it again?"

She coughed and choked, but a laugh sputtered out.

When he pulled her against him, her hands rested on his warm chest.
The kiss they shared was long and lingering and full of promise.

Taking a breath, she pulled away. "Now might not be the best time."

"You're right." He released her but reached for her hand as they
resumed their walk. "When can I see you again?"

"We'll be in Tahoe through the weekend, and then we'll be home. Why
don't you call me when you're finished communing with nature. I'll let
you take me on a real date."

"Dinner and a movie, that kind of date?"

She nodded. "This place is great, but it isn't exactly real life. It's like meeting on one of those reality TV shows."

"Except the poor suckers stuck on some deserted island don't have Ozzie around to cook for them."

"Too bad I don't have a couple dozen gorgeous bachelors throwing themselves at my feet."

"You have a half-dozen. There's me and Olmstead. He may not be gorgeous, but he'd probably kiss your toes if you'd let him. Then there's Chip and Bob and Curt."

"Curt, are you kidding? At this very moment, Curt and Tiffany are getting it on in their cabin."

"Well, I could be wrong about Curt, but old George would drop Rita in a heartbeat if you gave him a second glance. And don't get me started on Jed. The only reason my brother isn't actively pursuing you is because I can still whip his ass in a fight."

Rachel laughed so hard she had to sit down. "It's nice to know I have such amazing power over men."

"As long as you use your power for good, I won't hold it against you." Kane sat next to her on the fallen log and wrapped his arms around her.

"I thought you were the serious type, but deep down you're as nutty as my sister." Rachel leaned against his shoulder. "I'm going to miss your sense of humor."

"Is that all you'll miss?"

"Maybe not quite all."

He tilted her head and kissed her. His tongue stroked into her mouth, building her desire to flammable levels. When he released her, Rachel pressed a hand to her chest.

"Do you have this effect on every woman you meet?"

"Not that I've noticed."

"Then it must be me. My moral fiber is weak."

"Or maybe we're just good together." His hand covered hers.

Rachel sighed. "We'd better stop. Lark and Kevin seem to be drifting in this direction, and I don't want to give them any ideas."

"He's a fifteen-year-old boy. He already has ideas." Slowly Kane removed his hand. "We'd better keep walking, or I won't be responsible for my actions."

Following the well-beaten path along the lakeshore, Rachel threw pinecones for Daisy and studied Kane's profile. He had a strong nose and hard jaw, but there was kindness in the curve of his lips. Compassion—and caring—was reflected in his eyes. Her heart clenched as she searched for a neutral topic.

"Tell me about your dad. I think it's high time we got to know each other better."

Kane took her hand and swung it between them. "Well, you know he was a cop. He spent thirty-five years on the Reno police force. Now he's retired and plays a lot of golf."

"You said your mom died?"

"Yeah, breast cancer. It's been tough for Jed and me but worse for Dad. He comes up here fairly often, and I try to spend time with him during the holidays."

"What about you? Who do you socialize with?"

"I have a beer with the boys every now and then, but I spend most of my time at work. It used to make Diana crazy."

"Do you and your ex get along?" Rachel tugged the pinecone out of Daisy's jaws and tossed it into the woods.

"Sure. I don't blame her for leaving me. Maybe I wasn't as forgiving in the beginning, but now I can admit it must have been hell living with me. She's remarried and has a baby. Her husband's a good guy. They have the whole life in suburbia thing going on, which is what Diana always wanted."

"When my marriage crashed, it was anything but civilized." Rachel kicked a stick in the path. "Bryce didn't allow failure in his professional or personal life. He hated that I walked away from our marriage."

"Why did you?"

"He was cheating on me and had been for years. For a long time I fooled myself into believing he'd change. Then one day I snapped. I couldn't take it anymore, so I packed up the girls and moved back home to Vine Haven."

"Sounds like he was a complete idiot."

"He was a spoiled boy who grew up to be a spoiled man. He always got what he wanted, and he thought he could have it all."

"Why'd you marry him?"

"I was young and stupid and crazy in love. He was a god, the star college quarterback destined for greatness. And out of all the girls on campus, he chose me."

"Why wouldn't he? Jesus, Rachel, you're beautiful, not to mention funny and smart and sexy."

She smiled. "Bryce was always the one in the limelight, not me. Anyway, I got pregnant with Lark my senior year, so we got married."

"At least he did one thing right."

"I think it was his dad's idea. Ford is the salt of the earth. I know his mother was against the marriage from the beginning. She never thought I was good enough for her son. Then again, no woman would have been."

"Yet you're still going to see them?" He raised a brow.

"Hey, I do it for the girls. It's important for their grandparents to be a part of their lives. Anyway, I love Ford, and Olivia and I have an armed truce. Bryce's sister, Erica, can be a pain. She blamed me for leaving her brother, but I think she's finally coming around. For the girls' sake, I want a civil relationship with their aunt and grandmother."

"You're a good mom, Rachel."

"I try, though sometimes I wonder. It's tough being a single parent."

"Tell me about your life now. You own a bookstore?"

"Yep, The Book Nook is my baby."

"It sounds like you have a great life."

"I can't complain, well not much, anyway. Until yesterday, my sex life was nonexistent."

He reached for her hand and squeezed it. "Then I feel honored you chose me."

"That's a sweet thing to say. What about you? It's hard to believe there's no woman back in San Francisco waiting impatiently for your return."

"There hasn't been anyone important in my life since my divorce."

"You must have wanted it that way."

"Maybe, but I think I'm ready for a change. You mean a lot more to me than a single night in a canoe."

"Then I won't be waiting in vain for the phone to ring?" She tilted her head to look up at him.

"Not a chance. I want to make this work. I know the odds are against us, but I want to try."

They were almost back to camp when Kane stopped and took her into his arms. His lips were hot and demanding, eliciting an answer she was more than willing to give.

She pulled away from his heated kiss when the back of her neck tingled. "I think someone's watching us."

The sun was sinking behind the mountains, casting shadows across the forest.

His gaze scanned the woods. "I don't see anyone. Did you hear something?"

"No, just a feeling, but it gave me goose bumps. My imagination must be working overtime."

He rubbed his hands along her arms. "We should probably head back to camp anyway. The dinner bell is ringing."

"Will you join us at the campfire this evening?"

He ran a finger along her cheekbone then traced the curve of her lip. Rachel's breath caught.

"I'd love to."

"Good. Let's go eat. I'm starving, and if I know my girls, they probably aren't waiting."

"You go on ahead. I'll take Daisy back to the cabin and give her some dinner."

"Thanks, but you don't have to do that."

"I don't mind."

She reached up and kissed his cheek. "I'll see you in a few minutes."

As she hurried toward the picnic area, the prickling sensation at the base of her neck intensified. If the idea didn't seem so ridiculous, she'd swear someone was watching.

Chapter Nine

Kane unloaded the mules then helped stash their gear in the SUV while the girls fidgeted and grumbled. Now that the camping trip was over, they were eager to see their grandparents.

"Let's go, Mom." Jade boosted Daisy into the back of the car.

"I think you can wait two minutes while I tell everyone good-bye."

"Fine, but don't take forever."

They'd hiked out with the majority of their fellow campers. Only the Andrews along with George and Rita Dawson and their daughters had stayed on.

Rachel approached the group sorting out their possessions near the corral. "Tiff, I hope I'll see you again soon." She embraced the younger woman.

Tiffany grinned. "Of course you will. I wouldn't dream of passing up a free wine-tasting tour at your parents' vineyard, and neither will Mimi. Expect to see us in August."

"I'm counting on it." She turned to Curt with a smile. "It was nice meeting you. Too bad you have to leave before the rest of your family."

"Business first. You know how it is."

Rachel shook hands with Chip and Bob, but Dennis grabbed her in a quick, hard hug. His expression was reverent when he finally released her.

"I'll look forward to that hike we talked about."

Rachel ruffled Rex's hair and headed back to the car where Kane waited.

"Are you through spreading cheer and good wishes?" He took her hand.

"Jealous?"

"Damned straight. I'm going to miss you."

"I'll miss you, too."

"You still have my number?"

She nodded. Groaning, he pulled her hard against his body and kissed her. She came up gasping for air and flushed with embarrassment.

"Sorry, but I couldn't help myself."

"I'm not sorry at all." She reached up to touch his cheek. "Call me." Forcing herself to turn away, she climbed into the SUV and started the engine.

"Bye, girls. Have fun at your grandparents' house."

"We will. Bye, Kane."

With the two younger girls waving wildly through the open windows, they drove away.

Lark slumped in the passenger seat, her expression one of disgust. "Gee, Mom, next time why don't you rent a room?"

"It was just a kiss, Lark."

She rolled her eyes. "Whatever."

Rachel smiled. Even Lark couldn't disturb her good mood. After last night, she was confident she'd see Kane again. At the campfire, he'd joked with Jade and Ivy and tried to draw Lark out of her shell. He hadn't laid a finger on Rachel, but his eyes reflected his need. Without words, he'd told her he was willing to slow things down for the sake of her girls.

"Mom wasn't the only one kissing boys. I saw you and Kevin." Ivy's tone was guaranteed to infuriate her sister. "Lark and Kevin sitting in a tree, k-i-s-s-i-n-g...."

"Shut up, brat." Lark's face flushed pink.

"Ivy, leave your sister alone." Rachel spoke sharply. "Please, can't you try to get along? Enjoy the view." She pointed toward the right where the mountainside fell away from the freeway to a lake far below. "There's Donner Lake."

Ivy leaned out the open window. "I saw it first."

"You did not." Jade's voice rose. "I did."

Lark turned to glare into the back seat. "Can you two stop being such babies?"

"Girls, please."

At Rachel's final plea, they dropped the armed warfare as they exited the freeway in Truckee and followed the two-lane highway to Tahoe City. The senior Carpenters lived on the West Shore of Lake Tahoe a few miles from town in a gorgeous lakefront estate. Bryce had bought it with his first big signing bonus, and while Ford and Olivia had the use of the stately home for their lifetime, the girls actually owned it. Bryce's entire estate had passed to them on his death and was administered by a bevy of lawyers. Although Rachel never touched a penny of her ex-husband's money, it was comforting to know her girls were set for life financially.

She pulled off the road in front of an electronic gate and shifted the SUV into park. "Do you remember the code?"

Lark nodded and jumped out. A minute later, the gates opened. Rachel drove through then followed the driveway down to the main house. It was a beautiful natural wood and fieldstone structure with a magnificent view of Lake Tahoe. A three-car garage sat off to the left with a small caretaker cottage behind it. A lush green lawn lined with flowerbeds bursting with blooms spread in front of the house.

"There's Grandpa Ford." Ivy leaped out of the car the instant they stopped and threw herself at the tall, silver-haired man who had just exited the house.

Jade ran behind her. Lark followed more slowly but gave her grandfather a warm hug. Rachel released Daisy from the back of the SUV and was the last to be enfolded in his embrace.

"How are my girls?" Ford adjusted his wire-rimmed glasses, which Ivy had knocked askew.

"Great." Jade walked back to the SUV and yanked out a suitcase. "We had tons of fun camping."

"I painted some really neat pictures of wildflowers. I can't wait to show them to Grandma."

Lark rolled her eyes. "Ivy's the next Picasso, at least in her own mind."

White teeth flashed in his tanned face as Ford smiled. "How about you, Lark? Did you have fun?"

"I guess so. I made a couple of new friends, but Mom had the best time of all." Intercepting a warning look from her mother, she pressed her lips together.

"I'm glad to hear it." Ford wrapped an arm around Rachel's shoulders. "It's high time you enjoyed yourself."

"We all had fun. Where's Olivia?"

"She's inside getting lunch ready. Your timing is perfect."

"Can we go eat?" Jade dropped two more bags onto the driveway. "I'm hungry."

"Sure. We'll bring in your luggage later."

Olivia Carpenter greeted her granddaughters enthusiastically and gave Rachel a perfunctory kiss on the cheek. The petite woman with frosted blond hair cut in a chic look smelled of Chanel perfume.

"I'm so glad you're here. Everyone fix a plate and bring it out to the back patio. It's too nice a day to eat inside."

"That does sound good." Rachel gave her a warm smile, determined to make the weekend a success.

Before long, they were all enjoying Olivia's excellent Cobb salad along with the view. Lake Tahoe shimmered beneath a cloudless sky, the smooth surface of the water disturbed by the wake of an occasional boat roaring by.

Jade picked a piece of avocado out of her salad. "I want to try wakeboarding this summer."

"Maybe tomorrow." Ford set down his fork. "We thought we'd spend the day on the lake. Erica, Dan and Wes are coming, too. We just took the boat out of storage, and I'm looking forward to using it."

"Are they going to be here for dinner?"

"Not tonight." Olivia smiled at her granddaughter. "If you're finished eating, Ivy, why don't you bring in your paintings? I'm looking forward to seeing your progress."

"And I'll get the luggage." Her husband pushed back his chair.

Rachel spent the rest of the afternoon doing laundry. She and Lark each had a room of their own, while Jade and Ivy shared one with twin beds. Once the mounds of dirty clothes were washed and put away, Rachel tied on her running shoes and left the grounds for a quick jog down the bike path with Daisy. When she returned, Jade and Ivy were playing croquet with Ford on the front lawn.

"How was your run?"

"Nice but short. I went down to Hurricane Bay and tried to lure Daisy into the water with sticks."

"Good one, Mom." Jade knocked a red ball through a wire hoop. "Not in this lifetime."

Ivy snickered. "Her fur looks awfully dry to me."

Daisy lay in the shade of a Rhododendron bush with her tongue hanging.

Rachel grinned. "She didn't fall for it."

"You have plenty of time for a longer run before dinner if you want to take one." Ford waved a hand toward the road. "There's a great trail that winds through the woods along Ward Creek. It starts just across from the driveway."

"Maybe I'll try it tomorrow. I thought I'd help Olivia with dinner."

"I'm sure she'd love your company."

Rachel wasn't so certain. "Where's Lark?"

"Taking a shower." Ivy crowed in delight when she knocked her grandfather's ball away from the wicket.

"The thought of hot water's enticing, but I think I can survive until this evening."

Rachel left them to their game and found Olivia in the kitchen sliding a fat chicken in the oven to roast.

"What can I do to help?"

Her ex-mother-in-law shut the oven door and turned to face her. "I think I have it all under control."

"There must be something I can do."

"I suppose you can peel potatoes while I snap these green beans."

Rachel set to work with a bag of potatoes and a peeler. Olivia stood on the other side of the island, snapping beans. After a moment, the silence grew uncomfortable.

Rachel let out a slow breath. "Tell me about your winter in Scottsdale."

"It was pretty much the same as always. Ford played a lot of golf, and I painted and practiced my tennis. I did take a sculpting class, which was fun."

"You stayed in Arizona longer than usual, didn't you?"

Olivia nodded. "We enjoy it down there. As beautiful as this place is—" she waved toward the gleaming granite counter tops, stainless steel appliances and cherry wood cabinets "—I prefer our home there. Not that I miss it on a day like today when it's well over a hundred degrees outside."

"You probably don't miss Tahoe when the temperatures are below freezing, and it's snowing so hard you can't find your driveway."

"No, we have the best of both worlds. I spent my fair share of time shoveling snow when the kids were growing up, and I definitely don't miss it." She let out a deep sigh. "Bryce always loved the winters here. That's why he insisted on buying this house for us. He wanted his daughters to have a place to come to enjoy the snow."

"They do have a great time when they're here no matter what the season."

"So, how are the girls? Ford and I were sorry to miss Lark's and Jade's graduation ceremonies. Did you have a party?"

"My mom made a family dinner. Anything more elaborate wouldn't have been appropriate under the circumstances." Rachel dropped a bag full of peelings into the trash. "What would you like me to do with the potatoes?"

"Just cover them with cold water. That'll keep them fresh until I'm ready to add them to the chicken." Olivia glanced over. "What circumstances?"

Rachel found a bowl and ran water over the potatoes. "I'm sure you noticed Lark's hair."

"It's hard to miss." Her ex-mother-in-law's lips firmed. "I admit I had to bite my tongue when I saw her."

"Lark and I are having a few problems. The hair isn't the worst of it. I'm afraid she has a tattoo as well."

"That's horrible! I'm surprised you let her do something so drastic."

"Lark didn't ask my permission. Of course I didn't approve, and her behavior certainly didn't warrant a party."

Olivia released another deep sigh. "Bryce would have had a firmer hand with those girls."

Rachel sincerely doubted it, but she wasn't about to say so to his mother. "Lark misses her father very much. We all do."

"Is that what you were doing while we were camping, Mom, missing Dad?" Lark strolled into the kitchen, her hair still damp from her shower. "When were you missing him the most, when you were cuddled up next to Kane at the campfire or out in the canoe? Maybe the day he took you on that six-hour hike?"

Rachel closed her eyes for a long moment. "Don't use that tone when you speak to me."

"Then don't pretend you miss Dad! If you cared, you wouldn't have divorced him."

"We may have been divorced, but I never stopped caring about what happened to your father. You might think you know everything, Lark, but some relationships are complicated."

"Your relationship with Kane didn't seem very complicated. He kissed you, and you kissed him back."

Olivia drew in a breath. "This may not be my business, but who is this Kane person?"

"He's Mom's new boyfriend."

Rachel gave Lark a quelling look. "He's a friend. We met through my sister, Grace, and then again at the camp this past week."

"I suppose you have every right to date if you choose to." Olivia's voice quavered. "I can't expect you to remain faithful to my son's memory forever."

"Especially since we were divorced when he died." Rachel set down the bowl of potatoes with a thump.

Hold it together, Rachel.

"It's okay, Grandma." Lark squeezed Olivia's trembling shoulders. "I won't ever forget Dad."

"You're a good girl." Olivia wiped away a stray tear. "Thank you for your help, Rachel. I think we're finished in here for now."

After meeting Lark's defiant stare with a cool one, Rachel nodded to Olivia and left the kitchen. In her room, she dug her cell phone from her purse and headed down to the lake. She heaved a sigh of relief when Grace answered on the third ring.

"Tell me I can do this." Rachel pressed a hand to her throbbing temple. "Tell me I can take another couple of days of Olivia's tortured sighs."

"Trouble in paradise?"

"It only looks like paradise." She gazed across the water. "Why did I agree to spend the weekend here, do you remember?"

Grace snorted. "Because you love your daughters? Because Ford is awesome, and you don't want the girls to think you hate their grandmother?"

Jannine Gallant

"I don't hate her. She's sad and pathetic and will never believe her son was less than perfect, but her comments get on my nerves. Anyway, I only love two of my daughters. I want to wring the third one's neck."

"Twenty bucks says I can guess which one."

"No bet. Lark just told Olivia all about my new boyfriend. The woman thinks I'm besmirching her son's memory."

"That's priceless. Did my niece make it up just to spite you?"

Rachel was silent for a moment. "She didn't exactly make it up. She may have embellished the truth with a few unnecessary labels."

"What?" Grace's voice rose. "What boyfriend?"

"That's the label I'm talking about. I wouldn't call Kane my boyfriend, but we're sort of seeing each other. Maybe. If he calls—" Rachel stuttered to a halt. "All right, we made love. Once. Well, technically twice, but we didn't sleep together. We were in a canoe at the time." ˙

"Slow down. You aren't making a bit of sense. You had sex with Kane, and Lark knows about it?"

"No, of course she doesn't, not about the sex part. She just saw a little hand holding and a kiss and maybe a couple of hot glances."

"I thought you weren't going to get involved with Kane? We decided men with major emotional problems are bad relationship risks."

She sighed. "He's worth the risk. I really like him, Grace."

"So this wasn't just a vacation romance. You're planning to see him again when you get home?"

"I hope so. He said he'd call."

"Wow."

"It all happened sort of fast. One minute we were just friends on a hike, and the next we were making out and half-naked. The guy has the most amazing effect on me."

"I'll say. How long did you date old what's-his-name before you finally slept with him?"

"If you mean Alan, we dated for a couple of months."

"See. You're about the least spontaneous person I know."

"You don't have to tell me, but Kane makes me feel different. Better. He jolted me out of a boring rut."

"If he makes you happy, then I'll welcome him with open arms." Grace's voice rang with enthusiasm. "In fact, it's a win-win situation because I'll be seeing a lot more of you from now on."

"How do you figure?"

"Well, you'll be coming into the city to see Kane, so you can visit me at the same time."

"I wouldn't get my heart set on it. He's still pretty ambiguous about going back to work when his vacation leave is up. I'm hoping he'll spend a little time in Vine Haven while he decides what he wants to do."

"Is he planning to quit?"

"I'm not sure, so don't say anything to Nolan. You are still seeing Nolan, aren't you?"

"Of course I am." Her sister's tone took on an edge.

Rachel laughed. "What has it been, three weeks now?"

"For your information, it's been four."

"Wow, Grace Hanover has been with the same guy for a month. I'm surprised I didn't hear about it on the six o'clock news."

"Smartass. Do you feel any better?"

"Actually, I do. Talking to you always cheers me up."

"I'm glad I could help. Don't stew about Lark. If you and Kane really have something meaningful, she'll come around eventually."

"I hope so, but she's giving me a lot of grief."

"She's a teenager. That's her job."

"You're a fine one to talk. Lark reminds me of you when we were kids, and I guess you turned out okay, so maybe there's hope. Anyway, I appreciate the pep talk."

"I should get off the phone. I'm making dinner for Nolan, and he'll be here any minute."

"You're cooking? I couldn't have heard right." Rachel tapped her cell. "There must be something wrong with my phone."

"Of course I'm not cooking. I got take out. Drum roll please, it's not pizza."

"Amazing. Have fun tonight."

"I always do. Call me if you need another pep talk."

"I will. Bye, Gracie."

Chapter Ten

Rachel draped an armful of wet towels over the deck railing to dry before heading upstairs to change from her bathing suit to a tank top and shorts. The afternoon spent cruising on Lake Tahoe had gone better than she'd expected. Erica's high-energy intensity, while tiring at times, held no lingering resentment, though she'd seemed more stressed than usual. Olivia had actually relaxed and offered up a few hesitant smiles. The work Rachel had put into establishing a solid relationship with her in-laws seemed to be paying off. Still, after a full day of putting her best foot forward, she'd kill for some alone time.

Olivia stood at the counter slicing tomatoes when she entered the kitchen.

"If I promise to do the dishes tonight, can I beg off helping with dinner? I'd really like to go for a run."

"By all means, go. We aren't having anything fancy, and I did most of the prep work this morning."

"Thanks, Olivia. Do you know where the girls are?"

"Lark is reading a book on the front porch, and Jade went into town with Ford to get more milk. We're running low."

"That's because my girls drink so much."

"It's good for them. Bryce was a bottomless pit when it came to milk." Her sigh echoed through the kitchen. "I think Ivy and Wes are playing ping pong out on the patio."

"It doesn't sound like anyone will miss me. I'll be back before dinner."

Jannine Gallant

"We'll probably eat later than usual tonight, so take your time."

Rachel left the house, calling and whistling for Daisy. When the dog didn't appear, she decided not to waste time looking for her. Daisy would just have to miss out on the run. Rachel headed down the driveway and crossed the road then easily found the trail Ford had mentioned, which followed Ward Creek through an undeveloped area of state park land. She ran at a brisk pace, letting her tension fall away. Erica had made a few comments about the cost of the party then clammed up, leaving Rachel to wonder what her problem was. Bryce's sister usually didn't hesitate to tell anyone within earshot exactly what she thought.

The peacefulness of the forest worked its magic, filling Rachel with a sense of strength as she worked her muscles. Panting with exertion, she climbed steadily. It was after six o'clock, and the shadows across the trail had grown long. When a sleek coyote stepped onto the path, Rachel stopped. It stared at her through narrowed eyes. Breathing hard, she waited for the creature to move. Suddenly its eyes widened before the animal bolted into the forest.

Strong arms snaked around her chest and neck, holding her immobile.

"Let go!" Heart pounding, she screamed and kicked, trying to turn her head.

"Don't make me hurt you, Jordan." The voice whispered in her ear. "I've waited so long for this moment. Please don't spoil it."

"Let go of me, you freak!" Rachel kicked again, connecting with the heel of her shoe. "I'm not Jordan." She dug her nails into her attacker's arm.

He yelped but didn't release her. "That wasn't very nice. If you hurt me, I'll be forced to hurt you back."

"Who are you?" She struggled to turn, but he held onto her so she couldn't. "What do you want?"

"You belong to me. You betrayed me at the lake, but I'll try to forgive you. Don't fight me, Jordan."

"Let me go!"

Raising her foot, she kicked backward, connecting solidly with his shin. He swore and smacked the side of her head. Rachel's vision blurred.

"Stop it. If I have to, I'll knock you senseless and carry you out of here."

"Like hell."

She pried his fingers off her chest and bent them backward. He yelled and hit her again. She twisted and squirmed to free herself. When his erection pressed against her, she tensed with dread. As fear and exhaustion weakened her efforts, voices carried down the trail. Rachel sucked in a breath and screamed.

"No!" It was a bellow of anguish and rage. "Why couldn't you make this easy? Why?"

Pain exploded in her head, and she fell forward into blackness.

* * * *

Rachel's head throbbed. A whimper slipped past her lips as she fought to open her eyes. The world spun, and for a minute she was afraid she would be sick. When everything settled into place, her gaze focused on an unfamiliar face, young, male and wearing a bike helmet. With another scream, she struggled against him.

"Take it easy, lady. I'm not going to hurt you. My buddy and I heard you yell and found you lying on the trail. He's calling 9-1-1."

She gritted her teeth against the pain. "The man who had me?"

"We saw a dude in a white T-shirt and a baseball cap running down the trail. We were too worried about you to chase him. You were out cold."

"My head hurts."

"There's a big knot on the back of it. I'm afraid to move you. Does anything else hurt?"

"I don't think so." Her voice came out in a croak.

"Would you like some water?"

Rachel nodded then let out a moan. He held a water bottle to her lips, and she took a few sips.

"Hey, Isaac, an ambulance and the police are on the way." A second young man tossed down his bike. "I had to ride a ways to get cell reception. Is she awake?"

The boy holding her nodded. "Did you see the guy who attacked her? The police will want to know."

"He disappeared. Must have left the trail somewhere."

"Can I call my family?"

"Sure, but there isn't any reception right here." The second boy frowned. "I can ride down the trail and call them for you."

"Please, would you?"

He nodded. As she repeated the Carpenters' phone number, he punched it into his cell phone.

"Tell them where I am, but don't scare them. I don't want my kids to freak out."

"Sure thing. I'll be back in a few minutes."

"Do you know who grabbed you?" The boy, Isaac, eased her back down and put away the water bottle. "You scared the hell out of us when we saw you lying there, face down in the dirt."

"I have no idea. He was behind me the whole time. Then he must have hit me so hard I passed out."

"That sucks. Who would believe some maniac was on the loose out here? I always thought this was a safe area."

"Can you help me sit up? I feel pretty silly with my head in your lap."

"Are you sure you should move? You probably have a concussion or something."

"I'm okay, just a bit shaky."

Still looking doubtful, the boy helped her sit.

"I haven't thanked you. Isaac, isn't it?"

He nodded. "My friend is Cal."

"Thank heaven you came when you did. My name's Rachel."

"I'm glad we found you." His smile was hesitant. "I've never saved anyone before."

"Well, you have now, and that makes you a hero in my book. How old are you?"

"Seventeen."

"You and Cal have a lot to be proud of. You scared off my attacker, kept your heads and called for help. I can't thank you enough."

The boy's cheeks turned pink. "It was no big deal."

Cal appeared a moment later followed by two paramedics with a stretcher and the local sheriff with three deputies. The sheriff took her initial statement then sent his deputies out to search the woods for her assailant. The older paramedic, a gray-haired man with bushy eyebrows, carefully examined the lump on her head. During the confusion, Ford and Dan arrived.

"Rachel, honey, are you all right?" Ford knelt beside her.

"I think so, but my head is killing me."

"She has a concussion." The paramedic glanced up from his clipboard. "Also some bruising, but there don't appear to be any other injuries. They'll check her out more thoroughly at the hospital."

Rachel winced. "I really don't want to go to the hospital. I'm fine, honestly."

"I'll examine you and be the judge of that." Ford set down the black satchel he carried and moved closer.

"Hey, mister, I can't allow you to interfere with my patient."

His partner, a Hispanic woman with a beautiful smile, nudged his arm. "That's Dr. Carpenter. He worked at the hospital before he retired."

Ford smiled. "It's nice to be remembered." Taking out a penlight he shined it in Rachel's eyes and felt her head.

"You have a definite goose egg. How long were you unconscious?"

"I'm not sure."

"It couldn't have been more than a couple of minutes." Isaac rolled his bike out of the way. "We heard her scream when we were riding down the trail and reached her a few seconds later. I think she came to about a minute or so after that."

Jannine Gallant

"That's good news. How about dizziness or nausea?"

"A little of both initially."

"Your neck is bruised, and your throat feels swollen, which will make talking uncomfortable. Did he have his arm wrapped around your neck?"

Rachel nodded gingerly then held her head. "I have to stop doing that."

"I can give you something for the pain once we're home. You definitely have signs of a mild concussion, but I can keep an eye on you tonight." He looked up at the paramedics. "If I see anything unusual, I'll bring her in for a CAT scan, but I don't anticipate a problem."

"It's your call, Doc. I can't force a patient to go to the hospital against her will."

"We'll probably need the stretcher to get her back to the car." Ford stood. "I don't think she's up to the walk."

"No problem."

The sheriff finished questioning Cal and Isaac then approached Rachel. "I'll need you to answer some more questions first."

Dan stepped forward. "Can you question her back at the house? It's close by, and I'm sure Rachel would be more comfortable sitting in a chair than on the ground."

The middle-aged man with a droopy mustache and kind eyes who'd introduced himself as Sheriff Barns nodded. "I suppose so. Let me check in with my deputies, and then I'll follow you there."

The paramedics lifted her onto the stretcher and strapped her down. When they hoisted her, with Dan's help, Rachel protested.

"I came the other way."

"We parked on the far side of the creek." Ford patted her hand. "Don't worry, honey. We'll get you out of here."

They made it across the shallow creek without incident. When they reached the road, Ford eased her off the stretcher and into his big sedan.

"Are you certain you don't want to go to the hospital?" The senior paramedic raised a brow.

"I'm positive."

"Then sign this release." He handed her a clipboard. Rachel filled out the information they needed, signed it and thanked them for their help. When the sheriff arrived a few minutes later and gave them a thumbs up, Ford drove away.

"I can't believe some psycho attacked you." Dan turned in his seat to give her a commiserating smile. "I've lived in Tahoe City my whole life, and nothing like this has ever happened before. At least not that I've heard about. How're you doing?"

"Fine." She swallowed.

"She'll feel better once I get a couple of pain pills into her." Ford stopped the car. "Get the gate."

Dan jumped out to punch in the combination, then Ford and the sheriff drove through. All three girls, Wes and Daisy waited in the front yard.

Ivy ran forward. "Mom, what happened?"

"Are you okay?" Jade's face was pale beneath her tan.

"Give her some room, you two." Lark tugged her sisters away as they crowded closer.

Rachel's smile shook. "I'll be fine, but I do need a hug." She held each girl in a brief embrace then patted Daisy's head before letting Dan help her into the house. She sat on the couch then cautiously leaned her head against a cushion. When Ford handed her a couple of white tablets, a glass of water and an ice pack, she took them with a grateful smile.

"Thank you." After swallowing the pills, she placed the ice pack against the lump on her head.

"See, girls, I'm fine. Go eat your dinner while the sheriff asks me a few questions."

"Yes, why don't we all eat?" Erica shooed the girls toward the door. "It's long past dinner time."

"I'll stay with Rachel." Ford touched his wife's arm when she stepped up behind her daughter. "That way I can answer all your questions after we're finished, and Rachel won't have to go through it again."

Eyes wide, Olivia left the room, and Dan followed.

The sheriff pulled up a chair and opened his notebook. "Why don't you start at the beginning and tell me exactly what occurred. Don't leave anything out, even if you think it's not important."

"First, can you tell me if your deputies found the man?"

"Not yet, but they're still searching. Your information could help, so let's get started."

Rachel told him about her run, the coyote and the man grabbing her from behind. She went over how she struggled with him then had to go over it again.

"Now, I want every detail, Rachel. You probably know a lot more than you think. What part of this man did you see?"

"I saw his forearms and his hands and feet."

"Describe them for me, please."

"His arms and hands were lightly tanned and had brown hair on them. His fingers were bare, no rings." She closed her eyes. "He was wearing dirty navy and white running shoes. I didn't notice what kind."

"How tall was he?"

"I'm not sure. When he held me against him, his voice was just above my ear. When he spoke, he whispered. It was really freaky."

"It's possible he didn't want you to recognize his voice." The sheriff looked up from his notes. "You're what, five-five, five-six?"

"Five-six."

"Then that would probably make our suspect between five-nine and five-eleven. Was he thin or fat?"

"Sort of in-between. When he held me against him, he wasn't flabby, but not super muscular either. He was strong, though, a lot stronger than I am." Rachel hesitated. "He was...excited."

The sheriff's eyes held sympathy as he met her gaze. "Did you notice anything else about him, an unusual odor or maybe an accent when he spoke?"

"He smelled like sweat, not pot if that's what you mean, and he was breathing hard. I was running pretty fast before I stopped for the coyote and he caught me."

"So he isn't in top condition, but he was able to run a couple of miles." Sheriff Barns smiled. "You're doing great. Now, let's go over what he said again and anything you can remember about his voice."

Rachel shuddered. "He spoke in a whisper, except for once when he yelled, 'No!' It was hard to distinguish any kind of accent. He kept calling me Jordan and said I belonged to him." She drew in a breath. "He told me he'd been waiting a long time to have me and asked me not to ruin it. Oh, and he said something about me betraying him. When I fought, he threatened to hurt me. That's it."

"Why would he call you Jordan? A case of mistaken identity?"

"I doubt it. For five years I played a character named Jordan Hale on a soap opera, but that was a long time ago. People still recognize me occasionally."

The sheriff stopped writing. "It sounds like you have a stalker."

"That's what I'm afraid of."

"Has any stranger approached you lately, maybe tried to talk to you or follow you? Have you gotten any unusual letters or e-mails?"

"No mail, electronic or otherwise. I did feel like I was being watched a few times at work, but I thought it was just my imagination. I'm almost positive someone was following me up at Granite Lake."

"Where do you work?"

"I own a bookstore in Vine Haven. It's in Napa County."

"You don't live in Tahoe?"

"No, I'm just visiting my in-laws. My daughters and I were up at Granite Lake Retreat on Donner Summit for a week before we came here."

"You thought someone was following you there?"

"One day when we were out hiking, I heard someone on the trail behind us." Rachel shrugged. "I didn't think it was important at the time, but now I'm not so sure. Could this creep have actually been at the camp with us?"

"It's a possibility we'll look into, although it could have been someone hanging around the area. Now, what do you think he meant about betraying him? You told me you aren't married, but is there a man in your life?"

"There hasn't been, but I met someone at the camp." Her face heated. "We were together a couple of times in somewhat compromising circumstances. I suppose it's possible we were observed."

The sheriff's pen poised above the notebook. "The man's name?"

"Kane Lafferty."

He asked a few more questions before taking her full name, address and phone number. "I'll have this typed up. You'll need to come by the station tomorrow to sign it. Under the circumstances, I wouldn't advise going anywhere alone."

"I don't intend to. Thank you, Sheriff."

Ford walked him to the door and returned a few minutes later. "How's your head?"

"The pain medication you gave me is helping."

"Good. You can take the ice pack off if you'd like."

"Thank God, my head feels frozen."

Ford took the pack from her and felt the lump. He probed carefully and smiled. "The swelling has gone down some. Would you like something to eat?"

"I think I'll pass, but go ahead. You must be starving."

"You could sit with us."

"I'd rather just rest here if you don't mind fielding the questions all by yourself."

He patted her arm. "I don't mind at all. I'll check on you shortly if you're sure you don't need anything else."

"Actually, would you mind sending one of the girls up to my room for my purse? I'd like to make a phone call."

"One of them will be down with it in a jiffy."

Jade came in a minute later and handed her mother the leather bag. "Does your head still hurt?"

"A little. Thanks, honey. Go finish your dinner."

"I was done. Aren't you going to tell us what happened?"

"Right now I need to rest. Your grandfather knows all the details, so you can grill him."

"Okay." Jade hurried from the room.

Her daughter obviously didn't want to miss any of the excitement. Alone again, Rachel pulled out her cell and the business card Kane had given her. Her fingers caressed the SFPD emblem. Taking a breath, she sent up a prayer he'd answer and tapped in the number.

Chapter Eleven

"This is…surprise. Did…miss…so soon?" Kane's voice faded in and out.

Rachel let out a long breath. "I'm so glad I reached you. Can you hear me?"

"…sound funny. What's wrong?"

"Some lunatic attacked me. My throat is a bit sore."

"What did…say?"

"I was attacked."

"Shit, hold on…run up…hill…reception…better. If…lose…call back."

Rachel leaned against the couch cushions and closed her eyes. A minute later his voice was stronger in her ear.

"Now, explain what happened. I want to hear everything."

She gave him a brief synopsis. "The sheriff thinks some psycho fan from my past is stalking me. It could be a man from the camp."

"Why would he believe that?"

"Someone was following us the day the girls and I hiked to the waterfall. I told Jed about it, but I'm pretty sure he thought I was imagining things." She sighed. "It's hard to believe someone I've met would actually attack me."

He swore. "Give me your address, and I'll be there in an hour, maybe a little longer."

"Kane, you don't have to come. I'm sure I'll be safe if I stay close to the house. I shouldn't have called, but I wanted to tell you the sheriff will be investigating all the men who were at the camp with us."

"Of course I'm coming. This guy sounds like a serious lunatic. You don't know what his next move will be."

"I'm sure the sheriff would have left a deputy here if he thought I was in imminent danger."

"Honey, no disrespect to a fellow law enforcement officer, but your small town sheriff is more used to drunk and disorderlies than violent stalkers. I'll pack my stuff and be there as soon as I can. Now give me those directions."

Rachel recited the address and the code to the gate. "I might be asleep when you get here. I'm pretty tired."

"Then warn your in-laws I'm coming. I don't want them to mistake me for your attacker and shoot on sight."

"I'll tell them. Thanks, Kane."

"Take care of yourself. I'll see you soon."

Rachel put the phone back into her purse. She looked up when Olivia entered the room, followed by the rest of the family.

"Did you call your parents?"

"I spoke to my friend, Kane. He'll be here shortly."

Olivia frowned. "Do you really think that's appropriate under the circumstances?"

"He's a police detective, and he thinks I need protection."

"You mean this psycho following you might come here?" Erica frowned and pushed blond hair behind one ear.

"I don't know. I hope not."

"What about Mom's party tomorrow? We certainly don't need any problems at a family celebration." Her voice rose. "It's too late to cancel the caterer now."

"Cancelling is probably a little extreme." Dan rested a hand on his wife's shoulder.

Rachel straightened against the cushions. "I could go to a hotel."

"You aren't going anywhere." Ford sat beside her. "For one thing, with that concussion, you'll have to be watched tonight. We don't wake people up every couple of hours anymore, but someone needs to keep an eye on you to make sure your symptoms don't worsen."

"You and I can take turns, dear." Olivia touched her granddaughter's arm. "Maybe Lark can help, too?"

"Mom, you'll be exhausted for your party if you're up tonight." Erica frowned. "Dan can take Wes home, and I'll stay."

Rachel stared at the circle of concerned faces, her stomach churning. "No one has to stay with me. It's only a headache. I'll be fine."

"Ivy and I can help." Jade stepped forward. "We're not babies. We can stay up and make sure Mom is okay."

Ivy squeezed in next to her. "Why can't she just sleep all night?"

Ford cleared his throat. "She can, but we need to make sure she doesn't have any problems."

"I don't see why everyone is arguing about it. If Kane's coming, he can stay with her."

Relief flowed through Rachel as Ivy's words sank in. "You know, that's probably the best solution. I'm sure he won't mind losing a little sleep."

"What, now Kane is staying here?" A scowl twisted Lark's lips. "How convenient."

"I suppose I could make up the sleeper couch in the den."

"Please don't bother, Olivia. I'm sure he'll have his sleeping bag with him." Rachel forced a smile. "I wish everyone would quit worrying about me. I'm fine. All I need right now is a shower."

Ford patted her knee. "Lark will check on you in five minutes. I don't want you to pass out up there."

"Make it ten. I have a lot of dirt to wash off."

Jade touched her mother's hair. "You do look pretty gross, Mom. There's dirt on your face and pine needles in your hair."

"You couldn't have told me sooner?"

"I would have, but I was more worried about the bruises on your neck."

Ivy giggled. "Yeah, Mom, we didn't think dirt was your biggest problem."

Rachel steadied herself on the arm of the couch as she stood then gave each of her younger daughters a hug. She touched Lark's arm as she passed. "You'll make sure I don't drown in the shower?"

"Better me than Kane."

Rachel gritted her teeth.

As she headed slowly up the stairs, Erica spoke into the silence. "Sounds like the situation is under control. Let's go, Dan. It's long past Wes's bedtime."

Ivy's voice piped up. "Don't worry, Aunt Erica, we'll be fine with Grandpa and Kane to protect us."

"I certainly hope so. Good night, everyone." Erica's voice cut off when a door shut.

Exhaustion threatened as Rachel entered her bedroom. After stripping off her filthy clothes, she turned on the shower in the adjoining bathroom and stepped inside the stall. The hot spray eased her stiff muscles. Head hanging, she soaked in the warmth. Five minutes later, she worked up the energy to shampoo her hair.

A tap sounded on the door. "Mom, are you okay?"

"I'm fine, Lark. I'll be finished in a couple of minutes."

Rachel rinsed her hair and turned off the water. After drying on an oversized towel, she slipped on a pair of warm pajamas and a robe then ran a comb carefully through her hair and brushed her teeth. With a longing glance toward the bed, she went back downstairs.

Olivia and Ford were alone in the living room.

She sat on the couch beside her former father-in-law. "Where're the girls?"

Olivia clenched her hands in her lap. "I sent them up to bed. They looked tired."

"Thanks. It's awfully late." Rachel ran a hand through her damp hair. "I'm sorry for all the trouble I'm causing you."

"Don't be ridiculous." Ford patted her knee. "It's hardly your fault. We're just glad you're safe."

"Hopefully the sheriff will catch this person so you won't need to bother your friend for protection."

Rachel eyed the tight line of Olivia's lips. "I'm sorry if having Kane here upsets you, but I don't want to risk my girls' safety or yours. I have complete faith in his ability to protect us."

Ford gave his wife a warning look. "Safety is our main concern, of course, and any friend of yours is more than welcome in our home. Isn't that right, dear?"

"Yes, of course. Do you know when we can expect him?"

Rachel glanced at the old wooden clock on the fireplace mantle. Ten o'clock. "Soon."

As if on cue, the doorbell rang. Ford got up to answer it and a minute later led Kane into the room. He hurried straight across the hardwood floor to the couch and took Rachel's hand.

"How are you?"

She forced a smile. "I've been better."

He reached out to touch the dark blemish on her neck. "When I find the guy who put those bruises on your skin, he'll wish he'd never been born."

Olivia cleared her throat.

Rachel dragged her gaze away from Kane's. "Ford and Olivia Carpenter, meet Kane Lafferty."

He held out his hand, and Ford shook it.

"Please, make yourself at home." Olivia's tone was cool. "I'm sorry to greet you and run off, Mr. Lafferty, but I'm more than ready to turn in. I'm afraid we don't have an unoccupied bedroom to give you, but the couch in the den makes into a bed. Rachel can show you where everything is."

"Thank you, Mrs. Carpenter, and please call me Kane."

"Good night then, Kane. Good night, Rachel."

Ford's gaze followed his wife's progress. "I'll be up in a minute, dear."

Kane glanced over at the older man. "I hope I'm not imposing."

"Not in the least. The stress is getting to Olivia, what with the party tomorrow and worrying about Rachel. Now, we need to talk about Rachel's care. She has a concussion, so she should be watched tonight. She thought you wouldn't mind helping with that, but if you're tired, I'll stop by her room a few times."

"I can manage it. I don't need much sleep. What do I need to do?"

"You don't have to wake her every hour like they used to tell you to do when someone had a concussion. Maybe just a couple of times to make sure she's alert. If the headache or nausea worsens, let me know immediately."

Kane nodded. "Not a problem."

Rachel stood and gave Ford a hug. "Thanks. You went above and beyond the call of duty today."

"Honey, you know I'd do anything for you. Try to get some rest." He turned to Kane. "I'll see you in the morning."

"Yes, sir. Thank you." As soon as the older man disappeared up the stairs, Kane pulled her into his arms. "You scared ten years off my life when you said you'd been attacked. How are you really?"

"I'm sore all over, and my head is throbbing. I'm so glad you came. I was really scared. Still am." She leaned against his chest. "Who could have done this?"

"I don't know, but you can be sure I'll find him. Let's wait until tomorrow to hash it out, though. Right now you look dead on your feet."

"I feel half dead at least. Shall I show you to the den?"

"Nope. I'm coming up with you."

"Olivia will have a heart attack."

"I'm not planning a grand seduction. I don't think you're quite up to it." He touched her cheek. "It'll just be easier to watch you this way."

"There's a chaise lounge in my room, but it's short."

"I'll sack out on the floor with a blanket and a pillow. Come on, let's get you to bed."

With his arm around her, he led her from the room, pausing to grab the small duffle bag he'd left in the entry. When they reached the top of the stairs, she looked in on Jade and Ivy. Both girls were asleep. A light shone in Lark's room. Rachel knocked lightly.

"Come in."

Lark lay propped against her pillows, a book open on her knees. She glanced up when Rachel pushed open the door.

"Good night, honey."

Her daughter's gaze went straight to Kane. "You're here."

"I'm going to keep an eye on your mom tonight."

"I'll bet." She turned her shoulder. "Good night."

With a sigh, Rachel shut the door. "If you haven't guessed, she isn't thrilled by your presence."

"Neither is your mother-in-law."

"She's upset. Maybe calling you was a mistake."

Kane tipped her chin up with one finger. "You made the right choice. Your safety comes first." He indicated the girls' bedrooms. "*Their* safety comes first."

She walked into her room then hesitated when Kane shut the door. "You're right. Still..."

"Nothing is going to happen tonight that wouldn't have Olivia and Lark's full approval. I want you to get some sleep while I take a shower." He grinned. "A cold one."

Rachel smiled and dropped her robe on the carpet. With a sigh she slipped into bed. The water was still running when she drifted off to sleep.

* * * *

The light from the bathroom spilled across the carpet to caress Rachel's face. Bruises shadowed her neck, and a little scrape marred her cheek. Kane's fists clenched. He wanted to punch something—or someone. The bastard who'd put his filthy hands on her. The man who'd put a look of fear into her eyes.

He eased down on the edge of the bed but didn't touch her. She needed rest, and he had no intention of disturbing her. Watching her was enough, this woman he'd grown to care so much about in one short week. The timing sucked with his career in disarray, her resentful daughter and some nut job on the loose. Falling for Rachel would only complicate an already difficult situation. Too bad he couldn't control the way his pulse leaped every time he saw her.

Pulling the second pillow off the bed and an afghan from the back of a chair, he settled on the floor next to the bed. He probably wouldn't sleep, but he could at least rest his eyes…

Three hours later, he gently touched her shoulder. "Rachel, wake up."

Slowly she opened her eyes.

Kane grunted in satisfaction. "You're doing great, darlin'. Go back to sleep." He stroked her hair then lay down on the floor. Thank God she'd exhibited no signs the concussion was worsening. He wouldn't wake her again, not if her breathing remained even.

When she stirred an hour later, he sat up. "Everything okay?"

She slipped her legs over the side of the bed then switched on the lamp on the nightstand. "Bathroom."

He nodded and waited until the door opened again. "How're you feeling?"

"My head still aches but not as bad as before." The mattress sank as she sat on the edge. "You look exhausted."

Her hair hung around her face in soft waves. The bruising had darkened, but her eyes were a clear, beautiful green.

"I'll survive. Obviously you're fine, so I'll get a couple hours sleep now."

"Come here, then." She held out a hand. "The floor can't be very comfortable."

"It's not bad. The carpet is nice and thick."

"Well, the bed is better. Come on, Kane. You won't be any use to me or anyone else if you don't get some sleep."

"That's true." He stood and snapped off the light then stretched out beside her.

Rachel curled up against him. "Kane?"

"Yes." Turning on his side, he stroked the hair away from her face.

"Will that man come after me again?"

His hand stilled. He wouldn't sugarcoat the truth. "More than likely he will. Psychos who are fixated the way this one seems to be usually don't give up until they're caught."

"I'm scared."

He pulled her tight against him. "It's okay to be worried. It'll make you cautious." He pressed a hand to the soft curve of her breast. "Know in your heart I won't let anything happen to you. I'll keep you safe. You can count on it."

She hugged his hand against her. "Thank you."

His chest tightened with emotion. "Go back to sleep."

With Rachel in his arms, he finally let his guard down to relax into oblivion.

* * * *

He lay in a sleeping bag in the back of his pickup at the side of a little-used dirt road. Jordan was only a few miles away. So close—and yet so far. She should have been here in his arms. Tonight, she should have belonged to him.

He slammed his hand against the truck bed and cried out, the sound echoing in the silent night. It was near dawn, but he hadn't slept, hadn't taken his medication either. Instead, he'd thrown the pills into the bushes before crawling into his lonely bed. He didn't like the way taking them numbed his senses. He wanted to remember every horrible detail of his encounter with Jordan with crystal clarity.

Jordan screaming and kicking. Jordan calling him those awful names. Jordan struggling to get away. Worse, Jordan lying unconscious at his feet.

"I had to do it."

Tears ran down his cheeks as he wondered how it had gone so wrong. Should he have revealed himself to her? Would Jordan have come willingly if she'd known who he was? He hadn't been willing to take the risk.

He closed his eyes and remembered the feel of her in his arms. Even damp with sweat, she'd smelled incredibly sweet. The skin on her neck had been so soft beneath his arm, and his hand had touched her breasts. Just a brush, but enough to make him throb with need. His breath quickened.

"She wanted me." He moaned. "She wanted me, too."

His body surged. A wet stickiness flooded across his stomach and thighs, a tribute to his love for Jordan. Memories would have to sustain him until the next time.

There *would* be a next time, a better plan than the last one. Failure wasn't an option. He would watch every move she made and wait for his chance. Soon, Jordan would be his.

Chapter Twelve

The bed was empty when Rachel woke the next morning. Her head was still tender, but not nearly as painful as it had been. After swallowing a couple of ibuprofen, she dressed in a pair of shorts and a sleeveless blouse. Downstairs the house was strangely silent. A billow of white through the dining room window caught her eye. She stepped outside. A huge white tent had been set up on the back lawn. Most of the family was out there milling around it.

"Hi, Mom." Jade waved then ran toward her. "How're you feeling?"

"Much better." She nodded toward the tent. "You could fit a herd of elephants in there."

Olivia glanced her way from the edge of the lawn. "We're expecting over a hundred people for the party, and you never know when an afternoon thundershower will pop up. Erica ordered it as a precaution."

"I'm sure she knows what she's doing." Rachel crossed the patio and gave her mother-in-law a quick hug. "Happy birthday."

"Thank you, my dear. Are you sure you should be out of bed? Did Ford say it was okay?"

"I haven't seen him yet this morning, but I feel fine. My head's just a little sore."

"That's encouraging, but with a concussion you can't be too careful."

"Here he comes now. If it'll ease your mind, I'll have him take a look at my bump."

"I'm sure he'll insist on it." She raised her voice. "Ford, dear, Rachel is up."

He smiled as he crossed the patio. "Your color is better. Let's go inside, and I'll check your head." He directed her toward a chair in the dining room then felt the lump with gentle fingers. "Ah, much smaller. Have you had any dizziness or nausea this morning?"

"Not a bit. My head is still tender to the touch, but it isn't throbbing anymore. My throat's a little sore. I took a couple of ibuprofen."

He nodded then peered into her eyes. "I'd say you're recovering nicely. How did you sleep last night?"

"I was a little restless, which is probably why I got up so late this morning. I can't believe it's almost ten."

"You needed the sleep." He patted her cheek then stood. "Kane left for the sheriff's office about an hour ago. He said to tell you to stick close to the house and he'd be back soon."

"In that case, I think I'll get a bowl of cereal. Then I'll see what I can do to help."

"Erica is around somewhere. She has a list of chores for everyone. I love my wife dearly and would give her the moon if she asked for it, let alone a huge birthday party, but between you and me, I'd rather sneak off to the golf course than host this three-ring event."

Rachel laughed. "It'll be fun once the confusion of setting up is over. You'll see."

"You're probably right. Until then, I'll just do what I'm told and keep my mouth shut. If I've learned one thing in the last sixty-plus years, it's not to mess with a woman on an important day."

Rachel grinned. "You're a wise man."

"You bet. See you later, honey."

"Thanks, Ford."

After eating her breakfast, Rachel went looking for the girls. Ivy and Wes were throwing sticks for Daisy in the yard, and Jade was watering the containers of flowers on the front porch.

Rachel bent to scratch Daisy's ears when she ran up, tail wagging. "Where were you yesterday when I needed a protector? Now I wish I'd taken the time to find you before I left for my run."

Jade refilled the watering pot at the spigot. "She was at the store with me and Grandpa. She chased us down the driveway, so we took her with us."

"That explains why I couldn't find her. Where's Lark?"

Ivy and Wes, both breathless from running, plopped down on the porch steps.

"She went with Uncle Dan to pick up the cake. I think she's tired of Aunt Erica bossing everyone around." Ivy scrunched up her nose.

Wes giggled. "My mom is really good at bossing people. That's why we snuck out here."

"Why're they picking up the cake? Shouldn't the bakery be delivering it?"

"Yes, but there was some problem with their schedule. Aunt Erica was freaking out, so Uncle Dan said he'd get it himself." Jade emptied the watering can into the last pot of petunias and smiled. "Didn't you hear all the yelling?"

"I did, but I ignored it and finished my cereal."

"Smart move, Mom."

"I'm a smart woman." She looked up when an engine rumbled.

Kane's Jeep rolled down the driveway. He parked and jumped out. "You're awake."

"I would hope so. It's after eleven o'clock."

"How's the head?"

"Better. What did the sheriff have to say?"

"Let's go for a ride, and I'll tell you. He wants you to sign your statement."

Rachel nodded then went inside for her purse. On her way out, she paused beside Jade. "If anyone asks, tell them I went to the sheriff's station. Hopefully we'll be back by lunchtime."

"Can I go with you?"

"No, you can't. You can help out around here."

Smiling at her daughter's woebegone expression, Rachel climbed into the Jeep. Kane pulled up to the gate then closed it behind them.

"I warned everyone to be careful not to leave the gate open." He turned right onto the main road. "Your stalker could be hanging around, waiting for a chance to get near you. Although if he has any kind of a brain, he'll back off for a while before trying anything else."

"I guess that means Sheriff Barns didn't find him."

"I'm afraid not." He reached over to squeeze her hand. "Not yet, anyway. I called Jed's reservation service, and they're faxing over a list of addresses and phone numbers for the men who were at the lake. That'll give me a place to start."

"*If* I'm right about being followed while we were up there."

"You have good instincts, and this guy's pattern of behavior is escalating. It makes sense he would try to get close to you in a nonthreatening way before resorting to violence. The fact that he's now aggressively hunting you means he's taken his game to the next level."

She let out a long breath. "It's just so hard to believe a person I know would attack me."

"Honey, if this guy is someone from the camp, you don't know him at all. You only saw a façade, not the man beneath it. He's obviously good at disguising his emotions."

"I suppose so. It's just weird thinking some freak has been stalking me since I was on the soap, and I didn't know anything about it."

"He's been obsessed with you since then, but the stalking is probably a fairly recent development. There's a big difference between the two. One is passive and the other aggressive. Something may have happened to set him off."

"The whole situation is so strange. I never considered myself a real celebrity, not compared to Bryce. He was the one who got all the media attention. Women would literally throw themselves at him when he walked down the street. I can't believe some guy has similar urges toward me."

"Believe it. Has anything happened in your life recently that could have triggered his need to pursue you?" He pulled the Jeep into a parking slot in front of the sheriff's office and cut the engine.

Rachel frowned. "Nothing's changed. My life's been in a rut since my divorce. I'm really a very boring person."

"You're far from boring, but if your life hasn't changed, maybe his has." He jumped out of the Jeep and came around to open her door. "Let's go talk to the sheriff. Hopefully he'll have the fax by now."

The sheriff was on the phone. A female deputy rounded a desk to hand Rachel a typed statement.

"Let me know if there're any changes."

Kane stood close behind her and read over her shoulder. The breadth of his chest and the warmth emanating from his body were comforting. She glanced up when he stiffened.

"You didn't tell me he said you'd betrayed him."

She shuddered. "That bothered me. Do you think he could have been watching us the day we hiked to the little lake or when we were out in the canoe?"

"I guess it's possible, but it makes me feel like an idiot. I didn't have a clue, and that's inexcusable."

She touched his hand. "Your mind was otherwise occupied. Why would you need to be on alert for some sort of threat?"

He grunted and kept reading. When she finished, Rachel signed the statement and handed it back to the deputy.

Sheriff Barns left his office and smiled. "You look much better today."

"I feel better."

Kane turned to face him. "No lasting damage, thank God. Have you learned anything new?"

"I received the fax we were expecting. I also spoke with your brother, Jed, and a Mr. Ozzie Thompson." He gave Kane a penetrating look. "They both verified you were at Granite Lake during the time of the attack." He checked something off on the list he carried.

Rachel gasped. "You can't think Kane was responsible? Didn't he tell you he's a detective in San Francisco?"

Kane shrugged. "Some cops are dirty, and we have a personal relationship. Of course he would consider me a suspect."

"It never hurts to be certain." The sheriff's voice was tinged with amusement. "I'm glad you aren't holding it against me. We eliminated Jed and his employees, since they can alibi each other. Also George Dawson and his two sons-in-law. They're still at the camp."

Rachel drew in a breath. "So that leaves Chip, Bob, Curt Dawson and Dennis Olmstead as possibilities?"

"Don't forget Greg Andrews." Kane lifted one shoulder. "He left the camp yesterday morning. Having a wife and kids doesn't make him any less suspect."

"Except his family and two neighbors all swear he was home last night." The sheriff made another check mark. "None of the other four answered their phones when I called. I've contacted officials in their respective home towns to question them when they're located."

Kane frowned. "So we have four candidates if the attacker really was someone from the camp. Where do they each live?"

Sheriff Barns looked down at his list. "Dennis Olmstead lives about three blocks from your house, Mrs. Carpenter. Chip Stevens and Bob Mayfield both live in Vallejo, and Curt Dawson's home is in Santa Rosa. All are reasonably close to Vine Haven. I was hoping at least a couple of them had flown in from out of state for their vacation."

"Most of Jed's business comes from the Bay Area and Sacramento, so I'm not surprised. What about the dates the reservations were booked? Rachel didn't decide to come to the camp until a week before her stay, so that should narrow it down some."

"The Dawson party booked their reservation in May. One of the daughters reserved four cabins. The other two are more interesting.

Mr. Olmstead booked his stay the day before Mrs. Carpenter made her reservation, and Mr. Stevens booked a cabin for himself and his friend the day after."

"So we can eliminate Curt?" Rachel asked.

The sheriff shook his head. "Not necessarily, but I'd put him on the back burner unless he gives us a reason to think otherwise. Of course we'll still check out his whereabouts last night. The other three look more promising."

Kane rubbed her drooping shoulders. "You have to remember it might not be any of them. It could be someone who was up there on his own, camping nearby and watching you whenever he had an opportunity."

"We've got the Forest Service looking into that. They're searching for any recently used campsites in the vicinity and checking wilderness permits for overnight use."

Kane nodded. "Jed is out looking, too. I talked to him about it this morning."

"So, what do we do now?" Rachel pressed her lips together. "Pretend it didn't happen?"

"You should take it easy until you've fully recovered from the attack. Make sure you don't go anywhere alone. I'll have my deputies drive by your in-laws' place periodically to look for anyone who doesn't belong. In the meantime, we'll be checking alibis for our list of suspects."

"It's my mother-in-law's sixtieth birthday today, and we're holding a rather large party. We're expecting over a hundred guests."

The sheriff winced. "That'll make isolating any one individual tough, but you should be safe in a crowd. Make sure you stay with a group."

"What about my girls? Do you think they're in any danger?"

"I doubt it. These head cases usually stay focused on the object of their desire." Kane squeezed her shoulders. "Still, we won't take any chances."

"You don't think we should cancel the party?" Rachel glanced from one man to the other.

"Frankly, I think he's long gone." The sheriff looked toward his office when his phone rang. "He'll probably wait until you're home again to try something else, although I can't guarantee it."

"Great, so I'm safe until I go home. That'll be the day after tomorrow. Then what?"

Kane eased her toward the door. "I'll be there to make sure you're safe."

Her eyes widened. "I can't ask you to change your plans for me. Coming to Tahoe was enough of a sacrifice."

"You aren't asking. I volunteered. We'll get out of your way now, Sheriff. Thanks for the update."

"I'll pass along all this information to Sheriff Walker in Vine Haven. I already spoke with him about checking on an alibi for Mr. Olmstead. He'll be the man to see if you have any more problems."

Rachel and Kane left the building, and she let out a relieved breath. "At least we don't have to cancel Olivia's party. Erica would have had a breakdown. She put a ton of work into this event, and she's sort of freaking out about the cost. I think she's in over her head."

Kane opened the door of his Jeep for her. "Erica sounds…interesting."

"She's pretty high maintenance." Rachel slid onto the seat then pulled the door shut.

Kane smiled as he climbed in from his side. "I can't wait to meet this woman."

"We used to have a lot of issues, but she's really come around. Still, if I wanted someone to blame for the attack yesterday, it would have to be Erica."

Kane glanced over as he pulled away from the sheriff's office. "How do you figure?"

"I would never have gone running if I hadn't needed some down time after a day spent on the lake with her. She was more high-strung than usual, and it rubbed off on me. Now I wish I'd just challenged Ford to a game of ping pong to let off a little steam. It sure would have made my life less complicated."

They drove through town then waited in a line of cars for the single stoplight to turn green.

"The traffic alone would make a person tense. This place is packed." Kane nodded at the bumper-to-bumper traffic on the two-lane road around the lake. "Summer in Tahoe is busy."

"It'll be worse next weekend for the Fourth of July celebration. That's when we usually visit. The fireworks over the lake are spectacular, but this year we came early for Olivia's party."

"I guess we'll have to make our own fireworks."

Her cheeks heated, and she drew in a breath. "I can't think when you say things like that."

He grinned. "Good."

A panel van was leaving the estate when he turned into the driveway. Rachel climbed back into the Jeep after shutting the gate behind them.

Kane jerked his head toward the van. "Who was that?"

"The party supply people. They must have finished setting up the tent." A brow rose. "Tent?"

"Barnum and Bailey could put on quite a show in it. This party is costing a fortune, and Erica insisted on paying for the whole thing, which is why she's such a nutcase right now. It was her idea, and she made it clear it's her gift to her mom, but I'm tempted to offer to help."

He turned to stare. "Why would you do a thing like that?"

"Bryce left a fund to cover unexpected family expenses. We had huge issues, but money was never one of them. I wouldn't mind dipping into it to help with something like this. Olivia is the girls' grandmother, after all. We might not be best buds, but we'll always be connected through them."

"Wow, it would take balls on Erica's part to accept an offer like that. Does she have them?"

Rachel grinned. "I wouldn't know. You'd have to ask her husband. Speaking of whom..." She stepped out of the Jeep and waited for Kane to join her. "Dan, meet my friend, Kane Lafferty. Kane, this is my brother-in-law, Dan Selkirk."

Dan extended his hand. "How'd it go at the sheriff's office?"

Kane shook it. "They haven't caught the lunatic yet. The sheriff thinks he probably left town. The guests should be safe."

"Thank God. If we had to cancel, Erica..." He winced then gave Rachel's shoulders a light squeeze. "I just called the kids in for lunch. They've made themselves scarce all morning."

"I'll bet. My girls are allergic to work."

"So is Wes, and Erica has been on a mission. Anyway, we're pretty well set until the caterer gets here. Lark and I delivered the cake in one piece, so I'm enjoying hero status for the moment."

Lunch was uneventful, and Rachel insisted on cleaning up afterwards. The three men went outside with Erica to move lawn furniture, and Rachel commandeered Lark to help with the dishes.

"Why isn't Grandma helping?"

"Because it's her birthday, and she's pampering herself before the party. We'll have plenty of time to dress after we finish in the kitchen."

"I was planning to wear what I have on."

Rachel studied her daughter's frayed shorts and shirt that bared her midriff. The sun had faded the magenta streaks in her hair to a soft pink, but it stuck out in all directions.

"I was hoping for a dress and a tamer hairstyle."

Lark rolled her eyes. "In the first place, I didn't pack a dress. In the second, it took me a half-hour to get my hair to look this good."

Rachel rinsed the lunch plates and put them in the dishwasher. "Don't change for me. Do it for your grandmother."

Her daughter heaved a resigned sigh. "I may have packed a skirt. Are there going to be any kids my age at this party, or is it all old people?"

"I honestly don't know, but it's a family party. I think we'll have a mix."

"Then I refuse to look like a total dork. I'll change, but the hair stays the way it is."

The compromise was more than Rachel had expected. "If you're finished with the dishes, you can go find your sisters. I want you all to be ready well before the party starts. Please convince Jade to wear something nice."

Lark bolted out the door. Rachel wiped down the counters and then went looking for Kane. He was on the patio playing ping pong with Dan.

"Finished with the furniture moving detail?"

"Yep. We're all set." He returned Dan's serve, and the ball flew off the end of the table. "Damn, you distracted me."

"That's game." Ford held out his hand for the paddle. "Let an old pro show you how it's done."

"Sorry I made you miss your shot."

Kane leaned against the wall next to her and smiled. "I used that as an excuse. Dan was wiping the floor with me."

"You seem to be getting along all right with my in-laws."

"They're both nice guys."

"Since I got you into this, I want you to be comfortable at the party."

"Should I find something other than shorts and a T-shirt to wear? I get the feeling this isn't going to be casual."

"Did you bring anything?"

"I might have a pair of slacks and a button up shirt somewhere in my Jeep."

"Perfect." Rachel squeezed his arm. "Thanks for sticking by me."

He gave her a brief hug. "I'll keep you safe. Just make sure no one lures you away from the crowd. If we're wrong about your attacker being at the camp, you wouldn't know him from Adam."

"The only one who could lure me anywhere is you, but right now I should get dressed for the party."

He leaned down, his breath tickling her ear. "Let's find a quiet spot to make out instead."

Rachel's pulse thrummed, and her cheeks heated. "As tempting as that sounds, I'll have to pass. Anyway, if Dan's groans are anything to judge by, you're going to be facing Ford across the ping pong table in a matter of minutes."

"Terrific, I can get my ass kicked by a senior citizen."

Rachel patted his arm and gave him an encouraging smile. "You can handle it."

Upstairs, she took a quick shower then blew her hair dry. She applied makeup base, taking special care to cover the bruises on her neck, and chose a floral dress with a halter top that further hid more ugly marks. A pair of dangly turquoise earrings and a bracelet to match completed the outfit. Satisfied she didn't look like the victim of a mugging gone wrong, she went to check on the girls.

She tapped on the door and poked her head into the room Jade and Ivy shared. Her youngest wore a pink sundress and was struggling to tie a matching bow in her hair. Rachel took it from her and expertly tied it in place. "You look beautiful."

"Thanks, Mom, so do you. Jade is downstairs already. She's wearing the same outfit she wore for graduation, and she didn't even complain."

"I'm glad you two are being so cooperative. Are you ready to come down with me?"

"I have to find my sandals."

"Let me check on Lark while you get them."

Lark was dressed in a short denim skirt and a lace top that actually covered both her stomach and her tattoo. Her hair was a distraction, but at least she'd applied eye makeup with a light hand.

Rachel smiled. "You look great, honey."

She made a face. "My gift to Grandma—no visible tattoos."

"I'm sure she'll appreciate it."

"Are you ready?" Ivy skipped into the room. "Hey, that top is way cool."

"Thanks. Let's go."

The caterers were setting up the buffet table in the tent with Erica supervising their every move. The ping pong game had been abandoned, and the men were nowhere in sight. As Rachel crossed the lawn, Jade and Daisy raced around the side of the house and skidded to a stop.

"Can we tie that dog up?" Erica's tone dared anyone to argue.

"She won't jump on people, Aunt Erica. She's very well behaved, and I promise to keep a close eye on her."

"Take her to the front yard, Jade." Rachel sympathized with Erica. "There'll be a lot of people here shortly, and we don't need Daisy adding to the confusion. Now, what can I do to help?"

"You can take a bunch of balloons up to the front gate and tie them to the fence, if you don't mind. I want to make sure Mom and Dad's out-of-town friends find the house without a problem."

"You've got it." Rachel was tying the balloons in place when Kane and Dan pulled up in the Jeep.

"Where did you guys go?"

Dan jerked a thumb toward the rear seat. "To get a couple more cases of beer. We have plenty of wine and liquor, but Erica started worrying we might run low on beer."

"That would be a tragedy." Kane's smile faded. "What're you doing out here by yourself?"

"Tying up balloons."

He shook his head. "Not a smart move. Our friendly neighborhood psycho could pull up and grab you, and you wouldn't even have time to shout a warning."

She let out a breath. "I wasn't thinking."

"It's difficult to be on alert all the time, but you need to try."

"Message received. I'm finished here, anyway."

"We may as well prop the gate open." Kane climbed out. "The guests will be arriving shortly if the party starts at four."

Dan glanced at his watch. "Good God, look how late it is. I still have to change my clothes."

"I do, too. Can I use your room, Rachel? I'm sure Olivia would prefer not to have my stuff scattered around the den."

"Sure." When an older convertible slowed on the street, she gave him a push toward the Jeep. "Get moving. Those look like guests. Must mean the party's starting."

Chapter Thirteen

Rachel hadn't expected to enjoy herself after everything that had happened, but she was. The food was delicious, the guests friendly and the weather cooperating. Olivia looked gorgeous in a silver and gold dress, and far younger than her sixty years. She'd thrown off the air of depression she'd worn since her son's death and was having fun. When someone touched her shoulder, Rachel glanced up.

"I brought you a glass of wine." Kane pressed it into her hand.

She took it from him and smiled. "Thanks. I suppose one drink won't hurt. I didn't take any pain medication earlier."

"Does your head ache?"

"Actually, it doesn't. There's still a small lump, but it isn't painful to the touch."

He threaded his fingers through her hair. "Almost back to normal. I won't have an excuse to stay in your room tonight."

She quivered under his touch and drew in a breath. "Olivia made it very clear she expects you to use the den. She doesn't allow any 'hanky-panky' under her roof."

"Hanky-panky?" A broad grin split his face. "You've got to be kidding?"

"I wish. She certainly never allowed Bryce and me to share a room before we were married, even though I was five months pregnant and we were engaged at the time. Olivia has very old fashioned ideas when it comes to sex."

"Too bad for Ford."

Rachel almost choked on her wine.

"That's a pretty dress you're wearing, but looking at your bare back is giving me ideas."

"You don't clean up so bad either." She ran a finger down the line of buttons on his shirt front. "I've had a few ideas myself."

"Think anyone will miss us if we go upstairs?"

"My girls might. Lark has uncanny intuition when it comes to us. She'd probably know the second my dress hit the floor."

"I haven't seen her lately." His hand slid along her waist. "When I looked, Jade and Ivy were playing with some kids out front, but Lark wasn't with them."

"She's with the older teenagers hanging out down by the dock. I checked a few minutes ago." Rachel shaded her eyes and frowned. The group had disappeared. "That's strange. You don't think Lark would wander off alone, do you?"

"Let's take a walk. I'm sure she's around somewhere."

After searching the grounds, there was no sign of Lark.

Don't panic. She has to be somewhere close by.

"She knows better than to go off without telling me first, especially after what happened in the woods." Rachel bit her lip.

"Who else is missing?"

"I'm not sure. Maybe the older kids who were with her by the dock earlier."

"Let's check with Erica and find out who they are. Someone might know where they went."

Erica and Dan were drinking cocktails with another couple on the deck and laughing at something Dan had said.

Rachel gave the group a hesitant smile. "Did Lark mention going somewhere to either of you?"

Erica frowned. "No, isn't she here?"

"We can't find her, and some of the older teenagers are missing, too."

The woman next to Erica shook her head. "One of them is probably mine. Lucas said something about taking a walk along the lake."

"I saw him heading north with a few friends a half-hour ago." Her husband sipped his drink. "Is there a problem?"

"Not if Lark went with them. Did you notice a girl with pink-streaked blond hair wearing a denim skirt in the group?"

"I'm sorry, but I wasn't paying much attention. My kid is seventeen and responsible. He does his own thing."

Kane squeezed her hand. "She's probably with them. I'll find her."

"I'll go with you."

"In those shoes along a rocky shoreline? It'll be a lot faster if I go alone."

She nodded, regretting the choice of strappy heels. "I'm probably overreacting, but I need to be sure she's all right."

"She will be. Just stay close to the house while I'm gone."

He gave her an encouraging smile before heading down to the lake, his ground-covering stride taking him out of sight within minutes. When a hand touched her arm, Rachel jumped.

"I'm sure she's fine." Dan spoke quietly as Erica shot her a concerned look before heading toward the buffet with the other couple.

"I hope so. I'm praying Lark is just being Lark and hasn't put herself in any danger." Rachel's grip tightened on a chair back as she glanced up at him. "Is this what it's going to be like until they catch the guy who attacked me? Me freaking out every time one of the girls is out of my sight?"

He gave her shoulders a squeeze. "The authorities will find him soon. Kane knows what he's doing, and he won't let up until this creep has been put away. He seems to really care about you." His gaze met hers. "Are you two serious?"

"We haven't known each other very long. Our relationship's sort of been pushed ahead because of the circumstances." She stared down the beach where Kane had disappeared. "I really like him, though."

"Good. You deserve a guy who'll make you happy. I like Kane, and if he treats you right, I'll be the first to congratulate you."

"Thanks. I appreciate that."

"Look, I know Bryce was a cheating son of a bitch, and I didn't blame you a bit for divorcing him."

"Have you told Erica that?"

He rolled his eyes. "Erica and Olivia both thought Bryce walked on water. Since I value my marriage, I don't say anything negative about her brother. I'm not about to open that can of worms and neither is Ford. He was well aware of his son's less-than-stellar behavior."

"Well, I'm grateful to you both for the support."

"Speaking of support, you've been terrific this weekend. I know Erica has been a drill sergeant when it comes to this party. Thanks for putting up with her."

"I get the feeling the cost is worrying her. If she needs some help—"

"Thanks, but we have it covered. Ford realized the expenses got out of control and is going to cover the excess. Erica's relieved, and so am I." He gave her a half smile. "Now, what can I do to help take that strained look off your face? Would you like a glass of wine? It might calm your nerves."

"I had one, but I set it somewhere. Anyway, alcohol isn't going to help. Nothing but seeing Lark will steady me at this point. Darn that girl! Where do you suppose she is?"

* * * *

"Mind if I join you?" Kane slid onto an empty chair at the table. The missing kids were sitting on the deck of a lakefront restaurant eating fried zucchini and drinking something pink and icy. He reached for Lark's glass, took a sip and grimaced. "Unless I miss my guess, not one of you is twenty-one." His eyes narrowed. "I suggest you pay your tab and head back to the party before I report you to the manager for underage drinking."

"Oh, God, this is so embarrassing." Lark's face turned pinker than the drink. "I can't believe my mom sent you after me."

"Your mom is worried sick. I'm going to let one of these gentlemen pay for your drink. We're leaving. After yesterday, Rachel doesn't deserve one extra minute of anxiety."

"Fine." Lark stood and smiled shyly at the kids around the table. "Sorry I got you guys busted."

"Hey, no worries." A tall boy pulled a wad of cash from his pocket. "We'll see you back at the party."

"I doubt that. My mom will probably lock me in my room for the rest of my life."

"It would be no more than you deserve." Kane took her arm and led her down the steps to the beach. He stopped and flipped open his phone. "What's your mom's cell number?"

"What, you don't have it memorized?"

"Don't push me, Lark."

When she rattled off the number, Kane punched it into his phone.

"Did you find her?" The panic in Rachel's voice sent his anger level toward her daughter up another notch.

"She's fine. I'll bring her back in a few minutes, but first we're going to have a talk."

"Are you kidding me?" Lark screeched.

Kane smiled in grim amusement at the girl's protest. "I won't go into what she was doing. She'll tell you all about it when she gets back."

Rachel's sigh was heartfelt. "As long as she's safe."

"We won't be long." He clicked the phone shut.

"I don't have to talk to you." Lark's blue eyes flashed. "I'll go back to the house on my own."

"First of all, you don't go anywhere alone while the maniac who attacked your mother is on the loose. Is that clear?"

"Why?" Her tone was hostile. "It's Mom the guy wants, not me. I'm not in any danger."

"Are you sure about that?"

"Well, duh. He's got a thing for Jordan Hale, remember. I'm nothing like her."

"Maybe not, but he might use you to get to Rachel."

Lark's eyes widened. "That's not going to happen, is it?"

"Look, I'm not trying to scare you, but you need to be careful. This guy is a predator, and he's made it clear he's willing to take considerable risk in his pursuit of your mother. At this point, I wouldn't rule anything out. You need to be smart, and that means always telling your mother or me where you're going and never leaving the house alone."

"I wasn't alone today."

"No, but your mother didn't know that. She was really worried, and she doesn't need that kind of aggravation."

"Fine, I should have told her, but if I had she wouldn't have let me go."

"Come on, Lark. Rachel doesn't strike me as unreasonable."

She scuffed her sandal across the rocks. "She treats me like a baby."

"Can you blame her? You're fourteen, for God's sake. What were you thinking, drinking with those kids? And why in hell did the waitress serve you? Even if you have a fake ID, it would be obvious to anyone you aren't twenty-one."

She scowled. "You don't have to swear."

"Don't avoid the question."

"For your information, I don't have a fake ID. I ordered a virgin drink."

"Honey, I know tequila when I taste it." He stared down at her mutinous face. "Oh, I get it. One of the kids snuck in the booze. I should haul their asses—excuse me—their butts down to the sheriff's station just to scare some sense into them."

"You wouldn't! Kane, they'd know I ratted on them."

"Ah, hell, let their parents worry about their delinquent behavior. They aren't my problem. You are."

"No, I'm not." Lark fisted her hands on her hips. "Just because you're doing my mom doesn't give you the right to butt into my life."

"You have quite a mouth on you, young lady." He rubbed the back of his neck. "I'm going to say this once, and you'd better listen. What your mother and I may or may not be doing isn't anyone's business but our own."

"I notice you didn't deny it."

"I didn't confirm it either. It's not your business."

"It is my business. She's my mom. I don't want some jerk—namely you—thinking you can act like my dad or something."

"I'm not trying to be your father."

"You could have fooled me. This lecture seems awfully parent-like. You could have brought me home and let Mom yell at me. Now I'm going to have to listen to it twice."

"The only reason I'm still talking is to impress upon you the seriousness of the danger. I was hoping to avoid upsetting Rachel even more. Christ, you're a piece of work."

Lark smiled. "Thank you."

Kane stared at her in consternation but couldn't suppress a reluctant chuckle. "Look, can we call a truce for your mother's sake? I'm not saying you have to like me, but could you try to be civil? This situation with the stalker isn't going to end when we leave Tahoe, and if I have to maintain armed warfare with you indefinitely, it'll wear me out."

"What do you mean, indefinitely?"

"I mean, you'll be seeing a lot of me until we catch the guy. I promised your mom I would keep you all safe."

"Isn't that what the police are for?"

"I am the police."

Lark stared at him, eyes widening. "Do you think you're going to move in with us?"

Kane couldn't suppress a spurt of satisfaction. *That got her attention.* "Let's call it keeping an eye on you—up-close and personal."

"Mom agreed to this?"

"She will when I tell her. She knows I'm planning to come back to Vine Haven when you leave here, but we didn't get into any specific arrangements."

Lark's smile grew. "She won't allow it. What kind of example would she be setting if she let you move into the house after knowing you for a week?"

"All it would prove is she cares about your safety and her own. Think of me as a bodyguard."

"Grandma will have a cow. Nope. I don't have a thing to worry about."

"What does Olivia have to do with this?"

"Not Grandma Olivia. Grandma Audrey. She won't stand for her daughter shacking up with some guy she barely knows. Grandma Audrey has strong opinions on that subject, and she tells everyone what she thinks."

Kane gritted his teeth. "We aren't shacking up."

The girl gave him a very adult smile. "Sure you aren't. I've seen the way you look at my mom. I may not be as smart as Ivy, but I know you and Mom are more than just good buddies."

He rubbed a hand across his face and sighed. "I thought Ivy was the precocious one in the family."

"She is, but I know people. It's a talent."

"Your talent didn't tell you your mom would be angry if you left the party without permission?"

"Sure, but I decided it was worth it. You know, like the hair and the tattoo. Everything has a price. For example, the price you pay for dating my mom is me. That might be more than you bargained for."

"You may be right. Now, about that truce?"

"I would consider it if you leave out the part about the tequila when you tell Mom what I was doing."

"I'm not going to tell her a thing."

"You're not?" Lark's expression brightened.

"Nope. You're going to do it."

"That sucks."

Kane patted her shoulder then turned them both down the beach. When she didn't shrug him off immediately, his spirits lifted. "Sometimes life sucks. You just have to roll with it."

"Is that what you do?"

He nodded. "Do me a favor and try not to worry your mom again the way you did this afternoon."

"I'll think about it."

"That's all I can ask."

He'd given it his best shot. The rest was up to Lark.

Chapter Fourteen

Late Monday morning Kane squeezed his Jeep into the driveway next to Rachel's SUV. Car doors slammed.

"Nice place."

She glanced over at the pale blue Victorian complete with a wide front porch, wicker furniture and gingerbread trim. "We like it."

"Very Norman Rockwell, right down to the white picket fence and rose bushes. It suits you."

"Old Norman probably wouldn't approve of the overgrown lawn. I need to get out the mower."

"Your dog doesn't mind."

Daisy lay in the middle of the yard, wiggling vigorously as she scratched her back on the grass.

"She isn't the brightest bulb in the pack." Rachel turned back toward the vehicles.

Sleeping bags spilled onto the driveway, scattered everywhere by Daisy's mad scramble for freedom.

"I suppose we should unpack."

"We don't have time for that." Jade crossed the porch and raced down the walkway. In less than five minutes, she'd changed into soccer clothes and cleats and carried a bag lunch. "You have to take me straight to soccer camp, remember? We're late already."

"How could she possibly forget?" Lark stepped over a suitcase. "You reminded her at least ten times on the way home."

"I did promise." Rachel sighed. "Okay, back into the car."

Lark gave her an incredulous look. "I'll stay here."

"Sorry, not without an adult around."

"Mom, I'm a little old to need a babysitter."

"I'm sorry, Lark, but I'm not leaving you here alone until the police catch the person stalking me. We've been over this."

"You're only going to be gone fifteen minutes. What's going to happen in fifteen minutes?"

Kane dropped an armful of sleeping bags on the front porch. "Hopefully nothing, but we aren't taking any chances. Let's go, Ivy. Hop back into the car."

Lark crossed her arms over her chest and cast a dark look his way. "If you don't want us left alone, then you stay with us. I'm sick of the car."

"Get in." Kane frowned. "I'm not letting your mom drive around by herself either."

"This sucks!"

"Yes, it does. Hopefully it'll be over soon."

"It better be." Lark kicked a bag out of the way and climbed into the backseat.

Ivy sat next to her and pointed. "What about Daisy? Shouldn't she come, too?"

"Daisy will be fine in the yard." Rachel slammed the car door.

"What, you don't think the whack job is going to dognap her?" Lark's tone dripped sarcasm.

Rachel pulled out onto the street and headed away from the center of town. "This is going to be difficult for all of us, Lark. We need to make the best of it."

"I bet you and Kane plan to."

He could practically hear Rachel's teeth grinding.

"Lark." Rachel's voice held a warning.

"Fine. Whatever. I'll try to be cheerful while you have him babysitting me like a four-year-old. Are you happy?"

"Ecstatic."

Kane looked over his shoulder. "Are you always this much fun?"

"Sometimes she's worse." Jade jumped out of the car as soon as it stopped next to the soccer fields. "See you."

Rachel shut off the engine. "I'm going to go talk to her coach. I'll be back in a minute."

After she left, Kane turned in his seat. "I know this isn't fun, Lark, but can you lighten up on your mom?"

"It's always all about Mom. What about my feelings? I'm the one who has to have a babysitter twenty-four seven."

Ivy's brows lowered. "So do I."

"You're eight. You have to be watched, anyway. You won't even notice the difference."

Kane sighed. "Sacrificing a little personal freedom is better than getting abducted, don't you think?"

"What I think is you're both overreacting."

He eyed her steadily. "Maybe, but I'd rather err on the side of safety. All I'm asking is you cut us some slack. We'll all be happier if we work together."

"Not Lark." Ivy's eyes sparkled. "Lark is happiest when she's making someone mad."

"Drop dead, brat."

"Ivy, you aren't helping." Kane studied Rachel's youngest. Her angelic appearance was definitely misleading.

Lark's lips curved in a satisfied smirk. "See, I'm not the only problem child in this family. Little Miss Innocence is a pain in the butt. And don't get me started on Jade. She's even dorkier than Ivy. If you're smart, you'll dump all of us."

"Lucky for you, I don't quit. Here comes your mother. Let's surprise the hell out of her and get along for the ride home."

Ivy giggled hysterically, and even Lark smiled.

Rachel opened the door and glanced from Kane to the girls. "What's so funny?"

"Nothing. What's next on the agenda?"

"We go home and unpack. Then Ivy has a swim lesson. I also need to go to the grocery store."

Lark groaned. "Wow, I don't know if I can take that much excitement. Can I hang out with Grandma?"

"I guess so, but you have a dance class this afternoon."

"I haven't forgotten. It's obviously going to be the highlight of my day. I'll grab my stuff, and you can drop me at Grandma's when you take Ivy to her swim lesson."

"All right, but I was hoping to avoid telling Grandma and Grandpa about the stalker until tomorrow or the next day."

"I promise, my lips are zipped. I certainly don't want to be the one to break the news."

Rachel rolled her eyes. "Fine, are you happy now?"

"It beats following you around a grocery store." Lark sounded a little more cheerful. "Maybe I'll hang with Aunt Sharon in the gift shop. I want to talk to her about working there this summer. It'll be a good way to earn some money."

"That's a great idea, honey."

Rachel pulled into the driveway. Ivy and Lark jumped out.

"Hey, there's no stalker lurking in the bushes." Lark strolled toward the house, hands shoved in her pockets.

Rachel slammed the car door. "Enough with the sarcasm, and don't go inside empty-handed. We have the whole rear of the car to unload."

With an audible sigh, her daughter turned and came back, grabbed her duffle bag and guitar case and sauntered away. Rachel and Kane followed, loaded down with suitcases. They dropped them in the entry, and Kane took a look around.

"What do you think?"

"Someone did a terrific job restoring this place."

Rachel flexed her muscles. "That would be me. At least I did most of it. I hired a guy to refinish the floors, but I did the painting and wallpapering."

He pulled her close for a brief hug. "I can tell you put your heart into it. The crown molding in this place is amazing, and I do believe that banister is solid walnut." He nodded toward the stairway.

"It is. I sanded and lacquered it myself."

"You have to love a woman who can do her own household repairs." Slowly he released her. "Where do you want me to put my stuff?"

"I don't have a spare bedroom, but the couch in the living room makes into a bed. You're not going to have a whole lot of privacy." She frowned. "I suppose I could put Ivy and Jade together and give you one of their rooms."

"Leave the girls where they are. I don't need privacy, and I don't want you worrying about me. You should have seen some of the places I slept the year I worked undercover."

Rachel shuddered. "I'd rather not even imagine it. You can put your clothes in my office." She pushed open a door that led to a tiny room filled with bookshelves and a desk. "The bathroom is just down the hall. It has a shower, so at least you won't have to share the upstairs bath with the girls."

"This is fine, Rachel." He turned and rubbed her shoulders. "Stop treating me like a guest. Pretend I'm your cousin or something. You don't flip out over where family sleeps, do you?"

"Sorry. I guess I'm a little stressed."

He opened his mouth then shut it.

Ivy raced inside with Daisy on her heels. "I'm starving. What's for lunch?"

"How about a peanut butter and jelly sandwich? There should be a loaf of bread in the freezer."

The girl made a face. "I'm not in the mood for peanut butter."

Rachel ran a hand through her hair. "Well, there isn't a whole lot to choose from until I go to the store. Would you rather have tuna?"

"Tuna with pickles."

She paused in the doorway. "How about you, Kane?"

"Tuna is fine. While you're making the sandwiches, Ivy and I will take these bags upstairs."

Ivy twirled on one foot then skipped across the hall. "I'll tell him where they go."

"Rachel."

She glanced back over her shoulder. Shadows clouded her eyes.

"Relax. Everything will work out. I promise."

* * * *

Some of the tension drained away as Rachel headed toward the kitchen. A simple thing like dividing up the chores took the edge off her mood. It had been too long since she'd had someone around to share responsibility for the small jobs. Bryce, at least, had been decent about helping out. It was one of the things she'd missed after their marriage ended.

When Kane and the girls came back to the kitchen, they sat down together to eat the tuna sandwiches. Then Rachel called her mom to ask if she could bring Lark over for the afternoon.

"Of course she can come over. How was your trip, honey? Tell me all about it."

"It was fun, but I'm afraid I don't have time to go into details right now. I have to drop Lark off, then take Ivy to her swim lesson, and I really need to stop by the bookstore for an hour or two."

"That doesn't leave you much time to prepare a decent meal. Bring the girls over for dinner tonight, and we can talk then. Your dad and I would love to see you. We're having pot roast. I know it's one of your favorites."

"That sounds wonderful." She took a deep breath. "Uh, we have a guest."

"If one of the girls has a friend over, bring her along."

May as well face the inevitable and get it over with.

"We'll come for dinner, but our guest isn't one of the girls' friends. His name's Kane Lafferty. I met him through Grace."

"Really?"

Her mother's voice held more questions she didn't want to answer.

"It's not what you're thinking, Mom. I'll explain everything to you this evening."

"Now you really do have my curiosity roused."

"You'll just have to live with it for a few hours. Promise me you won't pump Lark for information. I want to explain this myself."

"Oh, all right. I'll see you in a few minutes."

"I take it we're dining with your parents." Kane stood in the kitchen doorway. He raised a brow. "I get the feeling you aren't too happy about it."

Rachel scowled. "I couldn't put her off. I hope you're ready for the inquisition."

"I've survived worse. The girls are ready to go if you are. I sent them out to the car."

"Does Lark have her dance stuff?"

"She does, and Ivy has her swimsuit and a towel."

"Very impressive. Maybe you should get out of law enforcement and consider a career as a nanny."

He choked on the soda he was drinking. "I think I'll pass." He crumpled the can and sent it sailing into the trash. "Speaking of law enforcement, I'm meeting with Sheriff Walker while you're at Ivy's swim lesson."

"Does he have any news?" Rachel locked the door to the house and handed Kane the key. "It's my spare."

He stuck it in his pocket. "None of our suspects have alibis, but he did get background info on a couple of them. I want to see what he found out and maybe set up some interviews." He took the car keys from her hand. "Do you mind?"

"Not in the least. Head north. You'll see the sign for the vineyard in about a mile."

They dropped Lark off in the driveway and pulled away. Her mother stood in the doorway waving, neck craned.

Rachel grinned. "She's trying to get a look at you."

"I don't blame her for wondering what's happening. You sounded very mysterious on the phone."

"I couldn't help it. I want to sit both my parents down and try to explain about the stalker without freaking them out."

Ivy laughed. "Good one, Mom. Grandma is going to lose it no matter how you tell her."

"You're probably right. Turn left at the light. The community swimming pool is a couple of blocks up the street."

"Got it." He pulled into the small parking lot near the pool, stopped then touched her hand. "I'll be back shortly to pick you up. If you want to make out a grocery list, Ivy and I can take care of the shopping while you check in at work."

"Really? You don't mind?"

"I'm happy to help out."

Emotion filled her, thankfulness for the simple gesture. "Better be careful. If I get used to this, I won't want to let you go."

"That's what I'm hoping."

* * * *

Sheriff Stan Walker was bald, stout and in his mid-sixties with penetrating gray eyes and a firm handshake. "Have a seat." He motioned toward a chair on the other side of his desk. "Would you like coffee or a soda?"

Kane sat. "Nothing, thanks. I appreciate your seeing me on such short notice."

"I'm happy to have your help. Frankly, I can't afford to spend a lot of time on this case when there hasn't been a crime committed here. I pulled the file." He nodded toward the manila folder on his desk and pushed it over. "Go ahead and take a look, but I want you to understand one thing. This is my jurisdiction. Anything you do will be cleared through me."

Kane opened the file then glanced up to meet his serious gaze. "I fully understand."

"Just so you know, I called your lieutenant to check you out. He vouched for you and then some, or I wouldn't be so willing to work with you."

"I appreciate it, sir."

"Call me Stan. Your lieutenant said you're currently on extended vacation?"

Kane nodded. "I don't intend to go back until this situation with the stalker is cleared up. Frankly, I think the man poses a serious threat to Rachel's safety. I'm hoping to flush him out before he escalates further."

"Which is why you asked for the background checks. See anything of interest?"

"The guy's been obsessed with Rachel since her days as a soap opera actress. That was years ago, but he only recently began to stalk her. I'm looking for a change in his life that could have triggered this new, aggressive behavior."

The sheriff pointed. "Dennis Olmstead's divorce was finalized about six months ago. That fits."

"Looks like Bob Mayfield recently inherited money and quit his job with a mail delivery service."

"That would give him a lot of time on his hands."

Kane nodded. "It certainly would. Chip Stevens has been working for the same company since he graduated high school. That's where he and Bob met. I don't see any major changes in his life, but maybe we haven't dug deeply enough yet."

"Who knows why these nut jobs do what they do. It could be as simple as his girlfriend dumped him."

"Maybe I'll have a talk with Chip first to see what I can learn."

Sheriff Walker leaned back in his chair. "How about our last guy, Curt Dawson?"

"Dawson moved to California several years ago. He has his own computer tech business. I don't see anything that stands out. Again, we might need to dig a little deeper."

"Isn't he the one who had the advanced reservation at Granite Lake?"

Kane glanced up. "His whole family was there for a reunion."

"So he probably isn't our man."

"I'm certainly not going to rule him out." He stood to offer his hand. "Thanks, Sheriff. I'll be in touch."

"Do you want to take one of my deputies along for these interviews you're planning?"

"Right now I'd like to keep it very non-official. If I'm talking to an innocent man, he should open up to me. I know from experience the sight of a cop can make some people nervous for no reason other than a few unpaid parking tickets."

The sheriff grinned. "Making people nervous isn't always a bad thing. Keep me posted."

Kane nodded and left. He barely made it back to the pool before Ivy's swim lesson ended.

Rachel climbed into the SUV and gave him an anxious look. "How'd it go?"

"Interesting. I'll tell you about it later. Did you make me that grocery list?"

Rachel handed over a sheet of paper. "I'm afraid it's pretty long."

"Ivy and I don't mind." He smiled at Ivy in the rearview mirror. "It'll keep us occupied until time to take Lark to her dance class."

"You don't have to do all this for me. I can manage, really. I feel like I'm taking advantage of you."

He pulled up at a stop sign and turned to look at her. "You didn't ask. I offered. Christ, Rachel, it's just running a few errands, not giving you a kidney."

Ivy leaned forward. "Are you two fighting?"

Rachel glanced over her shoulder. "No, we're not fighting. I'm just not used to anyone other than family helping me out this way."

"Get used to it," Kane broke in. "Where's your bookstore?"

"Two blocks up on the right."

He double-parked then reached over to squeeze her hand. "What time is Jade finished with soccer camp?"

"Four-thirty."

"I'll get her. Do you want to work until six or shall I pick you up sooner?"

"Six is good. Have fun, Ivy."

"We will. Bye, Mom."

"Bye, Rachel. I mean it. Don't worry."

All he wanted was to kiss the wary expression off her face. Instead, he drove away with her daughter in tow.

Chapter Fifteen

As the car pulled away, Rachel's heart swelled with gratitude. Kane was filling an empty place in her life she hadn't realized existed. She'd missed the friendship inherent in any good relationship more than anything, including physical intimacy. Still, the prospect of starting over scared her more than a little. Her life was complicated enough, and having a dangerous predator out there watching her only made it worse. She glanced down the busy street and shivered despite the heat. Pushing open the door to the bookstore, she hurried inside.

"Look who's back." Chandra stepped around the end of the counter. "Welcome home, Rachel."

"Thanks. How did everything go while I was away?"

"Fine. We were really busy over the weekend, but nothing we couldn't handle. Oh, there was a mix-up with a book order last week, but Ellen took care of it."

"Where is she?"

"I finally convinced her to take a break. She should be back soon."

"I need to talk to you both when she gets back. I'll be in my office until then."

"Sure. Is there a problem?"

"Just a complication. I'll tell you both all about it."

Rachel had just finished answering her most urgent e-mails when Ellen tapped on the office door.

"Welcome back."

Rachel glanced up and smiled. "I hear the place ran so smoothly while I was gone, you didn't even miss me."

"I don't know about that. There were a few issues, but I handled the major ones."

"I knew I left the place in competent hands."

"Thanks."

"Is it busy out there right now? I have something to discuss with you and Chandra."

"No, it's pretty slow. Chandra's helping a lady pick out a children's book, but I think they're almost finished."

"Good."

Rachel stood and followed her right-hand woman back to the front of the shop. Just as they reached the coffee bar, the door opened and Tim breezed through. With razor-cut hair and a diamond stud in one ear, he projected suave sophistication. A wide smile lit his face when he saw her.

"Hey, you're back."

"I got home this morning. What brings you in on your day off?"

"I wanted to let someone know I need to leave early tomorrow. I scored a pair of theater tickets and a hot date to go with them."

"Good for you, and your timing is perfect. Do you mind sticking around for a few minutes?"

"No problem. What's up?"

Rachel waited until Chandra finished with her customer and they had the shop to themselves then smiled at her gathered employees. "First, I want to thank you all for doing such a terrific job in my absence." She stopped for a moment to take a breath. "I also want you to be aware of a situation I had while I was on vacation."

Ellen's eyes widened. "What happened?"

Rachel took another deep breath. "I have a stalker."

"Holy shit."

She glanced over at Tim. "That about sums it up. A man attacked me while I was up in Tahoe. The police have reason to believe he may try again."

Chandra stepped forward to put a hand on her arm. "Oh, my God, were you hurt?"

"Not badly, but I was lucky to get away. Anyway, a friend is acting as a bodyguard, and he doesn't want me left alone. That means one of you needs to be around while I'm in the shop."

Ellen squeezed Rachel's other arm. "Of course we'll do anything you want. Do the police know who this person is?"

"They think it's someone who was up at Granite Lake with me, but there are several suspects."

Chandra shuddered. "Wow, that's scary. Why did this creep pick you to stalk? Did he like the way you looked in a bikini?"

Rachel had to laugh at that, then she shook her head. "Apparently he's been obsessed with me since I was an actress back in New York, but I haven't a clue why he chose now to come after me."

Tim stared. "You were an actress?"

She smiled at the question. "I was on a soap opera about a million years ago. It's not something I brag about."

"Which one?" Chandra's eyes lit up. "I love soaps."

"I played Jordan Hale on *Days of Desire*. It was back when you were just a little kid."

"Wow, that's so totally awesome. Everything but the stalker part."

"That part doesn't thrill me either. So, do you guys mind having a little less freedom? I think this man has watched me at work, maybe even come into the shop. Kane is worried about what he might do if he finds me in here alone."

Tim raised a brow. "Who's Kane?"

"He's a friend, but he's also a cop. He's on vacation right now and agreed to keep an eye on me until the police catch this guy."

"Must be a good friend if he volunteered to spend his time off keeping you safe." Chandra's tone was speculative. "What does he look like?"

Rachel cheeks heated. "You'll meet him soon. He'll be by to pick me up later." She grimaced. "I'm not allowed to drive anywhere by myself either."

Tim winked. "I'm guessing he's hot."

A harried-looking woman rushed through the door, and Rachel let his remark pass. "That's it. Thanks for being good sports about this."

"Why wouldn't we be?" Tim posed the question, and the others nodded.

After he left, Chandra went to help the stressed customer locate a book. A teenage girl came in soon after wanting a latte, and Ellen made it for her. Rachel escaped to her office.

With the payroll finished, she was ready and waiting when Ivy and Jade burst through the door shortly before six. Kane walked in behind them and glanced around the store.

Ivy skipped up to the counter. "Hi, Chandra. Hi, Ellen."

Rachel dropped a hand on Jade's shoulder. "How was soccer camp?"

"Really fun."

"Good. Ellen, Chandra, I'd like you to meet Kane Lafferty."

While Kane shook Ellen's hand, Chandra gave her two thumbs up behind his back.

Rachel grinned and picked up her purse. "We'd better go. I don't want Lark waiting around by herself if we're late."

"I agree. Girls, get back in the car. Ladies, it's been a pleasure." Kane followed the kids out the door.

Chandra grabbed Rachel's arm before she made it past the counter. "Wow, he's unbelievably hot. Way to go, girl."

Ellen's expression was wistful. "If you found a guy like that, maybe there's still hope for me."

"Any man would be lucky to have you."

Ellen smiled. "You'd better go. They're waiting."

"Have a good evening. I'll see you tomorrow." Rachel left the shop and climbed into the car then glanced at Kane. "How'd the shopping go?"

"It went great. We got everything on the list plus some other stuff."

Rachel looked over the back of the seat at Ivy. "What other stuff?"

Her daughter giggled. "Kane noticed you left all the good stuff like chips and popsicles off the list. We figured it must have been an oversight."

"I'll bet you did." She stared at Kane's profile. "Are you planning to turn my girls into junk food addicts?"

"I may feed a few of their bad habits."

"Terrific."

Jade laughed. "I knew having Kane around the house would be awesome."

Rachel sat forward and smiled. "I'm glad you're getting along so well. Did you talk to my mom when you picked Lark up earlier?"

"She was on the phone, so I hustled Lark out the door in a hurry. I did introduce myself to your dad. He shook my hand and sent us on our way."

"That's Dad's style. He goes with the flow, but my mom could pry information out of a rock."

"Sounds like we could use her as an interrogator down at the station. Maybe I should bring her along with me when I question our suspects."

"That's an idea. When we were kids, all she had to do was look at us and we'd spill our guts."

Kane pulled up to the door of the dance studio at the community college. Lark came out with her bag slung over her shoulder then climbed in next to Ivy.

Rachel glanced back. "I hope you didn't have to wait."

"No, I just finished changing a couple of minutes ago. The teacher was really cool. She taught us moves I'd never tried before. Most of the girls in the class are older than me."

"Is that going to be a problem?"

"The teacher said I have raw talent. She's hoping to refine it a little."

"I'm glad you enjoyed yourself. Are you ready for dinner?"

"Yeah, I'm pretty hungry. Grandma was dying to ask about Kane earlier, but she didn't. She kept opening her mouth then mumbling under her breath. It was hilarious. I've never seen her have that much self-control."

"Don't make fun of your grandmother, Lark."

"It was a compliment."

Rachel rolled her eyes.

Kane turned the SUV onto the dirt road that wound through the vineyard to the house. He parked next to a Volvo.

Rachel nodded at the car. "My brother's still here."

Lark slammed the car door. "He and Aunt Sharon are coming to dinner."

"We may as well tell everyone and get it over with."

Kane touched her arm. "True. Let's go do it."

Rachel couldn't remember ever walking into her mother's kitchen when it hadn't smelled like heaven. The scent of freshly baked cookies or a delicious meal always filled the air. Tonight the rich aroma of pot roast made her mouth water when she pushed open the kitchen door.

Kane took a deep breath. "Wow!"

"My mother's cooking is addictive. Chances are you'll put on a few pounds if you stick around long enough."

"Who cares? If it tastes half as good as it smells, I'm going to ask her to either adopt me or marry me."

Rachel's father, a heavyset man with dark hair, crossed the room and enfolded her in a hug. Brown eyes twinkled as he smiled down at her. "How's my girl? Did you have a good time in Tahoe?"

"I'm fine, Dad, and our vacation was...adventurous. I'll tell you all about it later. Did you meet my friend, Kane? This is my dad, Chet Hanover."

"We met. Welcome." He extended his hand. "We're happy to have you with us."

"Thanks, Chet. I'm sorry for that remark about stealing your wife."

"Who wants to steal me?" Rachel's mother hurried through the dining room doorway and smoothed back a wisp of gray-streaked red hair.

Her husband laughed. "Kane does, but he only wants you for your cooking. He wouldn't love you the way I do."

"You're full of bologna." She squeezed her husband's arm then hugged Rachel and kissed her cheek. "Introduce me to your friend."

"Mom, this is Kane Lafferty. Kane, this is my mother, Audrey, the creator of the fabulous pot roast you smell."

When Kane extended his hand, Audrey pushed it away and gave him a hug instead. "Any friend my daughter brings home to dinner gets a proper welcome."

"I'm pleased to meet you, Audrey, and I appreciate the dinner invitation."

"Any time. Chet, go pour the boy a drink and introduce him to Will and Sharon. Rachel, you can help me finish dishing up our meal."

"Sure. What can I do to help?"

Her mother waited until Kane and Chet left the room. "I'd like you to tell me where you met that gorgeous man. He's a friend of your sister's?"

"He works with Nolan. Have you met Nolan?"

"Not yet, and don't try to change the subject. So, Kane is a policeman?"

"He's a detective, but he's on vacation right now."

"He's staying in town? Have you known him long?"

"Just a few weeks, and yes, he's staying in town." Rachel took a deep breath. "Actually, he's staying with us."

Her mother frowned. "You know I'm pleased you're finally interested in someone, but do you really think having him stay in your home is a wise choice? After all, you have impressionable girls to consider."

"I know, and it isn't what you're thinking. Let's have dinner, and I'll explain everything."

"What's to explain?"

"Plenty. You make the gravy while I dish up the potatoes and carrots. Do you want me to carve the roast?"

"Your father will do it. There's a salad in the refrigerator and rolls in the oven." Her mother studied her with drawn brows. "I trust you have a reason for all this secrecy."

"I'm not trying to be secretive. I just want to explain in my own way. Which basket do you want to use for the rolls?"

"The big one. I made a double batch."

Sharon hurried into the kitchen and paused to give Rachel a hug. Short and plump with a head full of dark curls, her eyes were round with curiosity. "Where'd you find the hunk?"

"Through Grace."

"Don't tell me Gracie let that one get away? The girl needs to have her head examined, but her loss is your gain."

"They weren't dating."

"This must be serious if you're bringing him home to meet the family."

Rachel rolled her eyes. "You're as bad as Mom."

"Don't make it sound like such an insult." Audrey poured rich, fragrant gravy from the pan into a bowl.

"Would I do that?"

"Yes, you would. Go tell the men dinner is ready, and make sure the girls wash their hands."

Rachel laughed. "Yes, ma'am."

When they were all seated at the table, Chet said grace, then loaded their plates.

Kane took a big bite of pot roast and sighed. "This is delicious, Audrey."

"Thank you. Now, Rachel, we've all waited long enough. Why are you being so evasive about inviting a friend to dinner?"

Rachel exchanged a look with Kane then set her butter knife on her plate. "I had some trouble up in Tahoe. Kane is staying with us until we get it cleared up."

Her father frowned. "What sort of trouble?"

"Apparently, I have a stalker."

Her mother pressed a hand to her chest. "Honey, what happened?"

"Someone tried to grab me when I was out running."

"Oh, dear Lord."

Chet jumped up from his chair. "Were you hurt?"

"Just a few bruises, but Kane and a couple of sheriffs are afraid whoever grabbed me might try again."

"Do the police have a suspect?" Creases marred Will's forehead.

Kane laid down his fork. "There are a few suspects. It's possible the man was up at Granite Lake with us. I was helping out at my brother's camp, which is where Rachel and I ran into each other again. I'm personally pursuing all possible leads."

"Kane is staying with us to keep me and the girls safe." Rachel's lips firmed. "This guy won't be able to get anywhere near us."

"We're in your debt for looking after our girls." Chet resumed his seat. "Thank you, Kane."

"I'm happy to do it."

Will cleared his throat. "How can we help?"

"I don't feel comfortable leaving the girls alone, so I might need everyone to pitch in to help with that."

Audrey nodded. "Well, of course we will."

Kane rested his forearms on the table. "All of you can keep your eyes open for anyone hanging around who doesn't belong, especially when Rachel or the girls are here."

Sharon frowned. "We give tours of the vineyard and have wine tastings. There're frequently strangers around."

"If anyone strays away from the crowd, keep a close eye on him." Kane lifted a shoulder. "Otherwise, I don't think it'll be a problem."

Her father cleared his throat. "Why did this man choose Rachel to target?"

"He called me Jordan. He has some sort of fixation with me from when I was on TV."

"That was so long ago."

"I know, Mom. Something may have happened recently to trigger him to act on what was once only a harmless fantasy."

"I'll look into our suspects' backgrounds with that in mind." Kane picked his fork back up. "When I discover who he is, this nightmare will be over."

Rachel looked around the table. "Now you know why I was being so mysterious, so let's finish our dinner before it gets cold."

"You should have called us."

"There wasn't anything you could have done to help, Dad. I didn't call because I didn't want to worry you."

"You called Kane." Lark crossed her arms over her chest.

Rachel frowned. "I called him because he can protect us."

Audrey looked up, her eyes wide with alarm. "Are the girls in danger, too?"

Kane spoke up quickly. "Hopefully not, but we aren't going to take any chances. If this guy can't reach Rachel, I'm not sure what he'll try next."

"Sounds like you're covering your bases." Her father nodded in approval. "Please, everyone, let's not waste this good meal."

"And please, can we talk about something else while we do?" Rachel looked around the table and smiled. "I'm sure we'll get through this intact."

Amid murmurs of agreement, they went back to eating. When dinner was over, Rachel collected the dirty plates and headed to the kitchen. Her mother followed with a load of glasses.

"Don't tell me your relationship with Kane is purely professional. I may be getting old, but I'm not blind. I saw the way you looked at each other."

"We're friends, Mom."

Sharon came in with the serving dishes and snorted. "Friends with chemistry, the kind that could set a building on fire."

"All right, maybe there's a little more between us, but don't make a big deal out of nothing."

Her mother fisted her hands on her hips. "It doesn't seem like nothing when a man drops everything to look after a woman he's just met."

"He was already on extended vacation from his job, so it isn't some kind of noble sacrifice. I'm not pretending I don't find him attractive, but things are messed up right now. We aren't in a normal dating situation. My main concern is to keep the girls safe."

"Of course, but it doesn't hurt that the man protecting you is handsome, now does it?"

Rachel rolled her eyes. "You're hopeless, Mom."

"No, I'm hopeful."

"Fine, but keep your hopes to yourself. Right now I need Kane, and I don't want you to scare him off."

Audrey reared back. "Would I do that?"

"Yes!"

Sharon pressed her hand over her lips but couldn't hide a grin.

"What's so funny?" Lark strolled into the room.

Rachel started rinsing the dishes. "Nothing. Did you come to help clean up?"

"I came to see what happened to the dessert."

"We got a little distracted." Audrey headed toward the pantry. "I baked an apple pie. Get out the ice cream, honey, and you can help me serve it."

After everyone had finished dessert, Rachel cleared her throat. "I suppose we should talk about a schedule."

Her mother straightened. "We certainly should. Lark, you go first. What do you have in the way of activities this week?"

"Just dance. Can I work in the gift shop like we talked about, Aunt Sharon?"

"I could use another cashier if your mom approves."

"Mom, can I, please?"

"Of course you may, as long as you're not in the shop alone."

"She won't be," Sharon promised.

Rachel smiled at her sister-in-law. "Great, Lark is covered. I'll drop her off in the morning and pick her up before dance class."

"Next!" Chet called out in a jovial tone.

"Funny, Dad. Jade is easy. She has soccer camp all week. How about you, Ivy?"

"I just have swimming and a play date with Melissa on Wednesday. Her Mom called earlier to invite me."

"Then you can drop Ivy off tomorrow morning when you bring Lark. I'll take her to her swim lesson, and you can pick her up when you come back at four." Audrey smiled. "Easy."

"Are you sure you don't mind, Mom?"

"Of course I don't mind. Ivy can help me in the garden, and maybe I'll find that old easel I put up in the attic. You can paint when you're tired of picking vegetables, sweetheart."

"Cool."

"I guess we're all set then. It sounds like I'll be able to catch up at work." Rachel let out a relieved sigh.

"And I can get started on those interviews." Kane stood. "In fact, I'd like to set something up this evening. Are you ready to go?"

Rachel nodded. "Thanks for dinner, Mom."

"You're welcome. We'll see you in the morning."

With good-byes said all around, Rachel herded the girls out to the car. Kane ran out a minute later to join them. "You have a nice family."

"They were certainly very impressed with you."

He snorted as he backed up in the driveway. "I haven't done anything impressive yet. When I catch the deviant stalking you, then they can be impressed."

"Let's hope it's soon. Knowing someone might be watching me all the time gives me the creeps."

Chapter Sixteen

"Promise you'll be careful." Worry nagged at Rachel, and she bit her lip. "If Chip's the one who attacked me, who knows what he might do if he feels threatened."

Kane rolled his eyes. "I'm not afraid of Chip Stevens."

"You don't have to be afraid to be cautious."

"True, and I expect you to heed your own advice. Are you sure someone's in the bookstore?"

"Ellen's car is parked across the street."

"Then I'll see you around three-thirty." He cupped her chin in his hand and gave her a quick kiss. "Have a good day."

Rachel grimaced. "We're acting like a fifties sitcom, one where the parents sleep in twin beds and give each other a peck on the cheek before heading off to work."

Heat flared in his eyes as he pulled her hard against him and kissed her thoroughly. "Is that better?"

"Much." Her voice came out in a breathless gasp as she reached behind her for the door handle. With a last backward glance, she slid out of the car then carried the bags of muffins and scones into the Book Nook. Setting the baked goods on the counter, she leaned against the door.

"I'm not surprised your legs won't hold you." Ellen walked by with an open carton of books. "After witnessing that kiss, I need a cold shower."

Rachel blushed. "The man does know how to kiss."

"I bet that's not all he knows how to do."

"You're right about that." She pressed her hands to her hot cheeks. "I'm in trouble."

The other woman turned, eyes wide with concern. "What's wrong? Did that pervert come after you again?"

"No, nothing like that. I'm in trouble with Kane. I think I'm falling in love with him."

"That's wonderful. What's the problem?"

"When this is over and he leaves, it'll break my heart."

Ellen frowned. "Why would he leave? He dropped everything to help you out, and there's obviously chemistry between you."

"I know, but getting involved with me means taking on three half-grown girls. A few more days with Lark, and he'll be more than ready to go back to his old life."

"Is Lark being difficult?" She set down the box and pulled out the pastry trays to fill them with muffins.

"She's not exactly happy Kane and I are involved."

"Doesn't she like him?"

"I think she does, but she won't admit it. There's a lot of tension in the house, and I don't want my feelings for Kane to add to it. Sometimes I think even trying to have a relationship is a mistake. Life with Lark was tough enough before, and now it's worse."

Ellen gave her a commiserating smile. "No one ever said life's easy. Sometimes it's so hard you don't want to get up in the morning. But you do."

"You're right." Rachel sighed and glanced around the shop. "I suppose I should get busy."

"If you have paperwork, I'll be fine. Tim should be here soon."

"I do need to finish the inventory." She nodded toward the box on the counter. "Are those the self-help books I ordered?"

"They were just delivered. I'll shelve them this morning."

"Thanks, Ellen."

In her office, Rachel turned on the computer but couldn't concentrate. Her head ached with worrying about Kane and the interview scheduled with Chip Stevens. If Chip was her stalker, maybe he'd slip up and say something incriminating. Then this unbearable situation would be over.

* * * *

Kane was nearing the freeway when his cell phone rang. The number on the display wasn't one he recognized but looked vaguely familiar. He pulled to the side of the road to answer it since he had plenty of time to kill before his meeting with Stevens.

"Hello."

"Hey, Kane. Bob Mayfield here. I got your message. What can I do for you?"

"I hope you can answer a few questions. Any chance you'll have some free time today?"

"A cop was here to check on my whereabouts for last Friday. He said Rachel Carpenter was attacked up in Tahoe. Is that why you want to talk to me?"

"It is. I have a few follow up questions."

"Why would you think I know anything?" His tone took on an aggressive edge. "I met Rachel for the first time at Granite Lake. I have no reason to hurt her."

"Maybe if we talk, I can eliminate you as a suspect."

"Fine." An annoyed sigh echoed through the line. "I'll tell you anything you want to know. I plan to be home all morning."

"Great. I'll be there shortly."

"Do you need directions?"

"I have the address."

Kane smiled as he disconnected then pulled back onto the road. Chip was the only suspect he'd reached the night before, and their meeting wasn't scheduled until noon. This interview with Bob was an added bonus. He couldn't wait to hear what each man had to say about the other.

Twenty minutes later, Kane parked in the lot behind the complex where Mayfield lived. Smiling at a toddler eating a banana in a doorway two apartments down, he rang the bell. The door opened abruptly, and Bob waved him inside.

"You'll have to excuse the mess. I'm in the middle of packing." He gestured toward a chair. "Have a seat."

"Thanks for seeing me." Kane sat at the small dinette table and glanced around the room full of boxes. "You moving?"

"Yep. I'm out of this dump. I just bought a house in Marin close to the beach. I always wanted to live by the ocean."

Kane's brows rose. "That must have cost you a bundle."

"It's not large, a cottage really. My grandfather left me a good-sized inheritance."

"Congratulations."

Bob crossed into the kitchen then held up a coffee carafe. "Want a cup?"

"No thanks."

He poured a mug full of the fragrant brew then joined Kane at the table. "So, what do you want to know? Why am I a suspect in the first place? I don't understand why the police would even consider me a person of interest."

"Someone from the camp was following Rachel prior to the attack in Tahoe. We're looking at everyone at the retreat who had an opportunity."

He scowled. "So I'm being hassled because I don't have an airtight alibi for the night of the attack?"

"Our investigation shouldn't inconvenience you greatly. If you have nothing to hide, you won't mind helping us find the person responsible."

"Fine. Fire away."

"Whose idea was it to go camping at Granite Lake?"

"It was Chip's. We've been friends for years. When he got some extra vacation time, he called me."

"He knows you have plenty of free time now?"

"Would you still be working for a mail service if you inherited a few million dollars?" Bob swirled the coffee in his mug before taking a sip. He grimaced then added a teaspoon of sugar.

"Probably not. I understand you also inherited property up near Clear Lake."

"Yes, also half interest in a house in San Jose. My sister got the apartment in New York. I was in Lakeport the night Rachel was attacked. I told the police that."

"But you can't prove it?"

"No."

"Did you recognize Rachel when you saw her at Granite Lake?"

He shook his head.

"Did Chip recognize her?"

"He never mentioned it if he did."

"Do you have a girlfriend, Bob?"

The man frowned. "How is my personal life relevant?"

"Just curious. Do you have a lot of friends?"

"When you're rich, plenty of people want to be your friend. People who wouldn't give me the time of day before call to ask me to lunch. If I wanted a girlfriend, I could snap my fingers."

"So why don't you?"

"I'm not interested in a woman like that."

"But you are interested in women?"

"I'm not gay." His dark eyes glittered with annoyance.

"How about Chip? Does he have a girlfriend?"

"He was engaged, but they broke it off last Christmas. He hasn't dated much since then."

"Any particular reason why?"

Bob drained his mug then set it on the table. "He's still hoping to patch things up with Angie. She broke their engagement because she wants to go to law school. Chip's trying to convince her she can marry him and still get another degree. So far it isn't working."

"Ever been to Vine Haven?"

"I may have driven through the town a time or two, but I can't remember stopping."

Kane pushed back his chair and stood. "Thanks for your cooperation. If anything else comes up, I'll be in touch."

"You mean if Rachel is attacked again, I'd better have an ironclad alibi?"

"It certainly wouldn't hurt, but I hope it won't come to that." His fists clenched at his sides. "No one will get near Rachel on my watch."

"Sounds like you have a personal interest in this."

"Does that bother you?"

"Not in the least." Mayfield followed him to the door. "I hope you catch the guy."

"I will."

As he pulled out of the apartment complex, Kane glanced in the rearview mirror. Bob stood in his doorway, watching while he drove away.

Kane reached the diner where he was meeting Chip a half-hour early and spent the time writing down his impressions of Bob Mayfield. Something about the guy seemed a little off, but he wasn't sure exactly what. Maybe Chip would be able to give him some insight.

He looked up when Stevens entered the diner. The man limped down the aisle wearing a brown uniform. He slid onto the vinyl seat across from Kane and smiled.

"I hope you don't mind meeting here. I'm on my lunch break." Chip paused as a waitress set a glass of water in front of him then handed him a menu. "I'm ready to order if you are."

Kane nodded. "I'll have a turkey club and iced tea."

"A burger with onion rings and a Coke."

"I'll be right back with your drinks." The waitress favored Kane with a lingering smile.

After she left, he studied Chip. Lines radiated from the corners of the man's eyes. When he shifted in the seat, he winced.

"Did you injure yourself?"

"I tripped on a curb and sprained my ankle. It hurts like a mother."

"Have you wrapped it?"

Chip nodded. "It isn't helping. If my ankle doesn't feel better by tomorrow, I'll probably go see a doctor." He let out a disgusted snort. "Ironic, don't you think? I hike all over the Sierras without a scratch and then hurt myself in my own driveway."

"Sometimes life has a warped sense of humor." Kane squeezed lemon into the iced tea the waitress set in front of him. "Do you camp a lot?"

"I try to go at least a couple of times each summer."

"Was there any particular reason you chose Granite Lake for your vacation?"

"Bob agreed to go camping with me when I asked, but he didn't want to sleep in a tent or eat his own cooking. That narrowed down our choices. I would have been happy pitching a tent just about anywhere, but he volunteered to pay, so I didn't mind finding a place he liked."

"So you wanted to go camping, but he chose the place?"

"Technically I chose it, but we didn't have many options. It was the only camp that met his criteria within reasonable driving distance." Chip sipped his Coke. "Does it matter?"

"I want to get everything straight. I'm sure the police told you Rachel Carpenter was attacked after she left Granite Lake."

"They did, but I don't understand what that has to do with me. I barely know her."

"Someone followed Rachel a couple of times while she was at the camp, so every man who was there is a suspect."

"You don't really think I would hurt her, do you?" Chip frowned. "I liked Rachel."

"I'm just trying to sift through the facts. Our stalker likes her, too. He likes her a lot."

"That's not what I meant." He pushed a strand of hair out of his face and waited while the waitress delivered their food. "I meant she's a nice person, not that I have a thing for her. You're the one who had a romantic interest in the woman."

Kane took a bite of his sandwich and nodded. "The feeling's mutual. Does that bother you?"

"Why should it? I have my own woman problems. I'm not stupid enough to chase after a lady like Rachel who would never be interested in me in a million years. Check with that guy, Dennis. He was the one making a fool of himself over her."

They ate in silence for several minutes before Kane asked, "What about Bob? Was he interested in Rachel?"

"He thought she was pretty, but who wouldn't? Last time I checked, looking at a beautiful woman wasn't a crime."

"No, but stalking one is. Does Bob have a girlfriend?"

Chip swallowed a bite of his burger. "He's never had a steady girlfriend for as long as I've known him."

"Is he gay?"

"I don't think so. He makes sexual comments about women occasionally. I also saw him pick up a prostitute one night several months ago. I never asked him about it since it wasn't any of my business."

Kane finished his sandwich while Chip talked about the Giants' win the night before then took a final sip of his drink. "Thanks for answering my questions. I appreciate it."

"I don't mind. I have nothing to hide."

"I may need to speak with you again." He pulled his wallet out of his pocket and laid a twenty-dollar bill on the table then glanced over at Chip. "Have you ever been to Vine Haven?"

"Sure. It's not on my usual route, but I've made deliveries up there plenty of times."

"Did you make deliveries to Rachel's bookstore?"

"I didn't know she owned one."

Kane smiled. "I hope that ankle gets better real soon."

"I do, too. See you, Kane."

Kane paid little attention to the sparse traffic on the drive back to Vine Haven as he sifted through the nuances of the two interviews. His gut told him Chip was innocent, but he didn't have anything but a feeling to back it up. He wasn't sure about Bob.

When his phone rang, he checked the display. *Rachel.* His pulse quickened in a way that bothered him more than a little. Everything about her affected him, and he couldn't control his fascination. Listening to catch the sound of Rachel's voice. Watching her as she moved around her home. Dreaming about her while he slept alone on the lumpy hide-a-bed.... He shook off his preoccupation, which was starting to verge on a need only she could satisfy and answered the phone. "Hey, beautiful."

"How'd it go?" Rachel spoke in a breathless tone.

"Interesting. Bob may be hiding something."

"I thought you were meeting with Chip."

"I talked to them both. I didn't learn anything conclusive, but at the moment I'm more inclined to put my money on Bob. I'll know more after I question Dennis and Curt."

"Dennis called here a few minutes ago. He wants to see me. He's outraged the police suspect him of attacking me, and he isn't interested in talking to you."

"I can't force him to."

"I know. That's why I'm meeting him for lunch tomorrow."

He pulled to the side of the road and jerked on the emergency brake. "No way in hell are you going anywhere near him. What were you thinking?"

"I was thinking I'd be perfectly safe sitting in a busy restaurant with you somewhere close by. If Dennis is the one, he might be so overcome by my charming self he'll say something stupid."

Kane let out a breath. "I suppose you'll be safe enough, but do you really want to have lunch with the man?"

"I can eat a meal with him if it means ending this nightmare sooner. Anyway, I'm betting Dennis didn't do it."

"Any reason why?"

"I don't think he has that kind of violence in him. Let's face it—the man is a wimp."

Kane chuckled. "While I agree with your assessment of his character, I think Olmstead might surprise you. Often it's the mild mannered ones that lash out when they're pushed."

"I'll be careful. Where're you going now?"

"I told Sheriff Walker I'd keep him in the loop, so I'm headed to his office. How about you? Working hard?"

Rachel sighed. "I couldn't concentrate. I was too busy worrying about you."

"This is my job."

"I know. I also know you're good at what you do."

He stared through the windshield at a hawk circling in an air current, wondering if his profession would drive a wedge between them like it had with his ex-wife. "You're smart enough to realize we can't make a relationship between us work if you sit around biting your nails every time I leave the house."

"You're right. I'll work on it. I'd better go. It sounds like they need me up front."

"I'll see you in a couple of hours."

Chapter Seventeen

"I accuse Miss Scarlet in the library with the candlestick." Ivy pulled the three cards from the envelope, and groans went up around the table. "Oh, yeah. I won. I won." Standing up, she victory danced around the kitchen.

"And so graciously." Rachel scooped up the pile of weapons and dropped them into the game box.

"How the heck did you figure it out so fast?" Kane leaned an elbow on the table. "I wasn't even close."

Ivy laughed. "I guess I'm a better detective than you."

"You certainly have a more inflated ego." Lark pushed back her chair and stood. "I'm going to listen to music in my room."

"Don't you want to play another game?" Ivy sat back down. "I'll let you have a chance this time."

"You're *so* lame. Get a life, Ivy."

"We don't have time for another game." Rachel closed the box. "It's almost bedtime. You and Jade need to go get your pajamas on and brush your teeth."

Jade frowned. "I don't see why we have a bedtime in the summer. It's not like we have school in the morning."

"No, but you have soccer tomorrow, and you need a good night's sleep. Go upstairs. I'll be there in a minute."

"Fine." Jade yawned. "Good night, Kane."

"Good night, girls."

Ivy walked over to his chair and hugged him. "See you in the morning."

He put his arm up to hug her back then smiled. "You bet."

Footsteps echoed on the stairs followed by giggling and doors shutting. Kane glanced over with a mixture of surprise and pleasure in his eyes. "At least Ivy approves of me."

"She's always been the most demonstrative of my girls. I'm afraid she's becoming quite attached."

"Is that a problem?"

Rachel sighed. "I'm glad she cares so much, but she has some very real expectations about your place in our lives. I don't want her to be disappointed."

"I don't intend to disappoint her. Or you." His arm snaked out, and he pulled her down onto his lap. "What about you? Do you have expectations?" He pushed a lock of hair behind her ear.

"I'm trying to be realistic. The position we're in isn't exactly normal."

"It feels normal. Eating dinner together, playing games with the kids— it doesn't get much more normal than that."

"You've been forced into it. Don't tell me you usually spend your evenings playing *Clue*."

"No, I usually spend them working. This is much better."

"Really?"

He cupped her face in his palms and kissed her. "Yes, you're better than anything I've had in years."

Rachel wound her arms around his neck and kissed him back. His response was enthusiastic.

"Gross!" Lark's lip curled down. "Why don't you two get a room?"

Rachel made no move to jump off Kane's lap as her daughter walked across the kitchen.

"We were just kissing."

Lark picked up a book off the counter. "Whatever you say."

Kane cleared his throat. "I rented a movie, a romantic comedy since I'm surrounded by women. Would you like to watch it with us?"

"I think I'll pass. I see enough making out between the two of you." With the book pressed tightly to her chest, she left the room.

Rachel slid off Kane's lap. "I'd better go see if Jade and Ivy are in bed."

"Take your time. If you need to talk to Lark, the movie can wait."

"I don't think talking will make a difference. She needs time to adjust to seeing us together."

He nodded. "I'll be in the living room."

Upstairs Rachel kissed Jade good night then went into Ivy's room. She stepped over Daisy sleeping by the bed then pulled back the quilt her youngest had tucked up under her chin. "You'll be too hot. It's a warm night."

"It makes me feel cozy."

"Cozy is good." Rachel bent to kiss her.

"Is that how Kane makes you feel?"

She paused. "I suppose it is."

"Are you going to marry him? Brittany's mom got married again, and now she has two dads. If you married Kane, at least I'd have one."

Rachel stroked the hair away from her daughter's face. "It's too soon to talk about that. Kane and I haven't known each other very long."

"Well, you like him and he likes you, so why wait?"

"Because neither of us wants to make a mistake."

"Marrying Kane wouldn't be a mistake. I like having him here. He plays with us and tells us funny stories. Did Daddy do that?" Her eyes clouded. "Sometimes I forget what it was like when he was alive. Sometimes I have to look at his picture to remember what he looked like."

A photograph of Bryce sat on top of Ivy's dresser. She'd only been six when he died, and Rachel didn't want her to forget her father.

"He played with you as much as he could. Your dad had to work a lot."

"When Kane catches the man who hurt you, will he leave?"

She nodded. "That doesn't mean he'll stop seeing us, though. I don't know how things will work out between us." She squeezed her daughter's shoulder. "I don't want you to get your hopes up."

"If he leaves because Lark is mean to him, I'm going to be really mad."

"Nothing that happens between Kane and me will be Lark's fault or yours or Jade's. It's up to the two of us to work things out. Do you understand?"

Ivy yawned. "I guess."

"Go to sleep." Rachel kissed her forehead. "Sweet dreams."

Soft music came from Lark's room. Rachel paused outside the door then knocked softly.

"Come in if you have to."

She smiled and pushed it open. "I have to. I want to tell you good night."

"Good night."

Rachel sat down on the edge of the bed. "Don't read for too long."

"I won't."

"Your Aunt Sharon told me you were a big help in the gift shop today. Did you enjoy working there?"

Lark shrugged. "I guess. If you don't mind, I want to finish my book."

Rachel sighed. She wanted to pull her daughter into her arms and hug her until all the anger was gone. "It was just a kiss, honey."

"Whatever. Good night, Mom."

"Good night, Lark."

Kane glanced up when she entered the living room. "How'd it go?"

"Lark is resentful, and Ivy's already thinking *new daddy*." She sat down next to him on the couch. "You might want to go while the getting is good."

Kane pulled her close. "Are you worried?"

She sighed and leaned against his chest. "I wouldn't be much of a mother if I wasn't."

"How can I make things easier? Do you want me to keep my hands to myself?"

Rachel looked down at his hands. Strong and tanned with long fingers, she quivered when he rested one on her thigh and the other at her waist.

"That's not what I want."

His grip tightened. "Good because I doubt I could manage it."

Reluctantly she pulled away. "I think we'd better watch that movie before we forget my daughters are right upstairs."

With his gaze still locked with hers, he picked up the remote and pushed play. The movie was lighthearted and funny, but there was a sexy side to the romance that made Rachel squirm. When she glanced up at Kane, he looked as uncomfortable as she was.

"You couldn't have chosen an action-adventure flick with lots of blood and mayhem? Instead, you're forcing me to watch a hot guy who's younger than me take off his shirt?"

His brow rose. "You have a thing for younger men?"

"I'm not picky about age when they look like that. Jealous?"

"I can hold my own against those Hollywood types. Want me to show you?"

She gasped as his hand ran up the inside of her thigh into the leg of her shorts. Before she could think, let alone react, he had her stretched out full length on the couch. He kissed her until she couldn't breathe. The hard length of his erection pressing against the juncture of her thighs sent her up in flames.

"The office door locks."

Kane scooped her into his arms, carried her across the room and pushed the office door shut with his shoulder. The lock clicked. After setting her on the edge of her desk, he pulled her shirt over her head and dropped it on the floor. Her bra sailed across the room.

When his mouth tugged on first one breast and then the other, she moaned. The downward slide of her zipper brought a return of sanity.

"Kane, we can't."

His hand stilled. "Am I going too fast?"

She shook her head and rested her cheek against his chest. The muscle flexed as he exhaled a deep breath.

"It's not that I don't want to. I do, but the girls are right upstairs. What if one of them came down looking for me? I shouldn't have let it go this far. I'm sorry." Her voice quavered.

He pulled away slightly, and his thumb traced a tear as it ran down the side of her face. "Hey, none of that. We both got carried away."

She wrapped her arms around his waist. "You're not angry?"

"Of course not. We have plenty of time. We don't have to rush into anything."

Moonlight shone through the parted window blinds as he bent down to pick up her shirt. Outside, a porch board creaked. Her head jerked toward the window when a shadow passed, and her body tensed.

"Someone's out there."

Kane leaped toward the office door and threw it open. Seconds later, the front door slammed against the wall while she was still struggling to turn her shirt right side out. Finally, she shrugged it on and hurried out to the porch. Nothing moved. A minute later an engine started in the distance. Kane ran back up the sidewalk.

"Lock all the doors. I'll try to catch him." He jerked open the door to his Jeep, gunned the engine and raced down the street. The taillights disappeared into the night.

Lark stood at the foot of the stairs when she went inside.

"What happened?"

Rachel locked the door then pushed back her hair with a shaking hand. "Someone was out on the porch. Kane went after him."

Lark followed her into the living room. The movie credits were still rolling on the TV screen. "Did he see who it was?"

"I don't know." Rachel turned off the DVD player and sank onto the couch. Her stomach churned.

Lark sat next to her. "You don't look so good."

Rachel closed her eyes. Had someone seen her and Kane together, witnessed a private moment full of promise and caring? She pressed her hand to her lips and swallowed.

"Mom, are you okay?"

She opened her eyes and tried to offer a reassuring smile but couldn't. "I'm a little shaken up. I don't like feeling exposed in my own home."

"Should we call Grandpa or Uncle Will?"

"If Kane isn't back soon, I will. I don't want to take any chances with you girls."

Lark picked up her hand and held it. Rachel wasn't sure who was comforting whom, but she appreciated her daughter's presence more than she believed possible. They waited in silence. When a car pulled into the driveway, Rachel ran to the window with Lark behind her.

Her daughter dropped the curtain. "It's Kane."

Rachel unlocked the door and threw it open as he walked up the porch steps. "Did you—"

"He got away."

Her shoulders slumped. Kane wrapped one arm around them then used the other to give Lark a hug. The girl stood quietly for a moment before pulling away.

Rachel steadied her voice. "What happened?"

"The man took off through the neighbor's yard. I chased him, but he jumped into a pickup parked a couple of blocks over and drove away before I could get there. He must have run every red light in town because I never caught up. I called it in. The police are looking for him. We may get lucky."

"Could you tell who it was?"

Kane glanced over at Lark. "No, it was too dark, and he was smart enough to stay away from streetlights. I only saw him in shadows, average height and build. The pickup sounded like an older model, but I couldn't determine the color. Something dark."

"I guess you didn't get his license plate number either."

"There's never a full moon when you need one."

Lark crossed her arms over her chest. "That sucks. This whole nightmare would be over if you were a faster runner."

Rachel gasped. "Lark!"

Kane grinned. "I was closing in on him, but he had too much of a head start. Believe me, I gave it my best effort." He grimaced. "I'll probably be sore as hell tomorrow. I'm not used to sprinting."

Lark snorted. "I might as well go back to bed."

Rachel sighed. "Sorry the commotion woke you."

"I wasn't asleep. I was reading. Are you coming upstairs, Mom?"

"I'll be there as soon as I talk to the police. I'm sure they're on their way." She rested her hand on her daughter's shoulder. "Thanks for keeping me company tonight."

"No problem."

After she left, Kane pulled Rachel into his arms. "How are you really doing?"

"I've had better endings to a date. Do you think he saw us?"

"It was too dark in the office to see much. He probably saw shadows, not details."

"I hope you're right." She let out a deep breath. "What do we do now?"

"The sheriff should be here any minute. I asked him to call for an investigative unit to process the scene. Maybe we can get some prints." When a car slowed on the street, he walked over to the window. "Here's Stan now."

Sheriff Walker arrived with a fresh-faced deputy whom he introduced as Brandon Hendricks. The young man took Rachel's statement then stuffed his notebook in his pocket.

"We'll need to fingerprint your family to compare against any prints we find outside, but that can wait until tomorrow."

"Go to bed, Rachel." Kane stepped up behind her and squeezed her shoulders. "You look exhausted. I'll lock up after they finish with the porch."

"I'm pretty tired."

He walked her to the foot of the stairs then gave her a quick kiss. She pressed her forehead against his chest.

"I'm so glad you're here."

He stroked the hair away from her face. "I wouldn't be anywhere else. Good night. I'll see you in the morning."

* * * *

"Anything yet?" Kane joined the officers on the front walk.

Walker nodded toward the two men dusting for prints. "They found dirt under the windowsill at the end of the porch but no clear prints."

Kane swore. "He must have left something."

"He didn't touch the glass, but I have a partial on the sill." One officer looked over his shoulder and grinned. "It may be enough to get a match."

The sheriff rubbed a hand over his bald head. "The prints on the hand rails probably belong to family members, but we'll run them anyway."

"I suppose it's better than nothing."

"We'll check with the DMV to see if any of our suspects drives an older pickup. It won't be conclusive, but it may narrow the field." Walker yawned. "I'm getting too old for this. My wife's been at me to retire. Maybe I should consider it."

Kane clapped the man on the shoulder. "What, and miss all this excitement?"

"These days excitement is sneaking a donut. My doctor has me on a low cholesterol diet." He grimaced.

"I wouldn't mind a little less excitement on the job. I've been thinking about making a change myself." He let out a breath. "The stress is getting to me. There's never any down time, and after what happened—" He clamped his lips together. "I honestly don't know how much longer I can take it."

Gray eyes regarded him with sympathy and understanding. "You know, if I retire there'd be a damn fine job available right here in town. You might keep that in mind if you want to get away from the city.

People around here would probably be pleased to see someone with your experience run for sheriff."

Kane glanced at Rachel's dark bedroom window. "It's certainly something to consider."

"Brandon." The sheriff raised his voice. "Let's go. I need my sleep."

"Coming, chief."

The two left, followed a few minutes later by the investigative team. When the last vehicle disappeared down the street, Kane stood on the front walk. The darkness was thick beyond the spill of light from the porch. A dog barked in the distance then all was silent. Peace settled in, but it wouldn't last. The pervert stalking Rachel would be back. His fists clenched at his sides. Next time the shithead wouldn't get away.

* * * *

He slammed the door into the wall then threw his keys on the table. Slumping into a chair, he held his head in his hands.

Tonight had been a mistake. Approaching her house was a foolish risk, but he hadn't been able to stop himself. The need to see what Jordan was doing with Lafferty had overwhelmed his cautious nature. He drew in a sobbing breath. The two of them had been going at each other like animals.

Tears ran down his face.

She'd let the man touch her beautiful breasts, his filthy hands stroking.... Whimpering, he stared at the pictures of Jordan tacked to his wall and licked dry lips. The ungrateful bitch had given herself to Kane like a cheap whore, unwilling to wait for him.

He smacked the chair arm. He was tired of resorting to his own hand for the relief he needed, and obviously Jordan wasn't saving herself for him. Pulling the phone from his pocket, he punched buttons.

"Can you come over?"

"Now? It's late."

His voice lowered. "I'll make it worth your while."

When she mumbled an agreement, he hung up. He didn't like using another woman to satisfy his needs, but Jordan left him no choice. Standing, he paced the small room then went to pull each photograph from the wall and stack them in a neat pile. He couldn't allow her intimacy with Lafferty to continue any longer, couldn't wait for the perfect moment to claim his prize.

Divide and conquer. His lips curved. All it would take was a tiny error by a thoughtless child, and he would have his heart's desire.

Chapter Eighteen

The sheriff's office bustled with activity. Beyond a partially closed door, Sheriff Walker's voice rose in a heated conversation. In the outer office, the dispatcher relayed information over a radio to a deputy on patrol.

Rachel and her daughters stood clustered around Deputy Hendricks's desk. The young man wore immaculately pressed khakis and was so closely shaven, his cheeks were pink.

"Cool!" Ivy grinned from ear to ear as he rolled her fingers across the ink pad and pressed them to the paper.

Lark wrinkled her nose. "You like being covered with ink?"

"Hurry up, Ivy." Jade nudged her sister. "I'm going to be late for soccer."

"All finished." The deputy handed Ivy a tissue to wipe her fingers. "Thanks for stopping by. Now we can eliminate your prints from the ones we found on the porch. Hopefully, we'll know more by this afternoon."

Kane clicked his cell phone shut and dropped a hand on Rachel's shoulder. "Well, we can cross Chip Stevens off our list. The receptionist at his doctor's office confirmed he was treated for a severely sprained ankle an hour ago."

The deputy's brows shot up. "She told you that without a warrant? How in the world did you—"

"I can be pretty persuasive when I try."

Rachel let out a breath. "No one with a sprained ankle could run the way our Peeping Tom did last night."

Kane nodded. "Exactly. Chip was limping yesterday, and now we know he wasn't faking it. That leaves three suspects."

"Did you reach Curt yet?"

"He didn't return my call, but I'll try him again later. I'd like to meet with him after your lunch date with Olmstead."

Sheriff Walker hurried out of his office. "I can send Brandon over to keep an eye on things at the restaurant if you'd like."

"Thanks, but I think I can handle it. Rachel won't be out of my sight for even a minute."

Jade touched her mother's arm. "Can we go now?"

"Sure." Rachel smiled. "Thank you for your help, Sheriff."

"You're welcome. I'll let you know if the DMV turns up anything interesting."

Kane paused in the doorway as the girls headed outside. "That would be great. I'll stop by later."

Once everyone was in the SUV, he drove toward the soccer field. A light breeze took the edge off an already warm morning. When he stopped the car, Jade bolted through the open door and raced across the grass to join her friends. Kane pulled out of the parking lot and took a back road to the winery.

Rachel breathed in the scent of ripening grapes as she glanced his way. "You're driving like a local."

He pulled into her parents' driveway and stopped. "I have a good sense of direction. Here we are, girls. Everyone out."

Lark opened her door and dropped to the ground.

Ivy tightened her arms around the doll on her lap. "I have a play date today. Melissa got a new doll for her birthday, and we're having a tea party. That's why I brought Samantha."

Rachel groaned. "I forgot all about it."

"I tried to remind you earlier, but you weren't paying attention to a word I said."

"I was cleaning up dog barf. Whatever Daisy ate certainly didn't agree with her."

Ivy wrinkled her nose. "It was really gross."

"Tell me about it." Rachel frowned. "You don't think my stalker left poisoned meat for Daisy, do you?"

"I don't see why he would. She probably got into someone's garbage." Kane cleared his throat. "So, what are we doing?"

"I guess we're taking Ivy to her friend's house."

"Melissa's mom will drop me off at the bookstore before my swim lesson."

"Did you bring your suit?" Rachel ran a hand through her hair. "I forgot to remind you. I had other things on my mind this morning."

"I brought it."

Kane raised a brow. "Then we're out of here?"

She nodded and waved when her mother stepped out onto the front porch. "See you this afternoon."

Audrey smiled. "Have a good day."

Kane backed up then turned around in the driveway. "Your mom sounds awfully chipper. Must mean you didn't tell her about last night."

"I couldn't face another rehash. I'll call her later today if I have a spare minute."

"Which way?"

"Head toward town. The Hensleys live on Elm."

Several minutes later, Rachel walked Ivy up to the door of her friend's ranch-style home and thanked Debra Hensley for having her over.

"It's no problem at all." The slim brunette smiled. "Melissa's been missing her friends this summer."

"You're sure you don't mind dropping her off at the bookstore this afternoon?"

"Of course not. I have errands to run in town, anyway."

"Thanks, Debra. I'll see you around two."

Once Rachel was back in the car, Kane reached over and squeezed her hand. "How're you doing? If you were any more tense, you'd snap."

She leaned back in the seat and sighed. "I can't seem to relax."

"Nervous about having lunch with Olmstead?" He put the car in gear and backed out of the driveway.

"Not really. It's the whole situation. I just want life to be normal again."

When they arrived at the bookstore a few minutes later, Kane pulled into an empty parking spot and killed the engine.

With a soft touch, he stroked the hair away from her face. "Being constantly on alert is tiring. Just keep reminding yourself it'll be over soon."

"Will it?"

"I think so. He's escalating, taking bigger risks. Last night is proof of that. The next mistake he makes will be his last one."

"I hope so."

She stepped out of the car and slung her purse over her shoulder. Kane carried trays of nut bread while she grabbed bags of scones. They hurried across the street after a couple of cars had passed.

"Morning, Rachel." Tim glanced up as they entered the bookstore. "Hey, Kane." He studied her for a moment. "Dare I hope the bags under your eyes are because you two were out partying last night?"

"I'm afraid not. My stalker is back in business."

Tim's hands rested on the cash register. "You weren't hurt, were you?"

"No, but I didn't sleep well afterward. Hence the bags."

"Even with bags you're beautiful." Kane dropped a quick kiss on her upturned lips. "I'll see you at Palm Gardens at noon."

"I'll personally deliver her there safely."

"Thanks, Tim." With an encouraging smile Rachel's way, he left.

She stared at the closed door and sighed.

Tim shut the till drawer and came around the counter to give her arm a squeeze. "Chin up. This will all be over soon."

"That's what Kane keeps saying." She squared her shoulders. "It'd better be. I don't know what could be worse than this awful waiting."

* * * *

Kane pulled out his cell and called Curt Dawson. When the man answered on the second ring, he allowed himself a satisfied smile. "Dawson? It's Kane Lafferty."

"Hey, Kane, sorry I didn't get back to you sooner. I've been busy. What can I do for you?"

"I was hoping we could get together to talk later this afternoon."

"I assume this is regarding Rachel. I can't believe the police questioned me about where I was the evening she was attacked. Why in the world would I want to hurt Rachel?"

"I'm afraid everyone who was at Granite Lake with her is a suspect."

"Unbelievable."

"Maybe if we talk, I can clear you of suspicion."

"I'll cooperate, but I can't meet you today. I have a big project I've been working on, and I need to wrap up the final details. My client will be royally pissed if his computer system isn't up and running tomorrow morning."

Kane gritted his teeth. "When would be a good time?"

"If all goes well, I should be free by noon tomorrow."

"I can meet you in Santa Rosa for lunch if that works."

"I'll be downtown installing new software. There's a deli across the street from my client's office." He recited the address.

"Thanks, Curt. Good luck with your project." Kane clicked his phone off, drove back to the sheriff's office and headed through to Walker's inner sanctum. "Anything new?"

"I just got the report back from DMV. None of our suspects drives an older pickup, at least not one registered in their name."

"Damn. That would have made it too easy."

Stan Walker rubbed his bald head. "Nothing's ever easy. I've got Pete nosing around to see if any of our suspects has a friend or relative with a truck that matches your description. I'll let you know if he turns up anything."

"Thanks." Kane leaned forward. "I finally reached Curt Dawson. I'm meeting him tomorrow at noon."

"Good. You'll let me know how Rachel's lunch with Olmstead goes? He's our most likely suspect. Living three blocks away, it wouldn't be much of a chore for him to keep tabs on her, though I don't know why he'd drive to her house to do it."

"Maybe just as a precaution, in case something went wrong?"

"He wouldn't want to lead you straight back to his home if he had to make a hasty exit."

Kane nodded. "Exactly. Any word on the fingerprints the investigators pulled off Rachel's porch?"

"The partial on the sill wasn't enough for a match. They're still sorting through some of the others, but it isn't looking good."

"Christ, you'd think we could catch a break. This little shit isn't a professional. He should have left some evidence behind."

"It's a pisser." Sheriff Walker relaxed back in his chair. "Still, he's bound to screw up."

"Let's hope it's sooner rather than later."

* * * *

"That dress is a knockout!" Chandra admired Rachel from all sides. "One look at you should wring a confession from this guy."

"That's what I'm hoping." Rachel smoothed the silky fabric of her sundress.

"You weren't wearing that this morning." Tim whistled. "Chandra's right. You're definitely hot."

Rachel glanced down at the plunging neckline. "Is it too much?"

"No way."

Tim snorted. "*If* Kane lets you sit in the same room with the suspect. I bet your gorgeous cop friend is the reason you didn't put that little number on this morning."

"You're right about that." Rachel grinned. "He has a protective streak, but I don't mind taking a few risks if it will end this nightmare sooner."

Chandra gave Rachel a high-five. "You go, girl. I'd love to see this guy's face when he gets a look at you."

"I can't wait to see Kane's." Tim rubbed his hands together. "Let's head on over. It's almost noon now."

It was a short walk to Palm Gardens. Rachel was quiet as she held tightly to Tim's arm.

"Nervous?"

"A little. I don't believe Dennis Olmstead is my stalker, but I can't imagine any of the others are either. This seems like a bad dream, and I keep waiting to wake up."

They stopped in front of the Mexican restaurant, and Tim squeezed her hand. "If Olmstead's the one, you'll flush him out. You're a fighter, Rachel. Go get him."

She nodded. "Piece of cake. I was an actress for crying out loud. I can do this."

"Of course you can. I'll be waiting to hear all the details."

"Thanks, Tim. Well, here goes." With a deep breath, she pushed open the gaily-decorated wood door.

The inside was an attractive mish-mash of bright reds and yellows with colorful piñatas hanging from the ceiling. Forcing a sunny smile, Rachel crossed to the table where Dennis waited. His hand shook as he pulled out her chair.

"You look amazing."

"Thank you."

When a cocktail waitress appeared, Rachel ordered a margarita. Dennis followed suit. His hazel eyes glazed over when he sneaked a peek at her deep cleavage.

At a table in the rear of the restaurant, Kane held a newspaper in front of him. A plate of untouched nachos sat on the table. His brows lowered

Jannine Gallant

as well as his mouth when he met her gaze. One fist crumpled the paper. Rachel forced herself to focus on what Dennis was saying.

"You know I had nothing to do with the attack on you in Tahoe, don't you? I would never hurt you."

She hoped her smile appeared genuine. "I want to believe you, Dennis. I really do." She took a sip of her recently delivered margarita. "Up at Granite Lake I got the feeling you had a little crush on me. The fact I spent some time with Kane wouldn't have made you lash out, would it?"

"Of course not!" He shook his head in vehement denial as the server approached to take their lunch order. Halfway through the verbal list of specials, he interrupted. "I'll have a couple of tacos, beef please."

"And for the lady?" The young man's teeth gleamed white beneath his dark moustache.

"A chicken burrito." Rachel handed him the menu.

"Let me know if there's anything else you want, anything at all." His warm gaze settled on her face after a quick glance down. "More salsa?"

"We're fine." Dennis scowled but refrained from commenting until the man walked away. "Young punk, ogling you like that. He can't be a day over eighteen."

"See what I mean. If you get angry over a waiter smiling at me, I wonder what you'd do if you saw Kane...kiss me."

The anger slid from his face, replaced by confusion. "Nothing. I wouldn't do anything." He reached across the table to lay his hand over hers. "Sure I'd be thrilled if you dumped Kane and agreed to date me, but I wouldn't hurt you if you didn't. I'm not crazy. You have to believe me."

"I think I do. Let's not spoil our meal talking about it anymore. How's Rex? Do you spend a lot of time with him in the summer?"

"He's great. I get him three nights a week, which isn't enough in my opinion. I don't fight with my ex about it, though. I don't want to hurt Rex."

"You're a good father. Was Rex with you last night?"

"No, I have him on Mondays, Wednesdays and Saturdays, but I'll get him for a week in August. I planned a trip to Disneyland. We're both pretty excited about going." He described the vacation in detail, not stopping until the server delivered their food.

"Rex will love it." Rachel took a bite of her burrito. "What do you do in the evenings when you don't have your son?"

"I watch a lot of movies." His cheeks turned pink, and he glanced away to scoop lettuce back into his taco. "How about you?"

"I play games with my girls and read when I have a chance. I like movies, too. In fact, I watched one last night."

Dennis's expression didn't change. "What do you do during the day?"

"The bookstore keeps me pretty busy. I like to garden and run."

"I'm not much of a runner, but I'm a hiking enthusiast. I really enjoyed myself up at Granite Lake."

"The girls and I had a great time."

"Maybe we could hike together."

"That might not be such a good idea. I'm still seeing Kane."

Anger flashed in his eyes, but his tone was mild. "You just met the guy. Your relationship can't be all that serious. I want you to give me a chance."

Maybe if I give him a little encouragement, he'll slip up. "I'll think about it."

His smile was full of hope. "That's all I ask."

They finished their lunch, and Rachel declined another drink. "You go ahead."

"I'd better not. Alcohol goes straight to my head."

He reached across the table to stroke her hand. Gritting her teeth, Rachel didn't pull away.

"This has been great. I know if we spent more time together, we'd find we have a lot in common."

"We both like the outdoors. Do you garden, Dennis? I'd like to put in a little vegetable garden behind my house, but I need better soil. I don't suppose you have a pickup I could borrow to haul some dirt?"

"No, I drive a small hatchback." His eyes brightened. "My neighbor has a truck. He might let me borrow it to help you."

"Really?"

"Sure. He just got it. It's one of those huge ones with more power than anyone could possibly need. We're friends, so I don't think he'd mind loaning it to me."

"Maybe you could ask him about it and let me know."

"I'll do that."

Dennis insisted on paying the bill then came around the table to pull out Rachel's chair. As he hovered close, she forced herself to remember the stalker's arms around her in the woods. Dennis was the right height.

"Thank you for lunch."

"It was my pleasure. Can I give you a ride to the bookstore, or are you going home?"

"I'm going back to work, but I'd rather walk. It's a beautiful day."

"Not nearly as pretty as you." His cheeks flushed, and his gaze moved from her neckline back to her face. "I'll walk with you, if you don't mind. I hate to see our afternoon together end."

Rachel nodded. Behind Dennis's back, Kane stood and tossed a couple of bills on the table.

Her companion kept up a rambling conversation on the short walk then bent to hug her when they stopped in front of the Book Nook. He smelled of aftershave—a little too much aftershave.

Her assailant had smelled like sweat. If he'd worn aftershave, she hadn't caught any hint of it.

"I'll let you know about using the truck as soon as I talk to my neighbor."

"Thank you. I'd better go."

"Bye, Rachel."

She pushed open the bookstore door, shut it and let out a breath.

Chandra hurried around the end of the counter. "How did it go?"

"Give me a second. Kane should be along shortly."

Three women approached from the rear of the store, each carrying a stack of books.

"Shoot. I need to take care of these customers, but I want to hear every detail. Do you think Dennis Olmstead is the one?"

"I'm not sure. Where's Tim?"

"He's upstairs keeping an eye on things. We've been pretty busy."

Kane came in. Without a word, he strode straight past her. The office door hit the wall with a thud.

Chandra's eyes widened. "Someone's not happy."

Rachel winced. "I'd better go calm him down."

"Good luck."

"Thanks. I think I'm going to need it."

Chapter Nineteen

"I can explain."

Kane's gaze dropped to her exposed cleavage, but there was absolutely no hint of desire glowing in his eyes. He rubbed his temples. "This ought to be good."

"I thought if I gave Dennis a little...incentive, he might say something revealing."

"Honey, nothing would be as revealing as that dress. Jesus! Where did you get that thing?"

Rachel perched on the edge of her desk and picked up a pen she twisted between her fingers. "It's actually a designer original from when I was on the soap opera. Jordan Hale wore it all the time. The producers let me keep it after I quit. Since my stalker is so fixated on Jordan, I thought I could trip Dennis up if he was guilty."

"Did it work?"

"He didn't say anything about the dress, but he spent a lot of time looking at it."

"God, Rachel! He wasn't looking at the dress. He was looking at what's in it. So was every male in the restaurant!"

Her cheeks heated. "The dress isn't that revealing. Take a look at what women wear to the beach, for heaven's sake."

"It shows enough to make a man want to see the rest of the package. I'm mad as hell and still turned on."

Rachel's gaze dropped then flew up again. "That hardly counts. You're easy."

He let out a deep breath. "You have a point. If I promise to quit yelling will you tell me what happened?"

"Sure. Why don't you have a seat and relax." She pointed to the desk chair.

Kane walked over and dropped into it. "It's hard to relax when I want to forget about Olmstead and rip that dress off you." Wincing, he shifted in the seat. "I'll try to control myself. Tell me what your buddy had to say."

"He doesn't own a pickup, but his neighbor does. He said the neighbor just got it, and he thinks he might be able to borrow it to help haul dirt for my new vegetable garden."

"Hot damn. It's worth checking out. Maybe the guy bought a used truck." Kane pulled out his cell, relayed the information to Sheriff Walker then dropped the phone on the desk. "He's sending one of his deputies over to check it out. What else did you learn from good old Dennis?"

"Actually, I felt kind of sorry for him. The way he looked at me made me feel like I was back in high school with the class nerd asking me to the prom. It was painful turning him down."

"I hope to God you did."

"I mentioned I was still seeing you, which definitely didn't sit well with him. Still, he didn't go after me with a butter knife."

"Our stalker may have a little more self-control. I wasn't expecting him to confess."

"Maybe Dennis isn't the stalker. I think he's just a nice man who wants to date me. He can't help it if he's a geek."

"Do the kids still use that word?"

"Probably not, but it fits Dennis."

"You won't get an argument from me. Anything else?"

"He was home alone last night watching a movie—or so he says. I think he was hiding something. He acted weird when he mentioned it."

"Weird how?"

Rachel shrugged. "I don't know, sort of nervous or embarrassed. He wouldn't meet my gaze."

"That's interesting." Kane stared at her with a thoughtful look. "If his neighbor owns a dark-colored pickup, it'll be even more so. Is that all he had to say?"

She nodded. "I'd better change. "Debra Hensley will drop Ivy off shortly."

Standing, he pulled Rachel into his arms. "You can change but not before I get at least one kiss while you're wearing that dress."

She looped her arms around his neck. "Jordan Hale kissed a lot of men while wearing this dress."

"Has Rachel Carpenter?"

Her hair swayed around her face as she shook her head. "Not a single one."

"Good." He covered her mouth with his.

She was breathless when he released her.

"Go ahead and change. I'll wait outside."

"Was that payback?"

"For what?"

"Getting you all hot and bothered before."

Kane grinned. "I like the idea, but it backfired. I'm going to have to cool off in the darkest corner of the bookstore."

She laughed. "Tell Chandra I'll be out in a minute if she needs any help, and give her an update if she's not busy."

"Will do."

Rachel changed into the walking shorts and short-sleeved blouse she'd been wearing earlier then took a moment to run a brush through her hair. Studying herself in the mirror on the back of the office door, she decided she looked about as seductive as an old slipper.

Kane ought to be happy about that. Leaving the office, she headed toward the front of the shop where Kane stood talking to Chandra and Tim.

The front door burst open with a jangle of bells as Ivy and her friend entered.

"Mom, some man wanted me to get in his truck, but I didn't do it." Her daughter gulped for breath. "I ran away just like you taught me." Her hand shook when she flipped her ponytail over her shoulder.

"Oh, my God!" Rachel's throat closed. She dropped to her knees in front of Ivy and pulled her into her arms for a long hug. "Tell me what happened."

Debra Hensley shut the door and gave Rachel a trembling smile. "A man in a pickup approached the girls outside the library. We stopped on the way here to find a book for Melissa. While I was checking it out, the girls waited on the sidewalk. I could see them through the window. I swear they weren't out of my sight for a minute."

"I'm sure they weren't." Rachel eased to her feet and laid a hand on the distraught woman's arm.

"This truck pulled up, and the man in it said he was supposed to drive me to the bookstore." Ivy's eyes were wide. "He said you were hurt, and I was supposed to come with him. But I didn't know him, so I grabbed Melissa and ran back into the library. You aren't hurt, are you?"

"No, I'm not hurt. You did exactly the right thing." She glanced at Kane who was already on the phone. "How long ago did this happen, Debra?"

"Only a few minutes. I hurried the girls straight out to the car and called 9-1-1 while I was driving. Since it's only a couple of blocks, I didn't feel comfortable staying at the library with Ivy when you were so close. They're sending someone."

"I have Sheriff Walker on the line." Kane turned toward the two girls. "I need a description of the pickup."

"It was dark green." Ivy's eyes brightened. "One fender was grayish."

"Two doors or four?"

"Two." Both girls answered at the same time.

"Did it look new or old?"

"Old. There were dents on it and some rust."

"Do you know what kind of truck it was?"

When the girls shrugged, he looked to Debra.

"I couldn't tell. I just saw the back end as it pulled away, and I'm afraid I didn't see the license plate."

Kane relayed the information to the sheriff and hung up. "He's putting the description out now and will be right over." He squatted next to Ivy and Melissa. "I want you girls to tell me what this man looked like."

Ivy wrinkled her nose. "He just rolled the window down a little way, and it was kind of dark in the truck."

Melissa shook her head. "You couldn't see through the windows at all."

"They were tinted?"

Ivy nodded. "The man had on sunglasses, and he was wearing a baseball cap."

"His shirt was navy blue with a zipper."

"I don't think it was a shirt. I think it was a jacket." Ivy corrected her friend. "It was made out of that slick material."

"A nylon windbreaker?" Rachel asked.

"Yes!" Ivy's fear seemed to have disappeared in the excitement of having several adults hang on her every word.

Melissa nudged her. "He had a moustache. It was dark brown and bushy. I couldn't see what color his hair was."

"The ball cap covered his hair. It was blue with a little thingy in front."

"An emblem?" Kane asked.

"Yeah, like the SF on the Giants' caps, only this one was different. I can't remember what it was, but I think it was either orange or red."

Kane looked at Melissa.

She shook her head. "I don't remember either."

"Did you recognize the man, Ivy? Could he have been someone you've met before?"

"I don't know anyone with a moustache like that."

"Think about what he would have looked like without the moustache. Was his nose big or little?"

"Just normal. I couldn't see his face very well. He had his hand over his chin, and he kind of mumbled. Mom, we'd better leave for my swimming lesson, or we'll be late."

"I'm afraid you'll have to miss it today, honey. The sheriff will need to talk to you girls."

"But, Mom, if I don't go today, I won't graduate with my class tomorrow. The teacher gives out certificates on the last day, and I won't get one. Then I'll have to be a dumb dolphin again next summer instead of a shark."

Rachel sighed. "I'm sorry, but talking to the sheriff is more important."

Kane rested a hand on Ivy's shoulder. "I have most of what he'll need, at least for now."

"I'll take her to the lesson." Debra worried her bottom lip between her teeth. "This time I swear I won't let her out of my sight."

Rachel opened her mouth to answer then shut it when Sheriff Walker pushed open the bookstore door. His gaze dropped to the two girls.

"I hear you had a bit of a scare."

"We weren't scared. Can I go to my swim lesson now?"

The sheriff glanced at Kane.

"I have a description of the man, and we have a few things to discuss before you talk to them. I honestly think I have most of what you'll need."

"That'll be fine. I'll speak to you young ladies later."

Rachel stepped forward. "I don't want to trouble you, Debra."

"I'd like to help. I feel awful about letting the girls leave the library alone."

"It's not your fault. Normally I wouldn't hesitate to do the same thing." She glanced at the sheriff and bit her lip. "I'm worried that man will come back."

"I expect he's long gone, but I have deputies in the area, and one of them will keep an eye on Ivy until we get there."

Rachel nodded and hugged Ivy, only letting her go when her daughter tugged to get loose. She forced herself to turn away as Debra herded the two girls out the door. "Let's talk in my office. I'm afraid we're scaring away the customers."

Chandra squeezed her hand. "We'll take care of the store. You do what you need to do and don't be afraid to leave early."

Tim grimaced. "What a day."

"Somehow, I don't think it's going to get any better." Rachel ran a trembling hand through her hair. "Thanks for your help."

She followed both men back to her office. The sheriff finished talking into his radio and took the only chair while Kane leaned against the desk. Rachel shut the door and went straight to his side. He gave her waist a reassuring squeeze.

Sheriff Walker was the first to speak. "Did Ivy recognize the man in the pickup?"

Kane shook his head. "It sounds like he was wearing a fake moustache. He had on dark glasses, a windbreaker and a ball cap. Also, the truck had tinted windows. Obviously he didn't want to be recognized if he couldn't talk Ivy into coming with him. I doubt he would have forced the issue on a busy street."

"But he must have planned it ahead of time if he had a disguise ready." Rachel pressed a hand to her chest. "My God, what would he have done to my baby if she'd gotten into that truck?"

Kane's arm tightened around her. "Ivy's too smart to do something so stupid. The jerk took a chance, but it didn't pay off."

"He's right. Most kids know better than to get into a car with a stranger. It was a long shot, but it shows he's getting desperate." The sheriff leaned forward, and the desk chair squeaked beneath his weight.

"What about Jade and Lark? Jade's at soccer camp, and Lark is at the winery." Rachel pressed a hand to her chest and drew in a long breath. "Will he try to approach them?"

"I don't see how he possibly could if they're with other people. I know you're upset right now, but your girls are safe. Let's hear what happened at lunch with Olmstead. I don't suppose he was wearing a windbreaker and sporting a moustache."

She forced herself to focus on Walker's question. "He had on a polo shirt and was clean shaven. Dennis definitely has a crush on me, but I can't picture him as my stalker."

"Never say never." The sheriff asked her a few more questions.

With an effort, she answered them. All she wanted to do was run after Ivy and never let her youngest daughter out of her sight again.

Finally, Stan Walker cleared his throat and glanced at Kane. "What's your take on the situation?"

"In my opinion, Olmstead would give his left nut for a date with Rachel. The guy has it bad. Still, I'm not certain he would resort to stalking her. Did you find out what type of truck his neighbor drives?"

"Pete didn't see any pickups on the street, but he had an interesting conversation with Olmstead's neighbor. She's eighty if she's a day and was out watering her roses. She gave him a full description of the new truck the guy across the street bought last month. A big four-door Dodge, red, loud and smelly. Apparently, her neighbor two houses up also drives a pickup, an older two door Ford, but it's white. Everyone else on the block drives a car or an SUV."

"Any chance she's mistaken about the color?" Kane gave a half smile. "Possibly she doesn't see as well as she used to."

"According to Pete, the old lady is as sharp as a tack."

"I'd still be interested in knowing what Olmstead was doing last night."

"I would, too, but we can't do much more than question him. Maybe you'll have better luck with Dawson tomorrow."

"I sure as hell hope so."

"In the meantime, I have Brandon questioning people down near the library. Hopefully we'll find a witness who got a look at the license plate on that green pickup."

"Thank you for taking such a personal interest in my problems, Sheriff Walker." Rachel forced a smile. "I know you're busy."

"I want to find this guy before anything worse happens. I'm too old to deal with violent crimes. In fact, I've let my wife convince me to retire this fall instead of running for re-election."

"The town will certainly miss you. You've been the sheriff as long as I can remember."

He grunted. "That's long enough. Anyway, I know just the man to take my place." He winked at Kane then glanced back at Rachel. "I'd like to get an official statement from your daughter and her friend. Do you think she's about done with that swim lesson?"

She glanced at her watch. "It'll be over in fifteen minutes."

"Then let's meet at the pool. I don't think we can squeeze anyone else into your office."

"Thanks for giving Ivy a break. Her lessons are important to her."

"Well, of course they are, and there was no reason to upset her further. This is working out just fine." The older man heaved himself out of the desk chair. "I'll check in with my deputies and see you at the pool."

"Sounds good. Thank you." Rachel followed them out of the office then paused at the counter to speak to Chandra. "I'll be gone a half-hour or so while the sheriff talks to Ivy."

"Why don't you take the rest of the afternoon off? You look wiped out."

"If you're sure, I think I will. I need to have a serious talk with my family about this situation. It's time to take action."

"Good for you." Chandra leaned across the counter to give her a hug. "Be careful. This creep scares me, and I'm not even the one he's after."

"He scares me, too. That's why I intend to do something about it."

* * * *

Rachel climbed into the passenger seat and yanked the door shut. She gave the seatbelt a hard tug before snapping the buckle in place.

"I can't sit back while some freak threatens my children. Taking a shot at me is one thing, but no one hurts my kids."

Kane flipped on the blinker and pulled out onto the street. "We won't let him get anywhere near them. After what happened today, the girls will be on high alert. They'll know this isn't a game. Everyone will be more careful."

"That isn't good enough. You said he'd focus on me. You said my girls would be safe."

He glanced over at her before returning his gaze to the road. "I thought they would be. Hell, Rachel, I wouldn't begin to take chances with your daughters."

"Yet, the man actually spoke to Ivy! I want them completely out of the picture. I want them somewhere safe, and that means far away from wherever I am. They're everything to me. I won't take any more risks." Her voice cracked. "What if you're wrong again?"

Pain exploded in his chest. The last time he'd been wrong, it had cost his partner his life. *And a child had died.* His hands clenched on the wheel as he bent forward.

Rachel shifted in the seat and gave him a worried look. "What's wrong?"

"Nothing." *Nothing he intended to talk about.*

He parked next to the chain link fence surrounding the pool and turned to face her. "Your mom and dad would take them, or maybe Grace or Will."

She shook her head. "They're all too close. I have a brother in Portland and a sister in San Diego. Hopefully several hundred miles between my daughters and this...deviant will be enough."

"Will the girls go along with it?"

"I think so. Jade and Ivy won't mind. It's hard to tell with Lark. Who knows, she might be thrilled to put some distance between us."

"We can talk about it this evening. Let's go get Ivy and finish up with the sheriff."

Rachel let out a huge sigh before she pushed open the door.

As it turned out, the interview was over quickly and elicited no new information. Rachel thanked the sheriff and walked silently back to the car while Ivy ran ahead.

Kane squeezed her arm. "Is something else wrong?"

She shrugged. "I'm not sure. When Ivy described the truck and the man in it, I had the strangest sense of *déjà vu*. I can't for the life of me figure out why."

"Your subconscious will remember in the middle of the night while you're sleeping soundly. Of course once it happens, you can never go back to sleep."

"I hope so. It's really bugging me."

"Shall we head over to the soccer field? It's almost time to pick up Jade."

Rachel nodded. "I'm going to call Mom and invite us all for dinner. I need to tell them what happened, and I should probably do it in person."

"That's a good idea. You can talk to your parents while I take Lark to her dance class."

"You don't mind?"

Kane shut the rear door of the car after Ivy climbed in. "Of course I don't. Let's go get Jade."

* * * *

Audrey poked at the remains of her pork chop. "It makes my skin crawl knowing how close that man got to Ivy." Her shoulders shook. "To think he actually came right up onto your front porch last night, as bold as you please! A person should be safe in her own home. What will he do next?"

Rachel lay down her fork. "I don't know, but he won't be doing anything to my girls. I'm going to call Susan and Russ and see if either of them can take the kids until the police catch this lunatic. If we can book a flight, they'll be on a plane out of here first thing in the morning."

"What?" Jade stared across the table, a forkful of mashed potatoes suspended halfway to her mouth. "You've got to be kidding. I have soccer tomorrow."

"And I have swimming." Ivy's lip stuck out in a mutinous pout. "I'm not missing my last day."

Kane cleared his throat. "What if they go on Friday since their activities will be over?"

"I don't know, Kane. I hate to wait even a day."

"We've managed this long. We'll make it work."

"Go where exactly?" Lark walked in from the kitchen and returned to her chair. "What're you talking about?"

"I'm talking about you girls spending some time with either your Aunt Susan in San Diego or your Uncle Russ in Portland. I want you somewhere safe."

Jade swallowed a mouthful of food. "Do we get to vote on where we go? Because if we do, I vote for Aunt Susan's. Scott promised to teach me how to surf."

"Either place is fine with me, but it will depend on who can take you. It's possible your aunt may have plans for the holiday weekend."

"Can we at least ask her first? I really want to learn to surf."

"If your sisters agree."

Ivy bounced in her chair. "Fine with me. I haven't spent time with Tanya and Trista in forever. How long are we staying?"

"Yeah, Mom, how long?" Lark pushed away her half-eaten plate of food. "What if the police don't catch this creep? It could be the whole summer. I like working in the winery gift shop. I don't want to go to San Diego or Portland. Why can't I just stay here?"

"Because I want you to be safe. Because this man could have taken Ivy today if she hadn't been such a quick thinker. God only knows what he might try next."

Lark snorted. "Only a lame-brain would get in a car with a stranger. She wasn't in that much danger."

"Any danger is too much. You're all three going, and that's final."

"Not tomorrow. I need to finish my dance clinic."

Rachel let out a sigh. "All right, we'll book a flight for Friday. I'm not going to relax until I know you're safe."

"I'm glad that's settled." Audrey crossed her arms over her chest. "Since no one is eating anyway, you might as well go call your sister."

Rachel left the table, grabbed her purse, headed out to the patio and collapsed into a chair. She spent a moment pulling herself together before she punched in her sister's number. Thankfully, Susan was home.

"Mom told me about the attack on you in Tahoe, but I had no idea the stalker followed you home. Of course I'll take the girls."

Rachel leaned her head against the padded seatback. "You're sure? I can check with Russ and Dara if having the girls will cause a problem for you. I know how busy you are at the law office."

"Actually, I took a couple of weeks off so the kids and I could do some fun things together this summer. The timing's perfect."

"I can't tell you how much I appreciate this."

"Hey, that's what sisters are for. You'll call me with the flight times when you have them?"

"First thing in the morning."

"Good enough." Susan's voice took on a teasing quality. "I'd tell you to take care of yourself, but I hear you have this really gorgeous man to do it for you."

Rachel choked on a laugh. "Mom has a big mouth."

"Is it true?"

A sigh shook her. "Yeah, it's true."

"Good for you. I hope it works out."

"Right now, all I can think about is keeping my girls safe. Thanks, Susan."

"You're welcome."

Rachel clicked the phone shut and closed her eyes. When she opened them, Kane stood in front of her.

"Well?"

"Susan agreed to keep them."

"That's good." He took her hand and pulled her up from the chair.

As she rested her cheek against his chest, warmth spread through her.

"I can't tell you how relieved I am."

"I am, too." He dropped a kiss on her forehead. "Shall we go tell them?"

"In a minute. Right now, I don't want to move. I want to enjoy having you hold me just a second or two more."

His arms tightened. "Take all the time in the world."

Chapter Twenty

The scent of fresh bread, pickles and onions was thick in the air of the deli. Kane ordered a turkey with provolone on wheat and iced tea. Taking his food to an outside table, he claimed a chair facing the street and hoped Dawson would show. When the man hurried across the parking lot a moment later, Kane eased his grip on the sandwich.

"Sorry to keep you waiting." Curt flashed a quick smile. "Let me get something to eat, and I'll be right out."

He reappeared several minutes later carrying a meatball sub, a pickle spear and a bottle of water.

"Thanks for meeting with me." Kane pushed out an empty chair.

"Not a problem. I finally got my client's computer up and running, so I have plenty of time." He took a healthy bite of his sub and wiped tomato sauce off his fingers with a napkin. "So, how I can help you?"

"The authorities told you about the attack on Rachel Carpenter?"

"They did, although I'm not sure why they would question me. Rachel seemed nice enough, but I barely know her. Tiffany thinks she's terrific."

"You're still dating Tiffany?"

"Sure, though not as often as I'd like. Work has been overwhelming since we got back from Granite Lake."

"Must be tough keeping a beautiful girl like Tiffany hanging. I'd worry some other guy might snag her interest."

Curt shrugged. "Tiffany and I aren't exclusive, and lately I've had other priorities."

"Your business?"

He looked up from the dripping sandwich. "Yeah, it's really taking off. I neglected it for a week to attend my family reunion. Now I'm paying the price." He cocked his head as he looked at Kane. "Why, exactly, am I a suspect in a police investigation?"

"Someone followed Rachel up at Granite Lake, most likely a fellow camper. The authorities think it's the same guy who attacked her in Tahoe."

"Wow. None of those guys seemed the type."

"People can be good at hiding secrets." Kane sipped his tea. "I don't suppose you were with Tiffany Tuesday night or have an alibi for yesterday around two?"

"Why, what happened?"

"Let's just say Rachel's stalker has been busy."

Curt pulled several napkins from the dispenser and wiped his hands. "No, I was home alone with my computer Tuesday night and all day yesterday. Anyway, why would I hurt Rachel?"

"Her stalker doesn't want to hurt her. He just wants her."

"No offense to Rachel, but she's a lot older than me. Besides, I have a girl."

"Tiffany of the non-exclusive relationship?"

"That's right. It works for both of us."

"Must be nice."

"It is. Why are you involved in the investigation? I thought you worked in San Francisco."

"I do, but I'm on leave until we catch this creep. Rachel and I have grown close." His gaze never left the other man's face.

"Good for you." Dawson crumpled his napkins and dropped them into the basket holding the remains of his sandwich. He picked up the pickle and took a bite. "You should finish your lunch. The food here is excellent."

"I will. Don't let me keep you if you have someplace to go."

"I was thinking of driving into the city, taking in a ball game. I need a break after the hours I've put in lately."

"You like baseball?"

"Sure, but football's my game. Too bad the Niners stink."

"It's a shame. Not like the good old days when Bryce Carpenter was playing."

"He was a hell of a quarterback." Curt met his gaze with a steady regard. "Just because I was a fan of Carpenter's doesn't mean I'm stalking his ex-wife."

"Of course not." Kane finished his sandwich. "Will you be around if I have any more questions?"

"Sure. Good luck finding the man who's after Rachel."

"Thanks. I'll be in touch."

Curt crossed the street to head straight to a parking lot where he unlocked the door of a black sports car. When he pulled out onto the road, he waved.

Kane lifted a hand in response. The man hadn't seemed very concerned about being a suspect in an assault investigation. He wondered why. After finishing the iced tea, he tossed his trash into a nearby can. Then, using a napkin, he carried Curt's water bottle to his Jeep and slipped it into a plastic bag. The bottle had Dawson's prints all over it as well as his DNA. It wouldn't hurt to have a sample, just in case. He'd send it to the lab along with Dennis Olmstead's water glass, which he'd removed from the table when he left the restaurant the day before.

All he needed now was a sample of Bob Mayfield's DNA, and his collection would be complete.

* * * *

Rachel answered her office phone and smiled. "Hey, Grace, how's it going?"

"How's it going?" Her sister's voice was heavy with sarcasm. "It's going fine. I'm not the one with a predator watching my every move. Why didn't you call me?"

Rachel pictured her sister's green eyes snapping with indignation. Grace liked to be kept in the loop first hand.

"I was too tired to talk after we got home last night. Everything sort of caught up with me. Thank God for Kane. At least I was able to sleep knowing we'd be safe with him in the house."

"Mom told me you're shipping the girls off to Susan's."

"I want them someplace safe." Her gaze strayed to the framed photo resting on the desk. All three of her daughters smiling back at her. She'd taken it the previous Christmas, catching the girls laughing at Daisy's antics in a pile of wrapping paper. They looked the way children should, carefree and happy. Her voice caught. "I don't want this deviant anywhere near them ever again."

"They'll be safe in San Diego, and they'll have a great time."

"They're excited to go, at least two out of three are."

Grace laughed. "Let me guess, our little tattooed friend is putting up her usual resistance."

"I think it's more for show than anything. Once Lark's at Susan's, she'll enjoy herself."

"What's not to like about going to the beach or trips to the zoo and Sea World?"

"Exactly. Their flight leaves out of SFO at ten tomorrow morning."

"Why don't you stop by my apartment afterward? We can have lunch together."

"Kane will be with me, and I should come straight back to the bookstore. We're always busy over the Fourth of July with holiday shoppers."

"You can take a few extra hours off work. As for Kane, bring him along. I'll call Nolan to see if he can join us."

"I'd love to get together." She took a breath. "Let's do it." Making plans that didn't revolve around what her stalker might be doing lightened her mood.

"Great. I'll see you tomorrow."

Rachel hung up the phone and rubbed her temples. Despite getting a decent night's sleep, a tension headache nagged her. She shook a couple of aspirin out of the bottle in her desk drawer and downed them with a swallow of water. If she didn't eat something, the headache would only get worse. Grabbing her purse, she stood and nearly ran into Dennis Olmstead outside the office door.

"Rachel." A smile stretched his lips as he reached out a hand to steady her. "Sorry, I didn't mean to startle you."

She stepped away. "I wasn't expecting to see you there."

"I stopped by to tell you about the truck."

"The truck?"

He followed her into the office as she backed toward the desk.

"I asked my neighbor if I could borrow it, but he's going out of town this weekend. I'm sorry. I was hoping I could help you with your garden." His eyes brightened. "I don't suppose you'd like to take a hike with me instead?"

"I'm afraid I can't. I have to drive into the city tomorrow, but thanks for checking with your friend."

He blocked the only exit and stuffed his hands in his pockets. "What about next weekend? I could borrow the truck then."

"I'll probably just get the soil delivered, but thank you."

When Tim appeared behind Dennis's shoulder, she let out a breath.

"Rachel, we could use you up front."

"I'll be right there. Dennis, I'm afraid you'll have to excuse me. Duty calls."

"Oh, of course. I didn't mean to bother you at work."

"It wasn't a bother."

His shoulders slumped as he shifted to let her by. "I guess I'll see you around." Turning, he walked through the store, dodging around a line of customers at the counter.

Rachel nodded. "Wow, you really did need me."

"It's been busy with tourists getting a jump on the weekend." Chandra handed a man with a camera slung over his shoulder a cappuccino and a cinnamon muffin. "But I was worried when I saw that guy disappear into your office."

"That guy was Dennis Olmstead."

Chandra's dark eyes widened. "The man you had lunch with yesterday?"

Rachel nodded. She helped three more customers before there was a lull. "I still don't think Dennis is the one stalking me, but I was a little nervous."

"Kane isn't going to like this."

A family of four came down the stairs, followed by Tim.

Rachel rang up their purchases then smiled. "Have a great day."

The door closed behind them, and she glanced around the store. A woman with two young boys browsed in the children's area, but otherwise the shop was empty. "I guess the rush is over."

"I think I'll go get a sandwich while it's slow." Tim turned at the door. "Do you want me to bring you something?"

"A Caesar salad would be great." Rachel reached for her purse. "I intended to go eat when Dennis showed up."

"You stay here with Chandra. Kane would be pissed if I let you wander around town alone."

Rachel grimaced. "What was I thinking, planning a trip down the block all by myself?"

Chandra patted her arm. "Better safe than sorry."

The rest of the day passed without incident. When Kane picked Rachel up shortly before four, she smiled in satisfaction at the amount of work she'd accomplished. She shut the bookstore door behind them.

"Did Curt show up?"

"He did, but I couldn't read him. The man was pretty blasé about being a suspect in a police investigation."

He opened the car door for her then ran around the front of the SUV to climb inside.

"Maybe he wasn't concerned because he has nothing to hide."

"Or he's the cocky sort who doesn't believe he'll be caught."

Rachel studied Kane's chiseled profile and tight lips. Lines radiated from the corners of his eyes, and he tapped the steering wheel as traffic stalled. She wasn't the only one feeling the pressure.

"Curt didn't strike me as the super confident type, just an average guy getting through each day. I couldn't figure out what Tiffany saw in him. They didn't seem very well suited."

"She must see something. According to Dawson, they're still dating, although not exclusively."

"He doesn't mind?"

"Didn't seem to." Kane parked next to the soccer field and turned to face her. "How was your day?"

"Fine. I talked to Grace. She wants us to have lunch with her and Nolan tomorrow after we put the girls on their flight. I said we would."

He smiled. "Just like the first time we met."

She leaned back in the seat. "Can you believe that night was less than a month ago? It seems so much longer."

He picked up her hand and stroked her wrist with his thumb. "Is that good or bad?"

"Definitely good."

With a sigh, he placed her hand back in her lap. "Looks like soccer camp is over along with our quiet moment. The girls are headed this way."

Rachel released her seatbelt. "I want to go thank the coach."

"I'll come with you."

They left the car walking side by side. They weren't holding hands, but it felt like they were. Rachel's heart beat a little faster.

"Your stalker must be taking a vacation day. After what happened yesterday, maybe he'll back off."

Her chest tightened. "I almost forgot. Dennis came by the bookstore earlier."

Kane stopped and turned. "What for?"

"He wanted to let me know he can't borrow his neighbor's truck this weekend, but I think it was just an excuse to see me."

"Maybe I need to have a little talk with Dennis."

"Kane, don't." She touched his arm. The corded muscle flexed beneath her fingers. "I'm sure Dennis is harmless. Anyway, Tim kept an eye on me."

"Good for Tim." His jaw snapped closed as Jade ran toward them.

"Mom, Mom. The girls voted me MVP for soccer camp this week." She skidded to a stop. Grass stains covered her shirt. Her braids were ragged, but a smile lit her eyes.

"Congratulations, honey, that's terrific."

"Your daughter is a talented soccer player." The coach paused beside them. "I hope she'll pursue the sport."

"Oh, I will."

"She certainly enjoyed your camp." Rachel wrapped an arm around Jade's shoulders. "I'm sure we'll sign up again next year."

"Great. Enjoy the rest of your summer vacation."

"Way to go, Jade." Kane examined her certificate after the coach walked away. "Earning an MVP award is quite an honor."

"Thanks." She pushed her hair away from her face. "I'm hot. We worked really hard today."

"You can take a cool shower when we get home, but right now we have to go pick up your sisters."

"Then I have to pack. I can't wait to try surfing."

When she ran ahead to the car, Kane squeezed Rachel's hand.

"She certainly is single-minded when it comes to athletics."

"A regular chip off the old block. Bryce would have been so proud of her."

He dropped her hand and opened the car door. "Let's go gather the rest of the troops."

* * * *

The evening was beyond hectic. Rachel squeezed one more shirt into Ivy's overstuffed suitcase then let out a breath. "Those bags are going to be overweight." She eyed the pile of luggage in the entry hall. "I can't believe you girls really need to take so much stuff with you."

"It's not like we know how long we'll be staying." Lark dropped her suitcase with a thump. "I refuse to wear the same clothes over and over for the next month."

"Let's hope it doesn't come to that. I couldn't stand having you gone so long." Rachel's heart ached, the reality of their departure suddenly sinking in. "I'll miss you guys."

Ivy threw her arms around her mother's waist in a fierce hug. "I'll miss you, too."

Rachel hugged her back and forced a smile. "You'll have so much fun in San Diego you won't have time to miss me."

Daisy stuck her nose between them and whimpered softly. The dog knew something was up. Ivy released her mother to hug Daisy.

"I'll miss you, too." She pressed her face into the dog's fur. "Mom, you have to promise to play with Daisy while we're gone. She'll be sad if you don't."

"I will." She rubbed the dog's ears. "Now, off to bed so you'll have plenty of energy tomorrow morning."

After the girls were settled upstairs, Rachel sat down next to Kane on the couch and slumped against the cushions. An all-news channel droned on the TV. He turned it off then pulled her against him.

"How are you holding up?"

"Okay, I guess. My kids have never been away from me for more than a night or two at a time. It's going to be tough to let them go." She sighed. "I hope I'm making the right decision."

He stroked the hair away from her face. "You're *absolutely* making the right choice. This guy is willing to take risks, and that makes him unpredictable."

"Thank you."

"For what?"

"Reassuring me I'm not overreacting." She closed her eyes and pressed fingers against the bridge of her nose. "Lark thinks it's all an elaborate ploy on my part to get you alone in the house."

Kane laughed. "She's giving me a lot of credit."

"Lark's no dummy. She sees you're important to me."

"Look, I know your decision to send the girls to San Diego isn't about us."

She opened her eyes. "No, but their absence will change the dynamics around here. How do you feel about that?"

He picked up her hand and held it between both of his. "I'd like nothing better than to spend the next week in bed with you, but I'm not going to push."

"You wouldn't have to push very hard." Emotion churned inside her. She looked up and met his gaze. "Am I kidding myself, believing what's between us is more than mutual lust?"

"Is that how you see our relationship?"

"No, and it scares me. I don't want to get hurt."

"Before I met you, I was simply going through the motions. Some days I didn't want to get out of bed in the morning. I didn't want to go to work, and I didn't care about much of anything. You've changed that."

"Is it me or the situation? Maybe hunting for this predator has shown you what a difference you make. Your work is part of who you are."

He sighed. "I suppose, but this isn't about my career. When we were up at Granite Lake, I woke up eager to start the day because I looked forward to seeing you. You pulled me out of a sea of self-pity without even trying."

She tightened her grip on his hand. "You've given me something, too. You've made me realize I'm still a woman, not just someone's mother or daughter. After I left Bryce, I let those needs fade away. It's nice to know they're still there."

Kane pulled her across his lap and nuzzled her neck. "I'm more than willing to satisfy all your needs." His breath whispered across her face.

For a minute she let herself enjoy the feel of his lips against her skin. She allowed herself the luxury of touching the rough stubble of his beard, stroking his silky, overlong hair. When his hand caressed her breast, she pulled away.

"As much as I'd like to end this evening differently, I should go to bed. Alone. The girls—"

"You will. I understand your priorities." Taking her face between his hands, he kissed her. "Except I have to tell you, you're killing me here."

Rachel groaned. "I'm sorry about that. You make it hard."

"That's not the only thing hard. I respect your choices, but I still want you. We can't go on like this indefinitely."

Standing, she crossed the room to pause by the window with its drawn curtains. "I realize that. Once this is over—" She bit her lip. "Do you think he's out there?"

Kane stepped up behind her. "I can check around outside if it'll make you sleep better."

"Don't. Knowing you're here is enough."

He walked with her to the foot of the stairs. Daisy trailed at their heels.

"I think I'll check anyway, just to be sure. Sweet dreams, Rachel."

* * * *

Kane stood alone on the lawn, scanning the shrubs along the edge of the property for movement that didn't belong. Confident Rachel's stalker was nowhere in the vicinity, some of the tension drained out of him. His shoulders slumped, and he ran a hand through his hair.

She was safe. The girls were safe—for now.

He'd blown it completely, thinking this freak wouldn't target them. The same way he'd blown it, letting his partner go into the alley ahead of him that night. His fists clenched, remembering the dense, bone-chilling fog, the sharp crack of gunfire and thud as Mike hit the pavement. Knowing even as he shouted into his radio that help wouldn't come in time. A second, echoing shot, pain exploding in his chest as he returned fire…then nothing.

He took steadying breaths, anything to stave off a full-scale attack of anxiety. This time the situation would end differently. He couldn't live with the outcome if it didn't. Not again.

Not if it meant losing Rachel.

The woman made him ache with need. While she kept him at arm's length, he was falling hard—for the whole damn life-in-a-small-town-complete-with-kids-and-a-dog package. Not that she had any reason to keep him around once he put the bastard who threatened her away for good. He was nothing but a burned-out cop. The job he'd chosen just might kill him, but without it he had nothing to offer.

With a moan, he sunk to the grass. Pressing his hands against the cool blades, he took a few more deep breaths. When his phone vibrated in his pocket, it was a relief to let go of his churning thoughts.

He answered without looking at the display. "Lafferty."

"Are you still at Rachel's house?"

A half-smile tilted his lips. "Sitting in the middle of her front lawn in the dark wondering how the hell I ended up here—and how I can convince her to let me stay."

Jed snorted. "I was expecting a yes or no answer, but okay. Uh, should I call the men in the white coats to come get you?"

"Probably. I'm losing it." He pressed one hand to his chest. "Every time I think about the job waiting for me in San Francisco, I want to go hide in a hole."

"As long as Rachel's in that hole with you?"

"Yeah." He let out a sigh. "I'm so caught up in her life, I've forgotten I have one of my own. Maybe because this one's so much better." Flopping backward, he stared up at the star-filled sky. "Here, I'm making progress. Once I catch the goddamned asshole terrorizing Rachel and her family, it'll be over for good. For them. When—*if*—I go back to work, the shit never stops. There'll always be some new psycho spreading misery."

"I guess there's only one question to consider."

"Only one? I can think of a dozen."

"One that matters. Are you there for Rachel or to play hero and show the world you really can make a difference?"

"I don't give a damn about the world."

"Yet, you're still there. I rest my case."

"I care about Rachel. She's what matters—Rachel and her girls."

"Kane?"

"What?"

"Change can be positive. Healthy. Don't make a decision based on what's expected of you. Give yourself permission to be happy for once."

"What if I'm not the change she wants?"

"What if you are?"

His fingers tightened around the phone. "There's only one way to find out. But not until I stop this son of a bitch. Until then, life's on hold, and what I want doesn't matter."

"Then find him."

"I intend to."

Disconnecting the call, he lay still until the damp grass sent a shiver through him. Levering to a sitting position, he held his head in his hands. When this was over, Rachel might decide being with him was too complicated—or flat out not what she wanted—and send him back to the life he'd come to dread. Still, he had to try. A glance toward her darkened bedroom window quickened the steady beat of his heart. *This* was what he wanted. If he had to risk a piece of his soul to get it, so be it.

Rising to his feet, he strode across the lawn and entered the house, shutting the door behind him with a firm click.

Chapter Twenty-One

As her girls disappeared down the long hallway past the security gate leading to the loading area, Rachel held back tears as long as she could. Finally, she gave up.

Kane handed her a clean, but wrinkled, handkerchief. "It won't be for long."

"God, I hope not." She wiped her eyes and straightened her shoulders then crushed the handkerchief in her palm. "I want to hit something."

"You can take a swing at me if it'll make you feel better."

Her lips curved in a weak smile. "It wouldn't."

They walked to an observation area to wait. Standing at the window, she leaned against Kane Eventually, the big silver behemoth taxied slowly to the runway, roared down the tarmac then lifted into the dull gray sky. The weather was as gloomy as her mood, which hadn't been improved by the hassle she'd had at the security check point. Kane had flashed his badge, but the attendant still hadn't allowed them to accompany the girls to the gate.

She sniffed a couple more times and blew her nose. Once the plane was swallowed up by fog, she turned away. Neither spoke on their way to the short term parking garage as they dodged the hurrying crowds.

"Do you want to drive?" He pulled the keys from his pocket and gave them a little toss.

"Not really. I've never been a fan of city traffic. I'll give you directions to Grace's apartment."

"Is it okay with you if we stop by my place first? I should collect my mail and see if any of my plants are still alive."

"Of course. If it wasn't for me and my problems, your plants wouldn't be suffering."

Kane gave her a sideways glance before focusing on exiting the garage and merging into the stream of traffic leaving the terminal area. "They're just plants. If they're dead, I'll buy new ones."

Rachel wiped away a few stray tears. "I'm sorry. I'm not very good company." Her lips trembled, and she clamped them together.

He stopped at a red light and reached over to take her hand. "It's fine to miss your girls. Would it make you feel better to have a good cry and get it out of your system?"

She choked on a laugh. "No, it wouldn't make me feel better."

He let out a breath. "Thank God. I never know what to say to a crying woman."

She managed another weak smile. "Then it's doubly nice you offered."

Traffic was surprisingly light, and it didn't take long to reach Kane's apartment in an older but well-kept complex on the outskirts of the city. Rachel waited while he tugged a stack of mail out of his box then followed him up three flights of stairs.

He unlocked the apartment door and pushed it open.

Rachel stared. "It looks like a jungle in here."

Huge potted ferns stood by the sliding glass doors leading to the balcony. A row of African violets graced the kitchen windowsill, and the living room was crowded with a variety of plants.

"They're sort of overwhelming. My neighbor must be watering them for me. I gave her my spare key. I'll have to thank her."

Rachel wandered over to the balcony and stared out at the fog hanging low over the city. "Typical July weather in San Francisco."

Kane looked up from the mail he was sorting. "Ah, hell." His hand hovered over an envelope with childish printing on the front.

"What's wrong?" Rachel stepped up behind him.

He dropped into a chair and opened the envelope. The letter was printed in purple crayon. After a moment, he closed his eyes. "It's from Mikey, my old partner's son. He wants to know why his Uncle Kane never visits anymore."

"Why don't you?" Rachel rested her hands on his tense shoulders.

"It hurts too much. I look at those kids and know Mike would still be with his family if I'd gone into the alley first."

"What happened to your partner wasn't your fault."

"Maybe, maybe not. It doesn't make me feel any better either way. Mike had more to live for. He had a wife and two kids."

Rachel knelt beside him and grabbed his arms, giving them a shake. "You have people who love you. You matter to your father and your brother. You matter to me."

He pulled her into his arms and held her tight, his cheek resting against her hair. "I think I love you, Rachel."

She shifted to press a kiss to the side of his neck. "Good, because I think I love you, too."

His gaze locked with hers. "Now what?"

"We finish sorting this mail then go meet Grace and Nolan for lunch."

His eyes glimmered with amusement. "You're very nonchalant about my declaration."

"Inside, I'm turning cartwheels." She kissed him lightly on the lips. "Love doesn't make all our problems go away. Let's take it slowly and see what happens."

"Will you tell Grace?"

"Grace has a big mouth. Let's keep it to ourselves for a while."

"Maybe that's best. Once I catch the bastard harassing you we can have a serious talk about the future."

"Today we'll just have fun. I need to have fun, Kane."

He was slow to release her. "I know you do. Let me finish up here, and we'll go."

After sorting the rest of the mail, he laid Mikey's letter on the counter. "I'll call them. It was wrong of me to avoid those kids. They lost their dad. They don't need to lose me, too."

Rachel squeezed his arm. "You have a big heart."

"I don't know about that." He locked the apartment door behind them. "Sometimes I'm a selfish bastard."

She shook her head. "I don't believe that for a minute."

They hustled down the stairs then out to the street to climb into the car. Kane pulled into traffic. "Where to?"

"Take a right at the corner. I'll call Grace to tell her we're on our way." A minute later she snapped the phone shut. "She wants to meet us in Chinatown, said she has a yen for Chinese."

"Sounds good to me. Is Nolan going to make it?"

"According to Grace, he's already en route."

Traffic slowed to a crawl as they reached the congested streets of Chinatown. Kane glanced over. "Do you mind walking a couple of blocks? I see a parking spot up ahead."

"Of course not. I could use the exercise. I haven't been running at all since we got back from Tahoe."

He parked the SUV in the tight spot with remarkable ease. "I'll run with you. We can go this evening if you like."

"That would be great. I hate that this man has forced me to change my habits."

"It'll be easier to follow your usual routine without the girls to worry about."

"I know, but I'm going to miss them."

He squeezed her hand then took it again as they walked along the busy sidewalk. The shops they passed smelled of incense and were crowded with souvenirs. When they reached the restaurant Grace had chosen, a petite Chinese woman wearing traditional garb approached. "Table for two?"

Rachel shook her head. "We're meeting another couple."

"Aw, yes. I was told to be on the lookout for a pretty lady with red hair. You are she?"

"I am."

They followed the hostess toward the rear of the restaurant where tables overlooked a garden shrouded in fog. Grace and Nolan both waved.

"Well, finally." Her sister frowned. "I was expecting you ages ago. Was the girls' plane delayed?"

"We stopped to pick up a few things at Kane's apartment. Rachel took a seat and gave Nolan an easy smile. "You're still putting up with this crazy lady?"

"I certainly am." With an obvious effort, he tore his gaze away from Grace and greeted Kane. "I hear you're spending your vacation working."

He grimaced. "Hopefully it'll be over soon."

"Really? Do you know who this asshole is?"

"I've narrowed down the suspects. With the girls safely in San Diego, we should be able to draw him out."

"You're going to use Rachel as bait?" Grace's voice rose. "Is that necessary?"

"I'm not going to put her in any danger, but I'm hoping to goad this nutcase into making a mistake."

When Grace opened her mouth, Nolan stopped her with a look. "Kane knows what he's doing."

"It's okay." Rachel reached out to lay a hand on her arm. "Kane doesn't let me go anywhere alone. I'm lucky to shower without an audience."

Grace's gaze moved from her sister to Kane and back. A smile curved her lips. "With the girls gone, that may change."

Kane grinned. "I like the way you think. The server's hovering. Let's order."

When the food came, Rachel sniffed deeply. "The Chinese restaurant in Vine Haven isn't bad, but this is heavenly."

Grace nodded. "There're definite perks to living in the city, and food is one of them."

Kane dove into his Kung Pao chicken. "Just the way I like it—hot enough to blister your tongue." He nudged Nolan. "How's the shrimp?"

"Mild enough you can actually taste the flavor."

The two men grinned at each other.

Rachel looked from Nolan to Kane. "What's the joke?"

"He hates everything I like and vice-versa."

"Only when it comes to food. Is anyone going to eat the last egg roll?" Kane pushed his plate away. "It's all yours. How's work?"

"Business as usual." Nolan frowned. "I was lucky to get a couple of hours off. I'm in the middle of a double homicide investigation with too many suspects to count."

"I don't miss it."

"Some of the guys are wondering if you'll come back."

"I haven't made up my mind yet."

"You'll figure it out." Nolan's eyes filled with sympathy before he raised a hand to signal for a check. "I hate to break this up, but I have witnesses to question."

The men split the bill, and they left the restaurant.

Pausing on the sidewalk, Grace pulled Rachel aside and hugged her. "Be careful."

"I will."

"I meant with your heart. If Kane breaks it, I'm going to kill him."

"I don't think he will. He's a great guy."

"He'd better be." Grace pushed her long hair over her shoulder as they joined the men. "Nail the bastard who's harassing my sister, Kane."

"I intend to. It was good seeing you again, Grace."

"Likewise. I'll call you soon, sis."

Arm in arm, Grace and Nolan disappeared into the fog.

"You know, I think those two just might make it." Rachel turned toward Kane. "Wouldn't that be something?"

"Am I supposed to answer that?"

"Nope. Let's go home. If they aren't too busy in the bookstore, I think I'll take the rest of the day off."

Rachel called her daughters the minute she walked into the house. When she hung up the phone, relief mixed with an ache around her heart.

"How are they?" Kane entered the kitchen with Daisy at his heels.

"Excited. Susan and Evan have a pool. The kids were all out swimming when I called."

"They'll be fine." He pulled her into his arms.

She leaned against him and breathed in the clean scent of his skin. "I know. Even Lark sounded like she was having fun."

"Then maybe we should, too."

"Did you have something in mind?" Her lips curved in a smile against his throat.

"Let's see, we could go upstairs and get naked, or we could go for that run. Your choice."

"How about both? Run first then…" She lifted one brow.

Kane groaned. "Daisy and I will wait right here while you change. Otherwise we'll never make it out of the house."

"I'll be right back."

Rachel hummed while she pulled on shorts and a tank top. She dug her running shoes out of the closet and laced them up, then tied her hair back in a ponytail. Happiness filled her as she left the room, knowing Kane was waiting. She hadn't felt these flutters in her stomach over a man in a long time. The sight of Kane kneeling at the foot of the stairs, scratching Daisy's stomach, sent her heart soaring.

His eyes mirrored her happiness. "Ready to go?"

She nodded, and they set off down the street with Daisy galloping about madly. When they reached the main road, Kane stopped.

"Should we put her on a leash?"

Rachel patted her fanny pack. "I have one with me, but I don't usually use it. Believe it or not, she's smart enough to stay away from cars."

They ran side by side, their faces turned up to soak in the heat of a late afternoon sun. The air was redolent with the fragrance of grapes ripening on the vine and the dusty scent of baked earth. They turned onto a dirt path that ran along the edge of her parents' vineyard and followed it up into the rolling hills. When they reached the crest, Rachel paused to look out over the valley, her breathing short and deep.

Kane pulled off his T-shirt, used it to wipe his sweat-drenched body then tucked it into the back of his shorts. He offered her a drink from his water bottle. "Nice view."

The bit of breeze cooling her sweat-dampened skin felt heavenly. "It may not be as spectacular as the scenery around Granite Lake, but it has a restfulness that renews my soul." She smiled self-consciously. "That sounded pretty sappy."

He stepped up behind her to pull her against his damp chest. "It doesn't sound sappy at all. I know exactly what you mean." He let out a labored sigh. "There were plenty of times when I was in some dark, stinking alley that I wished for a place like this. I don't think I can go back."

"I'm glad." She turned in his arms and touched the scar on his chest. "I couldn't stand it if something happened to you."

"There aren't any guarantees, even if I leave the city. Any time you work in law enforcement you're taking a risk. Being a cop is all I know."

She laid her cheek against his shoulder. "Still, getting out of the city seems like a step in the right direction."

His arms tightened. "I want to make love to you right here."

"So what's stopping you?" She lifted her face for his kiss. Desire slammed through her as his mouth covered hers, hot and wet. A single kiss ignited her to a fever pitch. She whimpered as she pressed against the bulge in his shorts.

"This is a public trail." He groaned and cupped her bottom in his hands, drawing her closer still. "Anyone could come along."

"Daisy will bark if she hears someone."

Kane glanced at the dog lying in the shade of an old oak tree with eyes half closed. Her tail thumped the ground twice.

"Are you sure?"

"Pretty sure." When his hand delved into her shorts, she gasped. "Right now I don't care much. We'll be quick and hope for the best."

Kane stripped off her shorts and panties, dropping them in the grass. Tugging his own shorts down, he grasped her hips and lifted her in his arms. Her eyes widened as the length of him settled deep inside her, filling her body, mind and soul. His legs trembled as she jerked against him.

"Oh, my God, Kane. Oh, my God." She threw her head back and gritting her teeth as the first wave of pleasure crashed over her.

He let out a yell and surged within her, sinking to his knees. They rested in the grass for a long moment, their bodies still joined.

Daisy stood and let out a short bark. Tail wagging, she stared up the trail.

Rachel scrambled into her shorts and stuffed her underwear into her pocket. When a man appeared on the trail above them, she was clothed but disheveled.

"Is everything okay? I thought I heard a shout." He hesitated for a moment. "Rachel?"

She smiled weakly as he came closer. "Hi, Dennis."

Dennis Olmstead stopped a few feet away. "I thought you were going into the city today."

"I did. We just got back a little while ago."

"Oh." His eyes glazed as he studied her sweat dampened body and straggling ponytail. "I thought someone was hurt. Guess I was wrong."

Kane cleared his throat. "Were you following us?"

Dennis's face reddened. "No, I was out hiking. I hike out here a lot." His gaze moved from Kane's bare chest to Rachel's flushed cheeks. "I won't keep you, and I won't bother you anymore. I get the picture."

"Dennis..."

He left without a backward look.

"That was certainly interesting."

The man disappeared down the hillside.

Rachel pushed a hand through her hair. "Do you think he's the one? Do you think he'll leave me alone now?"

"I wouldn't count on it. He looked pretty angry."

"I think it was mostly embarrassment."

He glanced over. "That, too. I'm pretty sure he knew what we were doing."

"Oh, God. If he isn't my stalker, how am I ever going to face him again?"

"You won't have to. If he isn't your stalker, he'll avoid you like the plague. Don't worry about it."

"I'll try not to." She drew a long breath. "Well, that little encounter certainly killed the mood. We may as well head home."

Kane pushed a curling strand of hair away from her face. "We'll get this son of a bitch, Rachel. Whoever he is, I swear to you we'll get him."

With her eyes closed, she gave a short nod then opened them and took off running with Kane close behind.

Holiday traffic was heavy on the main road, and Rachel kept Daisy close to her side when they neared town. Kane touched her arm as a sports car and a pickup slowed then sped past. When they reached the house, she collapsed into one of the wicker chairs on the front porch.

"That was quite a run."

He took the chair opposite hers and smiled. "I can honestly say I've never enjoyed exercising more."

Heat that had nothing to do with exertion suffused her cheeks. "I don't know what I was thinking, doing what we did. If Dennis had come along two minutes sooner…"

"Hmm…that might be a good idea."

Rachel pushed to her feet then turned to face him. "What are you talking about?"

"Putting on a show for our Peeping Tom. If we piss him off enough, he may show himself. Then I'll bust his ass."

Her eyes widened. "You want to make love while some pervert watches?"

"We won't take it to that extreme. A little kissing and touching with the curtains open should do the trick."

"What if he isn't watching?"

Kane ran a finger down the length of her thigh. "Making out with you isn't exactly a chore. Since we'll have to miss the fireworks show tonight, we'll make our own."

"I almost hope he doesn't show up." She reached down to pull him out of his chair. "Let's go see what there is to eat. Lunch was hours ago, and I'm going to need sustenance to pull this off."

* * * *

He stood on his toes and stretched to reach the top shelf of the closet. Moving aside his winter sweaters, he pulled down a plastic box and carried it to the table to open the lid. A revolver rested on the padded lining. The metal of the short barrel gleamed dully beneath the light. His hands shook as he inserted a clip and checked the safety.

Lafferty needed to be taught a lesson. Jordan had looked up at the man and smiled, their bodies damp. His stomach churned, imagining what they'd been doing besides running to get so damned sweaty. He'd been tempted to jerk the steering wheel then and there to end it, but the risk of hitting Jordan instead of her shadow was too great. The cop stuck to her like dog shit on a shoe. Getting Jordan alone would take a drastic move. He'd failed to grab the little girl, but he wouldn't fail tonight.

The drive to the barn where the battered pickup was parked was a short one. His thoughts whirled as he traded one vehicle for another.

They'd left him no choice. If he wanted a chance with Jordan, he had to get Lafferty out of the way. He'd waited patiently through all the years of her marriage to Bryce Carpenter, and once she was finally free of the

Jannine Gallant

philandering asshole, he'd given Jordan a chance to make a new life for herself. He wasn't interested in a rebound relationship. He wanted forever.

Even a patient man like him had his limits. Right now, he was damned tired of waiting, sick of always losing out to someone else. Never again would he be second best. Once they were together, Jordan would discover Kane wasn't half the man he was.

Heart pounding, he carefully set the gun on the seat next to him then drove into the approaching darkness.

Chapter Twenty-Two

A light burned softly in the shadows as Kane and Rachel stood in front of the big living room window. He wrapped his arms around her and dropped a light kiss on her lips.

"Relax. There's no reason to be so tense."

"I can't help it. Do you think he's out there?"

"If he is, he'll have to come closer to see anything. The second he does, I'll hear him."

"That's why you opened the windows?"

He nodded and ran his lips down the side of her neck. "Pull my shirt off."

Rachel let out a breath and smiled. "Better you than me." Lifting the hem of his T-shirt, she tugged it over his head.

"Now, let's give him something to think about."

His lips fastened on hers, and his tongue moved in ways that made her forget all about their possible audience. Finally, he pulled back.

"I wasn't planning to get this turned on." His chest rose and fell, pressing against her breasts. "I never had to give chase with a boner before."

A giggle bubbled up. "Don't make me laugh, Kane. This is serious business."

"Very serious." He kissed her again.

A cry erupted in the darkness beyond the windows.

Kane's head jerked up. He turned sharply as something flashed outside. The front window shattered. Spinning, he threw Rachel to the floor then clamped a hand around his arm. Blood seeped between his fingers.

"Oh, my God, he shot you!"

"Stay down and call 9-1-1." He grabbed his T-shirt off the floor, pressed it hard against his flesh then tossed the shirt aside and ran toward the door.

"Oh, my God. Oh, my God." Rachel's hands shook as she picked up the phone off the coffee table and dialed 9-1-1. She scooted behind the couch to answer the operator's questions.

"Stay calm, ma'am. Help is on the way."

"Make sure they know my friend gave chase. I don't want someone to shoot him by mistake."

"Describe your friend."

"He's over six feet tall with brown hair, and he's not wearing a shirt. His name's Kane Lafferty. He's a detective with the SFPD."

"Thank you, ma'am, I'll make sure they're on the lookout for him."

"I hear a siren. The police just pulled up outside."

"That's great. You can hang up now and go talk to them."

Rachel's finger trembled as she stabbed the off button. Standing, she hurried to the door just as Deputy Hendricks raced up the porch steps.

"Someone shot Kane. He's bleeding, but he went after the guy."

"Was he badly hurt?"

"I don't think so. I hope not."

"Go back inside and lock the door. Stay away from the windows. The sheriff should be here in a couple of minutes."

Rachel nodded. "I'll be fine. Please go help Kane."

"Is he on foot?"

"Yes, but I didn't see which way he ran."

"Go inside." The deputy hurried back to his car and backed out of the driveway. The siren wailed and tires screeched as he drove away.

Rachel locked the door as instructed then stroked Daisy's head. The dog whimpered and pressed against her side. She retrieved the phone from the floor, sat down and punched in her brother's number. On the third ring, a sleepy voice answered.

"Will, my stalker shot Kane." Tears welled in her eyes. "He was bleeding."

"Rachel! My God, are you all right?"

"I'm fine. Kane went after the man. That young deputy was just here, and the sheriff is on his way."

"Did you call Mom and Dad?"

"No, I didn't want to worry them."

"I'll be right there. Sit tight." He hung up.

Rachel lowered the phone to her lap and leaned against the couch cushions. Holding a handful of Daisy's fur in a comforting grip, she closed her eyes and prayed. When flashing lights reflected off the ceiling, she went to the door to greet the sheriff.

His eyes were kind as he patted her shoulder. "Kane's fine. He's with my deputy. It's just a flesh wound. You, on the other hand, don't look so good. Let's make a hot cup of tea with lots of sugar. It'll help with the shakes." He walked with her to the kitchen, filled the teakettle with water then turned on the burner.

"Did they catch the guy?"

Daisy growled low in her throat when footsteps pounded up the porch steps. The sheriff swung around and reached for his weapon.

Rachel grabbed his hand. "It's my brother."

"Why's he here?"

"I called him."

"Rachel?" Will's voice called from the entry.

Daisy's tail wagged, and she ran out of the room.

"We're in the kitchen." She gave Sheriff Walker a feeble smile. "I needed the moral support."

When Will appeared followed by the dog, Rachel introduced him to the sheriff.

Will took a seat next to her at the table and squeezed her hand. "What happened?"

"She was just about to tell me." The sheriff settled his bulk onto a chair across the table. "First, I'll answer your question. The suspect got away in the same pickup as before. The license was obscured by mud, so Kane couldn't get a number. We have an APB out on the truck. Every cop in the area is looking for it."

"Is Kane coming back here?"

"He and Brandon are checking something out first."

Rachel pushed her hair away from her face with a shaking hand. "He should go to the hospital. I don't care if it's only a flesh wound."

"My deputy suggested it, but he's a hard man to convince."

"I'll convince him." Rachel's tone was grim.

Sheriff Walker smiled. "I bet you will. Now, let's hear what happened tonight."

The kettle whistled, and Will got up to make the tea.

"Kane thought we could flush out my stalker. Unfortunately, the plan worked a little too well."

Will's hand stilled with a teabag dangling over the cup before he dipped it a few times. "You set up the whole scenario?"

"Kane wasn't supposed to get shot. He wanted to provoke the man into exposing himself."

The sheriff leaned back in the chair. "Exactly what did you do?"

"My stalker has watched the house before, probably on more than one occasion. Kane thought if we could lure him in close enough, he'd be able to catch him."

Will handed her the freshly brewed tea. "What was the lure?"

Rachel's cheeks heated. "We turned down the lights and kissed in front of the living room window."

Walker grunted. "You got more of a response than you bargained for."

Using both hands, she lifted the cup to her lips to sip the steaming liquid. "That maniac shot Kane. He pushed me out of the way and took off after him. I called 9-1-1. That's about it."

"You took a risk." The sheriff eyed her steadily. "I guess Kane felt it was worth it."

"He knew he was in danger?" Rachel's voice rose.

"I imagine so." Sheriff Walker heaved himself out of his chair. "I'll go look for the bullet in the living room. I have Pete checking outside for evidence. We should be able to determine where the suspect was standing when he fired."

Will studied her with worried eyes while she drank her tea. "This is getting to be a regular habit."

"What is?"

"These late night phone calls. First the flat tire, and now this. You're playing hell with my sleeping habits."

Rachel's eyes widened. Tea slopped onto the table as she dropped her cup. "That's it!"

"What? What's wrong?"

"When Ivy described the truck the man was driving, I had the strangest feeling I'd seen it before. Now I know where it was. Do you remember a pickup was just leaving when you arrived to fix my flat tire?"

"You told me someone had stopped to offer help."

"Yes, he was driving an older, dark pickup."

Will sat straighter. "What did the driver look like? Could he have been one of the suspects?"

"I don't know. I never gave him a second thought."

"Try to remember."

"It was really dark." Rachel closed her eyes and forced the memory. "He had on a ball cap and sunglasses. I remember thinking it was odd the man wore dark glasses at night."

"What color was his hair?"

"I don't remember."

"What about his voice? Did any of the men at Granite Lake sound familiar when you first met them?"

"Just Dennis, and that's probably because I talked to him at school when Lark was one of his students."

"It wasn't because he's your stalker. We can eliminate Olmstead from the mix." Kane walked into the kitchen.

With a cry, Rachel jumped up and ran to him. "Are you okay?"

He hugged her to his side. "It's just a scratch. There's no reason to worry."

The *scratch* was wrapped in a gauze bandage sticky with blood. Kane wore a T-shirt Rachel didn't recognize.

"I'm taking you to the ER, and I don't want an argument."

"You can take him just as soon as we clear up a couple of details." Sheriff Walker followed his deputy into the room. "Sit down, Kane. You, too, Brandon. Now, let's hear what you found out."

Brandon Hendricks cleared his throat and flipped open his notebook, blue eyes bright with excitement. "I found Kane two blocks south of here. Blood ran down his arm, and he was swearing a blue streak."

"That's because I lost the bastard. He jumped in that rattletrap pickup and was gone before I reached him. I would have had him if I hadn't been so damned light-headed."

"That settles it. You're going to the emergency room. You might need a blood transfusion or something!"

The sheriff held up a hand. "He isn't going to keel over just yet. Let's hear the rest."

"I called in a description of the vehicle, our location, and the direction the suspect was headed. Then I slapped a bandage on Kane's arm to stop the bleeding and gave him a spare T-shirt I had in my car. I also offered to take him to the hospital, but he refused."

Kane sighed. "I wish people would stop harping about a little scratch. I wanted to check on Olmstead. He lives less than a block from where we were. If he was home in bed, then he couldn't be our man."

"You went to his house?" Sheriff Walker's brows rose.

"There was no sign of the pickup anywhere nearby." Brandon referred to his notes. "It took a while, but Olmstead answered the door when we pounded on it. He was wearing a flannel bathrobe. Kane barged in. The man put up a half-hearted protest, but he didn't refuse us entry."

The sheriff hit the table with his fist. "God damn it, Kane, without a warrant any evidence you found would have been thrown out in court."

"Good thing Olmstead's only crime is watching porn flicks and yanking his own chain. The movie was on pause on his bedroom TV. It was pretty obvious what he'd been doing."

Rachel glanced over at Kane. "That's why he looked guilty when he said he enjoyed movies."

Kane shrugged. "The man may be a bit of a pervert, but he's not your stalker."

"So it's either Bob or Curt?" Rachel glanced around the table.

"Looks that way." Kane squeezed her hand. "What were you and Will talking about when we came in?"

Rachel told them about the flat tire and the man who had stopped to help her.

Will gripped the edge of the table. "If I hadn't come when I did, this psycho could have taken Rachel then?"

"Shit." Kane's hand tightened on hers.

"You didn't recognize him, Rachel?" Sheriff Walker asked.

She shook her head. "It was too dark to see much of anything."

"So this son of a bitch was following her before she went up to Granite Lake." The vein throbbed at Kane's temple. "It's possible he's been following her for months."

"Now he's stepped up his game." The sheriff frowned. "He was obviously prepared to kill or injure Kane in order to get to Rachel. The man is extremely dangerous."

"Don't forget he was provoked." Will leaned back and frowned.

"That's a good point. Jealousy could be the trigger."

Kane drummed his fingers on the table. "We have a profiler on staff at the department. I'll get her take on this guy to see if it fits either Mayfield or Dawson. That way we can focus on the most likely suspect."

"Call her in the morning, Kane. I'll check our two remaining suspects for alibis. Maybe we'll get lucky and one of them was at a party with a dozen witnesses." The sheriff heaved himself out of his chair. "Right now I want to finish up out front then go home to bed. Brandon, let's see if Pete found anything besides that partial footprint. Rachel, you're free to take Kane to the emergency room if you can get him to go."

"Oh, he'll go."

Will stood. "I'll take off then. Sharon is probably worried sick."

"Thanks for coming." Rachel hugged her brother.

"I'm glad you called. Would you like me to break the news to Mom and Dad, or do you want to do the honors?"

"I may as well do it. I'll phone them from work in the morning."

Will nodded. "Take care of her, Kane."

"That's my plan."

Once they were alone in the kitchen, Rachel put her hands on her hips and studied him with a frown. "No more excuses. We're getting your arm checked out."

He rolled his eyes. "Let's get it over with."

* * * *

It was two o'clock before they returned home. Kane's wound had been cleaned and dressed, and the doctor had given him a shot of antibiotics to combat possible infection.

Rachel paused in the entry as Daisy rushed to greet her. She rubbed the dog's ears while her gaze turned toward the glass strewn across the living room floor.

"I forgot all about the broken window."

His hands dropped onto her shoulders. "You're exhausted. Go to bed. I'll clean up this mess in the morning."

"Aren't you coming with me?"

"I'll stay down here. Until that window is repaired, the house isn't secure. I won't take any more chances."

"He wouldn't come back tonight, would he?"

"Probably not, but I'd rather be safe than sorry. I'll take a look around upstairs just to make sure no one left any surprises while we were gone." Once Kane determined the house was undisturbed, he pulled Rachel into his arms and kissed her. "Try not to wake up at the crack of dawn. You need your rest."

"I can't sleep late. I have to take all the cinnamon rolls we baked earlier into the store." She leaned against his chest. "This isn't the way I pictured the night ending."

"That makes two of us." He kissed her again then pulled away with a groan. "I'll see you in the morning."

Rachel slept hard until the alarm sounded. After a quick shower, she went downstairs with Daisy at her heels. The smell of freshly brewed coffee and bacon drew her, but she paused to poke her head into the living room. It was neat, tidy and free of glass. Her lips tightened as she glanced toward the empty window frame.

Kane smiled as she headed straight to the coffee pot. "How do you like your eggs, scrambled or over easy?"

"However you're having them is fine."

"Over easy it is. Pop down that toast, please."

Rachel did as he asked then leaned against the counter. "You're very at home in the kitchen."

"I don't mind cooking. I've never been a big fan of those frozen meals, so it was either learn how to cook or starve."

"Or eat take out. Grace lives on pizza." Rachel sipped her steaming coffee.

Kane expertly tipped two eggs onto a plate. "Have a seat. I put butter and jam on the table." He handed her the dish and gave her a lingering kiss. "What's the plan for today?"

"I have to work. What about you?"

"I have a few phone calls to make, and I need to stop by the sheriff's office. Then I may go have more chats with Bob and Curt."

Rachel laid her toast back on her plate. Her stomach churned. "Who do you think it is?"

"My money's on Bob, but I wouldn't stake your life on it."

"Why do you think Bob's responsible?"

"Because the Dawson reservation for Granite Lake was made long before you decided to go up there. Still, it could have been a coincidence you chose the place where Curt was attending his family reunion. Coincidences do happen."

He sat next to her with a full plate of food. "Eat."

"I'm not very hungry."

"Tough. Would you let your kids skip breakfast?"

Rachel smiled. "No."

"Then eat."

She picked up her fork and took a bite of egg. "You're good for me, Kane. Thanks for making breakfast."

"You're welcome. I also called a glass shop. Someone will be out to replace the window this afternoon. Thankfully it's a size they have in stock."

"You are a marvel of efficiency, Mr. Lafferty."

"I certainly am." When they finished, he picked up their empty plates and stepped over Daisy on the way to the sink. "Where was she last night?"

"As close to me as she could get. At one point she tried to climb on the bed, but I kicked her off. She's been very worried about me."

"I guess we know where her loyalties lie." He looked into Daisy's soulful brown eyes. "I'm the one who got shot, and she hasn't given me a second glance."

"Speaking of which—how's the arm this morning? The bandage looks clean." She walked around the table to study the white gauze dressing with a critical eye.

"I changed it. It's a little sore but healing nicely."

Rachel linked her arms around his neck. "Did I thank you properly for being a hero last night?"

Kane snorted. "Getting shot doesn't make me a hero."

"I don't know. Seems pretty heroic to me." She kissed him, and her stomach fluttered. "I should make you leave. Being here with me put you in the line of fire."

"Do you actually think I'd go?" He pushed a lock of hair behind her ear.

"No, so I won't waste my breath."

"Smart woman. Go get ready for work while I wash these dishes."

"I'm ready to go now. I'll clean up the kitchen. Pour yourself another cup of coffee and relax for a change."

Kane reached down to rub Daisy's ears. "I'm not very good at relaxing."

"So I've noticed. If it'll make you feel better, you can help by feeding the dog."

"I suppose it's something. All I want to do is help. I want to make this madness go away for you."

Reaching up, she stroked his cheek. "Without you, I would have slipped over the edge into complete and utter panic. With you, I have the strength to cope. Don't ever doubt your worth, Kane. Having you beside me means everything."

"Good, because I'm not going anywhere."

Chapter Twenty-Three

Rachel shouldered her way through the bookstore door carrying a tray of cinnamon rolls and called out a greeting to Ellen.

"I hear you had some unwelcome excitement on my days off. Did the girls get to San Diego without a problem?"

"The girls are fine." She set the pastries on the counter. "They're planning to spend the day at the beach."

"Lucky them." Ellen shut the cash register and offered a sympathetic smile. "I imagine you miss them."

"I do, but I'm more thankful than I can say they weren't around last night."

"What happened now?"

When Rachel told her, Ellen's eyes widened behind her glasses.

"Are you kidding? There's no doubt this psycho is a real threat. Someone could get hurt—or worse."

"It might be a good idea if you, Chandra and Tim think about your own safety. Maybe you should each take some time off until this man is caught."

"How would you run the bookstore without us?"

Rachel shrugged. "I'd have to close for a while."

"You can't do that. This is our busiest time of the year."

"I know, but I wouldn't forgive myself if one of you was hurt. He shot Kane. God only knows what he'll do next."

"Do you really think we're in danger?"

"I don't know." Rachel rubbed her temples.

"Why do the police think he shot Kane?"

"He was probably motivated by jealousy. When he saw me with Kane, he lost control."

"If that's the case, there shouldn't be any danger to the three of us. We'll be fine."

Rachel squeezed her arm. "If you're certain, I'll go call my parents and tell them what happened last night."

"That doesn't sound like much fun. I'll let you know if it gets busy."

Rachel gave her a weak smile. "Thank you."

Dreading the conversation, she sat down at her desk and turned on the computer before reaching for the phone. Twenty minutes later, she hung up. It had taken some doing, but she'd finally convinced her mother she wouldn't be any safer if she moved back home with them. Determined to get some work done, she went online and pulled up her e-mails.

Her hand stilled above the keyboard before she jerked away as a chill crawled along her skin. Nestled amongst her business correspondence was an e-mail from *Jordan's True Love*. With a shaking hand, she picked up the phone and dialed.

"Hey, beautiful, what's up?"

Kane's voice calmed her jumping nerves.

"I have an e-mail from someone called *Jordan's True Love*. Should I open it?"

"Don't do anything. I'll be there in a few minutes."

Rachel hung up and left the office. She took over for Ellen at the coffee bar, needing the familiar routine of making lattes and selling pastries. Kane walked in a few minutes later accompanied by Brandon Hendricks.

She handed a cappuccino to a young mother then hurried over.

Kane took her hand. "Brandon is a computer whiz. If the guy who sent the e-mail left a trail, he'll find it. This could be a break for us."

"I hope so." She followed them through the store.

Reaching her office first, the deputy sat down at the desk to print out the e-mail. Then he spent the next half-hour trying to track its origins. Finally, he sat back in the chair with a frustrated sigh. "I'm hitting a blank wall. Whoever sent this is good."

Kane crossed his arms over his chest. "Should we consult an expert?"

"I don't like to brag, but I am an expert. This guy didn't leave a trace. He either knows his way around a computer or paid someone who does."

"Strange he'd suddenly contact Rachel through e-mail."

"You must have provoked him last night."

"That, or he's only now found a safe way to reach her electronically."

Brandon nodded. "What does our psycho have to say?"

Kane laid the printed copy on the desk.

The deputy read it and whistled. "He sounds pissed."

Rachel stepped closer. "Let me read it, Kane."

"It's not pleasant."

"I don't expect it to be, but I need to know what he's thinking."

He moved away from the desk and handed her the sheet of paper. Her hand was steady as she took it and read.

My beautiful Jordan—From the first moment I saw you, I knew you were destined to be my one true love. I've waited years for the time to be right. I wanted everything to be perfect. Now you've ruined it with your cheap relationship with that two-bit cop. You've become a slut and a grave disappointment. To my credit, I'm willing to overlook your transgressions. Once you're with me, you'll forget all about any other men you've known, but I'm losing patience. My time with you is now. If you continue to cheapen yourself, I'll be forced to resort to drastic measures. Come, my beautiful Jordan, accept your destiny. Let's not do this the hard way.

She dropped the paper on the desk and jerked back her hand. "Yuck. What do you think he'll do next?"

"I'll fax this to the profiler to get her opinion." Kane put his arm around her and hugged her close. "We'll catch him, Rachel."

"Should I close the bookstore?"

"I don't think that's necessary. The store's usually pretty busy, so reaching you here would be difficult."

"With this new development, Sheriff Walker will approve more frequent drive by patrols of the property. That should be an additional deterrent."

"Thank you, Deputy Hendricks."

The young cop's cheeks turned pink. "Call me Brandon."

"Thank you, Brandon." Rachel forced a smile.

"No problem. By the way, neither Dawson nor Mayfield has an alibi for last night. Both claim they were home alone."

Kane scowled. "Any news on the pickup?"

"A few similar vehicles were spotted last night, but none of them panned out."

Rachel ran a hand through her hair. "So where do we go from here?"

"I'll talk to Beth, the profiler I mentioned." Kane let out a frustrated sigh. "Maybe she'll be able to give us a starting point."

"Sheriff Walker wants to finish the in-depth background checks on our two suspects." Brandon stood. "Maybe that will turn up something."

"I guess I'll go back to work, then." Rachel stepped toward the door. "All this waiting is so frustrating."

"We're doing everything we can, Mrs. Carpenter."

"I know you are, and I appreciate it." She gave him a reassuring smile.

Kane touched her arm. "Do you mind if I use your office?"

"No, of course not. Make yourself at home."

The rest of the day flew by thanks to a steady flow of customers. At five o'clock, she left Ellen and Tim to close the store and drove with Kane to the sheriff's office. Sheriff Walker called them into a conference room where Brandon Hendricks and Pete Lowery were already seated. Two steaming pizza boxes, a six-pack of cola and a pile of paper plates sat in the middle of the table.

"Have a seat, Rachel." The sheriff pulled out a chair. "Help yourself to pizza if you're hungry."

She glanced up at him. "Doesn't your wife expect you for dinner?"

"It's my poker night with the boys. I'll head straight to the game as soon as we finish here." Sitting down, the sheriff picked up a slice and took a huge bite, chewed then swallowed. "So, let's get to it. What did we learn today? Kane, start with what the profiler had to say."

"Beth had some interesting observations about the stalker. He probably had self-confidence issues as a child but at some point overcame them. However, when it comes to Rachel, he still fears he's unworthy. That's why it's taken him so long to act. He probably hates the way she makes him feel, but his fixation won't allow him to let her go. I should say let go of his fantasy."

"Why does he always refer to her as Jordan?" Pete looked like he'd blow away in a stiff breeze, yet he'd demolished two slices of pizza.

"Beth believes he fixated on Rachel during the time she was on *Days of Desire* playing Jordan Hale. To this whack job, Rachel *is* Jordan, then and now."

"Let's hear a little about Jordan." Sheriff Walker glanced at Rachel. "What was this character like?"

"She was basically a good girl, wholesome but with a sexy side. It was always a man who lured her into compromising situations, and there were quite a few. The viewers loved her."

"So this sweet, naïve girl was led astray by bad men, just like Kane is doing now."

Kane looked up from his piece of pizza. "Good observation, Stan. Rachel's stalker doesn't blame her. He blames me."

"Too bad he's tired of waiting for Rachel—or Jordan—to see the light." Brandon popped the top on a soda.

The sheriff nodded. "Did your profiler have any insights as to his next move?"

Kane frowned and dropped his half-eaten slice back onto his plate. "She thinks he'll try to create a situation to draw Rachel away from me. He won't hesitate to use force again if he has to, but it wouldn't be his first option. She doesn't believe this man was the type of kid who tortured small animals. He isn't inherently violent."

"Would he hurt Rachel?" Pete asked the question, and Rachel subdued a shudder.

"Not unless he lost all hope of winning her over, and he isn't even close yet." Kane snorted. "He still thinks he can somehow earn her affection."

"But he wouldn't hesitate to take another shot at you if it served his purpose." The sheriff took a swig of his drink. "What about his childhood, any clues there?"

"Beth said it was probably fairly normal."

"That's not much help. All right, now for our two prime suspects. Pete, you start."

Pete swallowed the last of his pizza and wiped his hands on a napkin. "I checked into Curt Dawson's background. He grew up in Nebraska with two sisters and parents who are still married. From what I gathered through phone conversations, he wasn't a popular kid, but he dated quite a bit in high school. He went to college in Colorado then worked for a dot-com company that went broke several years ago. After holding a couple of short-term jobs, he started his own computer tech business in Santa Rosa. It seems to be doing fairly well." Pete paused to clear his throat then took a sip of cola. "He's currently dating a woman named Tiffany Randolph, but it doesn't appear to be serious. Dawson goes clubbing occasionally, though he isn't a real social guy. Most nights he spends alone."

"Anything else of interest?"

"He used to see a shrink but quit going after moving to California. There's no way to access those records without a court order."

"And we won't get one without a lot more evidence." The sheriff frowned. "What was your overall take on him?"

"On the surface he seems fairly well adjusted with no glaring hang-ups. His social life is a little curious. He's dated a lot but never had any lasting relationships. Maybe he's just not into commitment. A lot of thirty-year-old men aren't."

"True." The sheriff turned toward his younger deputy. "What about Bob Mayfield?"

Brandon looked down at the notes lined up on the table. "Mayfield is an interesting character. According to his sister, he was a loner growing up. Never more than one or two friends at a time. In high school he smoked some weed and skipped school a lot. According to his test scores, the guy was intelligent, but he wasn't motivated. After high school he went to work for a private mail company and quit recently when his grandfather died. Mayfield inherited a lot of money and property."

Kane leaned forward on one elbow. "If the grandfather was rich, why didn't he pay to send Bob to college?"

"Mayfield wasn't interested. The old man paid for the older sister's education. He was something of a hermit, lived up in Lakeport most of the year but didn't socialize with the locals."

"Does Mayfield date?" The sheriff reached for another piece of pizza.

"He doesn't appear to." Brandon glanced up from his notes. "He didn't have many friends at work, Chip Stevens being one of the few. According to Stevens, Mayfield has never had a girlfriend. He picked up a few women in bars and has used the services of prostitutes in the past, but that's about it. Right now he's moving to Marin from Vallejo. He bought a house by the beach courtesy of the inheritance."

Kane frowned. "The guy's a misfit. Is he still doing drugs?"

"From what I could learn, he smokes pot but isn't using anything harder."

The sheriff wiped his hands on his napkin. "So he's a loner with no girlfriend. Mayfield could fit our profile. On the other hand, so could Dawson. His social life is a little odd as well."

Kane sat back and crossed his arms over his chest. "I'd like to have a second talk with both men. I think I'll look Mayfield up tomorrow while Rachel's at work."

"Don't push too hard. I don't want any phone calls about police harassment."

"I don't work for you, Stan. I'll speak to him strictly as an interested civilian."

"I can't stop you from doing that." The sheriff gave a grunt as he pushed away from the table. "We're done for the night."

After helping to clean up the trash, Kane and Rachel left the building and headed home. He locked the door then pulled the shades on the first floor windows while Rachel fed Daisy. She smiled when he opened a bottle of wine and poured two glasses.

"Sit down and relax. You've had a rough day."

"No rougher than yours." Sipping the wine, some of her tension drained away. "Anyway, I can't relax for very long. I have muffins to make."

Kane leaned against the kitchen counter. "Wouldn't it be easier to use a bakery?"

"Not as profitable, and I enjoy baking." She set down her glass and went to the refrigerator, returning with eggs, milk and cream cheese. "You can get the flour and baking powder out of the pantry for me." She broke eggs into a bowl she'd pulled from the cupboard. "Bring those strawberries, too, please."

"What else can I do?"

Rachel raised an eyebrow. "Are you in a hurry?"

"Maybe. The window's repaired, so I don't have to sleep on the couch tonight."

Warmth coursed through her. She took a breath. "Wash the strawberries and cut them up into pieces. I'll call the girls while I'm mixing the batter."

"That's the spirit." He grinned as he passed her on the way to the sink. "Multi-tasking is a beautiful thing."

Rachel dialed her sister's number and updated her on the previous night's shooting.

"I can't believe this is happening." Susan lowered her voice. "Are you going to tell the girls?"

She positioned the receiver between one ear and her shoulder. "No, it would just worry them."

"It worries me. Are you sure you're safe?"

"The place is locked up tight, and Kane is with me." Rachel turned on the oven then folded the strawberries into the batter. "We'll be fine. How's everything there?"

"Wonderful. We had a great time at the beach. I promised everyone a trip to the zoo tomorrow."

"Susan, you don't have to entertain them so lavishly. They'd be happy spending the day in your pool or at the park."

"I don't mind. I'd planned to take my kids, anyway."

"At least let me pay. I gave Lark a credit card for emergencies. Charge the entrance fees."

"Paying for the zoo isn't going to break me."

"I feel guilty about it. You're already doing me a huge favor by keeping the girls."

"Don't feel guilty. We're enjoying having them. Do you want to talk to Jade? She's standing at my elbow, and I think she's going to explode if she doesn't tell you her news."

"Put her on. Thanks, Susan."

"You bet. Take care of yourself."

"Mom! Guess what?"

Jade told her all about her surfing lesson. Then Ivy relayed every detail of the giant sand castle she'd built with her cousins. Finally, Rachel spoke to Lark.

"Hi, honey. How was the beach?"

"Okay, I guess."

"Did you try surfing?"

"No, I just worked on my tan. Yes, I wore sunscreen."

"Good girl. I love you."

Lark was quiet for a moment. "When can we come home?"

"I'm not sure, but the police are making progress. They eliminated another suspect."

"Which one?"

"Mr. Olmstead."

"I guess that's good. It would have been weird if your stalker turned out to be my old teacher. Is Kane there?"

"He's helping me make muffins."

"Is that what people over thirty call it?" Lark's voice hardened.

"Lark!"

"It was a joke. Bye, Mom."

The phone went dead. Rachel hung up and smiled. "My daughter was in rare form."

"Lark usually is."

"They're having a terrific time. Susan is spoiling them rotten."

He put his arms around her. "Good for Susan. You deserve a little spoiling, too."

Rachel glanced over at the timer. "I'm counting on it, but not for another six minutes and forty seconds."

"I can think of several ways to spend the time."

His breath was warm on her neck.

Rachel quivered. "Washing dishes?"

"That wouldn't be my first choice, but let's get it done."

The kitchen sparkled in record time. Rachel left the muffins on the counter to cool with a dishtowel over the top of them.

"All finished."

"Good. Let's go to bed."

Chapter Twenty-Four

Outside, a bird chirped as dawn broke.

Eyes flickering open, Rachel stretched, her back coming up against a hard, warm chest. Smiling, she snuggled closer.

"If you keep wiggling that sweet little tush of yours, you're going to get more than you bargained for." Kane's voice rumbled in her ear.

"Who says?" She rolled over until they were nose to nose. "Maybe that's what I was counting on."

He slid between her legs. Taking her face in his hands, he kissed her. "Good morning, beautiful."

"It certainly is a good morning. I love you, Kane."

"I love you, too."

He pushed inside her, filling her soul.

Her breath whooshed out. "Oh, my."

Light streaked across the ceiling as they moved together in a rhythm as old as time. When they reached a mind-shattering end, he rolled with her until she lay across him, limp and sated. A cool breeze blew through the partially opened window, drying her damp skin. When she opened her eyes, Daisy's furry face was inches away.

"Go lay down."

"I am lying down. In fact, I may never get up again."

She smiled against his shoulder. "I was talking to the dog."

"Is that mutt still here?"

"Yep. I think she was critiquing your style."

"Oh, yeah? How'd I do?"

"A ten, definitely a ten."

Opening his eyes, he smiled. "Let's go take a shower and see how I score in the water sport category."

"I thought getting up was beyond your abilities?"

"I have amazing powers of recovery where you're concerned." He rolled her to her back and levered himself out of bed. "I'll go turn on the shower."

The man was truly gorgeous. A strong back rose above a firm butt and long, muscular legs. Her mouth went dry, and she licked her lips. When he turned in the doorway, she could barely drag her gaze above his waist.

"Don't be long."

"I wouldn't think of it." Rachel sat on the edge of the bed and pushed her hair out of her eyes. The shower started just as the phone rang. She reached for the bedside extension. "Hello."

"Mom, I forgot to pack the new shirt I bought, the blue one with the stringy things. I think it's in the dirty clothes. Can you mail it to me?"

"Good morning, Lark. You're up awfully early."

"Jade and Scott wanted to go surfing this morning before the zoo. I have to share a room with her, and she isn't exactly quiet. Can you send the shirt?"

"Sure, honey. I'll wash it for you today and mail it tomorrow."

"Thanks. What're you doing?"

"Shower then breakfast and work."

"Rachel, the shower's hot. What's taking you so long?" Kane's voice drifted into the bedroom before him. He paused in the doorway. "Sorry, I didn't realize you were on the phone."

"Mom, is that Kane? Is he in your bedroom? God, I knew this was going to happen. I knew you only wanted to get rid of us so you could sleep with him!"

"You know very well why I sent you girls to San Diego, and it had nothing to do with Kane."

"Sure it didn't. There probably isn't even a stalker. You probably made it up to get rid of us!"

"Lark, calm down please."

"I don't want to talk to you. This blows."

The dial tone buzzed. Rachel took a breath before placing the phone carefully in the cradle.

Kane sat next to her and wrapped an arm around her shoulders. "Should you give her some time to cool off before you call her back?"

"I suppose so."

"I'm sorry about that. I didn't know you were on the phone."

She gave him a half-hearted smile. "It's my fault. I shouldn't have been so anxious to jump into a relationship I wasn't ready to share with my children."

"You're a grown woman. You're entitled to a private life."

"I know, but this isn't just about me. I'm a package deal, and I have to think about how the two of us together will affect my girls."

"I hope they'll be affected in a positive way. The girls like me. Even Lark, although she won't admit it."

"That's an understatement. She wasn't exactly thrilled to find out you were in my bedroom at the crack of dawn."

"That's because she doesn't want to see her mother as a sexual being."

"I wasn't planning to throw it in her face."

"Let her spend the day at the zoo and calm down. You can talk to her about it tonight."

Rachel nodded. "That's probably best. I'll even promise not to obsess over it all day. At least I'll try not to." She straightened her shoulders. "Do you think there's any hot water left?"

"I sure hope so." Kane took her hands and pulled her off the bed then gave her a little push toward the bathroom. "Let's find out."

* * * *

Bob Mayfield's new home was a weathered gray redwood house with a bank of windows facing an incredible ocean view. It wasn't huge, but it was a far cry from the apartment in Vallejo. Kane's shoes crunched on the crushed shell walkway leading to the front door. He rang the bell and waited.

Mayfield opened the door wearing an old pair of cutoffs, a faded T-shirt and a surprised expression. "I wasn't expecting you, Lafferty, but come in. How do you like my new digs?"

Kane glanced around. "Nice. I hope you won't mind answering a few more questions. Rachel's stalker has been busy since we last spoke."

The man's lips twisted. "This is getting old. Should I call my lawyer?"

"You can if you want, but I'm not here in an official capacity."

"That was a joke. I've got nothing to hide." He led the way down a short hall to the kitchen. "Would you like a cup of coffee? There's still some in the pot."

"I'd prefer water."

Bob pulled two bottles from the refrigerator and handed one to Kane. "Let's go sit on the deck."

The Adirondack furniture was comfortable, and the view of waves crashing on the beach below them spectacular.

"Impressive."

"I'm not in Vallejo anymore. Did you hurt your arm?"

He glanced down at the bandage. "Gunshot wound. I got closer to Rachel than her stalker liked."

One brow rose. "This would be the reason you're questioning me again?"

Kane's mouth firmed as he regarded him. "You never seem to have an alibi when you need one."

"So that makes me suspect number one?"

"One or two, take your pick."

"How can I convince you I could care less about Rachel Carpenter? Should I hire someone to babysit me so I'll have an alibi the next time this whack job takes a shot at you?"

"That would do the trick."

"Sorry, but I like my privacy."

"I understand you always have. No girlfriend, not many friends, period. You're something of a loner, aren't you, Bob?"

"Is that a crime?"

"Depends on your reason. I noticed the computer set up you have inside. It looks state of the art."

"What good is having money if you don't spend it?"

"Have you spent a little of your new found wealth on sex?"

Bob scowled. "If it's any of your business, what if I have?"

"Now, that's illegal."

"So arrest me."

"I may, but it won't be for soliciting prostitutes."

"Look, I know you're worried about Rachel, but I've taken enough of your crap. I'm just a quiet guy who was lucky enough to inherit some money." His gaze veered away to rest on the horizon. "Maybe I have a few bad habits, but stalking women isn't one of them."

"Do you own a gun?"

"I own several. They belonged to my grandfather, and they're all properly registered."

"Do you know how to use them?"

"Sure. If I'd taken a shot at you, I wouldn't have missed."

Putting his hands on his thighs, Kane stood. "Do you mind if I use your john?"

"Help yourself. It's down the hall to the right."

Shutting the door to the small room, Kane looked around. Clean and uncluttered with no personal items in sight. Obviously designed for guests. One used tissue lay in the bottom of the waste basket. He lifted it with a piece of toilet paper and dropped it into a plastic bag he'd stuffed into his pocket.

Bob was waiting in the hall when he emerged.

"Thanks."

"I'll see you out."

"Sure." Kane paused when they got to the front door. "You may want to think about inviting a friend to stay with you for a while. Having an alibi would make your life a lot easier."

"I'm leaving town for a few days."

He eyed him thoughtfully. "Suit yourself. Thanks for your time."

"No offense, but I'm tired of these little chats. I'm done talking."

"That's fine. Next time there's a need to question you, it'll be official—and you may want to have that lawyer present."

Without looking back, Kane walked to his Jeep. Driving just out of sight of the house, he parked and circled the perimeter of the property on foot. There was a garage near the house, but the only vehicle in it was a shiny new SUV. No doubt another recent purchase. Returning to his Jeep, he cruised the neighborhood. No abandoned sheds or warehouses, not in this upscale area. If Mayfield had access to the old truck, he wasn't hiding it near his new home.

Leaving the high-end neighborhood of wealth, comfort and spectacular views, Kane merged onto the freeway. If luck and the traffic gods were with him, he'd be back in Vine Haven by noon. Pulling his cell from his pocket, he pushed the speed dial button for Rachel.

"Hi, beautiful. How was your morning?"

"Not bad. I talked to Grace, and she volunteered to call Lark. She thinks a little heart to heart with her cool aunt might help."

"What do you think?"

"I'm willing to try anything. Lark and Grace have always been close."

"Let's keep our fingers crossed. I'm on my way back. Will you have lunch with me?"

"I'd love to. What did Bob have to say?"

"Nothing definitive. We'll talk about it at lunch."

* * * *

After picking up Rachel, Kane drove straight through town and headed north. A breeze blew through the open windows of the Jeep as they wound through rolling hills, and some of her anxiety eased.

"I grabbed some sandwiches and drinks at the deli. I thought we'd have a picnic at Lake Berryessa."

"Sounds like heaven. I could use a big dose of fresh air and sunshine."

She inhaled deeply. The scent of dried grass was reminiscent of baking bread as they drove east through rolling hills. When they reached the lake, Kane turned onto a dirt road that bumped along the shore then parked. Grabbing their lunch from behind the seats, they walked down to the water.

He spread an old blanket in the shade of some willows. "I hope turkey and swiss is okay."

"It's fine." She sat and twisted the top off a bottle of lemonade to take a swallow. "How did your interview with Bob go?"

"The man has some definite hang-ups. I wish I was certain you were one of them." He ate a bite of his sandwich. "I did get a sample of his DNA off a used tissue."

She flicked away an ant. "How will that help?"

"Maybe it won't, but at least we have it. If your stalker sneezes on your window or scratches himself and drips a little blood on the front porch, we'll be prepared."

"That's disgusting."

"Evidence is evidence. I'm not picky about how we get it."

"You're covering all your bases."

"At this point, I'm grasping at straws. I just wish we could find that damn truck he drives. It would be covered with his prints."

"Sheriff Walker isn't any closer to locating it?"

Kane blew out a frustrated breath. "No, but something may still turn up. He's searching DMV records of the known relatives of both our suspects."

Rachel touched the tense muscle in his forearm. "We both need a break. And I'm not talking about evidence. It's so pretty here. Let's just enjoy the day."

"Yeah, let's."

They talked about everything under the sun except her stalker.

Ignoring her problems was a pleasure, but she couldn't forget them.

"I'm worried about Lark. I'm not sure what to say when I do talk to her."

"How about the truth? Tell her we love each other."

"That might freak her out even more than a summer romance. Love implies commitment, and commitment would mean change."

Kane pulled her back against his chest. "They'll have to know sometime."

His heart thumped steadily beneath her cheek. She tipped her head to look at him. "Talking about our relationship to my girls will make this very real."

"Don't you want it to be real?"

She pulled his face down to kiss him. "Yes, I do."

"Then what's the problem?"

"What about you? The weight of a readymade family is a lot to bear."

"Have the girls seemed like a burden to me?"

"You're wonderful with them, but I wouldn't blame you for having doubts."

"Once I make up my mind about something, I stick with it. That's why deciding to leave the force has been so difficult. I'm not a quitter."

"I know you're not, but there's a difference between quitting and changing directions."

He rested his chin on the top of her head. "I failed at one relationship that mattered to me. I won't screw up again."

"I'd like to take some time to make sure this is right for both of us before we tell the girls. They don't deserve to be hurt if you change your mind."

Kane pulled her around to look into her eyes. "Neither do you. My love isn't going to change. I know the difference between the real thing and a bad case of lust."

A desire to throw caution to the wind warred with her mother's instinct to protect her children. "I love you, Kane, and I trust you, but let's not say anything until after my stalker is caught. Everything is so tense right now." She touched his arm. The strength of his taut muscle beneath her fingertips was reassuring. "I'll make Lark understand what I do with you isn't any of her business. I just hope it won't influence her to make bad choices in the future."

"She knows this isn't about her mom hooking up for a one-night stand."

She pulled his face down for another long, slow kiss then reluctantly broke away. "As much as I'd like to stay here all afternoon, I really should get back to work."

"I need to stop by the sheriff's station to tell Stan about my interview with Mayfield."

He helped her to her feet then carried their trash to a nearby can while she folded the blanket.

He glanced her way. "Ready to go?"

"Yep. This was nice, but we can't avoid reality forever."

Chapter Twenty-Five

"What do you mean Susan can't find her?" Rachel's voice rose as panic grabbed her by the throat. "Where is she?"

"Susan and Evan are looking for her now. She probably just went down to the beach or something. Don't freak out yet."

"Tell me what happened, Grace." Taking a deep breath, Rachel let it out slowly.

"I phoned to talk to Lark like I promised. Susan said she'd been quiet all day and went straight to her room after they returned from the zoo. When she called her to the phone, Lark wasn't there."

"How long ago was this?"

"About a half-hour."

"And you're just now informing me?"

"Susan thought she must have gone outside. When she couldn't find her anywhere in the yard or their neighborhood, she called back to tell me. I offered to let you know so they could keep looking."

"You tried her cell?"

"Several times. It just goes to voicemail."

"Oh, God, where could she be?"

"You know your daughter. She probably wanted to be by herself because she's angry. I bet she just went for a walk."

"What if she didn't? Has Susan called the police?"

"Be reasonable, honey. The police aren't going to look for a teenager who's been missing a half-hour."

"They would if Kane called them."

The bells over the door jingled as it opened.

"Oh, thank God. Kane's here. He'll know what to do. I'll call Susan back."

"That's a good idea. Susan asked a neighbor to stay with the kids while she and Evan are out looking for Lark. Rachel, please call me as soon as you hear something."

"I will. Bye, Grace." Rachel clicked off the phone and stepped forward on trembling legs.

Tim dropped the cleaning rag next to the espresso machine and walked over to flip the sign to closed.

"What's wrong?" Kane took her cold hands in his warm ones. "Don't cry, Rachel. Tell me what's wrong?"

"Lark's missing. Susan and Evan are looking for her." She pulled away to wipe a hand across her face. "This is all my fault. Lark took off because we were together this morning. She was so angry!"

His expression hardened. "How long has she been gone?"

"They've been looking for her for a half-hour, but I don't know when she left the house."

"Check with Susan to get a timeframe. Call her cell phone."

With shaking fingers, Rachel punched in the number. "It's me."

"Oh, Rachel, I feel awful about this. She's not at the beach. Do you want me to call the police?"

Rachel looked up at Kane. "Should she call the police?"

He took the phone and put it on speaker.

"Susan, when did you last see Lark?"

"About two hours ago. She was quiet all day and spent a lot of time texting while we were at the zoo."

"Do you know who she was contacting?"

"She said it was a friend. What should I do?"

"Have you tried calling her recently?"

"Of course. She must have turned off her phone because it goes straight to voicemail."

"Keep looking for her. I'll make a few calls and see if I can find out anything. Did you notice if any of her stuff is missing?"

"I didn't look thoroughly when I checked her room, but her purse wasn't on the shelf where she keeps it."

"We'll call the house and have Jade and Ivy look." He disconnected.

Rachel left the phone on speaker as she connected to Susan's home number. Her nephew answered on the first ring.

"It's Aunt Rachel, Scott. Can I speak to Jade?"

"Sure, did Mom and Dad find Lark?"

"Not yet. They're still looking."

A moment later Jade's voice came over the line sounding young and scared. "Mom, where do you think Lark went?"

"I don't know, honey. Can you run up to the bedroom to see if any of her stuff is missing? Have Ivy help you look."

"Okay." There was a long pause with a few muffled thumps and the murmur of voices. Finally Jade came back on the line. "We can't find her purse, her laptop, or her smallest suitcase. Ivy thinks a few of her clothes are missing, a pair of jeans and some shorts and tops."

"Thanks, honey. I have to go now."

"Did Lark run away or something?"

"I'm not sure, but we'll find her." Rachel's voice held more confidence than she felt. "I don't want you and Ivy to worry."

"Lark is a total pain, but I don't want anything bad to happen to her. What can we do?"

"Just stay in the house. I'll check in with you later."

"Okay. Bye, Mom."

"Bye, honey." Rachel clicked off the phone.

Kane touched her arm. "Does she have much money with her?"

"I'd guess about fifty bucks." Her eyes widened. "She also has my extra credit card. I gave it to her for emergencies."

"Do you have the number? I can put a trace on it."

The minutes ticked by as Kane spoke on the phone. Finally, he hung up. "She paid online for a ticket on Southwest Airlines. The flight already left San Diego on route to SFO."

"Lark's on it?"

"She is. I'll call the airline, and they'll hold her at the gate."

They made a quick stop at the house to let Daisy out and switch vehicles. As Kane drove at a speed well above the legal limit, Rachel stared out at the darkening hills and talked to first Susan and then Grace.

"So Lark decided to come home without telling anyone." Grace's voice held an edge of anger. "She must have known everyone would be worried sick."

Rachel sighed. "Maybe that's what she wants. I'd ask her, but she's still not answering her cell."

"Have you called Mom and Dad yet?"

"Nope. I was thinking you could do it for me."

"Gee, thanks."

Rachel's smile was strained. "I need to save all my strength for the upcoming confrontation with my daughter."

"How do you suppose she planned to get home from the airport, hitchhike? What was she thinking?"

"I bet she called her friend, Rose." Rachel let out an exasperated breath. "She isn't thinking. She's mad as hell and running on emotion."

"She's gone too far this time. What are you going to do about it?"

"I haven't decided yet."

"At least she's safe."

"Thank God for that. I know I'd be angrier if I wasn't so relieved."

"You can't go easy on her, or she'll make your life a nightmare."

Rachel pushed a hand through her hair. "Thank you, oh wise, childless one."

"Hey, I might not have kids, but at one point I was even worse than Lark. I know how a troubled teenage girl thinks."

"Maybe you and Nolan should rectify the no-kid situation."

"After watching Lark in action, I may get my tubes tied."

Rachel let out a long sigh. "I'd better go, Gracie. I'll call you tomorrow."

"Sure. If you need me, I can get some time off work."

"Thanks. I appreciate the support. Don't forget to call Mom and Dad."

"I'll take care of it. Bye, Rachel."

She clicked her cell shut and rested her head against the seat.

Kane reached over and squeezed her hand. "Not too much longer."

"What do I say to her?"

"Why don't you let Lark do the talking?"

"She has a lot of explaining to do." Rachel was quiet for a moment. "Is it wrong of me to want a life of my own? Am I a horrible mother for once in a while putting my needs before my daughter's?"

"You know the answer to that. Maybe it would help if I talked to her. Obviously we have some issues to work out."

"She's not your problem, Kane. She's my daughter. I have to handle it."

He glanced over before returning his attention to the road. "She's our problem."

Rachel's heart swelled with emotion. How she loved this man, but the instinct to protect her child was fierce. Lark's emotional issues were something they had to work through together before she could commit to a relationship.

Turning into the airport, he parked in the short-term lot, and they walked quickly to the Southwest Airlines terminal. At the security checkpoint, Kane pulled out his badge. After the attendant verified their story, he let them through. Lark was waiting at the gate, blue eyes blazing with anger—and a touch of fear. When Rachel wrapped her in a hard hug, she stood stiffly and didn't hug back.

"I'm so glad you're safe."

"Why wouldn't I be?"

Rachel took a deep breath. "We'll talk about it in the car. Do you have everything?"

Lark nodded. They made the walk through the airport to the parking area in a silence which lasted all the way to the Bay Bridge.

"So, am I grounded for life or what? Not that I mind the silent treatment. I can do without the lecture."

Her daughter's voice echoed in the quiet interior of the car, full of bluster with an underlying hurt that made Rachel's heart ache.

She turned in her seat. "I'm waiting for an explanation. The whole family was sick with worry. How do you justify scaring us that way?"

Lark slouched, staring out the window. The lights of Oakland twinkled on the far side of the bay. "I didn't think anyone would notice."

"You need to do better than that. You may be angry with me, but your Aunt Susan and Uncle Evan didn't deserve what you put them through."

"I'm sorry about that, but I didn't want to stay in San Diego. I knew if I asked, you wouldn't let me come home."

"You're right. It's still not safe for you here. Nothing's changed."

Lark snorted. "Something's changed. You're sleeping with Kane while we're tucked away in San Diego."

"You may be my daughter, but my personal life is none of your business. My relationship with Kane has nothing to do with the choices I made regarding your safety."

"Sure it doesn't."

Rachel's blood heated. She clenched her fists in her lap. Kane reached over to lay a calming hand on her arm.

She drew in a long, steadying breath. "I don't deserve that kind of attitude."

"Well, I don't deserve to be shuttled off to San Diego. Jade is thrilled to spend her time learning to surf, and Ivy is happy playing with the twins. What about me? I don't have any friends there. There's nothing for me to do."

"It's rough spending your days at the beach." Rachel gritted her teeth. "I'm sure if you talked to Susan, she'd introduce you to some kids your own age."

"I'd feel like an idiot having my aunt make a play date for me. What am I, two?"

"Apparently. This stunt was worthy of a two year old. It's inexcusable."

"I'm sorry about worrying Aunt Susan. I'll call to apologize."

"You bet you will."

As she stared at her daughter's militant expression, the silence in the car weighed on Rachel like a shroud.

Kane cleared his throat. "What exactly is your problem with me, Lark?"

The girl's eyes drilled holes in the back of his head. "You're using my mom. She needs you because of the whack job following her around, and you're taking advantage of her."

When Rachel opened her mouth, Kane held up his hand. "That's a valid concern."

"It isn't like that at all, Lark. Kane certainly isn't using me. We have feelings for each other. Real feelings."

Lark snorted. "I'm sure he says he does."

"Are you're worried I don't care about your mom—or I care too much?"

Lark's voice trembled. "Both."

"I love your mom. When this situation is over, I'm not leaving. I'll be staying in Vine Haven."

Rachel drew in a sharp breath.

He smiled. "Surprised you, didn't I? I spoke to my lieutenant earlier today, told him I planned to hand in my resignation."

"You're going to quit your job? You're sure?" Emotion clogged her voice.

"I've never been surer about anything. I'm staying here—where I belong—while we work out our future. Right now, though, let's hear what Lark has to say."

"I had a dad. I don't need you trying to be another one."

"I'd settle for a shot at earning your respect and friendship. I'm not trying to take your dad's place."

"This bites."

Once again, Kane laid a warning hand on Rachel's arm. "Why's that?"

"Because I liked things the way they were. I don't need you telling me what to do. I get enough of that from Mom."

"I'm a reasonable man. Our relationship can be anything we choose." He paused. "Don't you want your mom to be happy?"

"Yes, but..." She shrugged. "You talk the talk, but why should I trust you?"

"Have I given you a reason not to? Give me a chance—" his voice hardened "—and I'll try not to hold the agony you put your mother through this evening against you."

Lark took a deep breath and let it out slowly. "I'm sorry, Mom. What are you going to do to me?"

"I'm not sure. I'd like to put you on the first plane back to San Diego, but I doubt Susan would take you. I do know I want you somewhere safe."

"She'd take me if you asked and I apologized."

"She probably would. I'll think about it tonight."

"Could I stay at home if I promise to be careful?"

Rachel turned around in her seat. "Absolutely not! This deviant, whoever he is, shot Kane. I'm not about to risk your life."

"What are you talking about?" Her daughter's voice rose. "When did this happen?"

"The night before last. I didn't want to worry you or your sisters, so I didn't say anything." She relayed an abbreviated version of the event.

"Just because he shot Kane doesn't mean he would hurt me. Kane pissed him off."

"That's not a risk I'm willing to take."

Kane pulled into the driveway and turned off the engine. "Let's all get some rest and decide what to do in the morning."

"Are you going to sleep with my mom?" Jumping out, Lark slammed the car door.

"Lark!"

He laughed. "Can I sleep with her if we don't have sex? That couch isn't the most comfortable bed in the world."

Lark's scowl morphed into a snort of laughter. "Are you trying to gross me out or what?"

"Or what. Give me the key, Rachel. I want to check the house."

They waited in the entry with Daisy dancing around in circles while Kane turned on lights and searched the upstairs. Lark's head hung as she drew the toe of her sandal along a crack in the floorboard.

"All clear."

"Do you want me to call Aunt Susan now?" She covered a yawn.

Rachel looked at her watch. "It's almost eleven. After the night you put her through, she might be asleep." She pushed a hand through her hair then shook her head. "You can call her in the morning." She touched her daughter's arm. "Don't think there won't be consequences for your actions. We'll talk about them tomorrow."

"Fine." Lark took three steps before turning around and flinging her arms around her mother. "I'm sorry." She bolted up the stairs with Daisy following.

Kane cleared his throat. "That went better than I thought it would."

She turned and smiled. "There may be hope for her yet, but I'm not ready to forgive and forget."

"She doesn't expect you to."

Rachel let out a sigh. "What next?"

"How about a stiff drink?" He touched her cheek in a gentle caress. "You look like you could use one."

"Probably, but I'd rather have a cup of tea."

He wrapped an arm around her shoulders as they walked into the kitchen. The light on the answering machine blinked furiously. Rachel filled the teakettle with water then pushed the button to listen to her messages. The first was from her mother expressing relief Lark was safe and promising to bake croissants and cinnamon rolls for the coffee bar. The second message was from Will offering his and Sharon's help if she needed it.

Kane stepped up behind her and rested his hands on her shoulders. "Your family is very supportive."

She nodded. The third message was from Susan volunteering to pick Lark up at the airport anytime she wanted to send her back.

Tears sprang to Rachel's eyes. "She's more generous than I deserve."

Kane turned off the burner and poured boiling water into her waiting cup. "Are you going to send her back?"

Rachel's brow knit as she dunked the teabag. "Do I have a choice? Lark won't be any happier in Portland with my brother and his family."

"I don't think she was unhappy in San Diego until she found out about us. Taking off was her way of expressing anger and frustration. Maybe if the three of us come to some sort of understanding, she won't act out again."

"Wow, are you a cop or a psychologist?" She picked up her cup and sipped the tea.

Kane's cheeks darkened. "You can tell me to shut up."

"Why would I do that? I think you nailed it perfectly. Maybe I'll hold off booking another flight until tomorrow. Lark and I need to have a talk before I send her back."

"That seems reasonable. Are you finished with your tea?"

She took another swallow then set the cup in the sink. Her chin snapped up as she swung around. "Oh, God, we didn't have any dinner. You must be starving."

"I'm a little hungry. Do you want a sandwich?"

"I'm too tired to eat."

"Then why don't you go to bed." He put his arms around her then kissed her slow and deep.

She let out a sigh when he released her. "What about you?"

"I think I'll sleep down here tonight. Lark will have to get used to seeing us together, but I don't think throwing it in her face right now is such a great idea."

"I hate to make you sleep on that lumpy couch."

"It's fine, Rachel. I only made the comment to lighten the mood. Go to bed."

"I will, but I haven't forgotten what you said." She touched his face. "Do you really want to stay here?"

"I do. I love you. I want to work through all our problems. I want a future together."

"I love you, too." She wrapped her arms around his neck. The kiss she pressed to his lips was full of emotion. "Thank you."

"For what?"

"Coming into my life and filling my heart."

"You fill mine, too."

She glanced out the kitchen window at the dark street. Some of her joy faded, and she let out a long breath. "Especially with everything the way it is now."

"I'll catch him, Rachel. I promise."

* * * *

He parked the battered pickup in the barn and retrieved his car then whistled softly as he drove down the dirt driveway. Things were looking up. Jordan had returned home accompanied by Kane and Lark. The one weakness in her line of defense. The whistle died on his lips. As if Jordan would ever need protection from him.

He'd waited so long for this day. Once they were together, Jordan would understand he was her true destiny. She would forget all about the men in her past, the unworthy men who'd never deserved her.

His body tightened and throbbed, aching for her. He considered calling someone to relieve his needs then shook his head. There wasn't a woman alive who was anything but a poor substitute. He could wait the short time remaining. It wouldn't be long.

Chapter Twenty-Six

"Terrific." Rachel groped beneath the bathroom sink for a tampon. "Just what I need to start my day." She took a quick shower and toweled dry. After dressing in a pair of bright blue Capri pants and a striped shirt, she blew dry her hair. Ready to face her daughter, she knocked on Lark's bedroom door.

"What?"

Rachel pushed open the door. "Time to get up."

Daisy raised her head and thumped her tail against the rug.

Lark grunted. "Do I have to?"

"Yes, it's seven-thirty, and I have to stop by Grandma's house before we go to the bookstore."

"We? Why can't I stay with Grandma?"

"Because I intend to keep an eye on you, personally, while I make a few decisions. We also need to have a serious talk."

Lark buried her head under her pillow. "Do I get a choice in this?"

"Probably not. Jump in the shower. We need to go soon."

The scent of freshly brewed coffee hung in the air as Rachel entered the kitchen.

"The coffee alone is reason enough to love you." She made a beeline for the mugs Kane had set out on the counter.

He grabbed her around the waist and swung her into his arms. "I'll give you another reason." When the kiss ended he smiled at her. "Did you get any sleep?"

"A little. I've decided to take Lark to the bookstore with me this morning. We won't stay long, but I want her close."

"Are you sending her back to San Diego?"

"I'm not sure. All I care about is her safety." She stirred sugar into her coffee and took a sip. "What do you think?"

"Maybe having her here isn't such a problem. With just Lark to worry about, it'll be easy enough to keep an eye on her. Let's give her at least a day or two before we do anything."

She nodded. "I was thinking the same thing. I'll call Susan to let her know. What's on your agenda?"

"My top priority is playing watchdog, but I'd also like to talk to Curt Dawson again."

Rachel rubbed her tired eyes. "I can't believe either Curt or Bob is the man stalking me. What if it isn't either of them? What if we've been wrong all along?"

"I don't think we are." Kane pulled her against his chest. "It's almost over, babe. Whoever it is will act again soon."

"Then what?"

"Then we catch him. I'll call Stan about putting a tail on both men. If the department balks at the expense, I'll hire someone myself."

"Money isn't a problem. I'll tap into Bryce's estate if I need to."

He kissed the top of her head. "I doubt it will come to that. This guy is getting tired of waiting."

"Gross." Lark walked into the room with Daisy at her heels. "Is this what I can expect to see every morning?" Her hair was still damp, and she hadn't bothered with makeup. Dressed in a pair of shorts, a tank top and flip-flops she looked like the fourteen-year-old girl she was.

"If I'm lucky." Kane grinned and stepped back.

"You can't blame me for needing an extra hug considering the circumstances." Rachel poured a glass of orange juice and handed it to her daughter.

"So what happens next?"

"You call your Aunt Susan and apologize."

"Let's do it." Lark reached for the phone. "I prefer to eat crow before my breakfast."

"That's the spirit." Kane's eyes twinkled above his coffee mug. "Crow may be the next breakfast of champions. It's full of protein."

Lark rolled her eyes and picked up the phone. To her credit, her apology was sincere. "Aunt Susan says she'll take me back."

"We've decided you can stay here for the time being if you promise to follow instructions to the letter."

"Seriously?"

Rachel nodded. Taking the phone, she spoke briefly with Susan before hanging up. "Nothing's changed Lark." She eyed her daughter's suddenly cheerful expression. "Someone will be watching you twenty-four seven."

"I get it. What's for breakfast?"

"Cold cereal. We don't have time for anything else."

"I'd better go get my cell. I left it upstairs."

When Lark entered the kitchen several minutes later, Kane was on the phone talking to the sheriff.

Rachel poured a second cup of coffee. "The cereal's on the table. Do you want a piece of toast with it?"

"I'll have an English muffin." Lark glanced toward the back door and stroked Daisy's ears. "First I'll let Daisy out."

Rachel dropped an English muffin into the toaster. "Why don't you feed her while you're at it?"

"Okay. Come on, Daisy."

It took a while for Kane to finish his conversation. While Rachel was still busy making Lark's breakfast, he hung up the phone. "Is that Daisy barking?"

She laid down the butter knife. "It's getting fainter. I hope she isn't chasing Florence Tate's cat again. She threatened to call animal control last time."

"Where's Lark?"

"She's feeding Daisy." Rachel frowned. "Maybe I shouldn't have let her go out on the porch alone."

"I'll check on her."

He went through the back door with Rachel at his heels. Neither Lark nor Daisy was anywhere in sight.

"Oh, no."

"She's probably just chasing the dog. Lark!" Kane shouted.

When she didn't answer, they ran out into the yard.

"Lark!" Rachel raised her voice. "Lark, answer me!"

Two houses over, a lawnmower started up. Next door, Florence Tate stepped into her yard carrying an orange tabby cat.

"What's all the hollering about?"

"Mrs. Tate, have you seen Lark this morning?"

"No, I was making a cup of tea when I heard you yelling."

"Rachel, over here." Kane bent over something behind the oak tree.

"Is it Lark?" Rachel ran toward him.

"No, this girl is out cold. Thank God she's still breathing. Go call 9-1-1."

Rachel pressed her hand to her lips. "It's Lark's friend, Rose."

Kane straightened. "Go inside." His voice was deadly serious. He gave her a firm shake when she didn't move. "Listen to me. Call 9-1-1 and then call Will or your dad. I'll go look for Lark. If he has her, he can't have much of a head start."

Rachel looked at him then had to blink to bring his face into focus. "I'll go get my cell then come back out here to stay with Rose."

* * * *

Kane waited only long enough to see Rachel head toward the house before running out to the street. There was no sign of Lark, but in the distance Daisy raced toward him. He ran to meet her. "Where's Lark, girl?"

The dog turned and ran back the way she'd come with Kane following. At the end of the block, she stopped. Sitting down on her furry rump, she whined softly.

"Shit!"

There was no vehicle in sight. He ran up to the nearest house and pounded on the door. A woman in a bathrobe answered it. Kane pulled out his wallet and flashed his badge.

"Did you see a man with a blond girl in the last few minutes?"

Her eyes widened. "No, there was an old pickup parked out front a while ago, but it's gone now. I think it was gray or maybe green. I wasn't paying much attention."

"Did you see the driver?"

"The truck was empty when I noticed it. You might try the other neighbors, but they've all probably left for work."

"Thank you." Pulling out his cell, he called Stan Walker's private line while he ran to the house next door and thumped on the door. "It's Kane. The asshole has Rachel's oldest daughter. A neighbor saw an old pickup, possibly gray or green, parked on the street, but she didn't see the driver or Lark."

"My deputies are on the way. I called the state police. I'll get an APB out on the truck. An ambulance is headed over to see to the girl you found in the yard. Rachel identified her to the 9-1-1 operator as Rose Zimmerman. Her parents have been notified. Any luck with the other neighbors?"

"I'm trying them now. He raced up the next walkway and used his fist to knock. "No one seems to be home except the woman I spoke to."

"Christ, this guy has balls, snatching Lark out of her own yard in broad daylight. Let's hope Rose got a good look at him."

"I'm heading back to the house. I don't like leaving Rachel alone."

"I'll meet you there."

Kane pocketed the phone, and with Daisy at his side, ran back to the house. He arrived just as a deputy's car and an ambulance turned into the driveway. Rachel ran up to him, her eyes pleading for news. He shook his head and pulled her into his arms. Her crying made him want to kill someone, but there was nothing he could do about it.

"We'll find her, Rachel. I swear I'll find her for you."

"Where's the injured girl?" The medic pulled a stretcher from the ambulance.

Rachel wiped the tears from her face. "She's in the backyard. My neighbor is sitting with her."

Pete Lowery joined them on the porch. "No reason we can't go on back, too. I'll get your statements while the medics are checking the girl. That way I'll see they do it without contaminating the crime scene."

While Rachel and Kane described the morning's events, the medics checked Rose for injuries and monitored her pulse.

He glanced at Florence Tate. "Has she been conscious?"

The older woman nodded. "Yes, but she's been pretty groggy."

"I'm concerned she has a concussion, but I don't see any other injuries. Looks like she's coming around again." The medic glanced at the deputy. "We need to get her to the hospital."

"It's important we question her."

"Try to keep it brief."

The young girl groaned then blinked. "My head hurts."

The deputy knelt beside her. "Rose, can you tell us what happened?"

She looked from Pete to Rachel. "Where's Lark?"

Rachel squatted beside her and squeezed her hand. "We don't know? Can you describe the man who hit you?"

She shook her head and winced. Tears ran down her cheeks. "Some guy called me early this morning and told me he found my wallet. He said he'd meet me in front of my house. I went outside, and there was an old pickup parked on the street. While I stood there wondering why it was empty, someone came up behind me and hit me." Sobs choked her voice. "When I woke up, I was in the truck parked a little ways from here."

"What did he look like, Rose?" Kane asked.

"I don't know. He had on a black ski mask. His eyes were brown, but I couldn't see his hair. He was wearing jeans and a blue T-shirt. He was average-sized, not as tall as you, more like him." She pointed to Lowery. "But not as skinny."

"Then what happened?"

"He made me call Lark. When she didn't answer, I could tell he was mad. His eyes were kind of wild. Then a minute later Lark called back. I asked her to meet me in the yard just like he told me to." Rose dissolved into tears. "I'm sorry, Mrs. Carpenter. I didn't want to, but I was so scared."

Rachel squeezed Rose's hand. "It's not your fault. Tell us what happened next."

"He pulled out a knife and said he'd use it if I didn't cooperate. He looked all around and then made me run down the street to your backyard."

The sheriff arrived with Brandon Hendricks. Rose paused to glance over at them.

Kane touched her shoulder. "Go on."

She took a breath. "When Lark came out, he hit her. Then he must have hit me again because I don't remember anything else."

"Son of a bitch!" Kane smacked his thigh with his fist. "I can't believe no one saw a man in a ski mask carrying a girl down the street."

Hendricks pulled out his notebook. "I'll check with the neighbors."

"You do that, Brandon. Rose, I want you to look at these two pictures." The sheriff held up photos of Bob Mayfield and Curt Dawson. "Does either of these men look like the one who took you?"

Rose squinted at the pictures. "I'm not certain. They both have brown eyes."

"What about his voice?" Kane asked. "Was there anything distinctive about it?"

"Not really, but I'm pretty sure I would recognize it if I heard it again. Oh, I did scratch his arm when he was marching me down the street." She looked at Rachel, and her lips trembled. "Is he going to hurt Lark?"

Kane shook his head. "I don't think he will. He didn't hurt you more than he had to. He's just using Lark to get to Rachel."

A moment later, a woman with dark hair and a worried expression ran around the side of the house. She knelt and stroked Rose's orange-streaked hair. "Is she okay? What happened?"

"Are you her mother?" At the woman's nod, the medics lifted the stretcher. "Someone can fill you in at the hospital. If you're through questioning her, sheriff, I'd like to take this girl to the emergency room to get her thoroughly checked out."

Walker glanced toward his remaining deputy. "Go with them, Pete. See if she remembers anything else. Make sure they collect samples from beneath her nails. We may have this bastard's DNA. I'll stay here and begin processing the scene. The state police should be arriving shortly to help."

Rachel's hand shook as she pushed back her hair. "What can I do, sheriff?"

"Just wait by the phone. The state boys will set up equipment to trace incoming calls. I've got local police trying to track down both Dawson and Mayfield. Neither is answering his phone."

"Let's get out of the way so Stan can do his job." Kane took her arm to guide her away. "Mrs. Tate, you can go home, now. Thank you for staying."

The elderly woman's eyes were wide in her wrinkled face. "What's the world coming to when a person isn't safe in her own yard?" She shook her head. "Rachel, you let me know if I can help."

"I will. Thank you, Florence."

The woman walked back to her house, the cat clutched tightly in her arms. With Daisy at her side, Rachel followed Kane inside then stood in the middle of the kitchen and stared at the cold English muffin on the table.

Her face crumbled as she brought her hands up to cover her eyes. "I can't believe this is happening."

Kane put his arms around her and pulled her shaking body close. He was still holding her when Audrey and Chet rushed into the kitchen. Only then did he release Rachel into her mother's embrace.

"What's being done to find Lark?" Rachel's father looked ten years older than the last time Kane had seen him. His face was pale beneath its usual ruddy color, and new lines were etched into his forehead.

"Everything that can be. The sheriff expects the man who kidnapped Lark to call. The state police will be here to trace it when he does."

"Do you think he will?"

Kane frowned. "I'm not sure. I don't know what he expects to accomplish by taking Lark. It's Rachel he wants."

Chet's shoulders heaved and when he spoke, his voice broke. "The bastard must be crazy as a loon."

"His obsession with Rachel seems to have pushed him over the edge. Still, he hasn't been overtly violent up until now."

"Hell, man, he shot you."

"I made him mad. He seems to treat women with more respect. The injuries he inflicted on Rachel in Tahoe and on Rose this morning weren't life-threatening. They served the purpose of allowing him to escape undetected. He doesn't get off on hurting women."

"You don't think he'll hurt Lark?"

Now it was Kane's voice that shook. "That's what I'm counting on."

Rachel pulled away from her mom's arms and wiped her eyes. "I should call the bookstore. Ellen must be wondering where I am."

"The cinnamon rolls and muffins are in the car." Audrey's voice trembled. "I was leaving to drop them off when you called."

Rachel spoke briefly to her employee then hung up just as the state police arrived. Once the officers had set up a trace on her home phone, she used her cell to call each of her relatives. She was in tears after speaking to Jade and Ivy.

Watching the woman he loved break down was killing him. Kane took the phone away from her when she finished. "You need to have something to eat."

"I'll make you some oatmeal." Audrey patted her arm.

"I'm not hungry, Mom."

"I don't care if you're hungry. You have to eat."

Rachel lowered her head and sat down at the table.

Kane walked over to pull the sheriff into the living room. "Anything new?"

He stuffed his cell phone back into his shirt pocket. "No, there's still no sign of either Mayfield or Dawson. None of their friends or relatives knows where they are."

"Mayfield told me he was heading out of town when I talked to him yesterday."

"That's convenient."

"Isn't it? The guy's never home when it matters, but neither is Dawson. Did you reach Tiffany Randolph? She may know where Curt is."

"I did, and she doesn't. She said she hasn't talked to him in a few days." The sheriff's phone rang again. He answered it, listened intently then hung up. "A DMV report shows Mayfield's grandfather owned a 1978 Ford truck. It was listed as non-operational the last time it was registered. Bob never changed the registration into his own name after his grandfather's death."

"Finally a break. It could be the vehicle we're looking for."

"It's a place to start, and it's certainly enough to get a search warrant for the property up in Lakeport Mayfield inherited. That's the address on the truck's registration."

Rachel walked into the room and came over to lean against Kane. "Do you think he took Lark up to Lakeport?"

"If Bob Mayfield's our man, it's a possibility." The sheriff smiled at her.

Rachel's fists clenched as she stared back at him. "Then why aren't you on your way up there?"

"We're waiting to hear from the local authorities."

"That's it? We just wait?"

Kane rested his hands on her tense shoulders. "It shouldn't be long."

Rachel buried her face against his chest. "It's already been too long."

Chapter Twenty-Seven

Doing nothing made Rachel want to fly into a million pieces. Grace arrived and held her in a tight embrace, her usual confidence missing. Having her sister beside her was a momentary comfort, but Rachel couldn't relax. She walked from window to window, staring out at the street, her mind full of images too frightening to contemplate. When Kane touched her shoulder, she jumped.

"They found the pickup in a shed on the property, and the house has been recently occupied."

"Lark?" She closed her eyes and prayed.

"There's no sign of her or Mayfield, but that doesn't mean they aren't in the area."

"Is the truck the right one?"

"They aren't sure, Rachel. It matches the general description. The paint is badly faded, but the original color was black not green. They were able to start the vehicle, but the engine was cold."

"He could have changed cars when he got there. It's been three hours since he took her, and it can't take much more than an hour to get to Lakeport."

"The local police are organizing a search. Stan is sending Brandon up to keep us fully informed."

Rachel clutched his arm. "Go with him, Kane. Please."

His brow creased. "I don't like leaving you. We can't lose sight of this bastard's main objective."

"Right now I only care about my daughter. I'll be fine." She waved her arm toward the half dozen people in the living room. "He can't touch me, but he could hurt my baby." Tears pooled in her eyes. "Lark's the one who needs you."

"I don't know. I feel like I should stay, like there's something we're missing."

"The only thing missing is my daughter. If Bob Mayfield is the sick, twisted pervert who took her, then you have to find her." Rachel took a deep breath. "I'd go up there myself, but I know the sheriff wants me here to talk to him in case he calls."

Kane gripped her shoulders. "You aren't to leave this house. Understand?"

Nodding, she walked into his arms, and they closed around her in a fierce hug. "Please find her. I can't stand this."

"If she's up there, I'll bring her back." He tilted her face to kiss her. "I'd better go."

"Please be careful."

His smile was tight. "Don't worry about me, but God help the sorry bastard who took Lark when I get a hold of him."

Rachel rested her hand on the windowsill as Kane crossed the yard. He stopped to speak to Stan Walker before he and Brandon Hendricks drove away in his Jeep. Her shoulders sagged.

"Kane looked pretty determined."

Rachel turned toward her sister. "He is. The police want to catch this man. I know they do, but to them Lark is just another teenage girl in trouble. Kane will do whatever it takes. I trust him to put Lark first the same way I would."

Grace squeezed her hand. "The guy really loves you."

"He's staying after this is over. We both want to make our relationship work, but right now I can't think about anything but finding my daughter."

"We'll get her back."

Rachel nodded. "We have to."

The afternoon dragged with no contact from the kidnapper. Rachel's nerves were at the breaking point.

"I expected to hear from him by now." The sheriff scratched his bald head and frowned. "This just doesn't make sense."

"Have something to eat." Rachel's mother took the sheriff's arm. "There's soup and sandwiches in the kitchen. You come, too, Chet."

"Thank you, Mrs. Hanover." Walker followed her across the room. "I wouldn't mind having a sandwich."

Grace touched Rachel's sleeve. "You should eat."

"Mom force-fed me a bowl of oatmeal earlier, but you go ahead."

"Are you sure? I don't want to leave you in here by yourself."

"I could use some alone time. What I'd really like is a little fresh air. I think I'll go sit on the front porch."

Grace paused in the doorway. "Are you sure you should?"

"No one is going to snatch me off the porch, Grace. Anyway, Pete Lowery is outside with one of the state cops. I'll be fine."

Grace left, and Rachel walked out the door, releasing a relieved sigh to find Lowery and his state counterpart had moved their work to the back of the house. The day was sunny and warm. A hummingbird darted by her and landed on the edge of the feeder. Down the street, the Johnson's car pulled into their driveway, and Cathy got out then waved. Standing on her front porch, Rachel wondered how the world could look so normal.

Daisy walked around the side of the house to lean against her leg. She reached down to scratch the dog's ears. "I need to do something."

Out on the street, the mail carrier stopped in front of the house. He thrust a handful of envelopes into her box before moving on.

Even collecting the mail was better than sitting still. Daisy accompanied her down the driveway. Rachel pulled out the small stack then went back to the porch. She settled on a rattan chair and sorted through the collection of bills, advertisements and catalogues. On the bottom of the pile was a plain white envelope with no stamp or return address. With shaking hands, she ripped it open and read the contents.

My Dearest Jordan,

I've waited so long for this day. Once we're together I'm confident you'll forgive me for this unfortunate scare. I promise I'll release Lark unharmed if you follow my instructions. Tell anyone about the meeting I've planned, and I'll see it as a breach of faith—which would force me to reconsider your daughter's safe release. Please don't make me hurt her.

Lark and I are enjoying a trip to the mountains. I thought it a fitting place for our reunion. Drive to the Soda Springs exit and ask for an envelope at the gas station. You'll find further instructions inside.

I'm counting the hours until we're finally together.

Your One True Love

Rachel read the letter a second time and bit her lip. Obviously Lark wasn't being held in Lakeport. Either Bob or Curt had taken her up to the Sierras. Quietly she slipped through the entry and climbed the stairs. In her room, she took a small penknife from a box of odds and ends and slipped it into her pocket. Too bad it wasn't a machete—or a gun. Not knowing what to expect, she packed a bag with a change of clothes and a few toiletries. In Lark's room, she grabbed a pair of jeans and a sweatshirt along with socks and tennis shoes. Her cell phone rang while she was writing a note.

"Kane?"

"Hey, beautiful. I just wanted to check in. We haven't located Lark or Mayfield yet, but we're still looking. The house has definitely been used recently."

"Do you think it was Bob?"

"We found footprints that match his shoe size in a patch of dirt near the driveway. The forensic guys are going through the pickup, but they haven't turned up any evidence yet."

"So the truck might not be the right one?"

"It's beginning to look that way. I'll head back if we don't find something soon."

"What if that's what he's waiting for? What if he has Lark hidden somewhere and is just waiting until the coast is clear?"

"The local police will still be around. No one intends to give up until we identify the person who's been using the house. It might not be Mayfield. He may have lent it to someone else."

"So Bob could still be the kidnapper, but he might have taken Lark somewhere other than Lakeport?"

"At this point we can't be certain of anything. I'm sorry, Rachel. I really expected this lead to pan out."

"I'm sorry, too."

"I don't understand why he hasn't tried to contact you. It doesn't make sense." Kane's voice was filled with frustration. "I know we're missing something."

"Maybe he'll call soon."

"Are you okay? Did someone slip you a sedative?"

"Of course not. Why would you ask a question like that?"

"Because you sound awfully calm. I expected you to lose it when I told you we hadn't found Lark."

Rachel swallowed. She sucked at keeping secrets—especially from someone she loved. "What good would freaking out do? I'm trying my best not to fall apart here."

"That's my girl." He blew out a shaky breath. "I'd better go. I'll see you in a couple of hours, okay?"

Her grip on the phone tightened. "I love you."

"I love you, too."

Blinking back tears, Rachel grabbed her bag, slipped down the stairs and hurried out the door. Thankfully the front yard was still empty although voices carried from the rear of the house. With fingers crossed, she started the SUV and backed out of the driveway. When she made it down the street without detection, she allowed herself to exhale. It was a long way to the mountains. Getting out of Vine Haven was just the first step. It was only a matter of time before someone discovered she was missing and all hell broke loose.

Rachel lifted one hand from the wheel to rub her forehead. Her parents would be beside themselves, and she wouldn't let herself think about Kane. He'd have an APB out on her car the second he was notified of her disappearance. Making a hard turn, she drove to the vineyard. Her father kept an old MG convertible in the garage. The spare key hung on a pegboard. As quickly as she could, she exchanged vehicles.

Feeling more confident by the minute, she drove through the vineyard and out to the highway. Her hair blew around her face as the MG ate up the miles. She stopped once to get gas and a bottle of water, using cash to pay for it. It was getting dark when she reached the Soda Springs exit. Long shadows from the towering pines crisscrossed the road. Rachel pulled into the gas station near the off-ramp and got out of the car.

Inside the open garage bay an older man wearing grease-stained coveralls glanced her way. "Need something?"

"Did someone leave directions here for me?"

"Is your name Jordan?" The man reached beneath the workbench for an envelope.

Rachel took it from him. "Could you tell me what time this was dropped off?"

"Must have been around noon because I was taking a lunch break."

She thanked him and went back to her car. She'd barely sat down when she ripped open the envelope.

My Dearest Jordan,

If you're reading this, we'll soon be together. I hope you haven't disobeyed my instructions as it wouldn't be in Lark's best interests. I'll know if you're followed. Don't disappoint me.

Take the road past the parking area for Granite Lake Retreat and follow it approximately two miles. When the paved road ends, continue on the dirt track for another half-mile.

I eagerly await your arrival.

Your Only Love

Rachel crushed the note in her hand. There was no turning back, not when Lark's safety was at stake. She followed the road as instructed, her heart contracting as she passed the entrance sign for Granite Lake Retreat. She'd fallen hard for Kane at the camp and prayed he'd forgive her for shutting him out. She blinked back a few more tears and swallowed.

The road wound past a few scattered homes that looked like vacation cabins and ended abruptly at a chain strung across the track with a private property sign hanging from two links. Rachel got out and unfastened a metal hook on one side. Leaving the chain lying on the road, she drove across it and bumped down the rutted drive, cringing when the MG scraped bottom. She certainly wouldn't be making a fast get-away with this car. Finally, the narrow lane opened up. The glare of her headlights revealed a small cabin.

Rachel parked next to an old green pickup and got out. Light shone through the multi-paned window near the door. Stepping up onto the porch, she peeked inside. Lark sat on a straight-backed chair with her hands behind her back. Heart pounding, Rachel threw open the door and ran to her daughter's side.

"Mom." Lark's voice broke.

Other than a streak of dirt on her face and a skinned knee, she appeared unharmed.

"Honey, are you okay?" Rachel touched her cheek then enfolded her in a tight embrace. "I've been going out of my mind with worry." "He didn't hurt me. Can you untie my hands? He's been gone a long time. Maybe we can get away before he gets back." "Not going to happen, Lark. No one's going anywhere, at least not tonight."

Rachel turned to meet Curt Dawson's warm brown gaze. A smile curved the corners of his lips. She shivered and looked away. A long hunting knife, strapped to his leg, gleamed in the light. "You promised you'd let Lark go if I came." Rachel held his gaze as she stepped forward. "I did as you asked. No one followed me, so I'm counting on you to uphold your end of the bargain."

"I'll let Lark go just as soon as you're ready to stay here with me. I'm not a fool, Jordan. I realize it may take a little time to convince you we belong together." He shut the cabin door and dropped her overnight bag and purse on the floor. "You left these in the car."

Rachel took a deep breath and smiled. "Thanks for bringing them in. Do you think we could untie Lark? Her wrists look raw. Maybe we could put some antibiotic ointment on them."

Crossing the room, he tore his gaze away from Rachel to glance down at Lark's wrists where they were secured to the chair. "They don't look so bad, and I'd really rather not have to worry about her trying to escape."

"I won't. I promise."

Lark's voice sounded so small, so vulnerable, Rachel's heart squeezed. Curt's chuckle grated across her nerves.

"I'd like to believe you, Lark, but your wrists wouldn't be chafed if you hadn't been struggling to get loose. I'll free your hands once dinner's ready."

When her daughter opened her mouth, Rachel shook her head. "That seems reasonable. Can I help with the meal?"

"Thanks for offering. I'm glad you're willing to cooperate." He came over to touch her hair. "We're going to get along just beautifully, Jordan. You'll see."

Rachel withheld a shudder as his fingers stroked her jaw. "What would you like me to do?"

His glazed eyes refocused. "You heat up a can of stew while I throw together a salad."

"I don't mind making the salad."

"I appreciate that, but I'm not willing to trust you with a knife just yet. The can opener is in the drawer by the stove, and there should be a corkscrew in there as well. I brought along a nice bottle of Merlot to go with our dinner."

Surely she was in some alternate universe. As she worked to prepare dinner beside the man who had terrorized her for so long, she wondered who owned the cabin. No pictures or other personal items sat on the bare shelves. The main room consisted of a living area and small kitchen. Two closed doors led to what she assumed were a bedroom and bath.

Lark sat quietly while Rachel heated the stew and buttered a loaf of bread. She gave her a reassuring smile whenever she could despite the fear twisting her stomach. When the food was on the table, their captor untied Lark's hands.

They ate in silence. After several long minutes, Lark pushed her plate away. "I can't stand this. What are we doing here? Let us go, you freak!"

Showing no real emotion, he kept his focus on his dinner. "We've talked about this. I have no more desire for your company than you do for mine. When Jordan and I reach an understanding, I'll turn you loose."

"Her name isn't Jordan. It's Rachel! Do you hear me?" Lark's voice pitched higher. "Why won't you let us go? My mom loves Kane, not you. She could never love you."

"Lark." Rachel gave her a brief head shake and a warning glance.

Dawson stiffened. Angry color suffused his face as he glanced up. "She may feel some attraction to that man, but I've no doubt Jordan will soon realize he could never satisfy her the way I will. You see, my Jordan is there inside Rachel, just waiting for me to release her."

His gaze moved from Lark to Rachel, and a smile lit his eyes. "For fourteen long years I've waited, knowing we'd be together someday. The time is now."

Pushing back his chair, he picked up his plate. "If you've finished eating, I believe I've waited long enough. Time for bed. Why don't you freshen up while Lark does the dishes? I see no reason why she can't help out." His head swiveled toward the girl. "For the time she's here, anyway."

"I'd like to wash my face." Rachel stood. "Lark, do as Curt asks and clean up in here. Would you please?"

Her daughter's gaze swung toward the bedroom door. "Mom, you can't."

"It's all right, honey." Rachel smiled. "Curt isn't a monster. He won't hurt me, but we do need to talk." She picked up her purse and headed toward the bathroom then turned to look at the animal who'd taken her daughter. "I'll be right back."

He cleared his throat and held out a large hand. "May I?"

Rachel handed him her purse. He looked inside and took out her cell phone before handing it back.

Fighting to walk slowly when she wanted only to run, she got to the bathroom then shut the door and locked it. She leaned against the wall with closed eyes as a wave of panic washed over her. She took a couple of deep breaths but her body wouldn't stop trembling.

"Okay, Plan B. I can do this." Opening her eyes, she straightened then stared at herself in the mirror, remembering getting into character during her New York days. She took a few long breaths and forced herself to focus. Soon, the face looking back was calm, almost serene.

"I wouldn't be much of an actress if I can't convince one deluded fool I'm interested in him." She squared her shoulders. "Tonight, I'll be Jordan Hale again, and when it's over Lark will be free."

She used the toilet then washed her face and hands. Pulling the penknife from her pocket, she looked for a hiding place. Her gaze rested on an open tissue box, and she slipped the knife inside. Her hand hovered over the box, questioning her decision. She could keep the weapon and try to use it on the pervert. If she failed, though, the game would be over. This way Lark had a better chance.

In the kitchen, her daughter stood at the sink washing dishes. Tears ran down her face, and she swiped at them with a wet hand. Rachel crossed the room to hug her.

"Everything's going to be fine. I don't want you to worry about me. I know exactly what I'm doing." She turned to smile at the sick, little man who blushed under her regard. "Curt and I are going to talk and get to know one another better."

He swallowed. "Lark, it's been a long day. I'd like you to use the bathroom, and then we'll get you settled for the night."

"Are you going to tie me up again?"

"I'm afraid I have to, but there's no need for you to be uncomfortable. I'll secure you to the couch."

"Go blow your nose." Rachel gave her daughter an intent look. "There really isn't any reason for tears. Take the overnight bag with you. I brought you a pair of jeans and a sweatshirt. You'll be a lot warmer sleeping in those. I remembered how cold it gets up here at night."

The deviant picked up the bag, unzipped it and looked through the contents before handing it to Lark.

"There's a spare blanket and pillow in the bedroom closet, Jordan. She'll be warm enough."

Without a word, Lark shut the bathroom door with a sharp click. Rachel headed into the bedroom. The sight of the king-sized bed covered with a patchwork quilt sent a shudder through her. She pulled the blanket and pillow off the closet shelf and went back into the main room.

"When I searched your bag, I couldn't help noticing you didn't bring a nightgown for yourself. Why not?"

Rachel looked him directly in the eye and smiled the way Jordan Hale had smiled at so many men. "Am I really going to need one?"

Keep him happy and focused. Give Lark the time she needs to get away. I can do this. She unclenched her fists and offered another smile.

Sweat broke out on the pervert's forehead.

The bathroom door opened. Lark's gaze went immediately to her mother, a hint of excitement in the depths of her blue eyes.

"Let's get you settled." With unsteady hands, he tied Lark's feet and hands then looped the rope around the couch, securing her to it.

Rachel spread the blanket over her daughter. "Good night, honey, sleep well."

"Good night, Mom."

Rachel bent to kiss her cheek.

"Got it!" The words were a bare whisper in her ear.

Rachel smiled then straightened. "I'll see you in the morning."

Lark stared at her kidnapper, her gaze fierce. "If you hurt my mother, Kane will kill you."

Anger darkened his eyes. "I have no intention of hurting her, and I'd rather not hear that man's name mentioned again." He indicated the bedroom door with a sweep of his arm. "After you, Jordan."

Rachel walked toward the bedroom with her head held high, fists clenched at her sides. She didn't plan to surrender easily. Once Lark was safely away, Curt Dawson was in for the fight of his life.

Chapter Twenty-Eight

Kane read Rachel's note for the tenth time, looking for a clue where none existed, then crushed it in his fist. Grace sat down next to him and squeezed his arm.

Head in his hands, he stared out the window into the early evening gloom. "Why'd she do it? Why didn't she let the police handle it? Why didn't she call me?"

"She was thinking of Lark's safety."

"By throwing herself to the lions? We could have put a tail on her the bastard would never have detected. For Christ's sake, this is what I do!" Kane pounded his fist against his thigh.

"The bastard has a name." Sheriff Walker closed his phone.

Kane jumped to his feet. "Which of them is it?"

"Curt Dawson. The lab rushed the DNA results on the skin sample taken from beneath Rose's fingernails. It matches the sample you took off his water bottle. Also, the Lakeport police have Bob Mayfield in custody. The reason Mayfield's been so secretive is because he's growing a nice crop of marijuana on his property. He flatly denied any involvement in Lark's kidnapping, and this time he has witnesses to verify his whereabouts. We charged him with possession of an illegal substance with intent to sell, but Dawson's our kidnapper."

"So the truck in Lakeport was just a coincidence?" Kane's chest rose on a long breath.

"I'm afraid so. I have men questioning Dawson's friends and relatives again. Maybe one of them will remember something significant."

"I want to personally question Tiffany Randolph. If Dawson's been harboring a secret obsession for Rachel the whole time they were dating, she must have known something was off. Maybe she'll remember some small detail that will help find them."

The sheriff nodded. "Go ahead, Kane. I'll call your cell if anything breaks. In the meantime, we'll be doing everything we can to pin down their location."

He fisted his hands on his hips. "The CHP hasn't spotted Rachel's SUV yet?"

"No, I don't understand how she could have traveled any distance without being seen. We had an APB out on her vehicle within forty-five minutes of her disappearance."

"Maybe they're somewhere nearby."

"That's one possibility." Walker frowned. "Another is Dawson picked her up, and she left her vehicle parked someplace secluded."

Kane pulled his keys from his pocket. "I'll be in touch as soon as I've talked to Tiffany."

He spent the forty-five minute drive to Tiffany Randolph's home in San Rafael trying not to imagine what Dawson was doing to Rachel. As the minutes ticked by, twilight deepened to darkness. Kane pulled into the condominium complex where the asshole's so-called girlfriend lived. Jumping out of his Jeep, he ran up to pound on her door.

She opened it almost immediately and waved him inside. "Have a seat. Can I get you something to drink?"

He shook his head and remained standing. "Thanks for agreeing to see me."

Tiffany sat on the edge of the couch, her hands clasped in her lap. She wore a pair of old jeans and a T-shirt that admirably displayed her assets, but the fun-loving smile was missing. "I can't believe Curt actually kidnapped Lark. Are you sure he's the one who did it?"

"We have DNA evidence. He's been harassing Rachel for weeks now. Apparently he's been fixated on her for the last fourteen years."

"How can that be? He would have been a boy all those years ago."

"He was a teenager with the hots for a beautiful actress." Kane clenched his fists. "It wouldn't be the first time a wet dream turned into a sick obsession. I'm looking for some help here. Anything you can tell me about Dawson and his habits could turn this investigation around for us."

"I wish I could help. Is that why he took me up to Granite Lake, so he'd have an excuse to be near Rachel? I thought he was sticking it to his mother."

"He never talked about Rachel while you were there?"

"Only casual comments, but he was horny as hell the whole time we were camping. We went at it like a couple of rabbits." Her lips twisted. "Now that I think about it, a couple of times during sex he whispered a name, but it wasn't Rachel. I asked him about it once, and he just gave me an odd look and said I imagined it."

"Rachel played a character named Jordan Hale on the soap opera. That's how he thinks of her."

Tiffany's hand shook as she pushed back her hair. "That's really perverted. I never could figure out what made Curt tick. We had an open relationship, which suited both of us."

"Why'd you date him?"

"He's good in the sack."

Kane cleared his throat. "Were there any special places he liked to go? Did he talk about a trip he hoped to take?"

"Not really. He grew up in Nebraska, but he hasn't been back there in years. Curt's not close to his family. He mentioned the reunion his sister was planning weeks before he asked me to go with him. I had the impression he didn't plan to attend. Then all of a sudden he was excited about going." She shrugged. "Anyway, he's mentioned that camping trip fondly a few times. He said he'd like to do it again without the excess baggage. I thought he meant his parents, but maybe he was referring to me."

"You think he might take Rachel back to the mountains?" A seed of hope sprang to life—not much to go on, but something.

"It's the only thing I can think of. When we were together, we didn't do a whole lot of talking. Curt may look like Joe Average, but he's anything but in bed." She picked at the edge of the couch with a shiny red fingernail. "Sorry. That's probably not what you want to hear."

Lips pressed tight, Kane walked over and handed her a business card. "You've been very helpful. My cell number's on the card. Call if you think of anything else."

"Of course." She stood and touched his arm. "Curt may have a sick fixation with Rachel, but he really isn't a violent person. He was always very considerate both in and out of bed. I don't think he'd actually hurt her or Lark."

"I hope you're right. Thanks for your cooperation, Tiffany."

"Just catch the son of a bitch. Rachel was so nice to me while we were camping." She grimaced then went on. "It creeps me out knowing Curt was thinking about her every time we had sex. I'd like to personally kill the freak."

"I doubt you're the only victim of Dawson's fantasy life. Don't worry. When I find him, he'll pay."

Kane's cell rang as he was leaving San Rafael. He glanced at the display and answered. "Do you have news?"

"We finally got an ID on the pickup he's been using." The sheriff paused. "It belongs to the father of one of Dawson's friends. Apparently he borrowed it to move some furniture a few months ago and has been helping himself to it ever since. The man keeps it at a farm outside Petaluma and rarely drives it. He only realized it was missing when his son asked him to check after we contacted him. I've released the license number, but so far no hits."

"No sign of Dawson in Petaluma?"

"None. His car was parked in the old barn where the truck was stored. Dawson obviously felt safe leaving it there. The elderly man who owns the place recently had hip surgery and hasn't been in the barn for weeks."

"Tiffany thinks he may have gone back to the mountains. Put the CHP near Donner Summit on alert for the truck and for Rachel's SUV. I'm heading up there now."

"Do you have anything concrete to go on?"

"Just a couple of comments Dawson made to Tiffany. Jesus, Stan, I have to do something. I can't sit around Vine Haven twiddling my thumbs. I'm going crazy, and this is the only lead we have."

"If you feel that strongly about it, I don't want you to go alone. Where are you now?"

"Just outside San Rafael headed for the 80 East interchange."

"I'll have Pete drive Brandon out to meet you at the junction of 80 and Highway 12. They should get there about the same time you do. Take Brandon with you for backup just in case you do find Dawson."

"Fine."

"Don't do anything stupid if you locate him." His voice took on a sharp edge. "I want this handled by the book. Technically, you're not involved in this investigation."

"I know that. I'll be in touch." He clicked off his phone. "Technically, I don't give a damn."

* * * *

Rachel sat on the edge of the bed and forced herself to remain calm. The pervert swallowed nervously a couple of times before finally sitting beside her.

"I'm sorry about scaring you. I never wanted to hurt you or Lark, but I couldn't think of any other way to get you up here."

"You could have asked."

"You wouldn't have come. You're so beautiful, Jordan." He ran a shaking finger along her arm. "So very, very beautiful. I couldn't risk you turning me down."

"Tiffany's beautiful, too. I'm no one special, Curt."

His face twisted. "That's not true. You're perfect. Tiffany was only after a good time. You're not like that."

"You don't know me at all. You don't know what I'm like."

"You're wrong." Emotion glistened in his eyes. "I've known you for a long time. I fell in love with you when I was just a teenager. You were amazing—your face so perfect, and your body..." His throat worked. "Watching you made me ache with desire, but I knew you wouldn't want me then. I had to become the man you deserved."

"How'd you do that?"

He scooted closer until their thighs touched. With a force of will, Rachel remained still.

Keep him talking. Give Lark a chance to escape.

"I wasn't a popular kid." A breath lifted his chest. "The other kids picked on me, but that stopped when I got older. You see I had something the boys envied, and pretty soon word got around. The girls showed a lot more interest, and I was happy to satisfy their curiosity." He gave her a smug look. "I don't like to brag, but I have what it takes to gratify your needs."

She pressed her lips together and fisted her hands on the quilt to keep them from shaking.

"I know I was no great lover back then, but practice makes perfect. You deserve the best, Jordan. I may not be as good-looking as those men on TV, but I compensate for it in other ways."

"A relationship isn't all about sex." She swallowed. "You know that, don't you, Curt?"

"It's an important element. Anyway, you were married. Then you left the show, and I didn't see you for a long time. I tried to forget about you. I went to a shrink, and he prescribed these stupid pills for me to take, but I couldn't let you go. When I saw stories in the tabloids about your cheating husband, I knew it was time to act. He wasn't good enough for you, Jordan. He never loved you the way I do."

Jannine Gallant

"Bryce wasn't a very good husband."

"He was an asshole. You filed for divorce, and I moved to California to be closer to you. I found your house and your bookstore, and sometimes I'd drive by just hoping for a glimpse of your beautiful face."

"You stalked me all these years?"

"Of course not. I never stalked you." His eyes clouded. "I was content to admire you. I knew you weren't ready yet. You were still hurting, still recovering from what that bastard did to you. I'm a patient man, and I was willing to wait until the time was right. I knew someday we'd be together."

"Then you got tired of waiting."

He nodded. "I suppose so. You made a new life for yourself, and you seemed happy. Still, you weren't dating. I saw that as a sign. In your heart, you were waiting for me. I watched you more often, and I knew the time for us to be together had come. I was working on a way to meet you when you booked the camping trip. It was perfect. Fate. My sister had that dumb family reunion planned, so I simply called and told her I changed my mind about going. She was annoyed because it meant crowding the kids to give me a place to stay."

"You brought Tiffany with you."

"Sure. She served a useful purpose. I was worried seeing you every day might cause me to act in haste. Tiffany was a buffer. I could talk to you, and you'd see what a nice person I was without feeling threatened. Then there's my mother. The old bat has been after me forever to marry a nice girl and settle down. I knew she'd hate Tiffany, and watching her squirm gave me some satisfaction." He smiled. "My mother will love you. She was a big fan of yours all those years ago."

She forced herself to stay calm, breathe evenly. *Keep him talking.* "Why didn't you just call and ask me out after we left the retreat? Why did you follow me to Tahoe and grab me in the woods? You hurt me."

His face darkened. "Because you ruined my plan. You spent all your time with Lafferty. You hardly knew I was there." He gulped in air. "I saw

you together at that little lake and again out in the canoe. You let him..."
His fists clenched. "I was angry. You belonged to me, not him. It was my
time to be with you. I had to get you alone and make you see that."

"So you attacked me and threatened my girls?"

"I didn't have a choice. Seeing you with Lafferty was killing me. He's
all wrong for you, Jordan. I knew once we were together you'd realize
I'm the man you need. We're meant for each other. Once you spend a little
time with me, you'll forget all about that stupid cop."

"I'm supposed to forgive you for kidnapping Lark and scaring me to
death?" Her voice rose, and she lowered it.

He stroked her arm. "You'll forgive me."

"Will the police forgive you? You committed a crime. A number of
crimes."

"You won't press charges. We'll work something out."

The man had lost his grip on reality. He was living in a fantasy world
where only Jordan Hale existed. Time was running out.

He licked his lips. "Enough talking. Let me love you. Let me show you
we're perfect for each other."

As an actress, dozens of men had kissed her. All part of the job. Some
she'd liked well enough, and some had been egotistical idiots. It hadn't
mattered. None of it was sexual.

This is no different.

A low moan of pleasure escaped his throat as he bent to kiss her. At the
last moment, she turned her face. His lips connected with her cheek. They
rested there before running down the side of her neck.

She closed her eyes, but no amount of pretending could convince her
this wasn't real. She forced her mind to another place. How long had she
been in this room? They'd been talking for what seemed like a long time.
Opening her eyes, she glanced at the bedside clock. Almost eleven. Had
Lark gotten safely away yet?

His lips quit assaulting her, and he stood. Her gaze flew up to meet his.

"Relax, Jordan, you're going to enjoy this." He unfastened the sheath holding the hunting knife and laid it aside then striped off his clothes. An erection pressed against his boxer shorts.

She turned away, heart pounding.

He glanced down then gazed at her and smiled. "Like what you see?"

Sick panic welled up inside her. She couldn't stand another minute of this. Time to play her trump card.

"You want everything to be perfect, don't you?"

He nodded. "It will be. Oh, Jordan, we'll be so good together."

"Then we'll have to wait."

His eyes darkened. "I'm through waiting."

"It won't be perfect. It's the wrong time of month for that."

Face twisted in anger, he sat down beside her again. "I don't believe you."

"I'm not lying. I wouldn't lie about something like that."

His shoulders sagged, and his eyes watered. "It isn't fair. I've waited so long, and it's supposed to be perfect."

She fought to keep her voice low and seductive. *Keep him happy. Don't piss him off.* "After all this time, will a couple more days matter?"

"I can't." He reached out to take her hand. "There are other ways. You could..."

"No." Her voice rang out in the still room, and she scooted away from him. "Please, don't make me. I can't do that."

He shuddered and let go of her. "All right, we'll wait until we know each other better to explore that particular pleasure. At least I can hold you. I want you to take off your clothes."

Rachel didn't argue. He was on the edge, ready to snap. If she pushed him, fought harder, he might turn on her. So far her plan was working. *Please, God, let Lark be on her way to get help.* Slowly she removed her pants and top, leaving only panties and bra to cover her.

His eyes glazed. "Keep going."

"I'm sorry. I can't." She called up Jordan Hale and forced a hesitant smile. "Maybe tomorrow..."

He looked away from her and sighed. "I'm losing patience, but I'll give you a little time." Lying down on the quilt, he pulled her tight against him. Tears ran down his face as he stroked her hair. His fingers burrowed into the thick mass.

"Our first time together *will* be perfect. I'll satisfy your every desire." He paused. "Maybe I could..."

It took all she had in her not to throw up. "No, I'm tired."

His chest rose and fell. "I'm sorry if I'm moving too fast, Jordan." Sitting up, he pulled back the quilt. "Get under the blanket."

"I'm not cold. I'll be fine out here."

His voice lowered. "Please don't make me angry."

"I don't want to do that."

She slid beneath the covers. He climbed in behind her and wrapped her in his arms. His erection pressed against her bottom. She lay perfectly still, afraid any movement...

After a few seconds, he reached across her to turn off the bedside lamp. The room plunged into darkness.

"I'll know if you try to leave." His breath touched her ear. "I'm a very light sleeper."

Dry-eyed, she waited silent and still until the sick pervert's breathing deepened. Somewhere in the night Lark was safe and sending help her way. She couldn't bring herself to believe anything else. She'd endured this freak's touch for a reason. Played her part and played it well. Her daughter was safe, and Kane was coming. She prayed he would arrive before the pervert's self-restraint crumbled. Before it was too late.

Chapter Twenty-Nine

The police radio squawked as the operator responded to the 9-1-1 call.

"Lark got away!" Kane pushed his foot to the floorboard, and the Jeep damn near went airborne as it sped up the freeway.

"We're close to her location, maybe ten minutes out." Brandon spoke into his radio. "We'll reach her before the local police can."

Kane's eyes never left the road. "I'm not waiting for backup."

Brandon grabbed the armrest. "That's why Sheriff Walker sent me along." He braced himself as they flew around a semi at ninety miles an hour. "Whoo-hoo, this is the most excitement I've had since I started this job."

Tires squealed around a corner. "Believe me, kid, you don't want this kind of excitement. I was like you once." Kane clamped his jaw shut and focused on the next bend. "You'll learn. I hope the lesson isn't as hard as mine was."

"Uh, sure. There's our exit."

Lark sat huddled near a phone booth when they roared into the gas station. Yanking on the emergency break, Kane jumped out of the Jeep and called to her.

"Kane!" She scrambled to her feet and launched into his arms.

He caught her and held on tight. "Are you okay? Did he hurt you?"

She shook her head. "We have to help Mom. She's still there." Her eyes filled with tears as she stared up at him. "She stayed with that sick freak so I could get away, and I'm afraid of what he's doing to her."

Kane put his arm around her as they ran back to the Jeep then boosted her in. "Let's go."

Following Lark's directions, they took off down the road. Brandon called in their destination.

Kane glanced in the rearview mirror. "How'd you get free?"

"The stupid pervert tied me up, but Mom hid a knife for me to find. Once they went into the bedroom, I started working on the ropes. It took forever." Her voice choked on a sob. "When I finally got loose, I ran for help. I couldn't believe no one was home in any of the houses along the road. I should have stayed. I shouldn't have left her alone!"

"You made the right choice. Don't cry, Lark. We'll help your mom."

"They want us to wait until the local police get here. They're about five minutes behind us." Brandon shut off his radio.

"I'm not waiting." Kane frowned as he slowed to enter the dirt road. "This leads to Jed's house. The bastard's holding her in my brother's home."

Lark leaned forward between the seats. "Why would he do that?"

"Probably because he knew it would be empty. Jed's up at Granite Lake all summer."

"That makes sense. The place is isolated and vacant. What better location to hold a hostage?" Brandon gripped the armrest as they hit a bump.

From the back seat, Lark let out a little squeak.

Parking the car a few hundred feet from the cabin, Kane turned off the headlights and cut the engine. He reached under the seat to remove his Glock then turned around to face Lark. "I want you to stay in the Jeep. If you come with us, you'll be a distraction I don't need. I have to focus all of my attention on helping your mom. When the other police get here, tell them we've gone inside."

Eyes wide, she nodded.

"Lock the doors behind us."

"Curt has a big knife he wears all the time. The only gun I saw was a rifle in the truck, but he could have one stashed somewhere."

"Thanks for the heads up. Don't leave the Jeep, no matter what. We'll be back with your mom in no time."

With Brandon following, Kane crept up to the cabin door and eased it open. Raising his Glock, he slipped inside. Dim moonlight illuminated the empty front room. The bedroom door was shut. As he moved forward, Brandon stumbled.

"Shit." Sacrificing silence for speed, he ran across the room and threw open the bedroom door. A shadow moved, leaping up from the bed. Moonlight glinted off metal as a scream of rage rent the air.

"Drop the weapon, Dawson! Drop it!" Kane shouted.

The man shook his head. "No! No! She's mine! Do you hear me, she's mine!"

When his arm swung up, Kane fired. Dawson crumpled to the floor. Approaching with caution, Kane crouched beside the still figure to feel for a pulse. Rising to his feet, he kicked the gun away.

Rachel huddled on the bed, a quilt clutched to her chest, bare legs folded beneath her. Her hair hung in tangles around her face, and moonlight illuminated shadowed eyes and trembling lips.

He sank onto the mattress beside her. "Rachel, honey, you're safe."

With a cry, she collapsed into his arms as all hell broke loose when the local police burst into the cabin. Kane let her go for only a second.

Long enough to call out they were all okay.

* * * *

The sun had risen well above the horizon when Kane and Rachel finally left the police station in Truckee. Brandon and Lark waited for them in the parking lot with Sheriff Walker who had arrived during the many hours of questioning.

Lark walked straight into her mother's arms and squeezed tight. "Can we go home?"

She touched the pink streaked hair. "We can go home."

"Is it over, Mom?"

"For now it is. Once they set a date for the trial, we'll have to testify."

"There won't be a trial. Dawson didn't make it through surgery." The sheriff's expression was sober as he faced her. "I got the word a few minutes before you came out." He turned to Kane. "I'm sorry, son. I know the next few weeks won't be pleasant until an investigation clears you."

Rachel glanced up at Kane's drawn face and squeezed his arm. "You did what you had to do."

He shrugged, but Rachel could feel his withdrawal as the three of them walked to the Jeep. Neither said much as he took the onramp to the freeway. An hour into the drive, Lark fell asleep.

Rachel turned to face him. "Do you want to talk about it?"

"There isn't anything to say." His throat worked, and he kept his eyes firmly on the road. "I killed the bastard. He deserved to die for what he did to you."

Rachel pushed her hair away from her face with a shaking hand. "I'll be fine. It could have been a lot worse."

"It was bad enough. I'm so sorry."

Her eyes widened. "Why are you sorry? You're the hero. You saved me."

"Some hero. I should have reached you sooner."

"Whose fault is it you didn't? Mine. I was so sure I could handle him by myself and save Lark."

"You did. Dawson didn't touch your daughter."

"No, he didn't." She leaned back against the seat. "We both did what we had to do."

Kane was silent for a long time. Rachel's eyes closed, and she started to doze off. On a head jerk, she opened them again and sat upright.

"Take a nap. You're exhausted."

She blinked and covered a yawn. "I'm thankful Brandon offered to drive the MG home. I don't think I could have stayed awake."

"Then get some rest."

"What about you? You're tired, too."

"I've gone longer without sleep. I'll be fine."

* * * *

Rachel fell asleep almost immediately. Her lashes formed dark crescents against her pale cheeks. Kane glanced over now and then, and his stomach churned. Listening to her halting description of Dawson's hands on her had made him sick. He wasn't certain he could put it behind him. He'd killed again. Not that he'd had a choice, but this one had been personal. Which might make getting past it even harder.

Except this time he had Rachel to help him mend. His grip on the wheel eased.

The woman he couldn't live without woke just as they entered Vine Haven.

He spoke softly. "Almost there."

She gave him a sleepy smile then turned to gently shake her daughter awake. "Lark, we're close to home."

She stretched, hitting the back of his seat with her knee. "Do you think everyone will be at our house?"

"I'm counting on it." Rachel smiled. "When I spoke to Susan, she said their flight landed at ten o'clock. They should all be home by now."

"I can't believe I'm saying this, but I'll be glad to see Jade and Ivy."

"They'll be happy to see you, too."

The driveway was filled with cars. Kane maneuvered the Jeep into a parking space behind Will's Volvo and helped Lark climb out of the back.

The front door burst open. Jade and Ivy flew across the lawn straight into Rachel's arms.

There were tears and hugs and relieved smiles. In the midst of the homecoming, Chet pulled Kane aside. Lines of strain were deeply etched in his face.

"I want the truth. Did that bastard rape my daughter?"

Kane shook his head. "No, Rachel did an amazing job of keeping the situation under control before we got there."

Some of the tension drained from the older man. "I was afraid she wasn't telling us everything. I was afraid she was trying to protect us from the truth."

"She might try to do that. Your daughter believes in protecting the people she loves, but she didn't need to lie."

He didn't mention the hours Rachel had spent alone with Curt Dawson. No one needed to know about them. If she woke up in a panic, reliving those moments, he'd be there to hold and comfort her. Let her know she'd be just fine.

After talking to Rachel's father, Kane kept to the fringes of the yard full of people. Rachel tried several times to draw him into the gathering, but he was content to watch from the sidelines. When Grace approached him, he couldn't avoid talking to her.

"You're not acting much like a hero."

"Probably because I don't feel like one."

"You saved my sister and my niece. That seems pretty heroic."

"They saved themselves. I just finished the job."

"Don't beat yourself up over shooting Curt Dawson. The way I hear it, you didn't have a choice."

Kane raised a brow. "Did Rachel tell you? I know the police haven't released any details to the general public."

Grace smiled. "Rachel didn't have to tell me. I'm an investigative reporter. I have my sources."

"Should I worry about reading this conversation in the paper tomorrow?"

"Nope. You're practically family. Rachel told me you two intend to make your relationship work. My sister isn't the only one who protects the people she loves." Grace gave his arm a pat. "You should remember that. We're all on your side."

Kane stopped her before she could walk away. "I'm not proud of what I did, but in the same circumstances, I'd do it again."

She gave him a long look. "Maybe that's what's bothering you most."

* * * *

It was several hours before people began to leave. Susan went home with her parents, and Grace announced she'd decided to drive back to the city.

Rachel touched her arm. "Are you sure, Gracie?"

"I'm positive. Anyway, you need some time alone with Kane and the girls." She hugged her tight. "Talk to him. I think he needs you as much as you need him."

"I will. Drive safely and tell Nolan I said hello."

"We broke up."

"Grace! You two were good together. I thought you were going to make it work with him."

"He was getting too serious, hinting around the *m*-word, so I cut him loose. I cared about him, but he wasn't *the one*."

"How do you know?" She fisted her hands on her hips. "You didn't give him a chance."

"I never looked at him the way you look at Kane. Don't worry about it, Rachel. I'm good with the decision."

"But I want you to find the kind of love I have."

"Someday I will, and in the meantime I'll enjoy looking."

Rachel shook her head as Grace sauntered toward her car. Kane came up behind her to wrap his arms around her waist. "Did I hear Grace say she dumped Nolan?"

"I'm afraid so."

"Poor guy."

"The last in a long line." Rachel turned toward the house with her arm tucked through his. "Where're the girls?"

"Ivy's throwing a stick for Daisy in the backyard, and Jade ran next door to talk to her friend. I promised to tell you. She said she'd be home soon. I'm not sure about Lark."

"That's fine. I know I don't have to worry about where they are every second any longer." She held on to him a little tighter. "It's a hard habit to break."

"Life will get back to normal, but it may take some time to adjust."

"I know." She let out a sigh. "Olivia called."

"Oh? Not Ford?"

"I talked to him, too. They were understandably worried. Olivia broke down when she told me how thankful she was Lark and I were both safe."

"Not half as thankful as I am. No one is as thankful as I am."

Rachel stopped and stretched up to kiss him before they entered the kitchen. Lark stood at the counter making dinner."

"Wow!" Rachel pressed a hand to her chest. "Be still my heart."

"It's no big deal." Her daughter glanced over. "I'm just heating up the leftover lasagna Grandma made." She slid the pan into the oven then turned. "You're probably tired."

"I am. Thank you, honey."

Lark's blue gaze met Rachel's. "It wouldn't kill me to help out more around here." She faced Kane. "I won't give you any more grief, either. You were there for us when it mattered."

Rachel opened her mouth then shut it and hugged her. "Thank you."

"Hey, don't get too used to it. I imagine the novelty of trying to be the perfect daughter will wear off shortly."

Kane laughed and patted her shoulder. "Now that sounds more like the Lark we know and love."

Ivy burst through the kitchen door with Daisy at her heels, and a minute later Jade walked in. The kitchen grew loud with talk about everyday topics as they settled into their usual routine. They ate her mother's delicious lasagna and cleaned the kitchen together. When the dishes were done, Rachel took her time mixing up a huge batch of muffins then baked four loaves of banana bread.

When the girls said good night and went up to their rooms, Kane stepped up behind her. "Your mom would have done the baking for a while longer."

She smiled at him. "I know, but I want everything to get back to normal, and baking for the coffee bar is my responsibility."

"You can't pretend nothing happened, Rachel."

She squeezed out the dishrag and draped it over the drainer. "I can try. Dwelling on it won't help."

"Mom, Ivy and Jade are already in bed." Lark stuck her head into the kitchen. "They want you to tell them good night."

"I'll head right up. I'm finished in here anyway."

Lark stopped her at the foot of the stairs. "It's okay if Kane stays with you tonight. I don't want you to be alone."

"I'll be fine, but what about you? Maybe you should bunk with one of your sisters."

She shook her head and let out a deep breath. "That guy was really sick, wasn't he?"

Rachel closed her eyes for a moment. "He was."

"Let Kane stay with you, Mom."

Rachel nodded and followed Lark up the stairs. She kissed the girls good night and was sitting at her dressing table, brushing her hair when Kane entered the bedroom.

"I let Daisy out to do her business, brought her back in then turned off all the lights. Are the girls asleep?"

"Yes, even Lark." Rachel's brow pleated, and her gaze met his in the mirror. "Do you think she's really okay?"

"It wouldn't hurt to have her talk about what happened with a counselor."

"She's been seeing one, anyway, but I'll make an extra appointment for her while she's still being so cooperative. I love my daughter dearly, but I can't see this sweetness and light stuff lasting long."

"Probably not. She's concerned about you. I overheard your conversation with her." Kane shut the bedroom door. Walking over to stand behind her, he rested his hands on her shoulders. "Is it all right with you if I stay here tonight?"

"Of course."

He pulled her to her feet and took her gently into his arms. "I would understand if you needed some time to sort out your emotions."

"I don't." She drew in a breath. "Does it bother you, knowing Curt touched me?"

"Hell, yes, it bothers me. I regret every second you spent with that sick pervert. I'm sorrier than I can say I wasn't able to prevent it."

"He made me feel dirty." She stepped out of his arms. "I'd like to take another shower before we go to bed, if you don't mind."

"Of course I don't mind."

Rachel walked into the bathroom and turned on the water. When the shower door opened a few minutes later, she jumped. Backing up beneath the steaming water, she brushed ineffectually at the tears on her cheeks.

"You aren't dirty." Kane pulled her close. "You don't need another shower."

She leaned against his chest, the water pouring over them. Her shoulders shook as she cried.

"I hated having him touch me. I wanted to scream at him to stop, but I was so afraid. I was afraid Lark hadn't gotten away yet. I was afraid he'd do something to her if I didn't cooperate. I was afraid the result would be even worse for me if I didn't play along."

He kissed the top of her head and stroked her back. "You did what you had to do, Rachel. I don't blame you for anything that happened. How could I?"

"I blame myself. I was so sure I was doing the right thing following his rules. I couldn't risk Lark's life by telling you or the police about the note. I thought I could handle either Curt or Bob all on my own. I was cocky and confident—and wrong."

"You did handle him." Kane squeezed her shoulders. "You made it possible for Lark to escape, and you kept Dawson from raping you. You were amazing, Rachel."

"When I was a soap actress, men touched me and kissed me all the time. I thought it wouldn't bother me when he did it." She shuddered. "It wasn't the same as acting. Having that pervert's hands on me violated everything decent and right."

He held her tight. "He might have touched your body, but he couldn't touch your soul. You're still the same beautiful, strong, loving woman you've always been. I love you, Rachel."

"I love you, too."

He turned off the water and ushered her out of the shower then gently dried every inch of her body. Slipping a nightgown over her head, he bundled her into bed then pulled her into the circle of his arms.

"In some ways, I can't help feeling sorry for Curt. He really thought he loved me."

"It wasn't you he loved. It was Jordan Hale, and she didn't exist anywhere but in his mind. He was sick and dangerous."

"I know. I keep thinking about his family, and Tiffany."

"Tiffany will recover." The arms around her tightened. "It's always tough on the family."

"You had to shoot him, Kane. He would have killed you—or me—if you hadn't."

"I know. It doesn't make it any easier."

She touched his face. "We all make difficult decisions. I made one out of desperation and fear for my daughter. You made one out of necessity. You acted in self-defense."

"You're right, but I was filled with hate and vengeance. I wanted to punish him for hurting you and Lark. Those feelings weren't professional."

"Neither was the situation. It was personal for both of us. I wasn't sorry you shot him. I wasn't sorry you ended it. Am I a bad person for feeling that way?"

"Of course not."

"Then give yourself a break." She kissed his lips. "No one's perfect, but you're perfect for me."

"If I promise to stop second guessing myself, will you do the same? Will you believe you're still the same incredible woman you were the first evening we met?"

Held tightly in his arms, Rachel let go of the shame and regret. There was only room for love. She put the fear and pain behind her and looked toward the future. With Kane beside her, it was bright with promise.

"I can." She gazed into his eyes and smiled. "Together, we both can."

Meet the Author

Write what you know. Jannine Gallant has taken this advice to heart, creating characters from small towns and plots that unfold in the great outdoors. She grew up in a tiny Northern California town and currently lives in beautiful Lake Tahoe with her husband and two daughters. When she isn't busy writing or being a full time mom, Jannine hikes or snowshoes in the woods around her home. Whether she's writing contemporary, historical or romantic suspense, Jannine brings the beauty of nature to her stories. To find out more about this author and her books, visit her website at www.janninegallant.com.